Past Lies

Holly Copella

ISBN:
ISBN-13: 978-1-947694-39-2

For Shiloh Byrnes:
Thank you for everything you do for Maverick!

ACKNOWLEDGMENTS

Copella Books: First Paperback Edition 2026
Cover Artist: Daniela Owergoor
Dani-owergoor.deviantart.com
Printed by KDP, an Amazon.com Company

PUBLISHER'S NOTE

Chapter 1

The old-fashioned study, rich with mahogany wood and deep leather, was a symbol of wealth. The massive desk, with its hand-carved trim and marble top, stood in front of double French doors opening to the patio. A tall, distinguished-looking man in his early fifties, Ransom, the homeowner, entered the study a little after ten that evening and collapsed behind the desk. He let out a low groan and began scrolling through the emails on his laptop. A short, petite woman in her early fifties, with wisps of silver in shoulder-length hair, paused in the open doorway and eyed the man behind the desk.

"I'm heading to bed, Ransom," Debra announced.

Ransom briefly looked up and smiled at his wife, Debra. "I'll be up in ten minutes," he said. "I just want to respond to this email from the accountant."

"I'll be waiting," Debra announced, flashing a knowing smile.

Ransom chuckled softly and returned to his email. Finishing in under ten minutes, he shut his laptop and rolled away from his desk. Ransom switched off the desktop light and strolled across the dimly lit room to the open study door and the brightly lit hallway, unaware that the small closet door was opening. He was almost to the doorway when he heard a floorboard creak behind him, stopping him. Ransom turned in time to see the blade of a hunting knife an instant before it plunged into his abdomen just below his sternum. Despite the pain, Ransom shoved the masked intruder away out of reflex, the knife tearing free from his body as the attacker stumbled backward. He immediately clutched his bleeding midsection and attempted to turn for the door. Ransom was yanked back into the study and thrown to the floor easily in his weakened condition. He landed on his back and could do little more than watch as the attacker dropped down beside him and stabbed him again. Ransom felt the steel of the blade drive into his lower abdomen, the killer deliberately letting him bleed out slowly rather than striking an instantly fatal blow.

Debra rounded the banister from the grand stairs, already dressed for bed, and approached the study. She wore an expensive white satin nightgown with a plunging neckline, wanting to surprise her husband. She entered the dimly lit study and stopped. Debra saw Ransom on the floor, his hands pressed over his bleeding knife wounds, blood seeping across his body and the floor beneath him. Debra was frozen for only a moment, then screamed for help and ran to her dying husband. When she touched his hand, he groaned softly. He was still alive! Debra bolted for the desk phone and snatched it from its base. It only took a second to realize there was no dial tone. She tossed the phone aside and ran into the hallway, screaming for help. Unfortunately, no one in the staff wing would hear unless they were upstairs. Debra ran for the kitchen door, but before she could reach it, the masked intruder stood before her. She barely saw him before he slashed her with his already bloodied knife.

Debra cried out, clutching her bleeding shoulder, and staggered back a step, then screamed and ran back down the hallway to her husband's study. Ransom had a gun in the desk drawer! Debra entered the study, quickly locked the door behind her, and ran for the desk. She yanked open the desk drawer and frantically searched, but the gun was missing! A thought then hit her. She pounced on the desk intercom to the staff wing, pounded the button with her bloodied hand, and shrieked for help. There was a thump against the door, cracking the doorjamb, making Debra scream in surprise. He was getting through! She bolted for the glass patio doors behind the desk and fumbled with the lock. Despite the blood on her hands, she unlocked the door and flung it open. Debra was about to dart outside when a hand grabbed her hair from behind and yanked her back into the study.

The intruder stabbed her in the abdomen, then released her. She stumbled a few steps, attempting to reach the open study door while the intruder followed casually, unhurried. When she was nearly there, he snatched away her hope as he grabbed her from behind and slit her throat. Debra staggered a step or two, clutching her throat as the blood gushed from the gaping wound. She fell beside her husband. Ransom forced his eyes open in time to witness his wife collapsing near him. The last thing Ransom heard was thundering footfalls in the grand hallway. Help was on the way, but it would be too late.

A detective in his forties and a young police officer observed the crime scene, watching as the coroner examined the victims more closely. As the detective visually inspected the rest of the study, the officer flipped through his notepad.

"The bodies were discovered by one of the maids moments after she and another maid returned home from bingo around eleven o'clock this evening," the officer announced. "The chauffeur, who lives above the garage, heard something that sounded like a gunshot just before the maids pulled up to the garage. He reached the study only a few minutes after one of the maids found the bodies, having heard her scream as he entered the house."

"And the weapon?" the detective asked.

"The knife used on the homeowners was found discarded between the husband and wife," the officer replied, nodding toward the blood-covered hunting knife still on the floor between the two bodies. "The chauffeur confirmed that his boss's antique, pearl-handled Cimarron .38 revolver is missing from the desk. It hasn't been recovered yet."

The detective scanned the crime scene again. He gazed past the bodies of Ransom and Debra to the neatly dressed man in his early thirties, lying unnaturally on his back, with blood soaking his shirt and the floor around him.

"And the third victim?" the detective asked.

"Their butler," the officer reported. "Single gunshot wound to the chest. Died instantly. Except for the chauffeur in the garage apartment, the butler was the only servant home at the time of the attack."

The detective studied the dead butler and the blood on the floor around him. "The body's been moved," he remarked.

"His wife was the maid that found him," the officer reported, then clearing his throat gently. "The chauffeur found her clinging to him on the floor."

The detective nodded.

"Blood on the intercom suggests the lady of the house may have contacted the butler in the staff wing," the officer continued. "We believe the butler rushed to the study and was ambushed. Shot with the missing gun from the desk."

"I doubt we'll find it," the detective informed the officer, shaking his head, "but we'll need to sweep the house and estate grounds for that missing gun. That fits with the gunshot the chauffeur heard just before the maids returned home. Probably wasn't sure what he'd heard, considering the distance, which explains why it took him so long to get here."

"The security system and the phone lines were disabled, and the lock on the dining room doors had been crudely picked," the officer remarked. "Looks like the work of a professional burglar. I'm guessing a home invasion gone wrong."

The detective was lost in thought for a moment, then finally glanced at the officer. "Do we have a next of kin to notify?" he asked.

"The chauffeur called the son who's staying at the family lake house about an hour from here," the officer replied.

"When the maids are up to it, we'll need them to check if anything is missing," the detective remarked and scanned the scene again, shaking his head.

"Something wrong?" the officer asked.

"This feels staged to me," the detective remarked, releasing a heavy sigh. "He leaves the knife but removes the gun. Why?"

"Feared someone may have heard the gunshot?" the officer questioned.

"If this were a robbery gone wrong," the detective informed him, "it might explain killing the man. And maybe the woman ***did*** happen to walk in at the wrong time, so he killed her, too. But that doesn't explain the butler's death."

"The blood trail around the room suggests the dead woman pressed the intercom button," the officer reminded him. "He obviously came to help."

"And the killer stayed after she called for help?" the detective asked, eyeing the officer. "You've just killed two people, and now someone else is alerted." He nodded toward the study door. "Why didn't he take off? Why wait for the butler to arrive?" He shook his head. "Our killer ***waited*** until the butler showed up. It makes no sense. I want alibis for everyone who hated or would benefit from the deaths of any of our victims."

"Even the butler?"

"Especially the butler," the detective announced. "His death is the one that makes no sense. The killer could have escaped before he arrived, but he chose to stay in the room. Now, maybe he wanted something here, explaining why he didn't leave, but nothing looks disturbed. I won't be satisfied until I know why the killer was still in this room when the butler arrived."

Chapter 2

Henry Westmore's two-story, custom-built home, with its broad, wraparound porch and thick, tree-trunk pillars, sat back on the corner lot just on the edge of town. Crafted mostly from fieldstone and old, stained wood, the house, built decades ago, remained solid and stable. As a craftsman carpenter, everything was custom-made from the rocking chairs to the covered fieldstone patio with its stone charcoal grill. The home, situated on an acre of land, was immaculately landscaped in an old development. Despite being a residential neighborhood, a long stone-lined driveway led to a large parcel of land behind the house. Partially hidden behind a line of mature trees stood what had once been the old two-story barn, now a stately eight-car garage. The exterior matched the house, while the double bay doors maintained the old-fashioned 'barn' look. A small panel truck backed against an open bay door where two men loaded handcrafted rocking chairs and benches into the back.

A young, attractive woman, dressed in jeans and a flannel shirt, spoke with a third man. Twenty-three-year-old Sidney Bristol had that classic 'girl next door' appeal. Her dark hair hung just below her shoulders, often kept in a messy ponytail while working in her grandpa's workshop. Wood stain was messy, and sanding sent wood dust everywhere. She wore little makeup since there was no one she was trying to impress. Most days, she didn't see anyone other than her own family. She stood roughly five-foot-six with a moderately athletic build. Her grandpa often required help moving larger pieces, and she was usually the only one available. Sidney was a country girl from her signature ponytail to her comfortable, military-style boots. The man supervising the truck loading operation, Evans, smiled at Sidney and handed her a check.

"Always a pleasure doing business with you, Sidney," Evans announced cheerfully. "I took a peek at the custom bar when I first got here. Looks like it's coming along nicely. Tell 'the old man' that my client is anxiously waiting for it. Anxious, meaning crabby."

"I'll tell him," Sidney replied with a smile that conveyed what 'the old man' would undoubtedly have to say.

Sidney waited until the men climbed into the truck and drove away before shutting the large bay door. She walked through the massive, open workshop filled with everything her grandpa was working on, from started projects to those nearly complete. Most were furniture. Everything from chairs to tables and bars. There was plenty of light through the large windows, keeping the meticulously clean work area cheerful. She approached her great-grandfather as he sanded the side of a massive, custom bar. She wasn't too surprised that he had disappeared the moment Evans arrived. He avoided small talk whenever possible. Her great-grandfather paused and ran his hand along the freshly sanded edges, feeling for any imperfections.

Henry Westmore was in excellent shape for a man in his mid-to-late seventies. He was a sturdy six-foot-tall with a mostly athletic build from decades of working long hours. His age showed around his eyes. He had a thick head of mostly white hair and a light gray mustache with plenty of white stubble that didn't quite constitute a beard. Most people saw him as a carpenter cowboy who wore flannel shirts, blue jeans, and cowboy boots every day. Despite his kind blue eyes, he could be somewhat 'ornery' and a little rough around the edges. Without looking up, Henry spoke to Sidney in his deep, gristly voice that tended to make him sound more intimidating than he actually was.

"Are they gone?" he asked while continuing to feel the edges of the bar.

"Yes, they're gone," she replied with a disapproving sigh. "You could have made an appearance, you know."

"Evans talks too much," Henry reminded her, then briefly glanced at her. "Did you get the check?"

"Paid in full," Sidney cheerfully replied while waving the check.

Henry snorted a laugh before straightening and admiring his labor of love. "I think this bar might be the most beautiful piece I've ever made," he remarked, then eyed Sidney. "Would look nice in your own home someday."

"We're a long way off from me having my own home," she reminded him, then grinned slyly. "My boss doesn't pay me enough."

Henry chuckled and again admired his work. "More like your mother wants to keep you around," he informed her.

"The benefits of living next door," Sidney remarked. "It takes me three minutes to walk to work."

He again straightened and set his sander on the nearby table. "I know," Henry announced. "My daughter and granddaughter have a decades-old path worn between our two houses."

"Dad said you helped them get the house next door," Sidney reminded him. "So I'm guessing that's your own fault."

"Seemed like a good idea at the time," Henry replied, then looked at her and smiled. "Got to see my great-granddaughter every day since the day she was born. Twenty-three years, and you're still here. Might be a record."

"Where else would I go?" she asked, now curious.

Henry shrugged. "Don't know," he replied. "Where do any kids these days go? City, I suppose."

Sidney snorted a laugh, humored by the comment. "That'll never happen," she muttered.

"Because you're not boy crazy," Henry informed her.

"I'm happy right here," Sidney replied. "I have 'boy' friends. I don't need a boyfriend. They're overrated."

Henry chuckled, amused at the comment. "Good to hear," he remarked. "Working here seems like a waste of your architecture degree, though."

"Can I let you in on a little secret?" Sidney asked while raising a curious brow.

Henry glanced at her and cocked his head, now interested. "Of course."

"I only got into architecture because I like drawing," she replied, now grinning.

Henry chuckled at the admission. "Sorry, honey," he announced. "You weren't fooling anyone. Kind of knew that already."

"Quitting time?" she eagerly asked as her eyes lit up.

"I've been looking forward to this weekend all month," he informed her and tossed his rag onto the counter.

"It's been months since we've gone to the cabin for the weekend," Sidney remarked.

"Why don't you pack the cooler and grab our bags, and I'll meet you out front with the boat," her grandpa informed her.

"You're the boss," she announced cheerfully, then hesitated and eyed him almost suspiciously. "Do you have enough ***bait***?"

"Got plenty of bait," he informed her as his grin increased. "You just make sure to pack the good snacks. I don't want any of that healthy crap your grandmother's been pushing on me." He then nodded across the shop. "I just need to hook up the boat to the truck."

"Meet you in twenty," Sidney announced, then hurried across the workshop.

Sidney continued through the building, across the office, and out the front door. She hesitated, then turned the sign in the window that now read, "Closed. Gone Fishing."

Chapter 3

Sidney entered the kitchen through the back door of her grandpa's house and nearly collided with her grandmother in the custom kitchen Henry lovingly handcrafted himself. It had granite countertops and a fieldstone island counter with plenty of workspace and functional counter seating. Helena Murdock, or G-ma as Sidney called her, was in her late fifties. Slightly robust and only five-foot-three, she was as feisty as ever, with short hair dyed platinum blonde, ruby red lipstick, and never without her dangly rhinestone earrings. She dressed as if she were ready to go out, even though she rarely did. The only thing sharper than G-ma's mind was her tongue. Helena was quick to exchange sharp barbs and to speak her mind freely, with little regard for who might be offended. She looked almost amused at Sidney's enthusiasm for the weekend fishing trip with Henry.

"Closing up shop early for the weekend?" Helena asked while attempting to contain her grin.

Sidney was beaming with delight over her weekend trip with her great-grandfather. "Grandpa is hooking up the boat," she announced. "As soon as I get the cooler and groceries together, we'll be heading out."

"The groceries are still bagged in the pantry," Helena reported. "I'll load the cooler with the perishables while you get the grocery bags."

Sidney headed for the pantry and opened the door to see several bags waiting. "That's a lot of groceries for one weekend," she remarked.

"And, judging by what I saw when I peeked inside, there's going to be very little healthy food," Helena informed her, then shook her head while loading refrigerated food and bags of ice into the large cooler. "I hope that man remembered to pack his heartburn medication."

"The cabin is only ten minutes from here," Sidney reminded her grandmother. "We can always run back for anything we've forgotten."

"Oh, no," Helena announced while hiding her humored grin. "You agreed to take him off my hands the entire weekend. I want the weekend to myself." She then casually shrugged. "I don't know. With my father gone for a few nights, maybe I'll have some boys over. Have one of those wild parties I never got to have when I was a teenager."

"It wasn't so long ago that I was a teenager," Sidney informed her grandmother. "And I've never had any burning desire to have any wild parties."

Helena shrugged while packing the cooler. "That's probably because you'd spent all your teen years with your grandpa."

Sidney snorted a laugh but didn't bother looking at her grandmother. "You like to portray Grandpa as the father from hell," she remarked. "But if he were really all that bad, you wouldn't have spent the last twenty-four years living with him."

"Let's see how you feel when you're my age and still living with your father," Helena remarked, then flashed a humored smile.

Sidney groaned and set the last grocery bag on the table. "I love my father, I honestly do," she announced, then made a face. "But I don't think I could live with him that long."

"Well, now you know how I feel," her grandmother reported. She finally turned, closing the cooler lid, and nodded across the kitchen. "Your grandpa's bag is in the hallway. I'll help you carry the provisions onto the porch."

§

Only a few minutes later, Sidney rolled the large cooler onto the porch by its handle with three bags of groceries sitting on top and her grandpa's overnight bag hanging on her shoulder. Helena followed, carrying several grocery bags in each hand, and set them down not far from the back porch steps. It seemed odd that Henry wasn't already waiting at the porch with the pickup truck and boat. Sidney glanced at her watch and then looked toward the garage, nearly one hundred yards from the house. The boat was already hitched to the pickup truck, but there was no sign of her grandpa.

"Think he's having a problem with the hitch?" Sidney asked.

"If he were, we'd hear him cursing from here," Helena remarked, then shook her head. "Hurry up and wait. He's good at that." She then glanced at Sidney. "Where's your overnight bag?"

"I stowed it in his truck this morning when I walked over for work," Sidney replied, then fidgeted while watching the motionless truck and boat. She groaned and shook her head. "I'd better run up there and see what's holding him up."

Sidney hurried from the porch and jogged the entire way to the garage. She slowed as she reached the truck with the large boat attached. The newer Regal 3760 Express boat was mostly blue and white fiberglass. It was approximately thirty-four feet long, with a well-appointed helm beneath a hardtop canopy, circular seating for four, and small sunning decks at both bow and stern.

"Waiting on you, Grandpa," Sidney called out. "I hope you didn't misplace the boat keys again."

As Sidney rounded the back of the boat, she didn't see her grandpa anywhere, but the driver's side door on the truck was open. She then looked back at the garage. The smaller office door was open as well, suggesting her grandpa had gone back inside for something. Sidney often wondered why he didn't just leave the boat at the cabin. Sure, there wasn't a garage there, but it would be fine alongside the log cabin, especially with the cover over it. Sidney briskly walked toward the open door and entered the office, brightly lit by sunlight streaming in through the open curtains. Sidney abruptly stopped when she saw her grandpa sprawled out on the floor with his cell phone not far from his outstretched hand. Sidney gasped in surprise and ran to his fallen side.

"Grandpa," she cried out while kneeling alongside him.

Sidney firmly nudged him, fearing moving him in case he had fallen. When he didn't wake or move, she swiftly rolled him onto his back.

"Grandpa?" she asked in a startled gasp.

When there was no response, panic swept through her entire body.

"Grandpa?" she announced again, a little louder, while nudging him.

When he still didn't rouse, she placed her hand to the side of his neck, feeling for a pulse. Sidney gasped in horror, then heard a faint voice from the cell phone. It was a 911 operator.

"Sir, can you hear me?" the faint female voice announced. "We have an ambulance en route to your location."

Sidney immediately began chest compressions despite the panic flooding her entire body. "My grandpa is unresponsive," she just about cried out to the voice on the phone.

"Okay, I need you to stay calm," the faint voice announced. "Do you know CPR?"

"I've already started," Sidney shouted before tilting her grandpa's head back, pinching his nose, and expelling several breaths into him.

Sidney concentrated on CPR and blocked out the flurry of noise suddenly surrounding her. The emergency dispatcher tried to keep her calm, but she didn't hear her. Even her grandmother's panicked screams seemed a thousand miles away. She heard the ambulance sirens, but Sidney remained focused. When the paramedics rushed in, her grandmother was sobbing. The male and female paramedics took over for Sidney, who could do little more than fall onto her backside, exhausted and shaken. As the female paramedic readied the portable defibrillator, the man checked for a pulse.

"I have a pulse," the male paramedic announced, then looked at Sidney, who remained sitting on the office floor staring blankly at her motionless grandpa. "You did good."

Despite her grandpa coming back to life, Sidney couldn't look away. Her grandmother soon knelt alongside her and clung to her while sobbing. Both watched as the paramedics kept Henry alive with IV lines and oxygen while simultaneously preparing to move him onto the stretcher. In record time, they rushed him out of the office and into the ambulance. Sidney and Helena got to their feet and hurried to the office door just in time to see the ambulance pull away, lights flashing and siren wailing.

Chapter 4

At the hospital a few hours later, Sidney sat by her great-grandfather's bedside on the right while Helena dozed off in the chair to his left. Her head lightly bobbed, and she woke. Helena looked around, then seemed to realize where she was. She looked from her motionless father in the hospital bed to her granddaughter, who remained solemn. Helena stretched in the chair, then stood.

"I'm going to find some tea," Helena reported. "Did you want to come along?"

"No," Sidney replied without taking her eyes off her grandpa in the bed. "I'll stay here in case he wakes."

Helena nodded, then left the room. Sidney drifted off into her own thoughts, back to a happier day.

Flashback. It had been decades since the cabin even saw better days. Despite its solid foundation and tightly mounted log walls, it needed a lot of work. The small covered porch was in worse shape than the cabin, and the old, single-pane windows needed replacing. Not far from the cabin was the old boat dock on the large lake. Halfway across the lake was an anchored, no-frills motorboat with

Henry and a little girl inside. Henry stared at his bobber in the water that hadn't moved in hours. He then looked at the ten-year-old girl across from him. Sidney was practically drowning in her orange life preserver and oversized cap, looking perfectly content with her fishing pole. Henry smiled then chuckled warmly.

"Enjoying yourself, sweetheart?"

Sidney looked back at her grandpa and grinned with the same enthusiasm she'd had since early that morning.

"Yes," she replied cheerfully. "I love sitting in the boat with you. Tell me another story."

Henry laughed without taking his eyes off the little girl. "How about we take a little spin around the lake instead?" he asked, catching her attention. His brows rose. "If you don't tell your mother or grandmother, I'll even let you drive."

Little Sidney's eyes lit up. "I can drive the boat?"

"You sure can."

Sidney was roused back to reality when she heard someone calling her name. She saw her mother and father just inside Henry's hospital room. Sidney's mother, Casandra, was only forty years old. Although shorter and slightly robust, she was a beautiful woman with shoulder-length, medium brown hair and hazel eyes. She carried herself with dignity and had a positive outlook on life. Always a warm and gentle soul, Sidney thought her mom was an amazing mother who rarely raised her voice. Although Sidney's father, Kingston, was only five years older than her mother, he somehow looked older than forty-five. He was shorter than average, only five-foot-eight, and far from athletic. Kingston wasn't considered handsome, but he was Leprechaun cute. His dark brown hair was already showing signs of gray, and his neatly trimmed beard was almost half gray, which may have made him look so much older. A gentle man and a gentleman. Considering Kingston and Casandra were both on the shorter side, at times, Sidney thought it almost ironic that she was slightly taller than average.

"Are you okay, Sidney?" her mother asked.

Sidney jumped up from her chair, hurried across the room, and hugged her mother. "No, not really," she replied, then sniffed and held back her tears.

Her mother again hugged her before her father moved in and held her as well.

"I'm sure he's going to be fine," her father insisted softly near her ear. "Your grandpa is a fighter. He doesn't give up that easily."

"Thanks, Dad," Sidney whispered while clinging to him.

Sidney's father always knew what to say to make her feel better. Sidney finally returned to her chair and stared at the once-strong man who now looked weak and frail.

"It was awful," Sidney whispered. "If I had stayed with him just a few minutes longer--"

"Don't start with that," Sidney's mother insisted firmly. "You couldn't have predicted this would happen. The man hasn't had so much as a sniffle in twenty years."

"I know," Sidney whispered. "I just keep reliving that moment over and over."

"Did he wake up at all?" her father asked and stared at the sleeping man, looking so helpless.

"No, not yet," Sidney replied. "I mean, he woke briefly, but I doubt he was aware of his surroundings."

An ICU nurse entered the room and eyed Sidney's parents. "I'm sorry," the nurse announced somewhat sympathetically. "Only two visitors at a time."

Kingston smiled politely and nodded. "Yes, we're sorry," he announced. "I'll wait outside."

Casandra took Helena's vacant chair and sat on the opposite side of her grandfather. She stared at him a moment, then finally met Sidney's gaze.

"You've been here for hours," Casandra remarked gently. "Why don't you go home with your father for a few hours, get something to eat, and get a little rest. G-ma and I will stay a while."

"I'd really like to be here when he wakes up," Sidney informed her mother.

"I know, honey," her mother replied sympathetically, "but that could be hours from now. You look exhausted."

Sidney eyed her watch and fiddled with it. "Grandpa and I should be sitting around the fire pit right about now," she remarked, then managed a tiny smile. "Exaggerating the size of the one that got away."

Casandra managed a tiny laugh. "I'll bet," she said, then sighed. "You'll have plenty of time for stories around the campfire. You should go home and rest."

Sidney eyed the nurse as she diligently worked as if awaiting her approval, but the nurse didn't offer any advice. As the nurse was leaving, Helena entered and paused when she saw her daughter in her seat. Sidney's mother stood and offered a warm, timid smile.

"I'm going to talk to your grandmother," Casandra announced. "When I get back, you're going home with your father."

Sidney frowned and nodded. Once her mother and grandmother left the room, Sidney returned her attention to her grandpa. She placed her hand on his and gave it a gentle squeeze.

"You heard the boss," Sidney muttered to the motionless man in the bed. "I'll be back in a few hours. I'll bring your favorite book and read a little to you. Not exactly campfire stories, but it'll be nice."

Henry weakly squeezed her hand, and his eyes fluttered open a moment after. They didn't remain open very long, but his head turned toward her.

"Sidney," he whispered through the oxygen mask.

Sidney practically jumped to his side and sat on the bed alongside him. She squeezed his hand with both of hers.

"Grandpa," she gasped as tears of joy escaped along with a sad smile. "You're awake."

"Where am I?" he whispered, barely able to keep his eyes open more than a second or two.

"You're in the hospital," she replied. "You collapsed in the office."

Henry groaned softly. "I hate hospitals," he muttered. "They're for sick people."

Sidney managed a tiny laugh while clinging to his hand. "I'll spring you just as soon as I can," she informed him. "Just a few more hours, I promise."

Her grandpa's eyes opened, and he met her gaze. "I'm so proud of you, honey," Henry whispered. "You're my reason for living."

"I love you too, Grandpa," she announced as the tears rolled freely down her cheek. "I'm going to get you out of here as soon as I can."

"Your birthday present is at the cabin," he informed her in little more than a whisper. "I hope you like it."

The comment seemed strange since her birthday wasn't for another six months. Maybe he was hallucinating.

"I'm sure I'll love it, Grandpa," she replied, offering a warm smile, even though his eyes were closed and he couldn't see it.

"I know," he whispered. "I just want you to be happy, Sidney."

Sidney watched as her grandpa drifted back to sleep. He'd had a long, exhausting day fighting for his life, and he needed to rest. When her mother and grandmother returned, Sidney released Henry's hand and stood.

"He was awake for a few minutes," Sidney informed them, then held her breath a moment. "I'll go home with Dad and let Grandpa sleep a while."

"And you should too," her mother announced, then kissed her quickly on the cheek. "Go home and get some rest."

§

Sidney's dreams that night were all over the place, but they mostly revolved around her grandpa and his cabin by the lake.

The small, cleared backyard had a massive stone fire pit with large, chiseled stones used as seats and a small picnic table not far from the stone charcoal grill. The rest of the backyard remained wooded. In her dreams, she walked the path around the entire lake with Henry. Grandpa told her many stories about the lake and his life as a young boy when he lived in the cabin with his mother and father. As she walked with her grandpa, she was once again a young girl, clinging to his hand and his words, and he was the handsome young man from his youth. He took her to his favorite spot not far from the cabin, where he used to go when he was just a boy. There was a large weeping willow tree near a long stone fence that seemed to extend forever. As they sat under the tree, he placed his arm around her shoulder and held her to his side while they stared across the peaceful countryside.

"One day, this will all be yours," Henry informed her while smiling reflectively. "You'll get married and have children of your own."

"Boys are gross," young Sidney informed him matter-of-factly.

Henry chuckled while hiding his smile. "Well, one day you may think differently," he announced, then kissed the top of her head. "And I may even approve of the lucky fella."

"You will," young Sidney replied. "He's going to be just like you."

Henry smiled and leaned his head back against the tree. "Well, then he's bound to have many flaws, sweetheart," her grandpa informed her. "I've made plenty of mistakes in my time."

"But Gammy loved you," she insisted, and glanced at the younger version of her great-grandfather sitting alongside her.

"Yes," he replied and nodded knowingly. "She did. I wish she'd been around so you could have known her. Your gammy tried to keep me honest, even when it was a losing battle. God bless her; she did her best with me."

Sidney turned onto her hip and clung to her grandpa. "Promise you'll never leave me."

He affectionately caressed her shoulder. "You grew up into a beautiful, intelligent, and independent woman, Sidney," Henry informed her and kissed the top of her head. "I know you're going to be just fine."

Sidney was no longer a little girl, but she remained clinging to her great-grandfather from his youth. She looked up and stared at his profile as he stared off in the distance. Sidney felt the tears welling in her eyes.

"Please, don't leave me," she whispered.

"Do you see her?" Henry then asked.

Sidney looked across the field and saw a young woman in a thin, elegant white dress. She was a vision of beauty with flowing dark hair and a broad, bright smile.

"Who is she?" Sidney asked while sitting up straight.

"That's your gammy," Henry replied without taking his eyes off the young woman.

Sidney stared at the oddly familiar woman for a long moment before seeing the older woman she only knew from photographs. Henry looked back at Sidney, then pointed to the field of purple wildflowers.

"Why don't you pick her a nice bouquet of wild flowers?" he suggested. "I'm going to go say 'hello'."

Sidney smiled and nodded, then eagerly jumped to her feet and began picking flowers. When she had a nice-sized bouquet, she looked back at the tree, but her grandpa was gone. Sidney looked across the field and saw her great-grandfather and great-grandmother together, as a young couple. Henry handed her a single purple flower. Sidney

stared at the loving couple for a moment, then felt a strange warm breeze blow past her face.

Sidney woke from her sleep and looked around her dimly lit bedroom, disoriented. The windows were open, and a breeze gently blew the curtains inward. It was three o'clock in the morning, and Sidney was suddenly wide awake. She couldn't deny the dream had both warmed and disturbed her, refusing to vanish from her mind. She shivered slightly, possibly from the light breeze blowing against her. There was a faint knocking on her door, but she already knew it was her father and what he was going to say. Her grandpa had died.

Chapter 5

Three days later. After the funeral, all of Henry's family and friends gathered at the Westmore house for the wake. Sidney sat on the back kitchen porch swing and stared at her grandpa's workshop in the distance, lost in her own thoughts. Although Sidney never wore dresses and didn't actually own any, she wore a simple, form-fitting black dress with short sleeves and a hemline that fell just below her knees. She had borrowed the dress and black high heels from her best friend, who was a few inches shorter than her, but it was the best she could do. She wanted to make a grand gesture for her grandpa's funeral, and she could think of nothing grander than wearing a dress. Sidney hadn't been out to the garage since the afternoon she performed CPR on her grandpa. She couldn't bring herself to go back there, but it was inevitable. If she didn't return phone calls and pay bills, her grandmother would. Considering her grandpa was the carpentry 'artist', sadly, the business would die with him.

Sidney knew it was only a matter of time before her grandmother had an uncomfortable talk with her about the fate of her grandpa's business. The thought turned Sidney's stomach. Of course, she hadn't eaten much the last three days, and both her mother and grandmother had been pushing anti-anxiety meds on her. It would only be natural that her stomach hurt, and she felt as if she were in a dark fog. Adding a glass or two of her grandpa's favorite whiskey on top of anti-anxiety medications and an empty stomach probably didn't help either.

"Hey," a familiar, timid voice announced through the kitchen screen door.

Sidney looked back and saw her best friend, Amber, stepping onto the porch. Twenty-three-year-old Amber Ford was a short, petite woman with wavy, shoulder-length, strawberry blonde hair and dazzling blue eyes. A beauty by any standards, Amber looked younger than her actual age, sometimes acting it as well. Sidney groaned, just about sprang to her feet, and threw her arms around her friend. Amber returned the embrace.

"Thanks for coming, Amber," Sidney moaned into her friend's hair.

"Sorry, we were late to the church," Amber remarked timidly as she pulled away and met Sidney's gaze. "Uncle Jackson feared erupting into flames crossing the church threshold."

Sidney managed a smile for the first time in three days and even chuckled. "I can't believe you actually got him here," she remarked.

"Yeah, he's not into public appearances," Amber insisted. "Especially since that time Naomi got his ass kicked at the bar when she dumped him."

"I don't understand why she goes out of her way to make your uncle's life so miserable," Sidney remarked. "Why would she want to 'poke the bear'?"

"His mouth writes checks his fists can't cash," Amber retorted. "You should know. You stood up to him a few times."

"That doesn't mean I don't still fear him," Sidney muttered.

Amber chuckled at the comment, then eyed her friend. "You look fabulous in my dress," she insisted. "Better than it looked on me. Of course, I don't have nearly as much cleavage."

"My first and ***only*** time wearing a dress," Sidney remarked and managed a tiny smile as she looked down at her cleavage. "Grandpa would be both proud and ashamed."

Amber had to laugh at the comment. She then turned serious. "Is there anything I can do for you?"

Sidney drew a deep breath, placed her head on Amber's shoulder, and sighed dramatically. "Get me through today without lashing out irrationally," she replied. "And don't let me near the booze. I've had enough already."

Amber patted Sidney's head on her shoulder. "You've got it," she replied. "Oh, and just so you know. The rest of the 'Brat Pack' has arrived."

Sidney lifted her head and managed a tiny smile. "The Three Stooges?"

"Yep," Amber announced proudly. "They're all here. Your 'best' bud, your 'ex' bud, and your 'never-would-I-ever' bud."

"My friends to the rescue," Sidney replied with a relieved sigh and a humored grin while clinging to Amber's arm. "Can you walk me inside? I'm high on anti-depressants and whiskey. The floor is swaying."

Sidney entered the kitchen through the porch door, using Amber as a crutch, and attempted a sober walk. She didn't feel like being lectured by her mother and grandmother, despite the fact that they were the ones pushing the antidepressants on her. Even though she was old enough to drink, there was still some disapproval. If they only knew how much of a bad influence her grandpa had been on her, she'd never hear the end of it. He'd often offer her a 'nip' from his emergency whiskey bottle in his office desk drawer, and that was since she was eighteen. Sidney's three guy friends had gathered around the island counter where the hard liquor was lined up for guests to help themselves. Greyson was a handsome, twenty-four-year-old man with short light-brown hair, a clean-shaven face, and dark eyes. He stood almost six feet with an impressive athletic build. Out of Sidney and Amber's guy friends, Greyson had the best personality and was considered the funny one in their group.

Leon was the same age as Sidney. He was a good-looking young man with sandy blonde hair, piercing blue eyes, and mostly clean-shaven with a hint of a five o'clock shadow. He was of average height with a leaner build. Leon was the charming one in their little group and her only guy friend that she had dated, although that ended back in high school. The last guy in their group was Miller. Miller, easily described as classically handsome, was also twenty-three, with thick, short, dark hair, dark eyes, and a clean-shaven face. He stood over six feet tall with a moderately athletic build. Although he was the loudest in their group, he was also the friendliest and the first one to lend a hand to a friend in need. Greyson and Leon saw Sidney and briefly hesitated when they noticed she was wearing a dress for the first time since kindergarten.

Once the shock wore off, both guys immediately approached her. Amber released her friend long enough for both young men to give her warm embraces and extend their condolences. Miller finished pouring his drink before noticing his guy friends with Sidney and Amber. Miller took in a sweeping eyeful of Sidney in the dress and did his best to hide his approving grin.

"Oh, wow," Miller announced while softly chuckling.

Greyson frowned and secretly elbowed Miller to silence him. If anyone had an inappropriate comment, it would be him. Miller then turned serious and hugged Sidney as well.

"Is there anything we can do for you, Sidney?" Greyson asked in genuine sincerity.

"If you really mean that--" Sidney began, then hesitated.

Leon swooped in and seemed a little too eager to lend his assistance. "Of course," he replied. "Anything you need."

"I'd appreciate it if someone could back the boat inside the garage," Sidney informed them, then fidgeted. "My father said he'd help me after the funeral, but I don't feel like going out to the workshop just yet."

Leon smacked Miller on the shoulder and indicated the back door. "Let's go move the beast before we get a few drinks in us," he announced.

"It doesn't have to be right this--"

"No, we've got this," Leon announced, then left the kitchen with Miller.

Miller could be heard talking to Leon as they walked off the porch. "Can you believe Sidney in that dress?" he remarked. "Who knew she was that hot?"

Greyson groaned and shook his head, knowing Sidney heard what he heard. "I suppose I should supervise those two," he remarked, then followed his friends with less enthusiasm.

Amber watched the guys leave with added interest. "Wonder what they're up to," she muttered.

"Well, I know what Leon is up to," Sidney replied. "And I'm guessing Miller is wondering how long he has to wait until he can ask to borrow the boat."

"If you believe that, then you're more clueless around guys than I am," Amber remarked with a tiny chuckle. "Did you see the way they were gawking at you in that dress?"

"No," Sidney replied, not even affected by the comment. "Let them gawk. It's the only time any of them are ever seeing me in a dress anyway." She then shrugged. "Besides, they're my friends. They don't think of me like that."

"Yeah, sure they don't," Amber muttered while hiding her smile.

"Guys get all giddy over trucks and boats," Sidney informed her friend. "And my grandpa did have some nice toys."

"Yep," Amber remarked with a tiny sigh. "I'm sure that's what had them all excited."

Amber and Sidney left the kitchen through the dining room doorway, where the massive buffet spread filled the long table. The sideboard was loaded with desserts. Despite having been picked through, there was still a lot of food for the taking. Dozens of men and women occupied chairs throughout the house, while others stood, picking at their plates. After sampling some of the fare, Sidney and Amber ventured down the hallway, mingling with other guests. All custom-designed by the craftsman himself, the living room was a work of art with its tall, broad stone fireplace and high hearth with a thick, carved wooden mantel. The fireplace climbed the cathedral ceiling, with exposed beams, up to the second floor ceiling.

"Your Grandpa certainly was popular," Amber remarked while looking around. "Looks like half the town is here."

"Including your uncle," Sidney replied, then managed a tiny laugh. "That has to be a first."

"I know," Amber announced. "It's not easy getting him out of the house these days, but I didn't even have to ask. He just assumed he had to come." Amber glanced at Sidney and offered a warm smile. "I mean, you ***are*** my best friend, and you have spent a lot of time at our place over the last few years."

"Training your uncle wasn't easy," Sidney informed her friend. "At times, it was a lot of work. He didn't make it easy for me, that's certain."

"Yes, he tolerates you nicely," Amber remarked, then offered a humored smile.

Sidney's mother and grandmother stood in the hallway, huddled together, staring into the front sitting room and talking quietly among themselves. They might have been gossiping. Despite not being all that old, they did enjoy good gossip from time to time. Something had them clucking away, which wasn't normal for either woman. Sidney silently approached them and followed their gaze, curious as to what had their undivided attention. She then saw the source of their gossip. Amber's uncle. Jackson Ford was a tall, moderately muscular man, standing about six-foot-two with broad shoulders and toned arms. Undeniably handsome, his short, jet black hair almost appeared slicked back for that classic Italian mobster look. His eyes somehow seemed even darker than his hair, giving him a slightly menacing appearance. Although he claimed to be only eight years older than Amber, the gray in his sparse beard made him look older.

Jackson was disturbingly quiet, particularly now that he was out in public, but when he did speak, he had a low, gruff baritone voice that carried a lot of authority. His demeanor, along with his grizzly voice, had a way of intimidating people, whether he meant to or not. Despite being a moderately quiet man in the crowded room, Jackson received more than his share of stares and whispers from the other guests. It was rare to spot Jackson outside of his natural habitat. Even Sidney, who had spent much time at Amber's house, was oddly awestruck seeing Jackson outside of his territory. Sporting a moderately casual suit made the sighting more surprising, even if he didn't wear a tie. As handsome as he was, Jackson looked out of place, like a caged panther looking for an escape. Sidney often wondered what made the man such a recluse. Or did he just despise people that much?

"It's not polite to stare," Sidney whispered over her mother's shoulder, causing her to cry out in surprise.

Helena and Casandra reacted to Sidney's taunt and looked back at the young woman.

"You really shouldn't sneak up on us like that," her grandmother scolded. "You're liable to give me a heart attack."

"Please, G-ma," Sidney moaned softly. "You're going to outlive us all." She then indicated Jackson across the room as he nervously fidgeted with his drink. "With the way everyone stares at him, it's no wonder he doesn't leave his farm."

"We didn't mean to stare," Sidney's mother remarked, then fidgeted slightly. "It's just that, well, we haven't really seen him since he first moved to town eight years ago. Just those few times he'd pick up Amber from school in his pickup truck, looking like the getaway driver at a bank heist."

"Mom," Sidney shamed her mother, rather surprised by the comment, then indicated her grandmother. "I'd expect that sort of thing from G-ma, but certainly not you."

"I didn't mean to be rude," Casandra informed her daughter and again looked at Jackson across the room. "I just don't remember him being so--"

"***Hunky***," Helena replied, finishing Casandra's thought.

Sidney looked from Jackson across the room to her mother and grandmother, who maintained their gazes. It then dawned on her.

"Oh, my God," Sidney gasped while attempting to keep her voice down. "I can't believe the two of you are checking him out!"

Her grandmother looked back at her, raising a skeptical brow. "And I can't believe you're not," Helena remarked matter-of-factly, then indicated Jackson. "He's got a great set of shoulders on him."

"Definitely the beard," Sidney's mother groaned and shook her head. "I can't believe ***Naomi*** dumped ***him***."

Amber approached Sidney's mother and grandmother, eyeing them almost suspiciously. "Are you okay?" she asked the two women. "You both look a little flushed."

Sidney eyed her friend while raising a cocky brow. "They're checking out your uncle."

"Checking him--?" Amber began, then abruptly silenced as horror crossed her face. "Oh! Ewe!" She conveyed her disgust. "He's all hairy and always smells like engine grease from working on his cars." She then waved them off while rolling her eyes. "And his tattoos!"

Casandra and Helena let out soft groans and tried to fan their rapidly reddening cheeks. Sidney and Amber stared at the two older women, realizing the description just made it worse.

"I'm going to be sick," Amber muttered.

Sidney ushered her friend away from Helena and Casandra.

Chapter 6

Sidney and Amber sat on the rustic, hand-carved staircase to avoid the excessively congested hallway. There wasn't any need for words, and both seemed to enjoy watching the throngs of well-dressed men and women socializing.

"What is it with older women gawking at my uncle?" Amber asked while frowning. "I mean, I want him to find someone and get his own life so he stays out of mine, but seriously--?"

"Well, maybe you'll luck out, and he'll get back together with Naomi," Sidney remarked.

Amber rolled her eyes somewhat dramatically. "Please," she moaned. "That woman was a nightmare, and he's not really into high-maintenance women. I mean, look at him. He's a mechanic."

"I wouldn't exactly call him a mechanic," Sidney reminded her friend. "He has quite the restoration operation going and makes a good living at it."

"Well, yeah," Amber replied. "Now, he does. Of course, that's almost all he does. That and that stupid gun collection of his. There are literally guns everywhere in our house."

"I know," Sidney remarked with a groan. "I've stayed overnight at your house many times. I once found a gun hidden in the towel closet."

"Yeah, now envision ***that*** with someone like Naomi," Amber muttered. "You're my only friend he'd ever even considered letting in our house."

"Only because I wore him down." Sidney smiled and snorted a laugh. "I remember you'd been living in town for almost two years and no one even knew who was living in that old farmhouse," she announced while grinning. "Grandpa was dead set on any of us ever getting to know you or your uncle. I think he thought you were terrorists."

"No big surprise there," Amber huffed while frowning. "My recluse of an uncle didn't want me playing with the other kids."

"Why was that anyway?" Sidney asked and eyed her friend's profile.

Amber waved her off without looking at her. "Some overly protective bull crap," she replied. "After my mother died, and he got custody of me, he was afraid to let me out of his sight for more than two minutes. And, naturally, other kids my age would be a bad influence."

"But ***you're*** the bad influence," Sidney reminded her.

Amber snorted a laugh. "Yeah, joke's on him, huh?"

Sidney maintained her smile as she sank back into a different time, not that long ago.

Flashback. Just outside the woods, seventeen-year-old Sidney sat on the bank of the large stream with her fishing pole and watched the red and white bobber lazily float on the water. The damned thing hadn't moved since she'd sat down half an hour earlier. Her grandpa approached while proudly holding up two large catfish on a chain stringer. Henry's grin was somewhat proud but mostly mocking.

"You used to be better at catching fish," Henry informed her.

"No one likes a braggart," Sidney scoffed while silently pouting over her lack of nibbles.

"Maybe you should try moving a little further downstream," her grandpa suggested.

"I'm fine here," Sidney insisted.

"Suit yourself," Henry replied, then nodded toward the distant four-wheeler. "I'll be over there, gutting our little friends. It's nearly lunchtime, so we should be heading back to the cabin soon."

"Give me another hour," Sidney announced, still discouraged.

"I really should get these on ice," Henry reminded her.

"Take the four-wheeler," Sidney insisted. "It's not that far. I'll walk back to the cabin."

Henry hesitated while eyeing her, as if considering the comment.

Sidney immediately groaned. "I know my way around these woods," she insisted. "I won't get lost."

"It's not that," Henry remarked, then looked past the stream and across a large field to a distant barn. "I'm not sure I like leaving you alone so close to 'that one'."

"Seriously, Grandpa," Sidney announced with a soft groan. "They've been living there for almost two years. I sincerely doubt he's a cannibalistic serial killer."

Henry frowned and shook his head, unable to take his eyes off the barely visible barn. "I find the whole thing particularly unnerving," he remarked. "A reclusive man and his teenage daughter living out here in the middle of nowhere. Only comes to town twice a month for groceries. I heard the girl hasn't even attended school since they moved in." He frowned in distaste. "She's homeschooled."

"Well, that is a thing, Grandpa," Sidney reminded him.

"Maybe so, but it's a 'strange' thing," he replied, then shook his head. "It's not healthy, keeping kids isolated from

other kids. Something about that whole thing just doesn't settle right."

"You're almost there, Grandpa," Sidney informed him, catching his attention.

"Almost where?"

"Becoming a busybody like G-ma," she replied.

Henry frowned, not appreciating the insult. "I'm nowhere near the busybody your grandmother is. Honestly, I don't know when my daughter turned into such a gossip."

As her grandpa walked away with his morning catch, or lunch, as he liked to call it, Sidney shook her head at the irony. It was true that her grandmother was a town busybody, but her great-grandfather wasn't really all that far behind her. Once she heard her grandpa drive away on the four-wheeler, Sidney returned to her tranquil, non-productive fishing excursion. The faint sounds of a girl screaming carried off in the distance. It seemed to come from the area near the barn. Sidney leapt to her feet and stared at the barn. Although faint, she heard raised voices, both male and female, in a shouting match. Sidney was instantly panicked by the angry voices. If she could hear it all the way out by the stream, the shouting had to be particularly loud at the old farmhouse. Even more frightening was that only the father and the teenage daughter were living there. That Sidney actually heard a screen door slamming was concerning.

Sidney fumbled for her cell phone in her pocket, quickly realizing there was no service anywhere near her grandpa's cabin, especially this far out in the woods. She reeled in her fishing line while plotting her next move. She certainly couldn't wander onto the remote farm and check on the shouting voices, but she also didn't feel safe remaining on the bank all by herself either. There was no telling what the father and daughter were arguing about, and everything she'd heard about him, he wasn't exactly someone she wanted to run into. Sidney decided the only course of action was to abandon her fishing gear and run back to the cabin.

She'd tell Grandpa about the argument and let him decide what they should do. Sidney had no sooner tossed her pole alongside her tackle box when she heard splashing in the stream. She immediately looked around, half-frightened out of her mind, when she saw a young teenage girl wading through the knee-deep water.

Seventeen-year-old Amber looked younger than her age. Her long strawberry blonde hair was somewhat unkempt, and her t-shirt was slightly worn. When their eyes met, both looked like deer in headlights, not expecting to see anyone so far out in the middle of nowhere. They both stood motionless and silent, staring at each other for the longest moment. Amber took the initiative and smiled.

"Uh, hi," Amber announced, staring at Sidney as if she'd never seen another teenager before.

"Uh, hi," Sidney replied, a little less sure of herself. "Are, uh, you okay?"

Amber stared at Sidney a moment longer, appearing almost puzzled. "Yeah, I'm fine," she replied, then touched her mussed hair. "Do I not look okay?"

"You look okay," Sidney replied, then hesitated. "But you didn't sound okay a minute ago."

Amber looked across the field at the barn before returning her gaze to Sidney and offering a slightly embarrassed smile.

"Oh, you heard that," she remarked, then managed a tiny, tense laugh. "That's my uncle. I love him to death, but he can be a real dick."

"Your uncle?" Sidney asked, somewhat surprised. "I thought he was your father."

"No, my father's been out of the picture for years," Amber replied while maintaining her smile. "My uncle got custody of me after my mother died. That's when we moved here." Amber relaxed, almost gleeful at that moment. "I'm Amber."

"I'm Sidney," she replied. "My grandpa has a cabin on the lake not far from here."

"There's a lake near here?" Amber asked, surprised.

Sidney wondered how the girl could live on the farm for two years without knowing about the lake. Despite being private property, many teenagers hiked to the lake for a swim.

"Yeah," Sidney replied while attempting to relax, although finding it difficult after the shouting she'd heard only moments earlier. "My grandpa and I were about to have lunch. You could join us, if you'd like."

Amber snorted a laugh. "As if my uncle would allow that," she scoffed. "He's already pissed at me."

"Oh?"

"I ordered mascara and lipstick online," Amber remarked, then batted her dark lashes and puckered her lips, showing Sidney. "Honestly, I didn't think he'd notice it." She groaned softly. "Boy, was I wrong!"

"Your uncle won't let you wear makeup?" Sidney asked, suspiciously.

"He says I'm not old enough," Amber insisted while adding an eye roll. "He's like a goddamned parrot."

"Aren't you my age?" Sidney asked. "Seventeen?"

Amber hesitated only a moment, then nodded. "Yeah," she announced. "Crazy, right?"

"Amber!" a deep male voice called from the distance. "Amber!"

Amber rolled her eyes and then shook her head. "He really hates when I run off like that," she announced. "He needs to get his blood pressure up about something once in a while. I like to think I'm helping him get 'it all out' by pushing his buttons. He wasn't bred for a life in captivity."

Sidney had no idea what Amber meant by that, but it certainly sounded as if she succeeded in elevating her uncle's blood pressure.

"Are you sure you're okay?" Sidney again asked. "If he's holding you against your will--"

Amber was taken aback by the comment before laughing it off. "Oh, God, no," she announced, humored. "It's not like that at all. I mean, he's paranoid, controlling, and can't cut the apron strings, but he's certainly not abusive by any means. We just, well, get on each other's nerves." She then considered her comment. *"Your grandpa's cabin--? Are you there all summer?"*

"No, just for the weekend," Sidney replied. "We live on the edge of town. We're local."

"Could I maybe come over this evening?" Amber asked. "I've never swam in a pond before."

"Didn't you just say that your uncle--?"

Amber grinned almost deviously. "That I need to elevate his blood pressure now and again?" she reminded her. "Absolutely!"

"If you're sure you won't get in any serious trouble," Sidney remarked.

Amber snorted a laugh, then gave a general nod back to the farm. "What's he going to do?" she demanded. "Ground me?"

"If you're sure," Sidney replied, then indicated the path not far from the stream. "Just follow that path and take the first path to the right. Walk for about fifteen minutes, and you'll see the lake. Take the path to the left, and in a few minutes, that'll bring you to the cabin. I'll leave the porch light on."

"Amber!" the gruff, baritone voice scolded from the opposite bank of the stream.

Sidney and Amber jumped and looked at the man in his early to mid-twenties standing on the opposite bank. Jackson was an imposing man. Although Sidney didn't get a very good look at his face, his bold stance was enough to unnerve her. When Amber's uncle saw Sidney, he seemed more surprised than Amber had been, possibly not expecting to see anyone so deep in the woods. Once the surprise wore off, his toughness returned.

"You're trespassing on private property," Jackson scoffed.

"Actually," Sidney announced in a somewhat cocky tone. "You're the one trespassing. My grandpa owns the stream and the land twenty yards on that side." Sidney gathered her fishing pole and tackle box. "He's also within shouting distance and packing a shotgun, so I suggest you maintain your distance or I'll scream." Sidney then looked back at Amber, offered a smile, and gave a general nod at Jackson. "Good luck with that."

Present day.

"Hey," Amber announced, returning Sidney to the present. When Sidney looked at her friend, Amber was staring at her. "Are you okay?"

Sidney finally smiled and nodded. "Yeah, I guess so," she replied with a sigh. "My grandpa could be overbearing at times, too, but I knew he meant well."

"At least your grandpa didn't suffocate you as Jackson does with me," Amber muttered. At that moment, she spotted her uncle entering the hallway. "I'm going to check on the boys. Make sure they didn't steal your grandpa's boat."

Sidney watched her friend make a quick getaway before Jackson was close enough to spot her. She didn't quite understand what went on between Amber and Jackson. Those two had a strange relationship. Overbearing would be the more accurate term. Initially, Sidney was convinced Jackson was abusive toward his niece, but he loosened Amber's leash two years ago, after she turned twenty-one. There had been quite the blowout between the uncle and niece after Sidney took Amber to the local bar to celebrate her legal drinking status. After that, he backed off some. Sidney would be lying if she said he didn't make her a little uneasy at times, especially in the beginning, but she always had a way with people. While watching him, she noticed Jackson looked somewhat awkward as he approached the staircase.

"How are you holding up?" Jackson asked, sounding more like a protective big brother than Amber's oddball uncle.

Sidney shrugged and managed a weak smile. "A little numb," she replied. "But that could be from drinking too much of my Grandpa's eighteen-year-old Crown Royal whiskey."

Jackson raised his brows at the comment. "I didn't know your great-grandfather appreciated fine whiskey," he remarked while offering a tiny smile.

"He was a simple man with a taste for some of the finer things," Sidney informed him. "There was no half-ass with my grandpa. He was pretty much an 'all or nothing' kind of guy."

"I probably would have liked him," Jackson remarked, and sat two steps below her, which put them at eye level.

Sidney wasn't used to one-on-one conversations with Jackson, and she'd only ever been this close to him on one other occasion. A very loud, confrontational encounter that she didn't care to repeat. When Sidney visited Amber at the farm, Jackson mostly stayed in his garage. He did make dinner on occasion, inviting her to stay, but Amber was always around as a buffer.

"After a round of insults, he probably would have liked you too," Sidney informed him. "He'd probably try to intimidate you by telling you he had a gun, you'd ask him what caliber, and the two of you would be hunting buddies before dark."

Jackson grinned and chuckled. "I keep forgetting you know me better than most people around town," he remarked.

"Well, I have helped Amber fold laundry on many occasions," Sidney reminded him while staring into his eyes, where he sat not all that far from her. "So I probably know you better than I want to."

The comment took him by surprise, but was soon followed by a humored smile and a chuckle. Sidney hid her smile and tensed slightly after practically admitting to Jackson that she'd folded his various colored boxer briefs. It was possible she embarrassed herself more than she had him. Sidney was suddenly having a difficult time looking him in the eyes, especially sitting so close to him.

"I'm guessing that embarrassed me more than it did you," Sidney admitted, to which Jackson just maintained his grin.

Sidney couldn't be sure, but Jackson seemed to be enjoying seeing her flustered. She needed to change the subject and fast.

"I'll bet you're dying to see my grandpa's gun collection."

"I didn't know he had a gun collection," Jackson replied without missing a beat, although his grin increased. "And, yes, I would absolutely love to see that."

When Sidney attempted to stand, she almost didn't make it. Jackson was quick to his feet and immediately stabilized her.

"You may want to cut back on the Crown Royal," Jackson remarked with a slightly humored grin while keeping her steady.

"I'm not drunk," Sidney insisted. If anything, it was the anti-anxiety pills G-ma kept pushing on her, but she wasn't going to tell Jackson she mixed alcohol with Xanax. "I wasn't meant to wear high heels." She then grimaced. "Or dresses, for that matter."

"I respectfully disagree," Jackson replied without missing a beat.

Sidney immediately met his gaze, somewhat surprised by the comment, although she was almost positive it was a compliment. She half expected to catch him sneaking a peek at her cleavage or her ass, but then she remembered he wasn't Miller or Leon. A tiny, humored smile crossed her face as she clutched his arm, then pointed up the stairs to the second floor.

"If you could see me safely to the top of the stairs," Sidney announced. "I'll ditch the shoes and maybe not fall down the steps on the return trip."

Chapter 7

Sidney entered her grandpa's bedroom, carrying her high heels, with Jackson only a step or two behind. Henry's master bedroom was exceptionally roomy with French doors leading to a small balcony. The king-sized bed, as well as the rest of the furniture, was Henry's own work. But the crowning glory of the bedroom was the massive, hand-carved gun cabinet on the wall alongside the bed, and nearly as long. The detail of the cabinet was breathtaking with rows of shotguns, rifles, and many handguns of various calibers. Jackson's eyes were immediately drawn to the hand-carved gun cabinet with two glass doors. When they paused before the cabinet, Jackson ran his hand along the heavily detailed wood and marveled at the masterpiece.

"Your great-grandfather was one hell of a carpenter," Jackson remarked.

"His profession and his hobby," Sidney replied. "I heard you're quite the carpenter yourself. You did a lot of work at your place, didn't you?"

"I fixed the house and barn, rebuilt the porch, and added a few closets here and there," he informed her. "Basic carpentry. Nothing detailed like this." Jackson then eyed some of the rifles through the glass, his interest peaking. "Did he hand-carve those rifle stocks?"

Sidney proudly opened the unlocked cabinet, extended her hand to the opening, and then stepped aside. "Some of the older ones he needed to restore," she informed Jackson, who eagerly checked out the weapons gently and lovingly. "He decided to make his own stock rather than order modern replacements."

Jackson aimed the rifle across the room and eyed the sights. "Do you know how to shoot?" he asked without looking at her.

Sidney suddenly chuckled at the question before drifting off into one of her fondest memories of her grandpa.

Flashback. Twelve-year-old Sidney held the custom-designed rifle in her hands and attempted to balance the rather long weapon. Her grandpa helped her steady it.

"Now, remember what I taught you," Henry informed her.

"Never curse in front of G-ma," Sidney replied and hid her smile while looking through the sights on the rifle.

"Well, that too," Henry remarked, then chuckled, knowing she was playing with him. "Don't squeeze the trigger until you have your sights locked onto the target, and make sure there's nothing behind the target."

Sidney attempted to nod, but it was difficult with the weight and size of the rifle in her hands. She steadied the rifle, checked her target, and then squeezed the trigger. There was some kick, being that she was smaller. The powerful rifle blast seemed to echo across the lake and the woods. Sidney lowered the rifle and stared at the distant target with a fresh tear through it, close to center.

"I did it!"

When Sidney looked back, her grandpa was almost as excited as she was.

"That's wonderful, Sidney," Henry announced joyfully. "A few more weekends at the cabin, and you'll be shooting better than me. We can even go hunting together."

Sidney looked at him and wrinkled her nose. "I'm not shooting Bambi and Thumper."

"Fine, you don't have to go hunting with me," Henry replied with some disappointment. His grin soon returned. "Are you ready to try the handguns?"

Sidney's eyes lit up. "Can I?"

"As long as you don't tell your mother or grandmother," Henry muttered with disgust. "They only need to know that we're 'fishing'."

"They're too girly to shoot guns," Sidney informed him. "I'm not going to be girly when I grow up."

"Well, sometimes it just happens," Henry replied with a groan. "You know, I taught your grandmother to shoot guns when she was your age."

Sidney stared at her grandpa, surprised. "You did?" she practically gasped, then turned skeptical. "I find that hard to believe."

"She wasn't always a proper young lady, you know," Henry reported while returning the rifle to the rifle bag, then removed a twelve-inch, pearl-handled revolver. "She was a crack shot. Kind of all went south when she turned fifteen or sixteen. Started wearing makeup and taking an interest in boys."

"I have boyfriends."

"I'm not talking about boys who are friends," Henry informed her, then raised a brow. "I'm talking about boyfriends. The kind that want to go on dates and make out at the movies."

"I'm never doing that," Sidney insisted matter-of-factly.

"Good," Henry announced while hiding his knowing smile. "I'm holding you to that." He then held up the large revolver. "This is a Smith & Wesson 610 revolver. It shoots six rounds." He indicated the weapon. "You keep your finger

off the trigger until you're ready to fire, and you never aim it at anything you don't intend to kill. Got it?"

Sidney nodded, gazing somewhat mesmerized at the weapon. As he handed it to her, handle-first, she gently accepted it in both hands, her eyes wide and sparkling.

Sidney slipped out of her memory and glanced at Jackson, who was now looking at her after her lengthy silence to his question. She offered a somewhat devious smile and looked at the pearl-handled Smith & Wesson 610 revolver proudly displayed in the case.

"Grandpa gave me some pointers," she casually replied while removing the revolver.

Jackson watched Sidney as she lovingly gazed at the weapon. Just then, voices were heard in the hallway. She was about to return the weapon to the cabinet when she heard a gasp from the doorway. Sidney and Jackson looked at her grandmother standing in the doorway, horror on her face.

"You shouldn't be playing with Grandpa's guns," Helena scolded her.

"It's okay, G-ma," Sidney insisted and replaced the gun. "Grandpa taught me how to handle weapons properly."

"As he taught me," Helena scoffed and shook her head. "It was a terrible idea then, too. I'll be happy when they're out of here."

Sidney was surprised by her grandmother's words. "What do you mean?"

Helena indicated the man standing just behind her in the doorway. The man was Randall, the diner owner, and also Naomi's father. Jackson's ex-girlfriend Naomi. If Sidney had been paying attention, she might have noticed the unfriendly stares between the two men.

"Randall offered me a thousand dollars for the entire lot of them," Helena reported. "Gun cabinet and all."

insane," Sidney scoffed. "The cabinet alone is worth more than that, and Grandpa wouldn't want you selling his gun collection."

"He knew how I felt about his guns," Helena reminded Sidney. "I don't like them, and I want them gone."

"Then I'll take them," Sidney boldly announced. "I'll gladly give you a thousand dollars for the entire cabinet and its contents."

"I'm sorry, Sidney," Helena informed her. "They're not staying here, and your mother won't let you take them to her house either."

"Dad will," Sidney scoffed while folding her arms proudly across her chest.

"Well, he's going to lose that argument, I promise," Helena insisted.

Sidney stared at her grandmother, even if it was all she could do at that moment. Her father would have her back, but if her mother were hell-bent on getting her way, he'd back off.

"I'll give you two thousand for the entire cabinet," Jackson announced to Helena.

Randall suddenly came to life, appearing almost horrified before sneering at Jackson, refusing to be bested by him. "I'll give you two and a half."

Helena glanced at Randall with some surprise.

"Five," Jackson countered without showing any emotion, then cocked his head and stared down Randall.

It was then that Sidney realized there was some hostility between the two men, possibly over Jackson's brief relationship with the man's daughter. Randall tensed, frowned, and left the room. Sidney shot a look between her grandmother and Jackson. The two stared at each other for a long moment.

Helena finally sighed and nodded. "You can stop by tomorrow with a check and take it then," she replied, then left the room without a word to Sidney.

The moment her grandmother was gone, Sidney [illegible] anger, facing Jackson. "You had no right," she scoffed, disregarding her feelings of intimidation.

"Says you," Jackson informed her somewhat arrogantly, "but G-ma said otherwise." He shut the cabinet door and turned to face her, jump-starting her heart and reminding her that she had a natural fear of the man. "Randall was exploiting your grandmother to make a quick buck by reselling the contents of that cabinet, whereas I'm an avid collector. The collection will remain intact with me. I did you a favor." Jackson cocked his head and cleverly raised his brows. "When you're in a situation where you can keep the cabinet at your own place, I'll happily sell it back to you." He shrugged with a tiny smirk. "Minus one or two pieces I'd like to keep for myself, but we have time to work out the details."

Sidney shifted uncomfortably and attempted to relax, although it was difficult with the way her blood had been boiling just a few seconds ago. She couldn't believe she had once again challenged Jackson like that.

"I want the Smith & Wesson," she announced in a stern tone, testing her boundaries with the intimidating man.

Jackson opened the cabinet door, removed the revolver, and handed it grip first to her. Sidney didn't actually mean at that moment, but she accepted the weapon regardless. If she didn't take it now, there was no guarantee it would still be there tomorrow. Her G-ma was acting strange since Grandpa's passing. Sidney hesitated and eyed the moderately form-fitting dress she wore. There was no place to hide the weapon to sneak it past her mother and grandmother, and since the dress was borrowed, she obviously didn't own a purse. Sidney thought about it only a moment, somehow managing to avoid Jackson's humored smirk. She stuffed the gun down the front of her dress into her cleavage, jamming it far enough down that the handle was securely hidden between her breasts. When she looked back at Jackson, he appeared somewhat stunned before hiding his smile and laughing.

"I was ***not*** expecting that," Jackson remarked while shaking his head and scratching his brow as he crossed the room for the door. "I'm beyond impressed."

Sidney grabbed her discarded shoes from the bed and followed him while frowning as she adjusted her cleavage. "I'm glad you're amused," she scoffed. "I'm going to have some nasty bruises."

Chapter 8

Early the following morning, Sidney sat on the back porch with her morning tea and stared at the workshop in the near distance. She had spent the better part of the night contemplating her next move regarding her current work situation, or lack thereof, and lost a lot of sleep doing so. She'd worked for her great-grandfather throughout high school and college. Once she graduated, she immediately began working full-time for him, never once considering this day. There was no business without the artist carpenter, and hiring another wouldn't be the same. He or she wouldn't carry on her Grandpa's style. Then, there was the issue of his unfinished work. Deposits had been made and would need to be refunded. Sidney assumed the business side of her grandpa's passing fell to her, since her grandmother never handled her father's business.

Sidney knew she'd need to suck it up and go into the office, preferably sometime today. She'd need to call the clients, cancel orders, and refund deposits. Her grandmother, being Henry's only child, would then decide what to do with the workshop, his machinery, and any other business-related items. Sidney just hoped her grandmother would consult with her before doing anything as irrational as she did with the guns and the gun cabinet. She couldn't handle even thinking about it anymore. It made her head hurt. As she sat in silence staring at the garage, she heard her grandmother and mother rustling around in the kitchen. There was a refrigerator full of leftover food from the wake, and Sidney's mother was helping Helena sort through the trays and freeze what they could. Since her father was off today, it wouldn't be long before he ventured over scrounging for something to eat. Sidney overheard her mother and grandmother's conversation in the kitchen and felt compelled to eavesdrop.

"Attorney Myers is stopping by this afternoon with the will," Helena announced to Casandra. "Once the property is officially transferred over, we'll need to discuss what to do with the workshop."

"Sidney has all the connections to the clients," Casandra reported. "I'm sure she'll have some ideas."

"Maybe we can rent out the workshop," Helena remarked. "If we find the right person, maybe Sidney can continue working in the office."

"Maybe it's time for Sidney to get into architecture and find work in her field," her mother announced. "She needs to think about her future."

"The workshop and garage are on their own parcel of land with a separate deed," Helena remarked. "Maybe we should consider selling it."

"I suppose that's an option," Casandra replied. There was a short pause. "What about the hunting cabin?"

"What about it?" Helena practically scoffed. "The land might be worth something, but that cabin is ancient. It didn't even have electricity and indoor plumbing until twenty years ago. All that money he put into plumbing and electricity was wasted. He should have torn it down and sold the land to those developers."

"Isn't there fifty acres with the cabin?" Casandra asked.

"Closer to one hundred," Helena replied. "With its own private lake."

Sidney felt her heart sink. Her grandmother was going to sell the cabin, where she had some of her best childhood memories of her grandpa. Sidney knew there was some tension between her grandmother and her great-grandfather. Something happened, but no one ever talked about it. Considering Helena moved in with her father a few years after her husband died, whatever their differences, it couldn't have been too bad. Helena had lived with him for the last twenty-four years, although she hadn't been nearly as close to him as Sidney had been. The thought of never visiting the cabin again reminded Sidney that her grandpa was never coming back. Her father crossed the yard and approached the back porch, smiling when he saw his daughter. Sidney managed a weak smile as he joined her on the porch and sat on the swing alongside her. Kingston affectionately placed his hand on her knee.

"Did you sleep last night?" he asked while studying her profile.

Sidney shrugged and frowned. "A little," she replied. "Xanax and whiskey. Bad bedfellows."

Kingston placed his arm around her shoulder and pulled her against his side as they both stared at the workshop in the distance.

"You and your grandpa were very close," her father remarked. "It's going to take time to adjust."

Sidney drew a deep breath while clutching her nearly empty tea mug. "It's going to take a lot of adjusting," she softly remarked so the women in the kitchen wouldn't overhear her concerns. "Mom and G-ma are deciding the fate of Grandpa's business and the cabin as we speak. It feels as if my life is being torn apart, and there's nothing I can do about it."

"I know," Kingston whispered. "I heard about the incident with your grandpa's gun cabinet yesterday."

"It's almost as if G-ma wants to eliminate all memories of Grandpa as fast as possible," Sidney muttered. "It's making me a little crazy. Although I will admit that I didn't handle the gun cabinet thing very well."

"Everyone grieves in their own way," Kingston replied. "Denial is sometimes easier than grief."

"Erasing someone's memory isn't grieving," she corrected. "And she isn't in denial."

Kingston released her shoulder and partially turned to face her. "Want to have breakfast at the diner?" he asked. "Seems to me you need to get away from here for a little while. Clear your head."

"I'd love that, Dad."

The retro diner was built in the 1950s and restored to maintain its old-time charm. Looking almost like a shiny silver tin can with windows, the lighted neon sign 'diner' was boldly displayed on top. The diner's interior had retro red walls, booths, and counter stools, while the floor was black-and-white checkered tile. Beyond the counter seating was the small, greasy kitchen, where patrons could watch the short-order cook fry up their meal. The diner was nearly empty early on the weekday morning. The breakfast crowd hadn't arrived yet, since it was before eight. Sidney and her father seated themselves in a booth not far from the counter. Before they even had a chance to look at the menu, Jackson's former girlfriend, Naomi, was at the table for their beverage order.

Naomi was a beautiful woman in her mid-twenties, with plenty of curves and an athletic build. She had dark, shoulder-length hair, thin eyebrows, and dark eyes. Although she spent a lot of money on her clothes, makeup, and hair, she dressed down to wait tables at her father's diner. Today, Naomi wore a low-cut tank top, skintight blue jeans, and black high-heeled boots. Kingston asked for coffee, while Sidney chose tea, despite already having one cup that morning. Sidney felt compelled to glance at Naomi as she left the table. Naomi dated Jackson for less than a month before breaking up with him. Despite being almost three years ago and her doing the dumping, Naomi still harbored ill feelings toward Jackson. She told people he was cold and unfeeling, which seemed to be her main reason for dumping him, but there had also been some scuttlebutt about a barroom brawl that labeled Jackson as weak and afraid to fight real men.

Sidney didn't know much about the fight that left Jackson battered and his ego bruised, but three years ago, Sidney may have described Jackson as cold and unfeeling, too. Now that she got to know him a little better, an emotionally unavailable recluse seemed the more accurate term, which was certainly better than her original fears that he was controlling and abusive. Kingston studied his daughter from across the table for nearly a minute before she finally realized he'd been staring at her. She immediately put on a false smile.

"So, are you and Mom looking forward to your trip to Hawaii?" Sidney asked, then turned concerned. "You're still going, aren't you?"

"Of course, we're going," Kingston replied, then stared at her a moment longer. "You know you can talk to me. Tell me what's bothering you."

Sidney shifted uncomfortably and then looked her father in the eyes. "Why does G-ma hate Grandpa?"

Kingston was taken by surprise and immediately fidgeted at the question. "She doesn't hate him," he replied, although his hesitation left room for doubt. "They just had a complex relationship, that's all."

"And what made it complex?" Sidney pressed.

Her father squirmed in his seat before meeting her gaze. "That's something you'll have to ask her," Kingston replied, telling her more than she needed to know.

Sidney groaned in frustration at the non-answer. She obviously wasn't going to drag any information out of her father.

"Is there any way you can convince G-ma not to sell the cabin?" Sidney finally blurted out her biggest concern.

"You have more pull with your grandmother than I'll ever have," he informed her. "You can try talking to her."

"I couldn't even convince her not to sell the gun cabinet," Sidney reminded him. "I don't think she's been to the cabin since she was a little girl, so, understandably, she has zero attachment to that place, but my best childhood memories were in that cabin and on that lake."

Naomi returned to their table and offered a pleasant smile. "Do you know what you're having?" she asked.

"Western omelet with toast," Sidney replied.

"Make that two," Kingston announced cheerfully.

Naomi wrote down their order, then smirked at Sidney. "I hear Jackson screwed you out of Henry's gun cabinet," she remarked and cleverly raised her brows. "Just like that asshole, huh?"

Sidney looked up, but Naomi was already returning to the counter with their order. She looked back at her father and shook her head.

"She's really got an axe to grind with Jackson, doesn't she?" Sidney remarked.

Kingston shrugged and leaned back in his seat. "She's high maintenance and used to getting her way," he informed her. "And I get the feeling Jackson didn't want to play her games."

"Yeah, but she broke up with him," Sidney reminded her father. "That's a known fact."

"Of course she did," Kingston remarked. "She's never been dumped. That girl is used to being showered with gifts, and I think she underestimated Jackson's financial situation." He gave a dismissive wave. "Randall spoiled that girl. Too much of a princess. She'll never be satisfied with any man. She goes through enough of them."

"I really don't understand the attraction to that," Sidney remarked. "I couldn't make it work with Leon, and he and I were friends first."

"Just because you were friends first, that doesn't mean you were meant to be together," Kingston reminded her.

Sidney leaned across the table and met her father's gaze. "Is there something wrong with me?" she asked almost timidly.

"Absolutely not," he replied without waiting for her to finish the question.

"I like guys as friends," Sidney informed him. "But the whole romantic notion just seems like nonsense."

Kingston stared at Sidney for a moment, surprised. "You honestly feel that way?"

"So you do think it's strange," she announced while straightening.

"No, it just means you haven't met the right guy," her father insisted.

"Can you look me in the eyes and honestly say you believe in love?" Sidney asked with a tiny smile while raising her brows.

His look was mildly shocked. "Of course, I do," Kingston replied. "When I met your mother, it was love at first sight."

"She tells a different fairy tale."

"That's because she's a princess and I'm the frog," he informed her. "She needed more time to warm up to me, but I knew it right away."

Sidney was silent for a moment as she sank into her thoughts. "I wish I could feel that," she remarked. "Even now, Leon seems to think we belong together, but I don't feel it. I can see us getting married ten years from now out of convenience, but that's all."

"Sounds like settling," Kingston remarked.

"I don't want to be alone the rest of my life," Sidney informed him. "I mean, Leon and I get along."

"What about the rest?"

"There is no 'rest'," she replied, then fidgeted and again leaned across the table. "Do you know why I broke up with him?"

"You weren't ready for a relationship," Kingston replied matter-of-factly while raising a knowing brow. "Your mother told me."

She shifted uncomfortably in her seat. "It goes beyond that," Sidney announced. "I was uncomfortable with the way he kissed and touched me."

"The way he ***touched*** you?" Kingston asked with a slight growl in his voice, turning protective.

"Not like that," she replied with a huff. "Just touching in general. It felt wrong. Weird. I'd make out with him because he was so into it, but it felt like a chore. Like cleaning the house. Just something you're expected to do." She sat back in her seat. "When he started talking about taking our relationship to the next level, I couldn't even stomach the thought."

Kingston drew a deep breath while studying her. "Sidney, there's nothing wrong with living by yourself," he informed her. "Despite what your mother and G-ma tell you, you don't need to date or get married. If you do it for the wrong reasons, you'll never be happy. Don't pressure yourself and don't let anyone else pressure you either."

Sidney smiled with some relief. "Thanks, Dad."

"You know, with the furniture shop going out of business, this might be a good time for you to make a fresh start," Kingston remarked. "Maybe you and Amber should find an apartment in town together and get away from those influencing you. Live your own lives. Have a little fun."

"Losing my job makes moving out a little unrealistic at the moment," Sidney informed him. "I have some money saved up, but not enough to hold me over in an apartment until I find a new job. Besides, there are no good-paying jobs in town. Grandpa paid well."

"Then you need to look outside of town," her father insisted. "Moving away from home might be the best thing for you and Amber."

"Jackson's not letting her go without a fight," Sidney remarked. "He sometimes still treats her like a child."

"Well, she's not," Kingston replied. "You're both adults now. Your mother and Jackson will just have to get used to the idea."

Chapter 9

Later that morning, Sidney sat behind the desk in the workshop office and leafed through her grandpa's work orders. He kept well-documented notes on each job, indicating how much had been completed and what remained to be done. She would need to call nearly a dozen people with pending orders. Even though her grandpa had purchased some of the material for the jobs, he hadn't taken deposits on most of them. More complex were the jobs he'd already started, for which he received a thirty percent deposit. There was enough money in the account to cover those jobs, but refunding the nearly completed jobs would empty the account. There was too much time and material already invested in those jobs. Sidney considered her options. For the jobs that were nearly complete, perhaps those clients would accept the pieces they'd ordered 'as is' for a discount.

Sidney snatched her grandpa's logbook with renewed determination and headed into the workshop. She knew exactly where to find each item he'd been working on and was familiar with the specific jobs. Each table, chair, bench, and cabinet had its own clipboard containing sketches of her grandpa's vision for the work, as described by the clients.

Sidney studied the sketches of the infamous bar her great-grandfather had poured so much of his blood, sweat, and tears into. Apart from stain and varnish, the magnificent bar had a five-foot piece of edging that still needed to be hand-tooled. One more day, and Grandpa would have had the tooling complete. Sidney picked up the sharpened tooling knife and then looked back at the bar. The edging was a detailed leaf-and-acorn design. Payment for that bar alone would cover the costs of refunds for all the remaining jobs. Sidney considered it another moment, then pulled the round rolling stool up to the bar and sat on it. She held her breath a moment, then gently chiseled into the wood.

§

Sidney entered the office from the workshop at a little after two as her father appeared through the main entrance. He seemed relieved when he saw her.

"You didn't answer your phone," Kingston announced. "You missed lunch."

"Yeah, I got caught up in something," she informed him, then picked up her cell phone from the office desk and offered a tiny smile. "I forgot my phone." She then shrugged. "I wasn't hungry anyway."

"We had a big breakfast," Kingston added. "Anyway, Grandpa's lawyer stopped by and dropped off his will. Your G-ma thought you'd like to be present when we looked at it. I wouldn't doubt he left you some of his guns."

"Then we'd better get to it," Sidney grumbled. "Before Jackson stops by with his check and takes them all."

"I believe he gave G-ma a check yesterday," Kingston remarked. "Would you like to join us?"

"Uh, yeah," Sidney replied, then waved her cell phone. "Just give me five minutes to text some pictures to one of Grandpa's clients."

"Take your time, dear," her father announced. "I'll tell G-ma to wait for you."

§

A few minutes later, Sidney entered her Grandpa's house and found her mother, father, and grandmother in the front sitting room. They were having a nip from what was left of Henry's favorite whiskey. However, Sidney hadn't left much in the bottle. Her father handed her a snifter of whiskey, which she gladly accepted, then sat in one of the chairs not far from where her mother and grandmother sat on the sofa. Her father chose the chair opposite the sofa. Helena smiled and held up her whiskey glass.

"A toast to Grandpa Henry," G-ma announced.

They all raised their glasses.

"If heaven has lakes, I'm sure he's already out fishing," Helena remarked.

They all chuckled and drained their glasses in honor of Henry. Helena set her glass down and picked up the manila envelope and letter opener. She opened the envelope without comment and removed the slim document.

"I hate legal documents," Helena muttered while scanning over the page. "So many unnecessary words." She then looked up and smiled. "I'm just going to skip over the sound mind and all that jargon." It took her another moment to scan through the document. She finally nodded and smiled. "To my dearest daughter, Helena." She easily skipped ahead. "I leave my house on 428 Westmore Road and all its contents with some exceptions." Helena continued to scan the document. "To my dearest granddaughter, Casandra, I leave the house on 432 Westmore Road, of which she and her husband, Kingston, have been renting."

Casandra and Kingston exchanged relieved smiles. Twenty-three years, and Sidney never knew her parents were renting their house from Grandpa.

"To my dearest, great granddaughter, Sidney," Helena continued, then offered Sidney a warm smile. "I leave my gun cabinet and all its contents--" Helena hesitated as her smile faded.

Sidney was now intrigued and leaned forward in her chair. She thought maybe he'd leave her one or two guns, but not the entire collection. Helena shifted uncomfortably, realizing she'd have to give Jackson his check back. She lost her place for a moment and fumbled to find it.

"As well as my truck and boat," Helena continued. A strange look then crossed her face. "I also leave Sidney my workshop and carpentry business in its entirety."

Sidney stared at her grandmother in complete shock. Kingston, Casandra, and Helena shared the same expression.

Helena gently cleared her throat, seeming slightly uncomfortable. "As for the cabin on the lake and ninety-eight acres, I leave to my dearest great granddaughter, Sidney. Since she was the only one who loved it as much as I did, it should be hers." Sidney's grandmother was now visibly uncomfortable and cleared her throat again. "Any money, stocks, and bonds I request be divided equally among my daughter, granddaughter, and great granddaughter."

There was an unusual silence as everyone processed what they'd just heard. Sidney couldn't believe her grandpa left her the business and the cabin on the lake. At the same time, she was relieved. Now, her grandmother couldn't sell the cabin. Her grandpa had been right. Sidney was the only one who loved that cabin as much as he did. Helena set the will down on the coffee table and immediately refilled her whiskey glass.

"Well," Kingston announced and refilled his glass as well. "I think that was very generous of Henry." He then smiled at Sidney and raised his glass. "With the business and the lake house, you have a pretty good start on the next chapter of your life."

"There is no business without Henry Westmore," Helena reminded him. "Dad ***was*** the company."

"Maybe," Kingston replied while sipping his whiskey, "but with the workshop, tools, and material, Sidney might find her own calling. If not, she can sell it and invest it in something she is interested in."

Sidney glanced from her father to her mother and grandmother. Her father seemed happy, but she wasn't so sure about her mother and grandmother.

"None of you are upset by Grandpa's decision, are you?" Sidney asked.

"Of course not," her mother announced while smiling pleasantly. "We each have our own place now, and Grandpa never could have expanded his carpentry business without you running the office. You were like his partner. He even said it many times."

Sidney then glanced at her grandmother. "You never really liked the cabin," she remarked. "You're not upset that he left it to me, right?"

Helena smiled even though she seemed troubled. "Of course not, dear," she replied. "The dust and cobwebs are the only things holding that old cabin together. I certainly wouldn't want it." She then came to life. "You know, you could sell the land and use the money to build a house next to the workshop." Her smile increased. "Then we can all live next door to each other."

"Secluded woods and a lake?" Kingston remarked, then raised his brows. "She might be better off selling the workshop and putting up a new home where the cabin sits."

Helena and Casandra cast disapproving looks at Kingston. He caught their glares and shifted in his chair.

"She'd be living out in the middle of nowhere," Casandra informed him.

"Exactly," Kingston replied. "That's the whole point. Besides, it's a ten-minute drive from town. It's not that far at all."

"But if she had a house by the workshop, she could just walk to either of our homes," Helena reminded him.

"That's not living on her own," Kingston remarked. "She may as well continue living with us, if that's the case."

"Are you suggesting she move out?" Casandra practically gasped.

"I didn't say that," Kingston remarked.

"Okay," Sidney announced with a groan. "Enough. Today, right now, nothing has changed. Can we just leave it at that? We can worry about the rest another day." Sidney then stood. "I have a little more work to do in the workshop."

"Will you be home for dinner?" her mother asked.

"No, I'm going out with Amber," Sidney replied.

Helena sighed and stood. "If you're going to see Amber, you may as well take Jackson's check back to him."

Chapter 10

Later, the following afternoon, Sidney stood before her grandpa's open gun cabinet, wrapped each rifle in cheap, store-bought towels, and then placed them in the box on the bed. Casandra entered the room, sat on the bed, and watched her daughter.

"You know, you don't have to move the gun cabinet to the workshop," Casandra informed her. "There's no rush."

"G-ma was pretty insistent that she didn't want it in the house," Sidney reminded her mother. "It's for the best that I move it. Besides, the guys all had time this afternoon."

Helena was heard calling up the stairs. "Sidney, you have company!"

Sidney looked at her watch, somewhat baffled. "The guys are early," she announced. "I'd better move a little faster."

They heard someone on the creaky steps, then in the hallway. When Sidney looked back, Amber appeared in the doorway and immediately smiled at Casandra.

"Good afternoon, Mrs. Bristol," Amber announced cheerfully.

"Hey, Amber," Casandra replied

"Where are the guys?" Sidney asked.

"They'll be here in half an hour," Amber informed her, then gently cleared her throat. "I wanted to talk to you in private before the guys got here."

Casandra sprang up from the bed, grinning. "I guess that's my cue," she announced, then left the room and shut the bedroom door behind her.

Sidney was now curious and sat on the bed facing her friend. "Is everything okay?" she asked, then turned concerned. "Was Jackson pissed when you gave him his check back?"

"No, this has nothing to do with Jackson," Amber replied, then hesitated and fumbled over herself a moment. "Well, maybe it has a little to do with him." Amber sat on the bed, facing Sidney, with a serious look. "Greyson asked me out on a date." She then grimaced. "A ***date*** date."

Sidney stared at her friend a moment, then grinned. "He did?" she asked, turning almost giddy. "No matter how much he denied it, I knew he liked you!" She then raised a curious brow. "What did you say?"

Amber hid her smile and appeared somewhat shy. "I said 'yes'," she replied.

Sidney squealed with glee. "That's wonderful," she cried out.

"Well, yes and no," Amber replied, then fidgeted. "Jackson can't know I'm going out on a date with Greyson."

Sidney cocked her head, surprised by what she heard. "You're twenty-three," she remarked. "You're allowed to go on dates with boys."

"I know," Amber replied while fidgeting. "I just don't want him to know yet. I know how he's going to react, and I don't want to deal with his overly protective uncle bullshit before our official first date."

"Jackson shouldn't have anything to say about it," Sidney huffed, then held her breath. "But I won't say anything to him."

"You need to cover for me," Amber insisted. "If he asks, we're all going out together this Friday night."

"I'll cover for you," Sidney reluctantly replied. "But you really need to deal with him once and for all. Don't let him bully you. If he throws a hissy fit, you can always move in with me."

"In the workshop or at the cabin?" Amber asked, now curious with a mocking smile.

"I'm going to stay in the workshop office for a week or so," Sidney informed her. "I have to figure some things out. After everything is settled, I'll move into the cabin."

"I'll keep in mind that you offered," Amber replied and managed a tiny smile. "I'm sure Jackson will be fine. I don't want him knocking me off my cloud just yet."

"You think he'll be fine?" Sidney asked while raising her brows. "Did you forget what happened on your twenty-first birthday?"

"I could have handled him," Amber interjected. "You're the one who poked the bear."

"Not how I remember it," Sidney muttered.

Two years ago. It was two o'clock in the morning when Henry's pickup truck pulled up the long driveway, approaching Amber's house. The twenty-one-year-old girls in the back seat were drunk and giggling. The truck stopped in front of the two-story, renovated farmhouse built in the 1800s. The exterior was old wood siding, freshly repainted red, with a large, cozy wraparound porch containing several rocking chairs and large hanging plants between each set of support beams. The two girls finally stopped giggling, and Sidney leaned between the front seats to speak to her grandpa.

"I'm going to walk Amber inside," Sidney announced, still giddy. "She's so wasted."

Henry turned his head, eyed Sidney, and hid his knowing smile. "Yeah, you do that," he replied.

Sidney and Amber climbed out of the back of the truck and nearly fell to the ground. Both women giggled as they headed for the porch.

As Amber fumbled with her house keys, she glanced at Sidney. "What time is it?"

"Uh," Sidney stammered and glanced at her watch. "I can't really tell. After two? Hurry up. I have to pee."

Amber cringed while attempting to find the right key. "Jackson is going to be so pissed," she now whispered. "We need to keep it quiet and not wake him."

Sidney reached past Amber and turned the knob. The door wasn't even locked.

Amber appeared surprised while staring at the open door. "Did you see that?" she remarked softly. "The door opened by itself."

"Creepy," Sidney replied, then followed her friend into the lit kitchen.

Since her great-grandfather was a carpenter, Sidney always appreciated the work Jackson had put into restoring the old farmhouse. The restored kitchen, connected to the living room by a large archway, had the same broad plank floorboards and barn wood as the living room. Modern appliances stood alongside the antique ice box and wood-burning stove, kept for their charm.

"Grab me a water. I have to pee," Sidney announced, then hurried to the bathroom just off the kitchen near the back stairs, almost not making it.

Once she had finished, she stumbled back into the kitchen while humming a song and immediately stopped when she saw Jackson, wearing a pair of shorts and an old t-shirt, standing in front of Amber. Jackson shot Sidney a look that nearly made her soul leave her body.

"Thanks for bringing her home, Sidney," Jackson grumbled. "Goodnight."

"I'm sorry about the late hour," Sidney attempted to smooth out the situation and lessen Jackson's wrath on his niece.

Jackson shot a look at Sidney, then pointed to the door. "Go home, Sidney! You've done enough!"

His irrational hostility surprised and even startled Sidney. If she had been sober, she probably would have been frightened of him, but she was feeling almost invincible from too much alcohol.

"What the fuck is your problem?" Sidney launched in anger. "You weren't going to take her out for her first legal drink. Someone needed to."

Jackson snorted an irritated laugh and shook his head before glaring at Amber. "You are in so much trouble," he muttered.

"I'm sorry we were out so late," Amber informed him, attempting to curb his hostility. "I should have called."

"Stop apologizing to him!" Sidney cried out, then turned her venomous glare on Jackson. "She's not a little girl anymore. She's twenty-one, and if she wants to go out to a bar and stay out until two in the morning, she's legally allowed to do so."

"Sidney," Amber pleaded softly with the appearance of a whipped puppy. "It's okay. I'll be fine."

"No, it's not okay," Sidney snapped back without taking her eyes off Jackson. "He's a controlling bully!"

"You know what, Sidney," Jackson announced in a gruff tone as he took two steps toward her. "Amber didn't get into trouble until she started hanging out with you. You're a bad influence."

"I'm a bad influence?" Sidney scoffed then laughed almost manically while shaking her head. "If it weren't for me, she'd be cowering under your thumb as she had for the last six years! You may be her uncle, but you don't own her, Jackson."

"You're getting very close to crossing the line," Jackson informed her while attempting to keep his temper in check. "Don't piss me off."

"Someone has to stand up to your abuse!"

"Abuse?" Jackson cried out, then looked back at Amber, who shirked and backed up a step. He shot his gaze back at Sidney. "I don't control her, and I certainly don't abuse her. I protect her, and right now, I'm protecting her from you!"

"And were you protecting her the first two years you lived here?" Sidney demanded. "Keeping her locked in this house, not letting her see anyone or make any friends. Is that how you protect her?"

"Yes!" Jackson shouted so loud it nearly sobered Sidney.

"Sidney, you should go home," Amber announced, now tense. "I'm fine. Really."

Jackson didn't take his eyes off Sidney, attempting to intimidate her with his stare, and it was working. Unfortunately, Sidney was drunk enough that it didn't affect her as much as it should have. Sidney didn't flinch and took a step closer to Jackson while maintaining eye contact. It was probably the longest she'd ever looked into his eyes, but she wasn't backing down. Amber appeared almost frightened at the confrontation.

"Okay, guys," Amber announced nervously. "Let's not compare gun calibers now. It's late."

"Fine," Jackson snarled without taking his eyes off Sidney. "We'll finish this discussion when everyone is sober."

Sidney returned to the present day and the current conversation with Amber. "Well, maybe I poked him a little," she remarked. "But he *was* out of line."

"When he first took me in, it was a bumpy road," Amber remarked, then offered a tiny smile. "Thankfully, we all survived. I suppose you did give him something to think about, confronting him like that."

"He seemed to loosen the apron strings after that," Sidney reminded her. "I guess no one stood up to him before."

"I doubt you were the first," Amber informed her, then giggled. "Although it was kind of fun to watch. Like a puppy yipping at a grizzly bear."

They heard lively voices in the hallway just before a knock upon the door.

"Hello?" Greyson was heard on the other side of the door. "Anyone home?"

"Come in," Sidney called out.

Greyson, Leon, and Miller entered the room in a flurry of activity.

"Three Guys Movers," Greyson announced cheerfully. "You have a job for us?"

Amber met Greyson's gaze, and there was a glowing, non-verbal exchange that Leon and Miller didn't seem to notice.

"Jesus," Miller cried out while staring at the gun cabinet. "That thing is massive!"

"Solid wood, too," Sidney replied while grinning. "Time to start flexing those muscles, boys."

Miller smirked, then looked at Leon and Greyson. "How much is this chick paying us?" he asked.

"Uh, nothing, I believe," Leon replied jokingly.

"Be nice, boys," Greyson announced almost sternly, then smiled. "Sidney is the proud new owner of a very nice boat and a beautiful lake."

"Yeah, I'm thinking party at the cabin on the lake," Miller replied cheerfully.

"That'll have to wait a couple of weeks," Sidney informed them. "I have a lot to do at the workshop. Once that's taken care of, we can spend a weekend at the cabin. You know, when you help me move."

There was a round of groans and laughter.

"There had better be a boat, beer, and fishing," Miller informed her.

"There will," Sidney informed them. "And even a bonfire, providing you chop some wood."

"She's good," Greyson remarked. "If we're not careful, she'll have us building furniture in the workshop."

"I do have an opening for a carpenter," Sidney casually replied, and was immediately met with groans.

Chapter 11

That evening, Sidney helped her mother and grandmother remove her grandpa's clothes from the closet and drawers. They were neatly folded and placed into boxes for donation. Sidney didn't understand her grandmother's rush to clear the house of all memory of Grandpa. Maybe her father was right, and it was just her way of grieving. Sidney placed several flannel shirts on a pile on the bed, catching her mother's attention.

"What's with the shirts?" Casandra asked.

"I'm going to use them as nightshirts," Sidney casually replied and immediately received a strange look from her grandmother, who then minded her own business.

Maybe Sidney wasn't meant to see that look, but she did. Now, she couldn't stop wondering why her grandmother was behaving the way she had been.

"Closet's done," Sidney announced and eyed her mother and grandmother. "What's next?"

"The armoire by the window," Helena reported, then straightened. "If you find any booze in the drawers, I call dibs."

Sidney approached the armoire that contained the television. She opened the side door and stared at several shelves of liquor. A tiny chuckle escaped her throat. She never knew her grandpa kept a minibar in his room. Apparently, G-ma knew about it, though.

"Found your booze," Sidney announced to Helena. "It's all yours."

Sidney then opened the top drawer beneath the television. The drawer was filled with photo albums, loose pictures, assorted belt buckles, and anything else that happened to find its way in. As she collected the loose photos, one picture caught her attention. She studied the photo of her grandmother and grandfather when they were younger. Sidney's mother was in the picture as well. She was just a little girl. It was the background that intrigued Sidney. Her grandmother and grandfather stood before a well-tended flower garden with a beautiful mansion behind them. Sidney turned the picture over. Casandra, eight years old. Miss you, Mom. Love Helena. Sidney turned and looked at her grandmother.

"Where was this taken, G-ma?" Sidney asked, catching Helena's attention.

Helena saw the picture and froze for a moment. "That was in his drawer?" she asked.

"Yeah," Sidney replied. "It's you with Mom and my grandfather."

Helena approached and gently took the photo from her. She stared at it for a long moment, then smiled warmly. "He was so handsome," she remarked of her deceased husband. "I wish you could have known him."

Casandra then approached and looked at the picture. "I barely had a chance to know him," Sidney's mother replied with a soft sigh.

"I have so few photos of him," Helena practically whispered. "We didn't have cameras on our phones like they do today, and there never seemed to be time to stop and take a picture. I didn't even own a camera back then."

"Where was this?" Sidney asked. "It's a beautiful photo."

"Yes, the flowers were exquisite that summer," Helena reported. "Probably the only reason we got a picture taken with the three of us."

"Looks like a museum," Sidney remarked.

Helena managed a tiny, humored laugh. "No, that wasn't a museum," she replied. "That was the mansion where your grandfather and I worked. Where your mother was raised."

Sidney was surprised by the admission. That was the first time she'd ever heard about where her mother grew up.

"You worked in a mansion?" Sidney asked.

"Yes," Helena replied and seemed to drift off for a moment in her thoughts while smiling. "Your grandfather was the assistant chauffeur when this picture was taken." She groaned softly. "He looked so handsome in his suits." She then returned to reality and managed an embarrassed smile. "I was the downstairs maid. Dreadful uniforms. Looked like I was attending a funeral every day." She then shrugged. "But the mansion was beautiful, and I loved my employers. Ransom and Debra Norwood." Helena then frowned. "After their passing, the son took over, and the job was never the same. I only stayed a few years after your grandfather's death."

"That's when you returned home and moved in with Grandpa?"

"Yes," Helena replied, then drew a deep breath and managed a smile. "Gave up the mansion but kept the same job."

"If you didn't like living here with Grandpa and keeping his house, why didn't you move out?" Sidney was compelled to ask.

The question made her grandmother visibly uncomfortable. “It’s not that I didn’t like living with your grandpa,” Helena remarked, then shrugged. “It’s just not how I envisioned my life. I thought I’d grow old with the man I loved. Moving back into my childhood house with my father when I was thirty-three years old was supposed to be temporary. Almost twenty-four years later is not so temporary.”

“I understand why you initially moved in with him,” Sidney remarked, then shook her head. “But why didn’t you eventually get a place of your own?”

Helena drew a deep breath and sighed. “Once your mother got married and you were born, how could I even consider moving out?” she commented. “I wanted to be close by if she needed anything.” Helena offered a warm smile and squeezed Sidney’s hand. “I didn’t want to miss a single moment watching you grow up. A mother will do anything for her child ***and*** her grandchild.”

She couldn’t argue with her grandmother’s logic. Sidney knew her mother was pregnant when she was only seventeen, and when she decided to keep her baby, Sidney’s father stepped up and took responsibility. Henry jumped in and got them the house next door. It wasn’t until she was in high school that she discovered the sacrifices her family made to support one another, and Sidney was grateful. Her childhood was filled with love and family.

Helena handed the picture to Sidney. “You keep this,” she announced. “I want you to have a picture of your grandfather to remember him.”

As Sidney accepted the picture, Helena straightened. “I should start dinner,” she announced. “I assume you’re staying for dinner.”

“Of course,” Casandra replied, then looked at Sidney. “Why don’t you sort out that drawer while I help your grandmother make dinner?” As Helena left the room,

Sidney's mother followed, then paused in the doorway and looked back at Sidney. "Keep whatever you want."

Once they were gone, Sidney placed items into a box, leaving what she wanted on the shelf with the television. When she reached the bottom, she found an old, leather-bound journal. Sidney picked up the book, surprised by the find. She didn't know her grandpa kept a journal. She sat on the bed and opened the old book. On the first page was the name of the book's owner. Elizabeth Westmore. To her surprise, it belonged to her great-grandmother. Sidney was overjoyed at the find. Her grandmother would undoubtedly be excited to have something that belonged to her mother. Before sharing her find, she decided to page through the book. Sidney read a couple of entertaining entries regarding her grandpa. She knew she should have been clearing the drawers, but she was enjoying a peek into her grandpa's youth through her great-grandmother's eyes.

It then dawned on Sidney that not all the entries would necessarily be pleasant, which forced her to skip to the last entry, in case there was something unpleasant around the time she died. The last entry was two months before her great-grandmother died, which seemed odd that she didn't continue writing up until the time of her death. Sidney read the last entry that would have been shortly after Helena moved back home. The entry read, "I'm so happy that Helena moved back home, and I finally get to spend time with my granddaughter. But, as with all things, it's bittersweet. Today, my sixteen-year-old granddaughter found out that she's pregnant! She doesn't even know who the father is! Some random guy she met at a party before they moved back home. Henry is going to be furious when he finds out."

Sidney sat on the bed, staring at the written words, unable to move. What did she just read?

§

Sidney entered the kitchen and found her mother and grandmother making dinner. Her father hadn't ventured over to Helena's house yet since he had just gotten home from work. Sidney clung to the journal as she approached the two women who were happily talking.

"Mom," Sidney announced, not caring that she interrupted them.

Casandra looked back at Sidney and smiled pleasantly. "Yes, dear?"

"I found great grandma's journal," Sidney informed her, now receiving her grandmother's attention as well. There was a tense silence, and it was apparent both were waiting to hear what she was about to say. "Is Dad not my real father?"

The tension immediately increased as her mother and grandmother appeared unable to respond.

"So it's true?" Sidney demanded in horror.

"Sidney," Casandra announced while fumbling over her words. "He may not be your biological father, but he's your father in every other sense of the word."

"Does he know?" Sidney gasped.

"It's complicated," Casandra informed her as gently as possible. "But he knows he's not your biological father."

Sidney stared at her mother while her grandmother now stared down at the floor, unable to look up. "So who is my real father?"

Casandra held her breath a moment, uncertain how to respond. Helena turned and hurried from the kitchen without a word.

"Sidney," her mother gently announced. "I was only with him the one time," she gently replied. "I don't even remember his name."

Sidney stared at her mother, a mixture of shock and horror on her face. "Are you kidding me?" she launched, feeling her anger spiking. "Why didn't you tell me? Why did I have to find this out from my deceased great-grandmother?"

"Your real father was a very bad man," Casandra replied. "If he isn't in prison, he's probably dead by now. How could I possibly tell you that?"

"I don't know," Sidney cried out. "You just do!"

Sidney turned and stormed from the house, slamming the porch door behind her.

Chapter 12

Henry's pickup truck flew down the long driveway and pulled up to Amber's house a little after five o'clock that evening. The truck skidded on the dirt and stone driveway as it came to an abrupt halt. Sidney jumped out with the old journal in her hand and slammed the truck door for good measure. She was on fire! Jackson appeared in the garage doorway beyond the house, possibly alerted to a speeding vehicle approaching. When he saw it was just Sidney, he shook his head and returned to the sanctuary of his garage. By the time Sidney reached the porch, Amber was already peering out the screen door, possibly having the same reaction as her uncle. She stepped into the open doorway when she saw Sidney bounding up the porch steps.

"Sidney," Amber announced, surprised and possibly alarmed. "Is everything okay?"

"No, not really," Sidney replied and flashed the journal. "My family has been lying to me, and I had to find out from my great-grandmother."

Amber was now curious as she ushered Sidney inside, shutting the screen door behind her. They entered the living room with its imposing fireplace, as old as the house itself, made of large stones, with a broad hearth and a large wooden mantel. The living room was a mixture of country and old leather with vintage signs, bottles, and antique guns tacked to the walls. Obviously, Jackson decorated the room in 'early man cave' style. Sidney flopped on the sofa and allowed her head to fall against the back while Amber sat nearby, facing her.

"What is it?" Amber asked. "What did you find out?"

Sidney sat forward and stared at her friend. "My father isn't my real father," she scoffed.

Amber was somewhat surprised by the news. "You're kidding," she responded and let the information sink in for a moment. "I always thought you two were so much alike. Are you sure? Did you ask them about it?"

"Yes," Sidney replied with a defeated groan. "My mother confessed it was true."

"So, who's your real father?" Amber asked the logical follow-up question.

"Some one-night-stand she had at some stoner party when she was sixteen," Sidney scoffed.

Amber was again stunned into silence. "***Your*** mother?" she finally responded. "Sidney, your mother is practically a saint."

"Well, maybe that came after her one-night stand with the sperm donor," Sidney huffed.

"Think you're being a bit harsh on her?" Amber asked. "I mean, she's been a fantastic mother to you."

"Maybe," Sidney muttered, but found it difficult to relax. "It's just, well, my father and I have always been so close. Now, I find out he's not even my real father."

"That doesn't change your relationship with him," Amber reminded her, then moved closer to the edge of the sofa. "My father was a horrible human being."

Sidney looked at her friend, surprised by the comment. Amber never talked about her father, only her mother. She always assumed she didn't like to talk about him because his death was too painful. Sidney remained silent, hoping Amber would finally open up about her parents.

"My, uh, father was partly responsible for my mother's death," Amber gently informed her. "I mean, he didn't kill her or anything, but they'd had a huge fight, and she was very upset when she got into her car. The night she died, he didn't stop her from driving away, and he should have."

Sidney was able to pull herself together as her friend finally opened up to her about her past. Amber drew a deep, slightly shaken breath.

"Although I had trouble admitting it at the time, he never treated her right," Amber continued while sinking into a darker time. "He was a bad man, and I'm glad he's out of my life."

"Amber," Jackson announced gruffly from the kitchen archway, alerting both women to his presence.

Jackson appeared almost emotionless and somewhat rigid. Amber immediately tensed when she realized her uncle overheard what she'd said.

"It's your turn to take out the trash," he remarked in an oddly stern tone.

Amber frowned, obediently stood, and headed into the kitchen without another word. Obviously, it wasn't about her taking out the trash. Sidney had to fight the anger she was feeling, now directed at Jackson. She feared it would be Amber's twenty-first birthday at the tavern all over again. Was he irritated about what Amber said regarding her father? Or was he pissed about losing the gun cabinet? It didn't really matter. He'd successfully made her mood worse than when she arrived. Despite his coarseness, he seemed tense with the way she stared at him.

"We're having hamburgers tonight, if you'd like to stay for dinner," Jackson announced, then headed into the kitchen.

Sidney was left feeling bewildered over what had just happened. What the hell was that all about? Jackson had some sort of Jekyll-and-Hyde personality. Sidney set down the journal and cautiously approached the kitchen, where Jackson was seasoning the hamburgers for the grill. Amber was conspicuously AWOL, but in their house, taking out the trash required driving to the end of the driveway for the garbage truck. Sidney folded her arms across her chest and leaned in the archway, silently studying Jackson's profile while he prepared the fresh hamburger patties. She had to wonder what went through his head.

"Onions and tomatoes need to be sliced," he informed her without even looking up from the plate of raw hamburgers.

Sidney straightened and approached the counter where the onions and tomatoes were set. She removed the cutting board and a knife from the butcher's block and began slicing the tomato.

"I know you've had a rough week," Jackson remarked. "Your entire life has changed dramatically overnight. Amber and I have been there. A roller coaster of emotions." He then hesitated. "You're more than welcome in our home, if you need someplace to escape."

"Are you sure about that?" Sidney replied, unable to hold back her irritation. "You came off pretty hostile just now in the living room."

Jackson released a low sigh, then turned to face her at the counter alongside him. Despite the fact that he gave her his full attention, she couldn't force herself to look at him. There were times she still felt like a little girl around him, especially when she was challenging his authority. Even though he was only eight years older than her, she still saw him as an authority figure. And a powerful, intimidating one, at that.

"Amber and I went through a lot when her mother died," he informed her in an unusually docile tone. "I didn't handle my sister's death with much dignity, and Amber was a mess. Drudging up those emotions won't do either of us any good, so we don't discuss it."

"But maybe she needs that to heal," Sidney remarked and finally glanced at him.

"It's a very delicate and complicated situation," Jackson informed her without taking his eyes off her.

Sidney only briefly met his gaze, but couldn't handle looking into his eyes for more than a second. In a way, Jackson reminded her of a wolf. Beautiful to look at, but approach with extreme caution. That tender moment on the stairs at her grandpa's wake was a rare occurrence.

"I know you have a low opinion of me, but I do what I do because I have to," Jackson announced, maintaining the same, non-threatening tone. "I wasn't there for my sister when she needed me, and from that moment on, I vowed I'd do whatever it takes to protect my niece."

Jackson's words struck her pretty hard. Sidney set down the knife and turned to face him, forcing herself to stare into his eyes. The look in his eyes was sincere, but there was a lot of pain hidden behind them.

"I ***don't*** have a low opinion of you," Sidney quietly corrected him.

"You accused me of being controlling and abusive," he reminded her.

"That was two years ago, and if you remember correctly, I was drunk when I said that," she remarked, surprised he held onto her less-than-flattering words all this time. She then leaned against the counter, releasing her gaze from his, and frowned. "At least you're honest. That's more than I can say about my family."

"What do you mean?" Jackson asked.

"I found my great-grandmother's journal this afternoon," she reluctantly replied. "My father isn't my real father. Apparently, my real father died in prison."

"It shouldn't matter," Jackson informed her. "Kingston loves you. You ***are*** his daughter. Blood doesn't make you family."

"Jackson being insightful and deep," Sidney remarked while managing a tiny smile along with a soft snort before shaking her head. "What a strange week."

Jackson chuckled, then took a step closer and held his arms open to her. "May as well make it the strangest week ever," he announced, for the first time inviting her into his personal space for a hug.

Sidney was hesitant, but she gave in and moved into Jackson's arms, accepting the offer of a hug. She placed her arms around his waist and immediately tensed as his arms tightened around her, holding her snuggly against him. For a moment, it was almost surreal. Once she pushed the awkwardness from her mind, Sidney felt oddly comforted, which allowed her to relax and lay her head against his chest. She could feel and hear his heart pounding. Or maybe that was her heart. When he nuzzled the top of her head with his face, Sidney realized she'd made some sort of impact on Jackson over the years. The way he embraced her showed how much he actually cared for her. She suddenly felt very special. His hands firmly caressed her back while reestablishing his hold, embracing her in a way she'd never felt before, meshed together as if they were one.

As Sidney nuzzled his chest, she let a tiny, contented moan escape. When she realized what she'd done, she internally panicked. Had she sexualized an innocent moment? Just then, she heard Amber's car pull up to the house. Jackson warmly kissed the top of her head, like a father to his child, and released her, casually returning to the plate of raw hamburgers as if she'd done nothing wrong. When Amber entered the house only a second later, Sidney didn't recover nearly as fast as Jackson had. She was still facing his profile when Amber paused and eyed her somewhat suspiciously.

"Everything okay?" Amber asked while giving strange looks.

"Yeah," Jackson replied a little too matter-of-factly without even looking at his niece. "Sidney is staying for dinner, which will be ready in twenty minutes."

Without further explanation, Jackson took his plate of hamburgers and headed outside to the gas grill. Amber suspiciously eyed her uncle as he left, then looked at Sidney, who attempted to slice onions while keeping her hands from trembling.

"Did I miss something?" Amber asked. "It almost feels as if the two of you were actually getting along."

"Yeah, it's strange," Sidney reported with a tiny crackle in her voice, unable to look at her friend. "He was actually being nice."

"Must be a full moon approaching," Amber muttered.

Sidney managed a soft chuckle as she continued with her work. As Amber grabbed some items from the refrigerator, Sidney wondered why she was so reluctant to tell her friend that her uncle had hugged her. It should have been front-page news, yet Sidney refused to share it. Why did she feel the need to keep it a secret? It was almost as if she'd done something wrong.

Chapter 13

After a pleasant dinner on the patio, Sidney was in a better mood than she had been in all week. There must have been some medicinal properties in Jackson's hug as the warmth of the moment seemed to linger. Although she attempted to hide it, Sidney couldn't help but cast stray glances at Jackson's profile while she and Amber helped him clean up after dinner. It wouldn't be the first time she secretly admired him for the handsome man he was. Despite having only eight years on her guy friends, he was far more distinguished than the others. Sidney found herself wondering when boys finally turned into men. When Jackson headed into the house with the leftover hamburgers, Sidney glanced after him.

"Stop it," Amber muttered close to her, startling her.

Sidney jumped and looked back at her friend as she collected the dirty paper plates. "Stop what?" she asked.

"Checking out Uncle Jackson's ass," Amber remarked, then sneered her distaste. "It freaks me out."

"I wasn't checking him out," Sidney practically gasped, feeling herself blush at the accusation. Or was she blushing because she was caught?

Amber rolled her eyes, then groaned softly. "Oh, please!" she cried out. "It wouldn't be the first time I caught you checking him out, which is weird because he's definitely not your type."

"I have a type?" Sidney asked, somewhat surprised. Ironic that Amber would know her type when she didn't.

"Of course you do," Amber insisted. "Preppy types, like Leon or even Miller. Certainly not bad boys like Uncle Jackson."

"You think your uncle is a 'bad boy'?" Sidney asked, almost humored.

"Well, not anymore because he's, you know, old," Amber insisted, then shrugged. "But he used to be before my mother died." She again rolled her eyes. "He and his delinquent friends used to troll for trashy girls every weekend at biker bars. Got into a lot of drunken barroom brawls. Usually over women. Talk about loud and obnoxious!" Amber then considered her comment. "Well, he's still loud and obnoxious, but only around me because I'm special."

"To be fair," Sidney remarked. "You incite him."

Amber was instantly offended. "I do not," she huffed. "Name one time."

"The first day I met you," Sidney replied. "You and Jackson were having a shouting match before you ended up by the stream."

Amber hesitated, considering their first meeting. "Name another time."

§

Sidney pulled up to her house around seven o'clock that evening, hoping her mother had returned from Grandpa's house. She needed to have a real discussion with her mother and at least hear her out. When she entered the house, Sidney found her parents sitting at the kitchen table having what appeared to be a serious, intimate conversation over a bottle of brandy. When they saw her, both fell silent. Her mother stared at her as if her world had shattered, while her father stared into his brandy glass, unable to look at her. Had her mother lied? Did her father not know the truth and just found out now, before Sidney could expose it?

Kingston gently cleared his throat and stood, now facing Sidney. "I'll, uh, give you two a little time alone to talk," he timidly announced, then left the kitchen, heading onto the porch.

Sidney felt her heart sink. The shattered look on her father's face was heartbreaking. She slowly moved into the vacant seat and looked at her mother across the table, not sure what she wanted to say or how to even start.

"I know you're upset with me, and you have every right to be," her mother remarked softly, blurting it out a little too quickly.

"Mom," Sidney replied. "It's okay. I overreacted."

Casandra stared at her daughter for a moment, surprised by the response. It would seem she had been expecting a long, groveling process.

"Your reaction was understandable," her mother replied, seeming less tense now, as if a tremendous weight had been lifted. "You have a right to know. If there's anything I can say to ease your mind, just ask."

Sidney held her breath a moment while staring at the turmoil on her mother's face. She couldn't believe she put her mother through that. Jackson's words of wisdom seemed to put all of it into perspective.

"I just want to know how Dad fits into all of this," Sidney announced somewhat delicately.

Casandra drew a deep breath, then released it. "When G-ma felt she could no longer continue working at the Norwood Estate, we moved back home to live with your grandpa," she informed her. "We weren't home more than a week or two when I found out I was pregnant." Her mother fidgeted slightly, reliving some unspeakable trauma. "Your great-grandmother, the great lady she was, decided she'd break the news to your grandpa. Of course, he was very upset."

Sidney knew her great-grandfather was somewhat old-fashioned. As someone of his generation would be, he probably didn't handle it well.

"It's a small town, and people loved to gossip back then," Casandra remarked, then hesitated. "Well, they still do, I suppose." She frowned and looked down while fiddling with her wedding band. "Your grandpa was adamant that I get married. Since your biological father was a non-starter, Grandpa turned to Kingston, who'd been helping him out in the workshop during the summer. He confided the situation to him, and he arranged for us to spend an afternoon together."

Sidney was momentarily horrified at what she was hearing. Her grandpa forced her mother to get married? She could barely believe it.

"We were married a week later," her mother admitted. "You were overdue almost a week, so it worked out perfectly. A few of the busybodies in town probably connected the dots, but they just naturally assumed Kingston was the father and we had to get married because of that."

"Dad rushed to marry you, even knowing I wasn't his?" Sidney asked, surprised, and then shook her head. "Why would he do that?"

"He said he liked me the moment we'd met," she replied, then managed a tiny smile. "You know your father, he's a stand-up kind of guy. He respected your grandpa, and he wanted to defend my honor."

"Did you love him?" Sidney asked.

Casandra hesitated, then managed a tiny smile, although it was difficult. "Not at first," she replied timidly. "I was just turning seventeen, dropping out of high school, and he was twenty-one and in college. But I learned to love him."

Sidney sank into thought for a moment, then suddenly cringed. "You were that young and didn't even love him," she remarked. "That's kind of icky. Technically, it's statutory rape."

Casandra snorted a tiny laugh, although Sidney didn't know what was funny about that. "We didn't even share a bed until I was eighteen," her mother reported. "And we didn't consummate the marriage until I was almost nineteen." She offered a warm smile. "Your father was very patient and understanding regarding our marriage of convenience. Even during those first uncertain two years, you were his pride and joy. Everything he did, he did for you and me, and he loves us very much."

"And you love him, right?"

There was a moment of hesitation. "I do now," she replied. "That's all that matters."

Sidney wanted to know the truth, but she possibly learned more than she wanted. Despite what her mother said, Sidney was still concerned that her mother sacrificed her happiness to marry a man she didn't love because of Grandpa. If her mother didn't love her father in the beginning, how long was she in a loveless marriage?

"I'm sorry we weren't more open with you from the beginning," her mother timidly informed her. "Your father has been so good to us. I just wanted you to believe he was your one and only father."

"I understand, Mom," Sidney replied. "Honestly, I just needed time to process everything." She hesitated, then frowned. "I just can't believe Grandpa forced you to get married."

"Well, there was a time when he was a little less forgiving," Casandra informed her. "Where he came up short with me, he more than made up with you. It took a few years, but I eventually forgave him."

"I think I should talk to Dad about this," Sidney informed her. "Let him know everything is okay between the three of us."

"I think he'd like that."

Chapter 14

Sidney sat silently on the porch across from her father, who fiddled with his brandy glass, and listened to him tell the story from his perspective. He didn't often drink, but this was one of those rare occasions.

"You'd probably heard it many times how your great-grandmother used to babysit me when I was around ten or eleven," Kingston announced and only occasionally looked up from his glass. "Helena was already married and had moved away. Your great-grandmother often talked about Helena, and she'd show me pictures of her granddaughter, your mother. Casandra was probably about five or six then." He again fiddled with his glass. "When I was a teenager, I would help your grandpa in his workshop. Mostly just sweeping and fetching tools for him. Your great-grandparents were like grandparents to me. Mine died when I was little, so I never got to know them."

"You worked for Grandpa while you were in college, too," Sidney remarked.

"Yes, but mostly on weekends and during the summer," he replied. "When your grandmother and mother moved back home, I was thrilled to finally meet them." He smiled warmly. "Your mother was the most beautiful young woman I'd ever seen. Definitely looked older than her actual age. Still, I was taken by her." He then frowned. "When your grandpa told me Casandra was pregnant, I was shattered. I had this bizarre fantasy that she'd one day fall in love with me, and we'd get married. Henry told me your mother needed to get married. That she couldn't have a baby without a husband." Kingston shrugged. "A little outdated thinking by today's standards, but things were a little different back then. In those days, being a single mother was more common in cities than in small towns. Your grandpa liked me, and I liked your mother."

"So you were on board with marrying Mom?"

"Onboard?" Kingston asked, then chuckled softly. "It was a dream come true. I know she only married me because she was pressured into it by her grandfather, but I was all-in." Her father smiled warmly. "When I saw her at the altar on our wedding day, I almost cried. Of course, she did cry, but for completely different reasons."

"It was wrong of Grandpa to insist Mom get married," Sidney informed her father, then frowned. "But I had an amazing childhood because I had the best parents. I can't help feeling a little guilty about that, knowing that Mom wasn't happy."

"Who said she wasn't happy?" Kingston asked with some surprise.

"She said it took time for her to warm up to you," Sidney replied, now feeling concerned that her father didn't know about her mother's feelings.

"While it's true that we didn't consummate the marriage for the first few years," her father announced. "We still enjoyed our life together. I'd bring her flowers and rub her feet, and she'd send me off to work every day with a kiss. After you were born, I made sure she had a few hours each night to herself. I'd even run baths for her so she could relax. Somewhere along the way, we turned into great friends."

"So neither of you were completely miserable in the beginning?"

"No, but I knew your mother would sometimes cry late at night," Kingston replied while shifting uncomfortably. "So I'd try even harder to make her happy." He seemed to sink into his own thoughts for a moment, and a tiny smile crossed his face. "One day, out of nowhere, she kissed me. I mean, she really kissed me." He managed a soft chuckle. "When she started wearing satin nightgowns and sending you to G-ma's for sleepovers, we were finally husband and wife, and we even went away for an official honeymoon. I think it was after that when she finally forgave Grandpa."

"Really?"

"Yes, she hugged him," Kingston replied. "It was the first time she'd hugged him. Remember, she was only sixteen when she met him for the first time. She resented him for insisting she get married even when she realized I wasn't so bad." He then held his breath. "Your G-ma wasn't quite as forgiving."

"Is that why there was friction between them?"

"Part of the reason, I'm sure," her father replied. "Those two always rubbed each other the wrong way."

§

Sidney sat across the kitchen table from her grandmother as Helena poured each of them a cup of tea. She couldn't deny that her grandmother looked uncomfortable about the current topic, barely able to look Sidney in the eyes at first.

"Back when I was sixteen, I started dating your grandfather," Helena informed her, then smiled while sinking back into her younger years. "He was so handsome and such a gentleman. Unlike any boy I'd ever met before. He was still a boy, I suppose. Not yet eighteen, but he was so mature. I fell in love with him the moment I met him, and he would have moved heaven and earth for me." Her smile slowly faded. "My father, your grandpa, didn't approve of him. Of course, he wouldn't. No boy would ever be good enough for his daughter, but I knew he'd come around." The light in her eyes diminished. "Your grandfather was a good man, but even good men and women make mistakes. When I found out I was pregnant, only a few months later, your grandpa was out of his mind. He wanted to hide the pregnancy and then have me and your grandfather put the baby up for adoption when it was born."

Helena shuddered slightly and took a sip of hot tea to ward off the chill of her past. She stared down at the teacup a moment before continuing.

"Your grandfather and I decided we'd get married instead," Helena announced, then raised her head proudly, meeting Sidney's sympathetic gaze. "We ran away, got married, and never looked back." Her smile soon returned. "It was hard, but I wouldn't have done a damned thing differently if I'd had it to do all over again. I loved that man. He found a job working at the country estate. The Norwoods were wonderful employers. We had a beautiful suite in the staff wing with plenty of room to raise your mother. And the lady of the house, oh, she adored your mother." She then sank into darker times. "I was only twenty-nine or thirty when your grandfather tragically died. Your mother was only thirteen when she lost her father."

Helena remained silent for a long moment, as if in another world. A much blacker world. She gripped her teacup tightly with both hands. For a moment, Sidney feared she'd break the delicate china cup. She loosened her grip on the cup, and her warm smile returned.

"Your grandfather and I had fourteen glorious years together," she remarked. "Thirteen of them were as husband and wife." Helena's sadness soon returned. "Unfortunately, the Norwoods died in the same tragic accident that claimed your grandfather's life." She drew a deep breath and sighed.

"I tried to make it work the next few years after her son took charge, but without your grandfather and without the lady of the house, I just couldn't bear staying any longer." She held her breath a moment, then looked back at Sidney and managed a tiny smile. "I was a thirty-three-year-old single mother with a sixteen-year-old daughter. I didn't know how I'd ever start over, especially without your grandfather. Your great-grandmother insisted I come home. With your mother in tow, we moved back to start the next chapter of our lives."

"But mom was pregnant," Sidney remarked softly.

"Yes, your mother found out she was pregnant shortly after we'd moved back," Helena replied while nodding. "Sixteen and pregnant. Just like her mother before her. Except she didn't have the love and support of her child's father as I did."

"That still doesn't excuse what Grandpa did," Sidney huffed.

"No, I suppose it doesn't," Helena replied, then managed a tiny smile. "But your mother loves your father very much, even if she didn't in the beginning." She raised her brows. "And he loves you. No matter what a paternity test would say, he's your father, and you're his daughter."

Chapter 15

Despite feeling better about the situation with her parents, Sidney felt like a caged panther the following day. She paced the workshop, feeling anger toward her grandpa for everything he'd put her mother and grandmother through. Realizing her grandmother ran away to be with the man she loved because Grandpa disapproved of Sidney's grandfather, and the baby she was carrying, was almost enough to drive her insane. It was as if her grandpa were some man she didn't even know. She'd think about how well they'd gotten along and how great he treated her growing up. How could this be the same man? Did he really change that much? Or was it because Sidney didn't date boys? Sure, she dated Leon for a few months in high school, but it's possible her grandpa didn't even know about that. Sidney finally paused alongside the freshly varnished bar and considered taking an axe to it. She hated how angry she was feeling. It was like some uncontrolled rage.

Amber would be home from work soon. Maybe talking to her would help. It then dawned on her. Today was Friday, and Amber didn't work. Her best friend had been off all day. Sidney spent the entire afternoon brooding in rage when she could have been venting to Amber. Sidney snatched her cell phone and called Amber. Unfortunately, it went directly to voicemail, which meant she was either on her phone or had it turned off. Sidney groaned with frustration and dialed the farmhouse phone.

"Sidney?" Jackson announced over her phone, obviously seeing her name on the caller ID. "Is Amber with you?"

"What?" Sidney asked, surprised and frustrated. "No, I was actually looking for her. I thought she had off today."

"She does," Jackson replied, then groaned. "She was pissed at me and took off about an hour ago. I assumed she went to your house."

"No, she's not here," Sidney replied. "At least, I don't think she is. I'm in the workshop. Maybe she's at my house with my mother."

"I'm sure you'll run into her," Jackson remarked with a defeated groan. "She's supposed to be going out with you and the guys tonight. Could you make sure she doesn't do anything stupid? I don't want her drinking and driving."

Sidney was about to correct him, since she didn't plan to go out with Amber and the guys, but then it dawned on her. This was the Friday Amber was going out with Greyson, and she was supposed to keep it a secret from Jackson.

"When I catch up to her later, I'll keep an eye on her," Sidney informed him.

"Thanks, Sidney."

Once Sidney disconnected her call with Jackson, she sank into thought. It was close to dinner time. Amber and Greyson were going to the restaurant just outside of town, but they'd probably circle back to the local bar for drinks and country line dancing. Sidney felt a little better now. She'd go to the bar and have dinner with Leon and Miller, who were undoubtedly there already. Going out and having a few drinks seemed like a good way to blow off some steam.

§

By the time Sidney arrived at the bar, there were already more than a dozen cars and trucks parked out front. The old two-story barn had been converted into the local bar with most of the original structure intact. Although the bar looked a little backwoods, the locals loved the idea of the renovated barn. It was going to be a particularly busy Friday night. Sidney recognized Miller's truck in the lot. At least she knew Miller was at the bar, which meant Leon was usually nearby. Sidney entered the bar and looked around. The converted interior was rustic with its finished plank wood floor and a large custom bar resembling an old west saloon. The walls were covered in old western décor, keeping in theme with the country vibe. Before Sidney could even finish her sweep of the patrons, she heard Miller calling to her above the crowd.

"Sidney!"

Sidney saw Miller with three other guys she recognized from high school, though she had never actually hung out with them. She approached their table, relieved to see at least one of her friends. Miller stood and offered her his seat while one of the guys found another chair for their table.

"Where's the rest of the crew?" Miller asked Sidney, who sat alongside her.

"I'm not sure," Sidney replied, knowing it was a lie. She wasn't sure if Amber and Greyson had told Miller and Leon that they were going out on an actual date. "Amber is MIA after having a tiff with her uncle." She looked around the crowded bar. "Where's Leon?"

"Don't get jealous or anything," Miller announced, barely hiding his grin. "He's on a date."

"I'm not jealous," Sidney informed him. "You do realize Leon and I haven't dated since high school, right?"

Miller laughed and nodded. "So I've heard," he teased, then indicated the guys at the table. "Speaking of high school. You remember the guys from the football team."

Yes, Sidney remembered them. Although Miller was her friend back in high school, his football buddies were not. If she remembered correctly, they snubbed her because she wasn't one of the popular girls. Sidney was the tomgirl who didn't wear dresses, makeup, or tops that revealed her cleavage. All three boys were at least six feet tall with broad shoulders and athletic builds. Everything you'd expect from former high school football players in their early twenties. Ray had dark, wavy hair that almost appeared curly now that it was a little longer. Although not unattractive, he certainly wasn't as handsome as Miller. Dawson also had dark hair, but he kept his hair short and neat. Possibly considered handsome by a lot of women, Sidney didn't think he was attractive in the least. His popularity might have had more to do with being on the football team than with his physical appearance. Dawson was also less masculine than Miller and Ray.

Jonas was the least attractive of the four. His hair was nearly black, long and unkempt. He had a baby face and a smile that could only be described as devious.

"It's been a while," Sidney informed Miller, then politely nodded at the three other guys.

"Jonas and Dawson finally stopped by for a visit," Miller informed her. "Ray wanted us all to get together."

"Oh, you guys probably want to catch up," Sidney remarked. "I shouldn't intrude."

"No," the three guys announced in unison, followed by a round of laughter.

"We could use a little female company tonight," Jonas remarked.

"Well, maybe I'll stay for one drink," Sidney replied and ordered a double shot of whiskey.

"She drinks the hard stuff," Dawson announced while chuckling.

"Sidney isn't your typical girl," Miller informed them. "She's more like one of the guys."

"Yeah, I remember you in high school," Jonas remarked, then grinned slyly. "You were dating Leon." He then nodded to her hair in a ponytail. "You still wear your hair in a ponytail, too." He laughed. "It was the only way we knew you were a girl."

Jonas, Dawson, and Ray laughed at the comment. Sidney smirked but didn't let their torment bother her. They were pretty much the same back in high school. It was a pack mentality.

"She's still a tomgirl," Miller informed them while whipping out his cell phone. "But now she has a cool pickup truck and a big boat."

Miller showed the guys a picture on his phone.

Sidney eyed her friend somewhat skeptically. "You took a picture of the truck?"

Miller looked back at her almost innocently. "And the boat," he added. He then laughed and pulled up another picture. "Sidney cleans up nicely. Check out this picture of her in a dress."

Sidney almost gasped at the comment. "You took a picture of me in that dress?"

"Absolutely," Miller cried out as the three guys gawked at the picture on his phone.

"Wow, you're hot," Dawson announced a little louder than necessary.

Sidney hid her embarrassment but managed a tiny smile. It was like high school all over again. Among her friends, Miller was the least mature, but he was better around guys like Leon and Greyson. Now that he was back with his 'pack', she remembered why she didn't hang out with him much in high school. None of his old friends, particularly those from the football team, seemed very mature. She had to hope Leon would show up and at least balance out some of the immaturity.

Chapter 16

Two hours later, Sidney remained at the table with Miller and his three friends. All five were laughing and having a good time, which was surprising since Sidney didn't think she'd get along with Miller's old jock buddies. Perhaps her moderately drunken state helped facilitate that process. They were crude, but she was used to crude. When a woman has mostly guy friends, it almost comes with the territory. Miller seemed almost as drunk as she was, so when he started hanging on her and flirting, it wasn't surprising. It was difficult to tell if Dawson, Ray, and Jonas were drunk, since they didn't act it.

Miller placed his arm around Sidney's shoulder and leaned in close, locking eyes with her. "I love you, Sidney," he announced in a drunken tone, then immediately waved his free hand. "I don't mean like wanting to bone you kind of love." His smile turned more sincere. "You're a cool friend."

"Thanks, I think," Sidney replied and had to giggle at Miller's excessively happy drunk talk.

"Don't listen to him," Dawson cried out. "He wants to bone you!"

Miller pulled Sidney against his side almost protectively and pointed at his friend. "She's my friend," he announced, then grinned. "And you guys are just jealous because I can have a 'girl' friend that's not a girlfriend."

Sidney happily hugged Miller, joining in on his drunken embrace. Naomi and her friend, Emily, approached their table, which seemed odd since Naomi had never shown any interest in socializing with Miller. Emily was a tall girl with a lean, almost athletic build, blonde hair, and ample cleavage, catching the attention of all four guys at the table.

"Hey," Naomi announced. "There aren't any tables left. Mind if we join you?"

Miller shoved Sidney away from him, nearly knocking her from her seat, and sprang to his feet. "Of course, we can squeeze in two more," he announced a little too quickly. "I'll find some extra chairs."

Over the next hour, Miller forgot how much he loved Sidney and flirted with Emily while Jonas attempted to make time with Naomi. Ray seemed stunned that Naomi was paying attention to Jonas. Apparently, he himself never got anywhere with her, and his friend getting her attention may have made him a little jealous. Once she got her buzz on, Naomi turned her attention to Sidney, which was out of character for her as well. Apart from visits to the diner, Naomi never found a reason to talk to Sidney.

"I'm surprised you aren't hanging out with Amber tonight," Naomi remarked in an almost sincere tone.

"She had other plans," Sidney replied, although she couldn't for the life of her remember what those plans were anymore.

When Miller took Emily's hand and led her onto the dance floor for a slow song, no one seemed to notice.

"I wouldn't doubt Jackson grounded her," Naomi scoffed, then snorted a laugh.

Dawson and Jonas were now interested in the conversation. Or perhaps it was just Naomi they were interested in.

"That's right," Dawson announced with a humored chuckle. "She was the chick with the psycho uncle." He then slapped Jonas on the shoulder hard enough to make him yelp. "Remember him?"

"No, not really," Jonas remarked. "I barely remember Amber."

"Her uncle would always pick her up at school," Dawson reminded him. "The moment she saw him pull up, she'd drop everything and jump in his truck."

"Didn't he beat her?" Jonas then asked.

"He didn't beat her," Sidney scoffed, defending her friend despite her drunken state.

Ray then looked at Naomi, appearing curious. "You dated Jackson," he remarked. "Think he beat her?"

"I doubt it," Naomi announced, then snorted a laugh. "He took controlling to a whole other level, but I doubt he was abusive. The guy's all bark and no bite. "

"That's right," Ray announced, somewhat humored. "Now, I remember. He got his ass kicked here in the bar a couple of years ago. Turned out to be nothing but a loudmouthed coward."

Sidney was becoming uncomfortable with the conversation regarding Amber's uncle.

"Is that why you broke up with him?" Jonas asked. "Because he was a controlling coward?"

"I broke up with him because he was emotionally unavailable," Naomi informed him. "We went out for almost a month, but he'd never take me back to his place. It was weird. Never talked about himself. Never offered anything personal, and if I'd ask, he'd shut down the conversation."

"I don't know why you went out with him in the first place," Ray muttered, now sounding drunk, while eyeing her. "Acted all tough but ran away, scared at the first sign of any real confrontation."

"I went out with him because he was tall and handsome," Naomi remarked, then seemed to consider the comment. "Once he had a few drinks in him, he was actually kind of fun. Back then, the girls all thought he was this unattainable, mysterious man. It was kind of exciting the first time I got him to go home with me." She snorted a laugh. "Unfortunately, his real personality returned in the morning, and he couldn't get out of my apartment fast enough."

"Yeah, but you dated a month or so," Ray reminded her, chuckling. "He must have done something right, or you wouldn't have gone out with him again. Every guy you've ever dated has proposed."

"My mistake was giving him a second chance," Naomi informed them, rolling her eyes in disgust. "He treated me more like a booty call than a girlfriend."

Sidney listened to the conversation, surprised by what she was hearing, although she probably shouldn't have been. Amber told her stories about Jackson trolling for women in trashy bars when he was younger. Maybe she was just disappointed that he treated Naomi, his girlfriend at the time, that way. Sidney shook her head in disgust and downed the rest of her drink. She was starting to think all men were pricks and needed to be avoided. Still, three-quarters of her friends were guys, so maybe she was being a bit hasty. Sidney ordered another drink, then got up to go to the bathroom for the tenth time since she started drinking. It wasn't until she got up that she realized how drunk she actually was, but that's how it was when drinking the hard stuff. By that point, she couldn't even remember how many drinks she had had. It probably didn't help that the guys took turns buying her drinks.

When she returned to the table, Naomi was gone, and Jonas was wiping beer from his lap. Sidney eyed Miller's three friends as she sat down and reclaimed her fresh drink.

"What happened?" she asked.

Ray glanced at her, grinned, and laughed. "Naomi said 'no'," he announced.

"Fucking tease," Jonas muttered with disgust.

Sidney sipped her whiskey then looked around the barroom, somewhat bewildered. "Where's Miller?"

"I guess Emily said 'yes'," Ray replied.

"He left?" Sidney asked with some surprise.

"Couldn't say," Dawson admitted. "They were on the dance floor, and now they're gone."

Sidney was now lost in thought. With Miller gone, she suddenly realized she was drinking with three guys she barely knew. She set her drink down and fumbled in her pocket for her cell phone.

"I should probably be heading home," she announced.

"You certainly can't drive in your condition," Dawson insisted.

"I'll call my father," she replied. "He'll come and get me."

"I'm the designated driver," Ray informed her, waving her off. "Don't worry. I'll give you a ride home. It's not even eleven o'clock. We're having fun. You can stay another hour or so."

Sidney nodded and attempted to relax, but found it difficult. She sipped her drink and subconsciously scanned the barroom, hoping to spot Miller. If he was still inside, she didn't see him. The guys were joking around and helped lighten the mood, and Sidney finally relaxed, although she now nursed her drink. It was time to sober up. Dawson moved into Miller's seat, and Sidney was wedged between him and Jonas. While the guys told jokes and goofed around, Jonas felt the need to place his hand on Sidney's leg. At first, she didn't even notice. When she finally did notice, she easily brushed it off. Dawson was also growing bolder, repeatedly resting his arm on her shoulder. She tried to remove his arm, but he kept putting it back.

"Stop it," she finally snapped at Dawson.

Dawson just laughed it off, although he did remove his arm. Ray and Jonas found her irritation humorous. Jonas's hand again found its way onto her leg, and she pushed it away more harshly.

"Come on, guys," Ray announced to his friends despite his smile. "Stop goofing around. You're upsetting her."

"It was okay when Miller did it," Dawson remarked while laughing.

"You're not Miller," Sidney scoffed in response.

Dawson put his arm around her, pulling her closer, and copped a feel on the side of her breast. She tried to push him away, but he refused to let go.

"You're so immature, Dawson," Ray remarked, although he laughed and didn't attempt to stop his friend's behavior.

Sidney finally pulled away from Dawson and thrust her palm into his chest. Unfortunately, she didn't hit him nearly as hard as she had thought, but at least he released her. She sprang up from her chair and immediately regretted it, suddenly off balance from the alcohol.

"Sit down before you fall down," Jonas remarked while laughing, and then pulled her onto his lap.

Sidney immediately protested, even though her actions weren't effective in her condition. They received several looks from those nearby.

"You guys are causing a scene," Ray informed his friends of the attention they were getting, but still did nothing to stop them.

Sidney managed to pull away from Jonas and his traveling hands. The moment she made it to her feet, Dawson grinned and patted his lap.

"My turn!"

Sidney aggressively stumbled away from the table but swore she heard several snickers from other men within the barroom. She collected herself, perfected a sober walk, and headed for the bathroom. Once in the bathroom, she leaned against the sink to collect herself before removing her cell phone. She pressed the button for her parents and listened to the phone ring. When the machine picked up, she disconnected the call. It was late, and they were probably already in bed. Frustrated, she tried Amber's cell phone again, but it went straight to voicemail. She must have turned her phone off and never turned it back on. Given the hour, she had to be at home by now. In desperation, Sidney pressed Amber's house phone number. It rang once and was picked up immediately.

"Amber?" Jackson asked over the phone.

"No, it's Sidney," she replied, feeling relieved just to hear a friendly, familiar voice. "Amber isn't home?"

"No," Jackson replied from the other end. "I thought she was with you."

"Uh, no," Sidney stammered into the phone as her emotions got away from her. She sniffed and attempted to pull herself together. "I, uh, hate to ask--"

"Are you okay?" Jackson asked, concern in his tone.

"Yeah, uh," she began and withheld her sniff. "I had too much to drink at the bar, and I, uh, I can't get a hold of my parents."

"Do you need a ride?"

Jackson's words immediately comforted her.

"Do you mind?" she gasped, jumping on the offer. "I really hate to ask."

"I can be there in ten minutes," he replied without hesitation.

"I really appreciate it," she whispered into the phone, attempting to keep from breaking down. Sidney then held her breath a moment, feeling a nervous pang. "Can you, uh, text me when you're out front? I don't want to wait outside alone."

"Yeah, sure," Jackson replied from the other end, then fell silent for a moment. "Is everything okay?"

"Yeah, just come and get me, okay?" Sidney whispered, finally breaking down.

"I'll be there in a couple of minutes," Jackson announced, his tone suddenly turning stern.

"Thanks," she whispered and disconnected the call before crying.

Apparently, everything that had happened since her grandpa's death had finally taken its toll on her. Or maybe it was just the alcohol. She felt she was being silly, but she couldn't seem to pull herself together.

Chapter 17

Sidney paced the bathroom for nearly five minutes, though it felt like a lifetime, when her phone dinged. She looked at the phone and saw Jackson's text. It simply read, "Outside". Sidney finally managed to collect her emotions, wiped her tears, and stumbled from the bathroom. Once she entered the bar area, she managed a sober walk and headed straight for the door. Ray caught up with her and stopped her, a sincere look on his face.

"Hey, there you are," Ray announced. "Are you okay? Sorry about the guys. I'll take you home if you're ready."

"I already have a ride," she informed him, matter-of-factly.

Dawson approached and pulled her into his arms while grinning. "You can ride in the back seat with me," he announced.

"Get your hands off me!" Sidney cried out in anger.

Several people looked up, but no one moved to stop it.

Dawson released her and laughed. "You're a bigger tease than Naomi," he remarked.

Jonas placed his arms around her from behind and held her against him. "I'm ready to go," he announced in her ear while laughing.

Sidney thrust her elbow backward but barely grazed him. She didn't have nearly as much force as when she was sober.

"Cool it, guys," Ray announced in a low tone, indicating the other patrons. "You're upsetting the drunks."

Dawson attempted to pull Sidney away from Jonas. "She's with me, asshole."

"Get your own girl," Jonas snapped back.

"Hey--!" a loud, baritone voice shouted, nearly raising the rafters.

The entire barroom fell silent except for the country music blaring on the jukebox. All eyes fell upon Jackson, standing just inside the doorway. The look on his face was somewhere between menacing and psychotic. Jackson walked across the barroom amid the stares and approached the three men with Sidney.

"Get your hands off her," Jackson snarled without taking his eyes off the young men.

Dawson laughed and faced Jackson, who was now practically in front of him, and puffed himself up, attempting to make himself appear bigger.

"What are you gonna do about it--?"

Jackson suddenly grabbed him by the back of the neck, practically pulled him off his feet, and bounced his head off the nearby table, startling those seated. Bottles and glasses bounced off the table and crashed to the floor as the patrons jumped up and away from their chairs. An enraged Jonas tossed Sidney into Ray.

"He's my friend," Jonas cried out as he swung his fist for Jackson's face.

Jackson caught his fist, surprising Jonas and everyone else within the bar. With speed and precision, Jackson punched Jonas in the gut, doubling him over before sweeping his legs out from under him. Jonas crashed to the floor with a loud thump. While his back was turned, Dawson grabbed a broken bottle and lunged for Jackson from behind. Sidney gasped in horror but didn't have time to scream a warning. Jackson immediately spun into a roundhouse kick and struck the broken bottle within Dawson's hand. The shattered remains easily cut into the man's hand. Jackson grabbed Dawson by the throat with one hand and stepped closer to him, staring him down from only inches away.

"Do that again, and I'll snap your fucking neck," he muttered just loud enough for Dawson to hear.

Dawson's eyes were wide with fear as he gasped for air beneath the hand gripping his throat. With his free hand, Jackson sharply punched him in the groin. As Dawson began to sink, Jackson released him, allowing him to fall to his knees, clutching himself in agony. Jackson then turned and focused his attention on Ray, who held onto Sidney after he'd caught her. Ray immediately released Sidney's arm and held his hands in the air.

"I didn't touch her, I swear," Ray cried out.

"Did you stop your friends from touching her?" Jackson snarled.

"I, uh--"

"Yeah," Jackson scoffed with a nod. "That's what I thought." Before Ray could flinch, Jackson punched him in the gut, doubling him over. "Learn to control your friends or find better ones."

With his booted foot, Jackson kicked Ray in the ass, knocking him to the floor. Jackson then held his hand out to Sidney while scanning the faces of those around them. She immediately clutched his hand, moved closer, and clung to his arm. Jackson only briefly met Naomi's gaze and the strange smile on her face before glaring at everyone else.

"You people are pathetic," Jackson snarled at them. "Fucking disgraceful."

Jackson escorted Sidney from the barroom and out to his haphazardly parked truck with long skid marks in the gravel behind it. When he saw them, Miller ran across the parking lot from one of the nearby cars.

"Sidney!" Miller called out, barely catching her attention.

Jackson opened the passenger side door for her and turned his attention to Miller as Sidney attempted to pull herself up and into the truck.

"Where the fuck were you?" Jackson demanded in a loud, threatening tone, stopping Miller in his tracks.

Emily made her way across the parking lot and paused several yards away while Miller stared at Jackson with apprehension and possible fear.

"I was--" Miller began, then hesitated. "What happened?"

"I'm not entirely sure," Jackson snarled back. "But it better never happen again."

As Jackson turned, he saw Sidney still attempting to pull herself into the truck. He swiftly grabbed her hips and just about launched her into the passenger seat. Once she was inside, he shut the door and rounded the vehicle to the driver's side. After slamming his door, Jackson's truck burned out in the loose gravel and jetted away, leaving Miller staring after it, dumbfounded.

Chapter 18

Sidney stared out the pickup truck's windshield at the dark back road, not even sure where she was. She glanced at Jackson, who appeared unusually relaxed, slouched in his seat with one hand on the wheel, considering his rage only a few minutes ago. Sidney stared at his profile in the dim glow of the dashboard lights, trying to gather everything she was feeling at that moment. Mostly, she was embarrassed about her behavior.

"I'm sorry," she finally whispered.

Jackson cast a strange look at her. "For what?" he asked, bewildered.

"Dragging you out here in the middle of the night," she replied softly. "Nearly getting you killed."

Jackson raised his brows and again eyed her. "There was little danger of that," he informed her, then glanced at his hand on the wheel. "Scuffed my knuckles a little, though." His tone turned more sincere. "Are you okay?"

"Feeling a little drunk and stupid," she muttered, then rested her head against the seatback.

"You're not stupid," he informed her almost sternly. "You're not to blame for the actions of others."

Sidney again tried to focus on the road ahead. It was familiar, but she was so drunk, she still didn't know where she was.

"Can I stay with you and Amber tonight?" she asked timidly, then sheepishly looked at his profile. "I don't want to go home. After everything that happened the last couple of days, I don't want my parents to see me like this. They'll think I'm still mad at them."

Without responding, Jackson slowed the truck, then turned around on the back road and headed in the opposite direction. They drove a few minutes in silence.

"So where is Amber?" he finally asked. "I thought she was with you tonight."

Sidney's mind immediately started reeling. She was supposed to lie and say Amber was with her. Now he would know Amber lied to him. She made a mess of everything she touched tonight.

"She went out with the guys and some other girls," Sidney easily lied. "They were going to see some movie I wasn't interested in seeing."

Jackson nodded while staring out the windshield at the dark road ahead of them. Sidney finally saw Jackson's farmhouse up ahead. There were several indoor and outdoor lights on, brightening the place despite the hour. Even in her inebriated condition, Sidney could tell that Amber's car was still missing. Once the truck stopped, Sidney attempted to release the seatbelt, although she had some trouble figuring it out. Jackson was already opening the passenger door by the time she unstrapped herself. As she fumbled for the step-down, Jackson attempted to keep her from falling. He finally groaned, grabbed her around the waist with one arm, and pulled her out of the truck. She cried out with surprise and clung to his neck, then laughed the moment her feet hit the ground. The swift action made her head spin in a fun sort of way.

"That was fun," she announced, now giddy while clinging to his neck with one arm.

The fresh air seemed to invigorate her inebriated state. Sidney shut her eyes, rested her head against his chest while leaning on him, and groaned softly.

"I'm tired," she cooed. "Carry me."

When Jackson swept her off her feet, Sidney cried out in surprise, clung to him with both arms, and laughed. That was even more fun than the leap from the truck.

"I didn't think you'd actually do it," she announced and continued laughing.

"It's been a long night," he casually informed her. "I don't need to spend another half an hour getting you into the house."

"It's not that late," she insisted, then rested her head on his shoulder as he effortlessly carried her up the porch steps. "It's only eleven or so."

"It's after one," he informed her as he pushed open the door.

Sidney looked around the brightly lit kitchen, wondering how they got into the house. "Did you open the door without putting me down?"

"I'm multi-talented," he replied.

"And strong," Sidney remarked while rubbing his shoulder, then giggled. "Tall, too."

Jackson closed the door with his foot, then turned his head to meet her gaze, his face only inches from hers. She stared into his eyes and immediately grinned.

"You're cute, you know that," Sidney informed him.

Jackson snorted a laugh and smirked. "Got our beer goggles on, huh?"

"I don't know what that means," Sidney replied while remaining giddy. "I don't even drink beer."

"I'll explain it to you another time," he remarked. "You really need to lay off the hard stuff." He then nodded across the kitchen to the nearby bathroom. "Do you need to puke before I put you to bed?"

Sidney grinned as she reached out and touched his beard. "You're getting gray in your beard," she informed him.

"Yes, I got those from living with Amber," he remarked. "Yes or no."

"What was the question?" Sidney asked and again laughed.

"Bathroom," he replied. "If you puke on me, I'll probably drop you."

"I don't have to puke, but I gotta pee."

Jackson set her down and pointed in the direction of the bathroom, in case she'd forgotten. Sidney stumbled to the bathroom and even remembered to shut the door behind her. While relieving herself, so many thoughts raced through her head in those few minutes. How did she get to Amber's house? Why was Jackson carrying her? And why did she have to pee so much when she didn't even consume a lot of liquid? The world may never know. She actually remembered to wash her hands before stumbling from the bathroom. Jackson pulled a bottle of water from the refrigerator and glanced at her as she stumbled across the kitchen.

"I'll have a glass of whiskey, if you're buying," she announced while remaining giddy.

Jackson held up the bottle of water. "Got your whiskey right here," he replied.

Sidney frowned at the comment, knowing damned well it was water. She immediately placed her arms around his neck and attempted to climb back up him.

"Second floor, Uncle Jackson."

Jackson groaned and easily swept her off her feet. She cried out in glee and clung to his neck.

"Oh, that's so much fun," she announced while laughing.

Before they even went one step, the front door opened, revealing Amber. She immediately stopped and eyed her uncle, who was holding Sidney.

"Do I want to know?" Amber muttered, not even fazed by it.

"Your friend got drunk and needed a ride home," Jackson informed her. "But you would know because you went out with her, isn't that right?"

Sidney looked back, saw Amber shutting the door, and cried out excitedly. "Hey, bestie! Want a ride upstairs? He's strong. I'm sure he could carry us both."

"We're not arguing about this now," Amber snapped back at her uncle. "Put Sidney down. It's creeping me out."

"Don't fight," Sidney announced, then looked at Amber. "I already told your uncle that you went to the movies with the guys and that girl, what's her name?"

"Are you sure that's the story you want to go with?" Jackson asked Sidney.

Sidney turned her head and again met his gaze, only inches from her face. Her smile increased. "I can't believe how cute you are," Sidney remarked and gently caressed the few visible gray hairs in his beard.

"I think I'm going to be ill," Amber muttered, then turned stern. "Sidney, you do realize that's my Uncle Jackson, right?"

"And he's so strong," Sidney announced as she looked back at Amber while again stroking Jackson's shoulder.

"Can we argue about this in the morning?" Jackson huffed. "I'd like to get Sidney into the guest bedroom before she pukes on me."

"Yes, gladly," Amber snapped back as she headed across the kitchen. "I'd rather not talk to you anymore tonight anyway."

"Right back at you," Jackson snarled as he followed Amber while carrying Sidney.

"Don't fight," Sidney muttered to Jackson while resting her head on his shoulder. "I love both of you too much for you to always fight like this."

Amber shot a look back at Sidney in Jackson's arms as they headed for the back stairs.

Jackson smirked at his niece. "Hear that?" he scoffed. "She loves me."

"She doesn't even know who you are," Amber snapped at him as she hurried up the stairs. "If she did, she wouldn't love you."

"Someone's bitchy tonight," Jackson scoffed under his breath as he followed his niece up the stairs, not slowed down by the young woman he carried.

"I'm pretty sure I get that from you," Amber snapped back as they headed down the second floor hallway for the guest bedroom.

"Don't listen to her," Sidney whispered close to Jackson's neck. "I love you even when you're bitchy."

"Back at you, Sidney," Jackson remarked.

Sidney wasn't sure if that was a compliment or an insult, but she giggled anyway. Amber entered the bedroom while glaring back at her uncle, carrying her best friend. The guest bedroom was more masculine than feminine, with a double bed that had only a headboard and some basic dressers.

"What are you two talking about?" Amber demanded.

"None of your business," Jackson snapped back. "Grab one of my shirts for her to sleep in."

Amber pulled the covers down on the bed, then spun to face her uncle with near horror. "You're not undressing her," she launched in anger.

"I didn't say I was," Jackson growled in response. "That would be dirty and wrong. Just get the fucking shirt."

"Someone's got a real potty mouth tonight," Amber scoffed, then left the room.

Jackson groaned in disgust. "I love that girl, but some days I'd like to put her in the ground," he remarked as he dropped Sidney's feet to the floor.

Sidney giggled at her own unsteadiness and refused to release his neck, forcing her to stand on her tippy toes as she pressed her body against his. She patted his chest with her free hand.

"Thanks for the ride," Sidney announced, unable to control her grin. "It was fun."

Jackson gently removed her hands from his chest and neck while simultaneously stepping away from her. "Amber will help you change." He removed the bottled water from his jacket pocket and set it on the nightstand. "Sip that, and if you have to puke, the trash can is right there." Jackson was about to turn and leave when Sidney spoke.

"I meant what I said," Sidney remarked, now serious.

He paused and looked back at her. "What's that?" Jackson asked.

"You and Amber are like family to me," she replied, smiling. "And I do love you."

Jackson took a step back to Sidney and pulled her into his arms, holding her against him in a warm embrace, which Sidney eagerly reciprocated.

"I really needed to hear that," he gently announced into her hair, then affectionately kissed the top of her head. As his arms tightened around her, he groaned softly near her ear. "I love you too, Sidney."

"You two are really starting to freak me out," Amber muttered from the doorway.

Jackson groaned as he released Sidney, then turned to face his niece. "Maybe I'll keep Sidney, and ***you*** can go live with her parents."

"That's the best idea you've had in years," Amber scoffed back at him.

Jackson muttered under his breath while leaving the guest bedroom. Amber slammed the door behind him as Sidney collapsed onto the bed.

"No," Amber cried out and hurried toward her with one of Jackson's old button shirts. "Change into this shirt before you even think about passing out."

Sidney groaned and sat up on the bed. "Fine."

Chapter 19

It was a little after three o'clock in the morning when Sidney woke in the spare bedroom. She looked around the dimly lit room, only the bedside clock illuminating it, and was momentarily disoriented. It took her a moment to realize where she was, having spent many nights in Amber's guest bedroom. She only remembered bits and pieces of last night. Her mouth was dry, her head was spinning, she was still feeling the effects of the whiskey, and she had to go to the bathroom. Sidney saw the bottle of water on the bedside table and took several sips as she padded out of the bedroom for the bathroom. While using the facility, she checked out the man's button shirt she wore as a nightshirt. Its origin was a mystery to her. Once she finished using the bathroom, she sipped more water and headed back to the dimly lit guest bedroom. Sidney set the water on the nightstand and crawled back into the nice, warm bed.

§

Something woke Sidney around five o'clock in the morning as pre-dawn was just peeking over the horizon.

Not even caring what had woken her, Sidney nuzzled the warm pillow that she clung to, re-establishing her hold on it.

"Sidney," a man softly muttered. "Sidney."

She groaned in her sleep, refusing to be roused by the voice. "It's too early to go fishing, Grandpa. The fish aren't even awake yet."

"Wrong bed, Sidney," the man announced a little louder.

Sidney opened her eyes only partway and saw Jackson halfway turned in his bed as she clung to his waist from behind. Apparently, it hadn't been a pillow after all.

"Wrong room," he insisted, and finally managed to turn onto his back while placing his arm above her when she didn't move, so he wouldn't hit her in the face.

Sidney lifted her head without opening her eyes more than tiny slits and looked around the room. She groaned, again moved closer to Jackson, and secured her arm across his abdomen while nuzzling her head against his chest.

"Don't care," she muttered and immediately drifted back to sleep.

§

An hour later, the sun was poking through the part in the curtains, rousing Sidney. She was completely exhausted, and her head was pounding from her hellish evening at the bar. It only took her a moment to realize she was nestled against Jackson, ensnared in his arms and legs, while their bodies were completely meshed together. He lightly snored against the top of her head while her face remained nestled against his bare chest. Sidney could feel his heart beating beneath her hand on his chest. Although somewhat disoriented, she remembered him waking her about accidentally being in his bed. Apparently, she disregarded his warning. Despite that she'd probably be embarrassed later, she was surprisingly comfortable and really just wanted to sleep a little longer. Since he didn't seem to mind, neither did she.

Jackson stirred in his sleep without waking and reestablished his hold on her by firmly running his hand down her back and along her buttocks. Sidney was immediately aware of his hand on her backside, but she was too tired to care. Without even waking, Jackson held her close to him and pressed his pelvis against her. Sidney just about gasped at the sensation of his morning arousal firmly poking her in a very sensitive area. If she hadn't been so tired, she might have protested, but she just wanted to sleep, and his body was nice and warm. Despite everything, Jackson never woke, and Sidney brushed it aside before quickly drifting back to sleep.

§

Around nine o'clock that morning, Sidney woke from possibly the deepest sleep of her life. Although still exhausted, she rolled onto her back, alone in the bed, and stretched. She hesitated, then suspiciously eyed the room from beneath the covers and wasn't sure where she was or how she got there. She slowly sat up and looked at the excessively large man's shirt she wore, then once more scanned the room. Sidney saw the many pictures of Amber and her mother on the walls. She felt her heart suddenly pound as she realized she was in Jackson's bedroom. She tried to piece together last night and vaguely remembered Amber's uncle driving her home. It took a few minutes, but she finally remembered Amber getting her settled into the guest bedroom. Her disorientation after her bathroom pit stop somehow brought her into Jackson's bedroom. The rest came flooding back to her in a tidal wave of embarrassment and shame.

Despite that nothing happened between her and Amber's uncle, Sidney remembered clinging to him in her sleep. She also remembered a particularly intimate moment when Jackson had his hand on her backside. Sidney allowed her head to fall into her hand as she groaned. She was never going to live this one down. Once she returned to the guest bedroom and found her clothes, she changed and headed downstairs, following the smell of freshly brewed coffee and bacon. Her stomach turned slightly at the thought of eating, but at the same time, she was somehow hungry. When she entered the kitchen, she saw Jackson alone at the stove. It was possible Amber wasn't even up yet, considering how late she'd gotten in as well.

Sidney paused at the bottom of the steps, attempting to think of what she was going to say to Amber's uncle after climbing into bed with him. She watched him make breakfast at the stove and suddenly felt a strange pang. She glanced over his tall frame, broad shoulders, and moderately muscular body, feeling her heart suddenly pound in response. She almost wished they were back in bed together. Sidney immediately scolded herself for even thinking something like that about Amber's uncle. Jackson glanced back, saw her, and chuckled.

"Look who's finally up," he announced in a moderately cheerful tone.

Sidney could almost feel the sensation of his hand firmly traveling her body and the way it felt when he pressed his body against hers. Despite being just a misunderstanding, she couldn't stop thinking about Jackson being a sexually desirable man and not just Amber's uncle. Sidney immediately fidgeted and had to look away, attempting to shake the reminder of Jackson's morning enthusiasm firmly pressed against her. It was possible he didn't even know he did it. Sidney, feeling insecure, folded her arms across her chest and avoided looking at him.

"I'm sorry about last night," Sidney remarked. "It was purely accidental. I hope you realize that."

He chuckled as he waved her off and turned back to the stove. "I thought it was funny," Jackson informed her while frying the bacon in the pan.

"You won't say anything to anyone, will you?" she asked timidly.

"You mean all the guys at the country club?" he asked, laughing again. "I don't think you have much to worry about. Besides, it was an honest mistake."

Sidney sighed with relief and allowed her arms to fall to her sides. "I appreciate that."

"No problem," Jackson replied. "Have a seat. Breakfast is almost ready."

"Do you need any help?"

"No, I've got this."

Amber entered the kitchen, paused in the archway, and grinned at Sidney. "I didn't interrupt anything, did I?" she asked with a giggle. "You know, the two of you could have slept in. I would have brought you breakfast in bed."

Sidney's expression dropped to near horror as she glared at Jackson.

He frowned and waved her off. "Ignore her," Jackson muttered. "She knows damned well nothing happened."

"I can't believe you crawled into bed with my Uncle Jackson," Amber announced while laughing and shaking her head. "You little slut."

"It was an accident," Sidney huffed and joined her friend at the table.

Amber poured coffee for all three of them but maintained her humor. "Yeah, sure," she announced. "Just keep your indiscretions in the confines of my uncle's bedroom."

"Amber," Sidney gasped as her cheeks reddened. "Don't say things like that."

"Oh, I wasn't trying to embarrass you, Sidney," Amber remarked, then indicated Jackson with a nod. "Just the dirty old man."

"I'm eight years older than you," Jackson huffed under his breath as he cast the plate of bacon onto the table.

"Doesn't make you any less old or dirty," Amber casually remarked.

Jackson shook his head and removed the scrambled eggs from the oven, where he had them warming. He then joined them at the table.

"Keep in mind, I don't embarrass nearly as easily as your friend," he informed her. "So don't get me started."

"Please don't involve me in whatever spat the two of you are having," Sidney remarked and quickly eyed both. "I'm really not in the mood."

"See," Jackson announced and lightly banged his hands on the table. "You've upset your Auntie Sidney."

Both looked at Jackson with horror in their eyes.

Amber waved her napkin in the air like a flag. "I surrender," she announced. "You win. Just don't call her that again."

Jackson smiled smugly and helped himself to a scoopful of scrambled eggs from the serving dish. "And he remains undefeated."

"God," Sidney groaned. "You're both weird."

"And yet you keep coming back," Jackson remarked to Sidney while grinning.

When she met his humored gaze, he winked at her. She couldn't deny the wink made her heart flutter slightly, and that bothered her.

"You should have thought about that before you slept with my uncle," Amber casually remarked, then exchanged grins with Jackson.

"Nice one," Jackson announced and held his fist out to her across the table.

"Thank you," Amber replied and bumped fists with him.

Sidney groaned, covered her eyes, and sank into her chair. "I think I like the two of you better when you're fighting with each other."

Chapter 20

Closer to noon, Amber gave Sidney a ride back to the bar to pick up her grandpa's truck. Well, technically, her truck. Once they were alone in Amber's car, Sidney was finally able to apologize to her friend.

"I'm sorry you had to suffer your uncle's wrath because I forgot I was covering for you," Sidney remarked while frowning. "Was he really as mad as he sounded?"

Amber waved her off, then started the car. "We were fighting long before I went on my date with Greyson," she informed her friend. "Nothing you said or did could have made things worse."

"So he knows you went out with Greyson?" Sidney asked as her friend turned around in the driveway, then drove up the long dirt road.

"My God, no," Amber replied. "I think he bought your drunken rambling about me going out with the guys and another girl. He just sometimes gets in his moods. Probably his time of month."

Sidney snorted a tiny laugh. She was relieved she hadn't made things worse for her friend.

"So? How did it go?"

"Oh, no," Amber announced boldly while casting quick looks at her friend. "First, I want to know what happened with you and Uncle Jackson."

"Nothing happened."

"I know ***nothing*** happened," Amber groaned while rolling her eyes, "but I want to know ***what*** happened."

"You're talking in riddles again."

"I want details."

"There are no details," Sidney insisted. "I got up to use the bathroom and wandered into the wrong room. End of story."

"Yeah, right," Amber scoffed while maintaining her grin. "If you don't give me specifics, I'm not telling you about my date."

"You don't need to tell me," Sidney reminded her. "Greyson will tell me all about it."

Amber groaned in frustration. "Stop being so wishy-washy and just tell me what happened," she insisted. "What was his reaction? Did he totally freak out? Details!"

"Fine," Sidney groaned and allowed her head to fall against the headrest. "He woke me when he'd discovered I was in his bed. I guess I was really tired and didn't leave. When I woke in the morning, he was already out of the room."

Amber frowned and shook her head. "Not exactly details," she remarked.

"There are no details."

"Then why were you so flustered all through breakfast?" Amber demanded. "You couldn't even look at him."

"I was embarrassed," Sidney insisted defensively. "I woke up in your uncle's bed. Isn't that enough?"

Amber raised her brow and eyed her friend skeptically. "Was he sleeping commando?"

"What?" Sidney gasped in horror, then shook her head. "No, of course not."

"Ha!" Amber cried out while pointing at Sidney. "How would you have known he hadn't gone commando if there's nothing else to tell?"

Sidney groaned and shook her head. "Okay, fine," she scoffed. "I was spooning against him."

Amber gasped, then squealed enthusiastically. "You were snuggling with my uncle!"

"We weren't snuggling," Sidney insisted, now becoming frustrated. "I thought he was a pillow."

"That must have given him a thrill," Amber remarked, then snorted a laugh. "Which explains his unusually good mood this morning." She groaned softly. "Jesus, that man needs to get laid."

Sidney couldn't exactly tell her friend that Jackson just about humped her in his sleep. It was far too embarrassing.

"I guess you're lucky he didn't hump you in his sleep," Amber remarked, catching Sidney's attention, almost as if having read her thoughts.

Sidney shifted uncomfortably at the comment, then hoped Amber hadn't noticed. Amber shot several looks at her friend, practically giving herself whiplash, as her expression dropped.

"Did he?" Amber just about gasped. "Did my uncle hump you?"

"No, of course not," Sidney cried out and had to hide her reddened cheeks.

Amber shot looks at Sidney in the passenger seat. "Oh, my God! He did!" Her expression then turned stern. "Be honest with me, Sidney. Did Uncle Jackson deflower you?"

Sidney groaned and looked out the side window. "You're impossible."

"He did!" Amber cried out. "No way!"

Sidney turned in her seat and glared at her friend. "I didn't have sex with your uncle," she scolded, then hesitated and fidgeted. "I suppose there ***was*** some unintentional cuddling, though." Sidney groaned and again held her head. "Do you have any idea how embarrassed I am right now?"

"There's no reason to be embarrassed," Amber groaned as they pulled into the bar parking lot. She put the car in park and turned to face Sidney. "Jackson certainly didn't mind." She snorted a laugh. "For as often as he's checked out your backside--"

"What?" Sidney gasped with surprise.

"It's going to take a lot more than wearing frumpy shirts and your hair in a ponytail to keep him from checking you out," Amber remarked. "He hasn't gotten laid in forever."

"I'm sure you exaggerate," Sidney muttered.

"No, I'm serious," Amber insisted. "That bitch Naomi soured him. She practically turned all the women in town against him. For a while after that, he would frequent some bar outside of town. He'd come home late at night, reeking of cheap perfume, but at least he was in a good mood for a few days. Then, he stopped going out altogether." She shook her head. "Maybe if he had a girlfriend, he wouldn't have time to worry about what I'm doing." Amber sighed and threw her head back against the seat rest. "I can just see it now. The two of us living together forever, sad and lonely. Kind of like your grandmother and great-grandfather."

Sidney twitched at the comment. Her evening at the bar and waking up in bed with Jackson had taken her mind off that business with her grandpa for a while, but now it was back.

Chapter 21

Sidney spent the better part of her Saturday afternoon in the workshop hand-sanding a nearly completed table. She was lost in her own thoughts, unable to focus on anything except sanding the table. When she heard a commotion in the office, she sprang up from her stool, not sure what was happening. Greyson was the first to enter, with Leon and Miller a couple of steps behind him. The concerned look on his face meant that he'd heard about what happened last night at the bar.

"You don't get any say in this," Leon snapped at Miller, who looked upset and guilt-ridden.

Greyson paused before Sidney and visually checked her over. "Are you okay?" he asked in a gentle, sympathetic tone, then turned gruff. "Did Miller's ill-mannered friends hurt you?"

"I'm going to beat the piss out of them," Leon snarled as his adrenaline spiked.

Miller attempted to get closer to Sidney with a shattered look on his face. "I didn't know, Sidney," he insisted. "I didn't leave you there. Emily and I were just hanging out in her car in the parking lot. I thought you'd be okay in the crowded bar."

"I'm fine," Sidney replied to her three friends. "I was drunk, and those bastards took advantage of the situation." She then looked at Miller. "When I saw you outside, I knew you hadn't abandoned me."

"Don't let him off that easy," Leon scoffed.

"Is it true?" Greyson asked while just about squinting in disbelief. "Did Jackson beat the crap out of those guys?"

"Honestly, I'd never seen anything like it," Sidney informed them. "He was scary calm. If he wanted to, I think he could have seriously hurt them."

"It's all anyone in town is talking about," Greyson informed her, then fidgeted. "I think you should know, they're already starting rumors about you and Jackson."

Sidney shuddered at the comment and was immediately reminded of her intimate moment in Jackson's bedroom. She suddenly felt as if she were hiding some dirty secret.

"You mean, Naomi is spreading rumors about Jackson and Sidney," Leon corrected. "She's had a real hard-on for Jackson ever since they broke up."

"She broke up with him," Miller reminded him. "Why would she have it out for him?"

"Jackson is Amber's uncle," Sidney informed them. "Starting rumors about me and him is insane. Don't they have anything better to talk about?"

"Apparently not," Leon muttered. "There isn't anything between you two, is there?"

Sidney eyed her ex-boyfriend and commandingly raised her brows. "Are you serious?"

"Give your hormones a rest," Greyson scoffed at Leon, then focused his attention back on Sidney. "Are you sure you're okay?"

"I'm fine," Sidney replied and even offered a warm smile. "Really, I am."

"We should have a nice, quiet get-together tonight," Miller remarked, then grinned at Sidney. "We should go to the lake house for the rest of the afternoon. Camp out, have a bonfire, and spend the night."

"No," Sidney remarked and fidgeted. "I don't want to go to the cabin. I'm still dealing with my grandpa's passing, and being there will bring back more memories."

That was only partly true, but she wasn't going to tell them she was feeling hostility toward the man she loved dearly after finding out what he'd done to her mother and grandmother. She didn't want to think about her grandpa right now. Even being in the workshop was difficult, but she needed to keep working.

"If you don't want to go to the cabin, we can camp on the other side of the lake," Leon suggested. "There's road access to that clearing by the lake."

"Isn't there a dock there as well?" Miller then asked. "And a massive fire pit too?"

All three of her guy friends suddenly became enthusiastic, as if they had come up with the same plan.

"We could take the boat, pitch tents, and have a bonfire," Leon announced excitedly.

"Sounds like a lot of work for an overnight," Sidney remarked, then noticed the enthusiasm from the guys.

"We could take the boat out and do some fishing, have a cookout, bring a keg of beer," Greyson added, ignoring Sidney's comment.

"Pee in the woods," Sidney muttered. "Snakes in our sleeping bags."

The guys seemed to ignore Sidney's negative comments and continued with their own ideas.

"Bring some girls," Miller announced while grinning. "Cuddle in sleeping bags."

"Mosquito bites," Sidney remarked while sneering. "Poison ivy."

Greyson turned to Sidney, placed both hands on her shoulders, and stared into her eyes. "Please, Sidney," he announced with sincerity. "If you ever cared about me, agree to go camping by the lake."

Sidney knew Greyson just wanted a chance to play musical sleeping bags with Amber. It was the perfect opportunity to get Amber away from her uncle without creating another shit storm between them.

"Fine," Sidney groaned.

Just because her life sucked, that didn't mean she wanted to stand in the way of Greyson and Amber's happiness. All three guys cheered excitedly and each took turns hugging her.

"You don't have to worry about a thing," Miller insisted. "The three of us will get provisions, wood for the fire, and sleeping accommodations."

"We'll pitch all the tents, launch the boat, and build the bonfire," Leon added.

"All you need to do is ask Amber," Greyson announced while cleverly raising his brows.

Sidney groaned, knowing she'd have to go over to Amber's house and ask. After Amber lied to her uncle last night, he wasn't about to agree to letting her go on an overnight without making sure it was a group thing. Even then, Jackson might cause problems.

§

As Sidney drove down the long driveway to Amber's farmhouse, her stomach was already tied in knots. She couldn't stop thinking about her 'sleepover' with Jackson. She could almost feel his hands on her and his morning arousal pressing against her. At least her embarrassing night with Jackson helped keep her mind off her grandpa. Maybe camping in the woods would help get her mind off Jackson and her grandpa. As she pulled up to the house, Sidney felt her heart pounding. She dreaded talking to Amber about tonight. Her friend shouldn't need her uncle's permission to spend the night in the woods. She was a grown woman and shouldn't need his permission to do anything. A thought then occurred to her. She had the workshop and the cabin. Amber could move in with her, and there wasn't a damned thing Jackson could do to stop her. She could finally get out from under his controlling thumb.

Sidney jumped out of her truck and approached the house with renewed confidence. She didn't even make it up the porch steps when Amber greeted her at the screen door. It was difficult to sneak up on the farmhouse with its long driveway. The two of them usually heard someone coming a mile away.

"Hey," Amber announced cheerfully and held the door open for Sidney. "I wasn't expecting you back here anytime soon. Is this a social call or a booty call?"

"That's not funny," Sidney scoffed at her friend, then entered the house and nervously looked around for signs of Jackson.

"Don't worry," Amber announced with a tiny giggle. "Uncle Jackson is in the garage tinkering on his cars. Are we going out tonight?"

"That's what I wanted to talk to you about," Sidney remarked, then cringed at what she needed to say next. "The guys want to camp overnight at the lake."

Amber's eyes lit up only for a moment. Dread quickly replaced her enthusiasm. "You'd better get out there and open the cabin windows," she remarked. "The place is probably damp and stale. Will there be enough time to wash the linens?"

"I nixed staying in the cabin," Sidney informed her. "I don't want to be reminded of my grandpa right now. We're going on the far side of the lake, where the second dock is located. The guys are bringing tents and sleeping bags."

"Already a step above the cabin," Amber teased, amused by her comment. "Do I need to bring anything?"

"Bug spray," Sidney muttered, then gave her friend a curious look. "Do you think Jackson will give you a hard time after last night?"

"Of course he will," Amber casually replied. "But I'll think of something while packing my overnight bag. In the meantime, you can go into the garage and soften the blow for me." She then shrugged. "If you're really my friend, you'd offer him a hand job."

"Amber," Sidney cried out, surprised by her friend's amount of teasing.

"I'm just having a little fun at your expense," Amber insisted, somewhat humored before her expression turned stern. "Seriously, though. A hand job wouldn't hurt."

Sidney ignored the crude joke. "I don't think I can face Jackson right now," she remarked while shifting uncomfortably. "I'm still a little embarrassed about last night."

"There's no reason to be," Amber insisted. "You said nothing happened."

Sidney groaned and ran her fingers through her hair. "Okay," she huffed softly. "He did kind of hump me in his sleep." She then turned stern. "Just a little."

"You were a warm body in his cold and lonely bed," Amber announced, then casually shrugged. "Of course he humped you."

"Which is why I don't want to see him right now," Sidney insisted. "I'd like to get over my embarrassment first."

"Big baby," Amber muttered, then pushed Sidney toward the back door. "Now, go out there and ask my uncle if I can go camping with you."

Sidney cast a look back at her friend and considered the irony.

Chapter 22

Beyond the farmhouse was the old, twelve-stall, two-story stone barn that Jackson renovated several years ago. Amber's uncle was quite handy. The outer stall doors were replaced with three sets of garage doors. And the second floor was possibly renovated into living quarters or a workshop with an entrance and stairs to the upper floor. Attached to the side of the barn was a large hangar of sorts. Sidney lightly tapped on the lower barn door before opening it and looking inside. She'd actually never been in Jackson's restoration garage. The lower level of the barn was entirely open with concrete flooring and was cleaner than most houses. There were four completely restored muscle cars as well as two others in various stages of restoration. Among the fully restored cars was a beautiful purple 1970 Plymouth Hemi Barracuda, a black Chevrolet Chevelle SS 454 LS6, and an old 1953 Chevrolet 3100 truck in hunter green.

Sidney checked out the two, junky looking muscle cars awaiting restoration. Jackson had quite the operation and enough tools to run his own chop shop. She knew he made a decent living buying and selling cars he restored, considering he had enough money to fix up both the house and the barn. Both had been in pretty sad condition when he bought the farm several years ago. Sidney followed the sound of a hammer pounding steel and found Jackson toward the back of the shop, straightening a dented metal fender. There was a door beyond where he was working that led into the hangar. From what Sidney could see, there was a restored prop plane occupying the hangar. When Jackson looked up, he seemed surprised to see her and not his niece. He set the hammer down and actually smiled, giving Sidney his full attention.

"You're the last person I expected to see out here in my lair," Jackson remarked as he wiped his hands on a rag while approaching her.

"Yeah, me too," Sidney informed him. "I wanted a quiet afternoon at home, but my annoying friends had other ideas."

"They didn't talk you into going to the bar again tonight, did they?" Jackson scoffed, now frowning.

"No," Sidney remarked while insecurely rubbing her shoulders, then shuddered. "It might be a while before I go back there again."

"Yeah, you and me both," he muttered, then flexed his hand with the scraped knuckles.

"Sorry about your hand," she announced somewhat timidly. "I feel bad for putting you in that position in the first place."

Jackson leaned against the nearby car, partially sitting on it, so they were at eye level. "You aren't responsible for my actions," he informed her.

"No, but it's my fault you were there," she reminded him.

"I was due for some social interaction anyway," Jackson remarked while grinning slyly.

Sidney looked at him with some surprise, then smiled and laughed, finally relaxing. She inadvertently took in a sweeping eyeful of Jackson and his unintended sexy pose against the car. She could almost feel his body against hers from last night, and it made her heart skip a beat. Sidney felt her cheeks redden, and she looked away, embarrassed at her thoughts. She was once again stiff and awkward around him.

"Sorry," Sidney remarked. "I didn't think this would be so awkward."

"Oh, I don't know," Jackson announced while grinning. "I like seeing you all flustered. Restores the balance of power in my favor."

Sidney met his gaze, and her eyes narrowed as she sneered at him. "Not surprising," she scoffed.

Jackson chuckled. "And she's back." He then straightened and returned to his workstation, replacing the tools in their proper places. "You don't need to be uncomfortable around me because of anything that happened last night," he insisted. "You didn't puke on me, that's what's important."

Sidney couldn't help but admire his profile while he worked. When he turned and leaned his back against the counter, Sidney quickly met his gaze, afraid he'd catch her checking him out.

"Was there something else you wanted?" Jackson then asked, offering a tiny smirk. "I assume you didn't come out here to talk 'shop'."

She wanted to kick herself for hesitating on her real reason for being out here. Had last night destroyed any headway she'd made with Jackson over the years? Was she back to being intimidated by him just because he put his ***manly*** hands on her last night?

"Well, there was one thing," she remarked, and again hesitated.

Great! Now, she couldn't get her mind off his hands grasping the counter on either side of him, reminding her that he'd had his hand on her ass! Her eyes then strayed past his crotch, perfectly outlined by the creases in his pants and his legs crossed casually at the ankles. She couldn't even go there! She could almost feel the sensation of his morning glory pressed against her, reliving that moment. Sidney knew the color was again rising to her cheeks, and she quickly met his gaze, hoping he hadn't noticed her stray look. She needed to say something. Amber would be so disappointed in her if she didn't at least try.

"We're, uh, camping overnight by the lake tonight," Sidney forced the words from her mouth.

Jackson suddenly turned curious as he straightened. "An overnight?"

Sidney knew he would squash the idea and forbid Amber from going, even though she was old enough to do as she pleased. As her mind raced, she knew she had to sell it, and sell it fast.

"Obviously, there will be girls' and boys' tents," she informed him. "Fishing on my grandpa's boat. A cookout and bonfire. It'll be fun."

His look turned somewhat stern. "Booze and skinny dipping in the lake," Jackson added in a dry, matter-of-factly tone.

"Hard pass on the skinny dipping," Sidney announced, then shifted uncomfortably.

There was no way Jackson was going for it, and she hated that Amber needed his approval in the first place, but those were the rules.

"My friends aren't so bad once you get to know them," she remarked.

Jackson's look was hard to read. Sidney drew a sharp breath and kept her eyes locked on his.

"You said you needed more social interaction," she announced as casually as possible.

Jackson seemed to come back to life, now curious. "You're asking me to come along?"

"Yeah," Sidney replied as her heartbeat quickened, just about stealing her breath away. She offered a slightly tense smile. "It'll be fun."

There was a long moment of silence as Jackson stared at her, possibly attempting to read her mind. His silence and stare made Sidney almost uncomfortable. Jackson finally nodded.

"Well, if Amber wants to go, we can go," he finally replied.

Sidney attempted to smile more naturally, then took two steps backward and away from him. "Great," she announced. "I'll, uh, draw you a map, and you guys can meet us there in a couple of hours." Her uneasiness grew dramatically, and she was almost certain Jackson was picking up on her anxiety. "Bring sleeping bags and bug spray."

Sidney hurried from the garage and just about ran into Amber, who had obviously been hanging around outside, avoiding interrupting while Sidney did the dirty work for her.

"Well?" Amber eagerly asked.

"Well, you're coming," Sidney informed her while just about dragging her by her wrist back to the house. "And so is your uncle."

"Sidney," Amber gasped, her eyes wide in horror. "What did you do?"

"I couldn't help it," Sidney gasped. "He was just staring at me, waiting for me to break. I broke."

"Never look the devil in the eyes," Amber scoffed. "You know better." She groaned and shook her head. "Such a rookie move."

"Well, you're more than welcome to uninvite him," Sidney scoffed.

"Are you insane?" Amber gasped, then shook her head while offering a tense laugh. "I had trouble asking him if you could sleep over during our senior year in high school. There's no way I'd ever be able to ask him if I can go on a co-ed camping trip."

"Amber, you're twenty-three," Sidney reminded her. "Stop letting him intimidate you."

"Hmm, that's great advice," Amber remarked. "Remind me how that worked for you?"

Chapter 23

While Miller and Leon set up the last of the four tents, Greyson was in a huff while following Sidney around the makeshift camp alongside her grandpa's private lake. The campsite was basically a large clearing deep within the vast woods, with an old, twelve-foot fire pit crudely made from large stones and makeshift benches from old split logs. The crude campsite was just a few yards from the older boat dock, which was on the far side of the lake from the old cabin. The boat dock had a railed walkway approximately twenty feet long that opened to a large docking area. The lake was big enough that the cabin on the other side couldn't be seen from their current location, mostly obstructed by a small island. As promised, Sidney's friends had her grandpa's boat docked and waiting for her arrival.

"What were you thinking?" Greyson demanded while following her around. "Why would you invite Jackson along? How is that supposed to work?"

"I'm sorry," Sidney huffed in response as she headed toward the docked boat with two bags filled with provisions. "Maybe you and Amber need to come out and announce you're dating. Why do I have to be the go-between with the two of you and her uncle?"

"Because you're the only one around here who isn't afraid of him," Greyson snapped back.

Sidney stopped on the dock and spun to face her friend with a look of shock on her face. Her sudden action forced Greyson to take a step back.

"Are you kidding?" she squawked. "I'm terrified of the guy!" Sidney then waved him off and continued along the dock toward the boat. "It's not my problem. The two of you need to make it work."

"Make it work?" he cried out and followed her to the boat. "We want to ***share*** a tent, Sidney. Even Jackson knows that's code for sex. He's never going to allow that."

Sidney placed the bags on the boat deck and then made the small jump to the deck herself. "Not my problem," she chirped, now disinterested.

Greyson jumped onto the deck with her and helped carry the bags toward the bridge. "I'm begging you, Sidney," he announced. "If you ever cared about either of us, you'd help us here."

Sidney headed through the narrow opening and down the small set of steps to the cramped crew quarters, which consisted of a sofa within the galley and a private bedroom. Although the leather sofa could be converted into a double bed, four people would be extremely tight in the small living quarters, but it was nice for day trips with Sidney and her grandpa. There was also a tiny bathroom, only a little bigger than those found on a plane. The bedroom was separate from the galley, but it was basically a double bed against three of the four walls, with a narrow walkway alongside it. Nowhere near as big as most of the ships some people owned, the boat was still almost two hundred thousand dollars when her grandpa bought it new a few years back. Sidney placed her bag on the small kitchen counter, then did the same with Greyson's bags.

"You want my help?" she asked while sharply eyeing him. "Fine. I'll tell you what you should do, but it's up to you to execute the plan."

"I love the plan already," Greyson replied, almost cheerfully, and attempted to relax.

"Amber and I were supposed to be sharing one of the four tents," Sidney informed him. "Instead, we'll take the sleeping quarters here on the boat. You take the tent closest to the dock and give Jackson the one furthest from it. After Jackson falls asleep, you and I will switch places, giving you and Amber the crew quarters and a locked door."

Greyson grinned. "Awesome plan," he replied and kissed her on the cheek. "You're the best!"

"Yeah, yeah," she groaned and waved him off. "Get out of my sight."

§

With still no sign of Amber and Jackson almost an hour later, Greyson was beginning to panic that Jackson had changed his mind or somehow found out why Amber really wanted to go camping in the first place. Being there wasn't any cell phone service in most of the woods, they couldn't contact them either. Although there was room to park near the lake, they heard a vehicle stop on the narrow, overgrown lane. Greyson practically dropped his armful of wood and attempted a more casual look so that Jackson wouldn't notice his enthusiasm for their arrival. To Greyson and Sidney's surprise, they saw a young woman they'd only seen around town a few times approaching with a backpack. Leon immediately grinned and hurried to greet her. He eagerly took her bag, placed his arm around her, and guided her toward his friends, who were preparing the wood in the pit for the bonfire.

"Hey," Leon announced to them, indicating the young woman. "This is Carrie. We went out last night. I hope it's all right that I invited her to join us."

Carrie was an attractive woman in her early twenties, although definitely younger than the rest of them. She had wavy blonde hair and big, innocent brown eyes. Leon definitely had a type, which was tomgirls, and Carrie fit that type, being a bit like Sidney. Little to no makeup, low maintenance, and less feminine. Sidney and Greyson exchanged glances since neither of them had been aware of any changes to the plan. Of course, Sidney had also altered the plan when she invited Jackson.

"Yes, of course," Sidney replied, almost reluctantly, but immediately wondered where she'd be sleeping. The tents were big enough for two people, and only then if they really liked each other.

"Obviously, she'd be staying in my tent," Leon then added, answering their silent question.

"Amber and I will take the cabin in the boat," Sidney informed them, and added a smile. "I'm sure it'll all work out."

Greyson then chimed in. "Jackson's coming with Amber," he informed them.

"He is?" Miller asked, surprised.

It was possible Miller might still be a little gun-shy about being around Jackson after what happened in the parking lot last night.

"Of course, he's coming," Greyson informed Miller, matter-of-factly, then left it at that.

"There are enough tents for each of you guys to have your own," Sidney reminded them. "Amber and I are the only ones who have to share our quarters."

"That's good," Miller announced. "Because I invited Emily to share my tent."

"Nice," Leon remarked while grinning.

Another unexpected revelation, but it really didn't matter. Greyson still had his own tent, which was necessary since he and Sidney would be switching places after lights out, and she certainly wasn't sharing a tent with Miller. When another car parked off to the side of the lane, Sidney assumed it was Emily. Miller ran to greet her, then stopped, his expression dropping. He looked back at Sidney with noticeable concern. Miller's reaction seemed odd because there was nothing that could make the overnight camping trip more uncomfortable than Jackson. When Sidney saw Naomi approaching with Emily, she realized she'd been mistaken. Miller hurried back to Sidney with his head hanging down almost shamefully.

"Please tell me Jackson isn't going to kill me," Miller practically whispered.

"He might," Sidney muttered as every muscle in her body tensed at once. "Did you know Emily was bringing Naomi?"

"No, of course not," Miller insisted. "I'm not into threesomes."

Miller received disapproving glares from Greyson and Sidney.

"That was a joke," Miller insisted, then considered the comment. "I mean, I'm not into threesomes, but I honestly thought Emily and I were sharing a tent." Horror then crossed his face. "Does this mean I have to share a tent with Jackson? Please, don't tell me I have to share a tent with Jackson."

"Sharing a tent with Jackson is the least of your worries," Sidney informed him in a gruff tone. "If Jackson has a problem with Naomi being here, Naomi goes. Because if Jackson goes, then Amber will have to go too, and that's not happening."

"Dude seriously has to cut the apron strings," Miller informed her.

"Well, you can talk to him about that when you're sharing your tent with him tonight," Greyson scoffed, then indicated Emily and Naomi, who were getting closer. "Go sort your shit out."

Miller groaned softly, then roused his best smile before approaching the two women. "Hey," he announced, his cheerfulness sounding forced. "Did you have any trouble finding the place?"

"No, none at all," Emily replied, humored. "When we were teenagers, we used to hike up here to swim in the pond. Finding the old driveway was a bit challenging, but we found it after a couple of drive-bys."

Miller remained tense while nodding, pretending there wasn't more on his mind as he glanced at Naomi several times.

"I hope you don't mind that Naomi tagged along," Emily announced, indicating her friend.

"No, I don't mind at all," Miller insisted, then practically fumbled over himself. "It's just, well." He hesitated. "This could be kind of awkward--"

Emily immediately placed her hand on Miller's lower arm and smiled almost slyly. "No, it's okay," she announced. "I knew you wanted me to share a tent with you. It's not awkward at all."

Miller was momentarily set back, though instantly pleased. "I'm glad to hear that," he announced, then tensed. "But that's not the awkward part."

Jackson's truck drove past them and pulled up closer to the dock. As Naomi's eyes followed the familiar truck, her smile was replaced with a frown.

"I think I can guess the awkward part," Naomi muttered.

Despite parking his truck, neither Jackson nor Amber got out, concerning Sidney. She was almost positive he saw Naomi when they pulled up. When Jackson and Amber finally got out of the truck, as if on cue, Leon ran stark naked past them and across the dock before jumping into the lake. Jackson briefly glanced at the streaking man, rolled his eyes, and then helped Amber unload their camping gear from the back of the truck. Greyson was quick to assist with Amber's things while Sidney approached Jackson and forced a tiny, tense smile.

"Sorry about the guys," Sidney sheepishly remarked. "They tend to go a little wild in the wilderness."

"I'd like to say I'm shocked and surprised," Jackson replied with little emotion, then met her gaze. "But I know how immature young guys can be."

"Behave, Uncle Jackson," Amber scoffed, casting a glare at him. "You promised."

"That was before," Jackson reminded her.

Sidney took a step closer to Jackson while fidgeting and met his gaze. "Is it Naomi?" she asked somewhat delicately. "I didn't know she had invited herself, and if her being here is a problem for you, Miller's been instructed to ask her to leave."

Jackson stared into Sidney's eyes only a moment before chuckling. "No, I'm a grown-ass adult," he reminded her. "I can be in the same room with Naomi without causing a scene. That's more ***her*** thing." He drew a deep breath, then proudly straightened. "That being said, if she starts anything with me, just know, I'm finishing it."

"Hey, Leon was a whiny little bitch after we broke up," Sidney informed him, then casually shrugged. "The only reason we get along now is because I called him out on all of his bullshit. If you want to tell her off, the trash will take itself out."

"A concern for another time," Jackson announced, then managed a smile as he removed a bottle of whiskey from the bag and handed it to Sidney. It was her grandpa's favorite whiskey, Crown Royal. The expensive stuff. "My contribution." He then pulled a large cooler from the back of the truck. "And some provisions for breakfast as well."

"That was nice of you, although unnecessary," Sidney replied. "We're putting all the coolers with food in truck cabs or on the boat." She grimaced. "We don't want uninvited guests in the middle of the night."

"Bear?" Amber asked as her smile faded.

"More like raccoons," Sidney informed her. "Although there could be bear."

Jackson removed a shotgun from the front of the truck. "That's okay," he announced with a sly grin. "I brought bear repellent."

"You certainly come prepared," Sidney remarked.

Jackson shrugged and smirked. "I'm a good Boy Scout."

"You're a scary Boy Scout," Amber muttered.

Sidney hid her smile at her friend's comment, although Jackson grinned and seemed to take perverse pleasure in the insult.

"We would have been here sooner, but Jackson couldn't decide which shotgun he wanted to bring," Amber remarked with an added eye roll.

Sidney snorted a soft laugh at Amber's joke meant to embarrass her uncle.

"Joke all you want," Jackson informed his niece. "But if a bear charges you, you'll be grateful I went with the fourteen-round rather than the double-barreled."

Sidney was left momentarily silenced. Amber ***hadn't*** been joking. Only Jackson would put that much thought into what gun to bring to which occasion. Amber was right. Jackson was scary.

"So, Amber and I are sleeping in the crew's quarters of the boat," Sidney announced, wanting to change the conversation as quickly as possible, and then indicated the tent furthest from the dock. "And Jackson can have the last tent to himself."

Jackson indicated the bed of his truck. "Actually, I have a blow-up mattress and my sleeping bag in the back of the truck. I'll be fine there."

Sidney eyed his truck, parked with a direct line of sight to the dock. That could make things a little tricky for Greyson to sneak onto the boat after 'lights out'. With the way Greyson's expression dropped, he had the same thought.

"Well, there's a tent available for you," Sidney informed him without missing a beat. "In case you change your mind." She then looked at Amber and managed a smile, although somewhat tense. "Let's get your bag stowed on the boat before Greyson takes it out to do some fishing."

"Who's all going fishing?" Amber asked.

"Leon was supposed to go, but I think he's having too much fun swimming," Greyson announced.

"So it's just Greyson at the moment," Sidney informed her friend.

"I don't know about fishing," Amber remarked, "but I'd like to go along on the boat, if there's room."

"Plenty of room," Sidney informed her while casting a quick look at Greyson before shifting her gaze to Jackson. "Did you want to go fishing on the boat?"

"No, I'd rather explore the woods a little," he replied and slung the shotgun over his shoulder. "Get a lay of the land."

Sidney was pretty sure it sounded more like 'patrol the perimeter'.

"Don't get lost," Sidney remarked with a teasing smile. "There's no cell phone service out here."

Jackson eyed Sidney and snorted a laugh, clearly mocking her. "I won't get lost," he insisted.

"Famous last words," Sidney muttered.

"If you're worried about it, you could come along," Jackson informed her while meeting her gaze.

Sidney stared at him a moment, feeling her entire body tense before smiling and nodding. "Certainly a better offer than skinny dipping with the guys," she remarked, then indicated the dock. "Let me show Amber her sleeping accommodations for the night, and I'll be right back."

Jackson nodded and casually leaned against his truck while Sidney walked with Amber toward the dock. Greyson hung out with Jackson for only a moment in an uncomfortable silence before indicating the women heading onto the dock.

"I'll, uh, be on the boat," Greyson announced, then hurried after Sidney and Amber.

Chapter 24

Jackson and Sidney walked along the well-groomed path around the lake, which encompassed several acres and featured a tiny island in the middle, though it was covered in trees. She told him which path would eventually lead to his farm, although it was quite a distance from their current location. Being alone in the woods with him was both frightening and exciting. That he actually seemed interested was almost baffling. Each time she glanced at him to see if he was bored, he seemed to be smiling at nothing in particular, as if he enjoyed the lengthy hike.

"You can take this main path completely around the lake," Sidney informed him. "On the other side from where we're camping is my grandpa's cabin."

"The one he left you?" Jackson asked.

Sidney frowned and nodded. "Yeah, that one," she muttered.

Jackson studied her as they walked. "Something wrong?" he asked while tilting his head. "You haven't been yourself lately."

"You mean my drunken escapades and climbing into bed with strange men?" she remarked while raising a skeptical brow.

"I'm not 'strange men'," he countered. "I've known you for several years."

"I know," she replied. "But you are strange."

Jackson shook his head and chuckled. "We're alone in the woods far enough away that no one would hear you scream," he remarked, then eyed her almost humored. "Mind your manners."

"I said you were strange," she reminded him. "Not a serial killer." Sidney stopped on the path and nodded further ahead. "The cabin is up there. This is as far as I'm going."

Jackson eyed her somewhat suspiciously. "Why?" he asked. "Your great-grandfather left you that cabin. Don't you want to visit it?"

"No," she replied, almost too quickly, then spun and headed back.

Jackson turned and followed her. "Well, something's bugging you," he remarked.

"My grandpa wasn't who I thought he was," she informed him. "He was a bastard to my mother and grandmother, and I'm having a hard time forgiving him for that."

"You're not really being fair," Jackson informed her, now walking alongside her, keeping up with her brisk pace. "He's not here to defend himself. Perhaps tell you his side of the story."

"I'm not really sure he has a side of the story," Sidney remarked, then groaned and slowed her pace. "My grandmother ran away from home when she was sixteen and pregnant because my grandpa didn't approve of my grandfather. Then, when my grandmother finally moved back home after my grandfather died, my mother found out she was pregnant." She eyed Jackson while raising her brows. "If that wasn't bad enough, my grandpa more or less forced my mother to marry my father, who isn't even my real father."

"You were your great-grandfather's pride and joy," Jackson reminded her. "The two of you were very close. So close, he gave you everything he cherished. Perhaps he made some mistakes with your grandmother and even your mother, but he had a chance to be a better man with you. That should count for something."

"I know," Sidney moaned. "That's why it bothers me so much."

Jackson groaned softly and raked his fingers through his hair. "I made a lot of mistakes in my life, Sidney," he informed her. "I would hate for Amber to judge me on who I was before my sister died rather than who I've become after I took her in."

Sidney paused on the path and looked at Jackson. "I can see where you're coming from with that," she remarked, then fidgeted slightly. "There were rumors about you around town about how some loudmouth beat you up. People were claiming you were weak. All bark and no bite. I know what I saw last night." She studied him a moment before gently taking his right hand and holding it up, revealing his scraped knuckles. "You obviously know how to fight."

"Actually, I'm a little too good at it," Jackson remarked and easily maneuvered her hand into his. "Avoiding confrontation is in everyone's best interest." He gently caressed her hand in his. "Don't judge Henry on his past. Anyone can change."

"You're right," she replied without taking her eyes off his. Sidney knew Jackson was looking for his own redemption and perhaps even her approval. "I suppose it's unfair to tarnish his memory when he was always good to me."

"I'm sure he'd be happy knowing you feel that way," Jackson replied.

"I know you weren't exactly a saint, Jackson," Sidney remarked almost timidly. "And I don't think any less of you either."

She affectionately squeezed his hand before releasing it, feeling the color once again rising to her cheeks. Sidney turned and continued on the path back to camp, unable to look Jackson in the eyes. Jackson walked alongside her in silence until they saw the camp up ahead. He caught her hand, surprising her, forcing her to stop. Sidney had little choice but to face him and was compelled to look into his eyes.

"Did you invite me here because you wanted me here or because you didn't think I'd let Amber come?" he boldly asked.

Sidney stared into his eyes a moment, surprised by the bluntness of his question, and flashed a tiny smile. "Yes," she replied.

"Not really an answer," he remarked.

"I really wanted Amber to come camping with us," she informed him. "But I also needed to overcome this awkwardness between us after last night."

"Any awkwardness between us is in your head," he insisted. "Just let it go."

Sidney snorted a laugh and fidgeted slightly. "How am I supposed to do that?" she asked as her eyes flicked upward and met his gaze. "I can't stop thinking about--" Sidney held her breath a moment and had to look away with embarrassment. "--about the extremely intimate cuddling with inappropriate sexual overtones."

Jackson chuckled softly, further frustrating Sidney. Her gaze turned stern.

"It's not funny," she insisted, now flustered. "You're my best friend's uncle, and I literally crawled into bed with you." She sharply raised her brows. "You had your hand on my ass, and your--" She groaned and again looked away while placing her hand over her eyes. "You wouldn't understand."

"Guys can't exactly control what they do in their sleep," he reminded her. "If you were awake and bothered by what I did in my sleep, why didn't you wake me, hit me, or even get up and leave?"

Sidney stared at him while searching for a reasonable response. Why didn't she speak up? Was she really that tired? Or did she just enjoy being held?

"I, uh, don't know," she responded.

"Maybe you're uncomfortable because it ***didn't*** bother you," he remarked.

Was that why she was so embarrassed about last night? Did she want to be in Jackson's arms? Sidney stared at the man standing before her for a moment longer. She saw Jackson as a grown man but couldn't stop thinking of herself as a teenager. Perhaps if he didn't seem so grown up and represent an authority figure, it wouldn't be as big a deal. That couldn't be right.

"I think you're just messing with my head now," she remarked somewhat bluntly.

"Well, there's one way to find out," Jackson announced. "Let me ask you something--"

"Okay," Sidney replied and anxiously awaited the question.

Jackson pulled her into his arms, his hand on her face, and kissed her with surprising passion. Sidney was momentarily startled by the aggressive action and the kiss itself. The eagerness of his kiss just about stole her breath away, sending shockwaves throughout her entire body. Her heart was pounding so hard, she almost couldn't breathe. She couldn't believe Jackson was kissing her! Jackson broke off the kiss as quickly as he had initiated it, leaving her almost dizzy, and met her gaze. Sidney just stared at him, completely astonished and unable to move. She never expected Jackson would kiss her. A woman's shrill scream came from their camp, startling them. Jackson swiftly pulled the shotgun from his shoulder and ran back to the nearby camp. Sidney took a moment longer to recover and then hurried after him.

Both arrived just in time to witness Emily, holding a shirt to her wet, naked body, giggling as she ran for the nearby tent. Miller, completely naked, chased after her, disappearing inside the tent behind her. There were more playful screams and then silence. Sidney grimaced at what she'd just witnessed while Jackson groaned and shook his head.

"Clearly, this camping trip needed a chaperone," Jackson muttered.

Sidney was several shades of red, mostly from the kiss but partly from seeing Miller naked. Sadly, it wasn't the first time she'd unintentionally seen him naked. Leon and his 'date' were a little more discreet, wearing clothes on their way to their tent. Leon insisted they were just going to dry off and change before dinner, but Sidney knew better. The giggling and moaning coming from both tents made her very uncomfortable while alone with Jackson. Thankfully, Greyson and Amber returned on the boat only a few minutes later. Sidney headed for the dock with Jackson, only a few steps behind, to help them tie off the boat. For some reason, Jackson seemed a little distrustful of his niece alone with Greyson on their two-hour fishing excursion. Perhaps the two couples moaning in the nearby tents aroused his suspicions.

"Did you catch anything?" Jackson asked Greyson while somehow looking intimidating.

Greyson smiled, although appearing somewhat tense, and opened a cooler. Two large catfish were flopping around in several inches of water on the bottom of the cooler.

"Beginner's luck," Amber announced cheerfully.

"Not sure if it counts," Greyson informed her. "You wouldn't put the worm on the hook."

Amber wrinkled her nose. "Yeah, because that part is gross."

Greyson grinned slyly. "You know you have to clean your own catch."

"And they can go right back in the lake," Amber informed him.

"Fine," Greyson groaned. "I'll clean your fish."

Greyson carried the cooler from the dock to the campfire while Amber remained near Sidney and Jackson, grimacing as she stared after Greyson.

"I'm not watching that," Amber muttered, then appeared curious and looked around. "Where are our skinny dippers?"

"Helping dry each other off in their tents," Sidney remarked.

"I'm so glad we're sleeping on the boat," Amber scoffed. "Otherwise, we wouldn't get any sleep."

"So," Jackson announced with a curious tilt of his head. "You had fun fishing, huh?"

Amber shrugged, seeming neutral. "Nothing to write home about," she insisted, then insecurely shoved her hands into her pockets.

Sidney glanced toward the boat and was surprised to see Naomi, in her bikini, disembark. When Sidney looked back at Amber, she raised her brows in such a manner that Sidney knew her friend was cursing because Naomi 'tagged along'. Thankfully, Jackson lost interest the moment he saw Naomi and wasn't even paying attention to his niece's exchange with Sidney. When Jackson finally looked back at her, Amber smiled, appearing enthusiastic, and eyed the two of them.

"How was the ***nature*** walk?" Amber asked, suggestively raising her brows.

Sidney fidgeted at the subtle sexual innuendo by her friend but managed a smile, although not without blushing. "Buggy."

Chapter 25

After dinner, everyone sat around the bonfire while drinking and roasting marshmallows. Jackson made a half-hearted effort to socialize with Greyson, who was the only one brave enough to interact with him. Leon kept Carrie entertained, and they seemed to be getting along rather well. Sidney preferred being around her ex-boyfriend when he had a steady girlfriend. It kept him from delusions of getting back together with her. Miller was busy monopolizing Emily's time, leaving Naomi to fend for herself with a group of people she either didn't like or didn't know. Unfortunately, that meant Sidney was the only person left for her to socialize with. Amber and Naomi didn't get along because Naomi mocked and trash-talked her uncle. That being said, Sidney wasn't exactly a fan of Naomi's either, but she didn't want to be rude to the woman who handled her food at the diner.

All things considered, the evening seemed to be going better than Sidney had expected, although maybe not as well as Amber and Greyson had originally intended. Sidney couldn't help sneaking peeks at Jackson, thinking about that mind-blowing kiss. Somehow, that eight-year age gap made all the difference in the world. Greyson, Leon, and Miller were just boys compared to Jackson. And even though Jackson was Amber's uncle, he was still a fine specimen of a man. Everything from the way he sat to the way he interacted with her friends seemed commanding and manly. Each time Sidney gazed at Jackson, he seemed to catch her looking, and a strange smile would cross his face, making her heart flutter. According to Amber, it had been a while since Jackson had gotten laid. Sidney assumed he was sizing her up as his next conquest, possibly unaware that she'd never been with anyone before. She knew she should tell him so he'd realize he was wasting his time.

Ever since Jackson had kissed her out in the woods earlier that afternoon, Sidney couldn't stop thinking about Jackson's past intimate relationship with the woman sitting alongside her. Was she jealous of Naomi? She never even fantasized about having sex with Leon, and here she was wondering how Naomi felt while Jackson made love to her. It only took a moment or two for Sidney to realize that she wished Jackson had made love to her instead. No! She needed to turn off the voices in her head for the rest of the night before they got her into trouble. Sidney excused herself from Naomi's tedious small talk. When she stood, she immediately felt Jackson's gaze upon her. Sidney rounded the bonfire and sat on the log alongside him. Despite the warmth of the fire, she still shivered.

"I was wondering if you'd ever get back to me with an answer," he remarked while offering a tiny grin.

"An answer?"

"To the question I'd asked you on our walk," he reminded her.

She was compelled to stare into his eyes for a moment while reliving that kiss. Sidney managed a tiny smile and indicated the opened bottle of Crown Royal on the ground between him and Greyson.

"How about a drink first?" she suggested.

Jackson offered her his plastic cup with a slightly humored smile. Sidney immediately accepted it and took a healthy swallow. She didn't want to get drunk, just dull her senses a little and maybe curb the thoughts racing through her mind. Despite being an innocent gesture, Leon and Naomi both took notice that Sidney had taken a sip from Jackson's cup. It didn't necessarily mean anything. All Sidney's friends shared cups at some time or another. It was merely a symbol of comfort, yet that level of comfort with Jackson didn't go unnoticed. Sidney had to force herself to stare into his eyes without fidgeting or looking away. She needed to be strong.

"You know this is awkward, right?"

Jackson suddenly chuckled without taking his eyes off hers. "Oh, absolutely."

Sidney then noticed they were getting some stares from everyone except Amber and Greyson, who seized the opportunity for their own, intimate conversation. Sidney fidgeted, avoided looking at Jackson, and took another swallow from the cup.

"Everyone is staring," she whispered. "Maybe we should go somewhere private to talk."

"If we do that, they'll be whispering instead of staring," Jackson reminded her.

She finally met his gaze. "Are you okay with that?" Sidney asked. "Because I really think we should talk."

Jackson casually refilled his cup and then indicated the dock in the near distance. "Then let's take a little walk," he replied, standing.

As if on cue, everyone except Greyson and Amber watched Jackson and Sidney head onto the boat dock. Both leaned on the railing and stared out onto the dark lake.

Sidney cleared her throat and again fidgeted while glancing sheepishly at Jackson.

"I don't know if I somehow gave you the wrong impression," she gently remarked, "but I'm not, well, ***that*** kind of girl."

"What kind of girl?" Jackson asked somewhat playfully, although he obviously knew what she meant.

"You know, easy," she replied with some discomfort, even vaguely discussing something sexual in nature with the man she mostly knew as Amber's uncle.

"Yeah, I kind of knew that," he casually replied while maintaining his humor.

Sidney was a little surprised by the admission. "If you know I'm not that kind of girl, then why did you kiss me?" she asked, now curious.

Jackson chuckled at the comment and met her gaze. "Because I wanted to kiss you," he remarked. "You do realize that those two things aren't necessarily interconnected, right?"

Sidney stared into his eyes for a long moment, then shifted uncomfortably. "With the way Amber talks about your, well, barroom exploits, I just assumed--"

Jackson groaned lowly and took a swallow of whiskey from the cup. "Did she call me a 'man whore' again?" he demanded.

His comment surprised her, considering Amber had never used those words to describe her uncle before, at least, not in her company.

"Well, no," Sidney replied, stumbling over herself. "It's just that, well, you're older and more experienced. And she likes teasing that you need to, well, get laid."

"I'd condemn her for her filthy mouth, but she probably gets it from me," Jackson muttered, then turned to face Sidney. "I'll admit that I was a horny young man, and I ran with a pretty wild crowd, but that was years ago. Since then, I had Amber to consider, and I didn't want to give her the wrong impression. I tried dating, but that was a disaster. Better known as Naomi." He stared into her eyes. "I've been celibate for over two years, Sidney. Do you honestly think I'd go after my niece's best friend for a cheap, one-night stand? I'd never forgive myself, and Amber would hate me forever."

"If not sex, what could you possibly want?" Sidney asked, again confused.

Jackson stared at her for a long moment, possibly wondering if she was serious. "Something I've never had with a woman until last night," he informed her. "Intimacy." He groaned softly. "I know you were drunk, but I was kind of hoping on some sort of subconscious level you actually liked me."

"Jackson," Sidney announced softly while studying him. "I do like you. I like you on ***every*** level. It's just that, well, I find you sexually intimidating."

"That doesn't sound good," he remarked.

"No, not in a predatory way or anything," she insisted, then hesitated and actually stared into his eyes. "Just worldly, manly, and, you know, more experienced." Sidney hesitated again and tried to convey the seriousness of her situation. "And me, well, I have ***zero*** experience. I mean ***none***."

Jackson shifted a moment uncomfortably, then managed a tiny smile. "Yes, I'd heard," he replied. "Amber mentioned your 'situation' the first time she called me a 'man whore' two years ago."

"You may have to explain that one to me," Sidney remarked.

Jackson groaned softly and insecurely rubbed the back of his neck. "After you ripped me a new one, the night the two of you came home drunk," he began. "Amber caught me, well, checking you out. She told me to keep my filthy 'man whoring' hands off you because you were a good girl and deserved someone, well, not me."

"Ouch," Sidney muttered while grimacing. She then considered what he had actually said and grew curious. "Wait. You were checking me out ***after*** I screamed at you that night?"

Jackson stared at her a moment before raising a clever brow. "Come on, Sidney," he announced. "This is me. When you stood up to me and literally got in my face, it was an instant turn-on." His look then turned serious. "Zero pressure, Sidney. Sex is completely off the table until you say otherwise."

"Do you really mean that?"

"You're Amber's best friend," he reminded her. "I need to tread lightly."

Sidney smiled and then nodded. "I think we both do," she remarked. "Can we talk more about this tomorrow when we have fewer prying eyes?"

"Of course," Jackson replied, seeming pleased with her response.

When Sidney and Jackson returned to the campfire, they were greeted with strange looks by everyone, including Greyson and Amber. It was painfully obvious that everyone wanted to know what that private meeting had been about, but none were brave enough to ask.

Chapter 26

It was almost one o'clock in the morning, and an hour after everyone had gone to bed. Sidney disembarked the boat onto the dock right on time, except she didn't see Greyson. She thought he'd already be on the boat waiting for her to vacate his spot in the cabin below. Sidney casually but quietly walked along the dock, noting Jackson's truck to the left of the tall crackling campfire, and Greyson's tent to the right. Sidney was almost positive her friend hadn't overslept. It was an important rendezvous for him. Greyson's first time with Amber, and Amber's very first time. As she got closer to the campsite, Sidney saw what possibly deterred Greyson's plans. Jackson sat reclined in the bed of his truck and stared at the stars. Perhaps that was why he parked so close to the clearing. He wanted to sleep under the stars. Unfortunately, for Greyson, Jackson also had a perfect view of his tent flap, making it nearly impossible for him to slip out unnoticed.

Sidney could have aborted the mission without being seen, but she chose to approach Jackson's truck bed instead. She paused alongside the truck and leaned on the fender, immediately catching Jackson's attention. He smiled when he saw her.

"I was hoping you'd sneak out after lights out," Jackson teased. "Trouble sleeping? Or did you just miss me?"

"A little of both," she replied.

Jackson grinned and patted the vacant spot on the sleeping bag on top of the air mattress. "Plenty of room, if you'd like to join me. I could get the tailgate for--"

Sidney used the side step and easily climbed into the back of the truck. Jackson watched her with mild fascination, then shook his head as she made herself comfortable alongside him.

"Gotta love country girls," Jackson announced with a tiny chuckle.

Sidney could feel his stare before finally glancing at him and the tiny smile etched on his face. She wasn't sure what she was doing. It was like some bizarre dream, but she didn't really want to wake from it.

"I don't know what I'm supposed to do," she whispered while fidgeting.

Jackson placed his hand on hers and gently caressed it. "You don't ***have*** to do anything," he informed her while smiling warmly. "We can just sit here and gaze at the stars. Zero pressure."

Sidney considered the comment only a moment before reaching out and gently touching his stubbly beard. She was oddly fascinated with his facial hair, being the first time she'd touched a man's beard since she was a little girl and would tug on her grandpa's beard. Jackson affectionately placed his hand over hers, enjoying the way she touched him, then captured her hand and warmly kissed the back of it. Sidney felt an erotic shockwave ripple through her entire body at the sensation. When she giggled, Jackson met her gaze and leaned closer to her, lowering his mouth to hers. Sidney held her breath a moment, then leaned into it. Jackson warmly kissed her on the lips as his hand moved to her neck. Sidney returned the kiss while slowly placing her hand on his chest. Her heart was pounding as her body ached for him. She didn't remember feeling this way when Leon kissed her. His slow, insanely erotic kiss turned more passionate and even a little aggressive, but Sidney didn't mind.

Greyson slipped out of his tent and crept closer to the dock before spotting Sidney and Jackson kissing quite passionately in the bed of his truck. Greyson suddenly stopped, straightened, and stared a moment in surprise. He mouthed 'what the fuck' then hurried for the dock and the awaiting boat.

Jackson broke off the kiss and met her gaze with a warm smile. "Want to sleep under the stars with me?" he asked, then grinned. "Fully clothed, I promise."

Sidney affectionately ran her hand along his chest before meeting his gaze. "What if Amber comes looking for me and finds us together?" she asked.

"I'm sure Greyson will keep her occupied," Jackson remarked.

Sidney stared at Jackson with a stunned look, not sure what to say in Amber's defense. Jackson chuckled and gently brushed the hair from her face.

"Come on, Sidney," he announced. "Give me some credit here. I'm smarter than I look. I know ***why*** she wanted to come here tonight."

"I'm a little surprised you didn't try to stop them," Sidney remarked.

"She's a grown woman," Jackson announced with a defeated sigh. "And he's the best out of the three of them, so she could do worse. If he were a bad guy, I'm sure you'd talk her out of it."

"Greyson has been my best friend since I was just a little girl," Sidney informed him. "He's about as good as they get."

"I'm glad to hear that," Jackson announced while gently caressing her hand. "Honestly, your father is the one I feel sorry for."

"My father?" Sidney asked, somewhat surprised. "Why would you feel sorry for my father?"

"Every father dreams that his little princess will find a prince," Jackson informed her, then met her gaze. "Instead, his princess found a dragon."

Sidney managed a smile and laughed softly. "You're not that bad, Jackson," she insisted.

He shrugged, taking his eyes off hers. "That's up for debate," Jackson replied. "And a worry for another day. I just want to enjoy tonight."

Sidney warmly caressed his beard, forcing him to meet her gaze. "I think I would like to sleep under the stars with you," she replied. "As long as you promise to be ninety percent gentleman."

"What about the other ten percent?" he asked, somewhat humored.

"You can have the remaining ten percent," she informed him. "I like the way you kiss."

"Hmm, I like that," Jackson replied, grinning almost deviously. "Sounds kind of dirty." He suddenly hesitated, turning concerned. "I probably shouldn't talk like that. I don't want to make things any more awkward for you than they already are."

Sidney was a little surprised by how quickly he reversed course, realizing her lack of experience might make ***him*** uncomfortable. She turned on her hip, facing him, and insecurely placed her hand on his chest while meeting his gaze. Initiating any physical touch was going to be extremely awkward for a while.

"I'm willing to work through the awkwardness," Sidney informed him. "I've already seen the good, the bad, and the ugly sides of you over the years."

"But you haven't seen the dirty, perverted side," he reminded her. "I'm afraid I might give you the wrong idea of my intentions with bullshit talk and scare you away."

"Have you met Miller?" Sidney asked, raising an arrogant brow. "I wouldn't be friends with quite so many guys if I couldn't handle their dirty sides." She again tensed while staring at him, enjoying the feeling of his heart beating against her hand. "I want you to be you. Whoever that person is." She tensed slightly while gently caressing his chest. "And, so that you know, you'll probably need to initiate physical contact for a while." Sidney held her breath a moment and grimaced slightly. "I still find you a little ***imposing***."

"I am imposing," Jackson informed her with a soft chuckle before placing his hand on her face and kissing her warmly on the lips.

Sidney returned the kiss while sinking against him. As his kiss intensified, bordering on aggressive, a strange flood of desire swept over her, and she had to convince herself to behave. She never had the urge to throw herself at Leon, but the feeling was incredibly strong in Jackson's arms. Despite that he held her in a tight embrace, it didn't feel like enough. Her mind was suddenly all over the place, contemplating what it would feel like if he made love to her. And it wasn't just the heart-pounding, 'take her breath away' kiss, but the way his hands traveled her body, respectfully avoiding the 'danger zones' yet somehow making love to her with each caress. Jackson broke off the kiss and lowered his mouth to her neck, nearly driving her out of her mind while practically devouring her throat. He briefly paused while nuzzling her neck.

"Am I overstepping your boundaries?" he whispered close to her ear, sending tiny goosebumps across her entire body.

"No," she gasped while just about clinging to him. "As long as we stick to the 'fully clothed' promise."

Jackson chuckled into her neck, which somehow aroused her further. "You'd be surprised what I'm capable of doing without breaking that promise."

"I accept the challenge," Sidney whispered back.

Jackson groaned lowly right before he maneuvered her from a sitting position down onto the sleeping bag beneath them. The action was so swift, it made her head just about spin. She was practically pinned to the sleeping bag beneath his body, his arms and legs taking up every inch of available space between them. 'Manhandled' was the only appropriate term that came to mind. Despite feeling incredibly vulnerable at that moment, it was exactly where she wanted to be.

Chapter 27

Sidney woke just before sunrise to the smell of the smoldering bonfire and the faint sounds of loons on the lake. Some of her happiest memories were waking up in the cabin in the early morning. It was so familiar, yet completely different for obvious reasons. Sidney was consciously aware of Jackson nestled firmly against her from behind in the sleeping bag, his arms wrapped around her and his body keeping her warm and cozy. She caressed his arm, anchored around her, and sighed contentedly. Jackson groaned into her neck and caressed her abdomen as he pressed his morning enthusiasm against her backside. It was possible he wasn't even awake. Sidney again caressed his arm, this time waking him. Jackson tensed a moment, then groaned softly near her ear.

"Was I humping you in my sleep again?" he teased.

"I believe so," she replied with a tiny giggle.

"Sorry," he whispered and attempted to move away.

"It's okay," Sidney assured him, stopping him. "I kind of like it."

Jackson groaned and pressed firmly against her. "I'm happy to hear you say that," he muttered softly while nuzzling the back of her neck.

"Is it like this every morning?" she remarked as she gently caressed his arm.

"Hmm, pretty much," Jackson muttered, now kissing her neck, then chuckled lowly. "Of course, it's always nicer when I have someone to share it with."

The sensation of Jackson kissing the back of her neck, coupled with his body firmly pressing against her, was almost overwhelming but so incredibly enjoyable. He felt so good against her, and he was definitely enjoying his morning. As Sidney turned over in the sleeping bag to face him, he gathered her in his arms, holding every inch of her against him. He warmly kissed her lips before pulling her head to his chest, cuddling her.

"I really enjoyed sharing my sleeping bag with you," Jackson announced into the top of her head. "Honestly, I didn't think we'd achieve dry humping for at least a month or two."

Sidney giggled softly into his chest while nuzzling him. "I think you should know. Just because I haven't had sex before that doesn't mean I'm necessarily waiting until marriage," she informed him. "When I was eighteen, I wasn't ready, and Leon definitely wasn't the right guy." She hesitated a moment, then groaned softly. "You're a lot harder to resist."

"As much as I like hearing that, I can't imagine I'm the right guy," Jackson informed her. "Unless you have a warped sense of 'right', but I'll gladly take the compliment." He rolled onto his back, taking her with him. She immediately nestled against him while he held her. "The irony is astounding."

"What irony?"

He groaned softly as he stared at the stars, which were slowly fading with the sunrise. "That you let me touch you at all," Jackson remarked. "Let alone consider me 'hard to resist'."

"You need to try looking in the mirror once in a while," Sidney informed him. "Even my G-ma thinks you're hot." She shivered at the thought.

"I don't look at myself in the mirror," Jackson informed her somewhat timidly. "I don't like what I see."

Sidney suddenly moved onto her elbow and looked at him, a little surprised. "Well, that's profound."

Jackson avoided looking at her while maintaining his frown. "I wasn't going for philosophical," he remarked. "Just an image of myself I can't get past." He groaned and placed his arm over his eyes, almost as if attempting to hide from her. "It was selfish of me to pursue you the way I did. I guess I never thought you'd be interested in me, and then I could stop thinking about you. Stick with the trash, where I belong."

Sidney immediately moved against him and clung to him as if her life depended upon it. "You're not trash," she insisted firmly. "I don't know what happened in your past that made you hate yourself so much, but you deserve happiness."

Jackson gathered her in his arms and held her so tightly against him that she almost couldn't breathe. "I'm sorry," he whispered into her hair. "Escaping my past is like being in rehab. I'm still making amends with myself, but I don't forgive easily."

"Well, I happen to like Jackson," Sidney informed him. "So you tell that other guy he'd better cut you some slack, because I won't let him mentally torment you. Your past is dead and buried, and it needs to stay there."

Jackson managed a tiny chuckle and, while clinging to her, warmly caressed her. "I'll have it out with him later," he insisted, then affectionately kissed her forehead. "Thank you, Sidney."

Sidney was fully aware of his fingers lazily caressing her hip while working his way down her shorts to her bare leg. She was pretty sure she knew what was on his mind.

"It's so peaceful out here pre-dawn," she remarked while nuzzling his chest. "Probably another hour before anyone is up. You might want to take advantage of that."

Jackson chuckled softly and caressed her bare thigh beneath the sleeping bag. "I should, should I?" he lightly teased while pulling her leg alongside his hip and firmly holding her against him.

Sidney affectionately caressed his chest. "Maybe lose the shirt."

"Hmm," Jackson groaned softly. "Would you be willing to do the same?"

She seriously considered his question. Sidney really wanted to feel his bare chest, and it seemed like a small price to pay for the privilege.

"With the understanding that I'm not coming out of this sleeping bag," she replied.

Jackson immediately tensed and pulled back just far enough to meet her gaze. "I was actually kidding," he informed her. "I don't want you to feel pressured into anything."

Sidney smiled warmly and affectionately caressed his beard. "No, it's okay," she insisted. "I'm comfortable with you touching me, and, you know, other stuff."

She barely had a chance to finish the sentence before Jackson practically tore off his shirt and kissed her with a renewed sense of urgency. Maybe she shouldn't have, but his aggression made her giggle. Soon after he removed her shirt, her giggles were replaced with groans. She tensed the first time he fondled her, the sensation being almost overwhelming, but his enthusiastic desire made her want to please him in any way possible. When his mouth and tongue replaced his hand, Sidney's entire body stiffened as she clutched his shoulders. A voice inside of her was screaming a dire warning, 'It's Jackson!' For a moment, she nearly panicked. As intense pleasure swept over her, she just about clutched his head to her bosom. That panicked internal voice suddenly became enthusiastic, realizing it was Jackson, and sent shockwaves of desire throughout her entire body. She writhed against him, clinging to him with every inch of her body. At that moment, he could have done whatever he wanted, and she wouldn't have protested.

Jackson finally moved on top of her and kissed her with renewed aggression, while she continued clutching and clinging to his body. That he remained respectful both relieved and disappointed her. By the movement of the mass within the sleeping bag, most would speculate about the couple's activity. The low moans and soft groans almost confirmed it, although it wasn't quite as it appeared. Despite being clothed from the waist down, Sidney could almost imagine what it would be like having Jackson make love to her, in a PG-13 sort of way. The loons provided a romantic, lakeside serenade for the aggressively tussling couple in the bed of the pickup truck.

Sidney arched against Jackson as a strange wave seemed to flood her entire body, making her instantly dizzy. She gasped, attempting to keep from crying out. Jackson groaned softly, becoming still. After a moment, he kissed Sidney affectionately before pulling back just far enough to meet her gaze.

"That's enough to put a permanent smile on my face," Jackson remarked with a soft chuckle. "Everyone will wonder why I'm suddenly in such a good mood."

Sidney giggled while caressing the light coating of hair on his chest. "And they'll wonder why I'm giddy," she replied. "I don't know that I've ever been 'giddy' before."

"I know a lot of ways to make you giddy," he teased, then lunged for her neck.

Sidney withheld her giggle and enjoyed the sensation.

"Jackson," a woman whispered, startling Sidney.

When the tailgate lowered with a metallic scraping, Sidney and Jackson jumped, still within their compromising position, at the sound. Both looked at the tailgate and saw Naomi at the back, prepared to climb inside, staring at them like a deer caught in headlights. Sidney cried out with embarrassment, having been caught half-naked in Jackson's sleeping bag with him, but her embarrassment quickly turned to irritation when she realized it was Naomi and not Amber. As irritated as she was, she wasn't half as pissed as Jackson had been.

"What the fuck--" Jackson cried out, glaring at Naomi. "What the hell do you think you're doing?"

"***You're*** with ***her***?" Naomi cried out, shocked by what she was witnessing, their bare shoulders giving the distinct impression that they were naked together.

"Yes," Jackson snarled while practically shooting up in the sleeping bag, blocking Sidney's naked upper body behind his. "Now leave us the hell alone!"

Naomi couldn't help but eye Sidney several times before hurrying away from the pickup truck. Sidney sat up, having hurriedly slipped back into her shirt, and watched Naomi, only in her tank top and underwear, dash across the campsite and back to her tent at the far end.

"What the hell's gotten into her?" Jackson muttered softly, returning his attention to Sidney. "She's been a boil on my ass for years, and she picks ***now*** to reconcile."

"You became more desirable when she thought I was interested in you," Sidney informed him. "I saw the way she reacted last night when we came back from the dock."

"More like she was looking for a new way to ruin my life," Jackson muttered. "She's not exactly my number one fan."

"If it makes you feel any better, she doesn't like me much either," Sidney remarked with a sigh.

"I'm really sorry about that," Jackson announced almost timidly. "I hope you're not too upset by it."

"No, of course not," Sidney replied, then smiled warmly. "I understand, believe me." She then cringed slightly. "Would you be terribly offended if I snuck out before anyone else catches us together? I don't want my friends jumping to the same conclusion. Especially Amber."

"Honestly, I'd rather introduce her to the idea of us a little slower as well," Jackson replied.

Sidney kissed him quickly on the lips, smiled, and then slipped into her shoes before climbing out of the truck bed. Although she was trying to be quiet, she was almost halfway to the dock when she heard someone calling from the campsite, surprising her.

"Sidney--"

As Sidney turned to see Leon approaching her, she spotted Greyson slipping off the boat deck at the same time. When Greyson saw Leon, he jumped back onto the boat and ducked down, out of sight.

"This is like a nightmare," Sidney muttered, then roused a smile as Leon approached. "Hey. I didn't think anyone was up yet. I was looking for some matches to get the gas grill started for the kettle."

"I think they're by the grill," Leon informed her, then attempted to walk with her to the dock.

Sidney saw Greyson poking his head around the entranceway of the boat before she swiftly changed direction back to the gas grill not far from the bonfire. Leon automatically turned and followed.

"I wanted to talk to you before the others got up," Leon informed her.

"Oh?" she asked, now curious. "About what?"

Leon took a moment to light the gas grill and placed the kettle on it before turning to face her.

"About, well, things," Leon replied.

Sidney eyed him almost suspiciously. "What sort of things?" she asked.

"Mostly, well, you and me," Leon replied, taking a step closer to her. "I know I was a jerk for pressuring you back when we were dating in high school. I want you to know that I've done a lot of growing since then, and I really think we should try again."

Sidney stared at Leon in silent disbelief. Her eyes strayed past her ex-boyfriend to Jackson, who now sat on the fender of his pickup truck, observing their exchange. She was certain he could hear them, too.

"Leon," Sidney announced somewhat sternly. "You're here with Carrie. You picked a truly bizarre time to want to reconcile."

Leon's back was turned to Jackson's pickup truck, so he had no way of knowing he was listening in on their conversation.

"That's not important," Leon informed her as he placed his hands on her shoulders. "I saw the way Jackson was sizing you up last night, and I don't want a guy like that corrupting you."

"Jackson is Amber's uncle," Sidney reminded him. "He'd never do anything to disrespect me."

"Sidney, the guy's been around the block a few times," Leon informed her. "Give him a little time, and he'll have you in his bed."

"Oh, so that's what's bothering you," Sidney replied, slightly humored, then playfully patted his chest. "You don't have to worry about that happening, Leon. The only way Jackson is getting me into his bed is if I want to be in his bed."

Leon eyed her, confused by the comment. "What do you mean by that?" he asked.

Sidney smiled and leaned closer to Leon. "It means, if I want to sleep with Jackson, I will," she replied and patted his shoulder. "If you like Carrie, I suggest you worry about her wants and needs; not mine."

When Sidney saw Greyson dart into the woods behind his tent, she walked past Leon, heading toward the dock. Leon turned to watch her and saw Jackson casually sitting on the side of his truck, staring at him.

"Good morning, Leon," Jackson announced with a strange smirk on his face.

Chapter 28

From the moment they packed up everything but the boat and left the campsite, Sidney couldn't stop thinking about Jackson. She replayed every kiss, every caress, and every inappropriate comment between them. Her body ached for him in a way she'd never felt before, and she wanted to act upon it. She wished she'd jumped on him and begged him to take her. Maybe the reason she wasn't ready for sex with Leon was that she wanted a man and not a boy. With her parents leaving on their trip to Hawaii that afternoon, Sidney couldn't stop thinking about how perfect the timing was. It didn't take much. She had herself convinced. The next time she saw Jackson, she would seduce him! Although her plan was flawed. She didn't want to leave her poor G-ma all alone, especially the first night her parents would be gone. Seducing Jackson would have to wait until tomorrow night. She just needed Greyson to get Amber out of the house for the evening, or, even better, for an overnight.

Later that afternoon, Sidney saw her parents off on their two-week tropical vacation, then joined her G-ma for dinner. Her G-ma was by no means an old woman, but it would be the first time she was by herself in decades. Without her father; without her daughter. Although not necessarily in the same room, Grandpa was often nearby. On the rare occasions when he was at the cabin for the weekend, her daughter was just next door. It was close to seven o'clock that evening when Helena glanced at Sidney across the living room.

"Are you sure there isn't someplace else you'd rather be tonight?" Helena asked.

Sidney smiled warmly at her grandmother. "No, I want to spend time with you," she replied. "I hate seeing you all alone with Mom and Dad away for two weeks."

Helena drew a deep breath, then smiled at Sidney. "I appreciate the sentiment, dear," she announced. "But if you're doing it for my benefit, it's not necessary. For the first time, I have time to myself. I'd love to take a hot bubble bath, have a glass of wine, and watch a good movie." She hesitated only a moment. "By myself."

"Oh," Sidney replied and shifted uncomfortably at what was obviously a less-than-subtle hint. "Why didn't you say something?"

Helena shrugged and smiled weakly. "I was afraid ***you*** didn't want to be alone."

Sidney laughed softly and stood. "I'll leave you to your bubble bath, G-ma."

She kissed her grandmother on the cheek, then left through the kitchen entrance. As she walked along the worn path between her grandmother's and her parents' houses, she took out her cell phone and texted Amber.

"G-ma kicked me out," she texted. "Too early for bed. What are you doing?"

Amber almost immediately texted back. "Jackson is driving me insane! Need a buffer. Can you come over? Preferably now!"

"On my way," Sidney texted back, then added a smiling face emoji and headed straight for her grandpa's truck in the driveway.

§

As Sidney pulled up to Amber's farmhouse in her grandpa's truck, her heart began pounding with anticipation. It had only been a few hours since she'd seen Jackson, and she was already missing him. How was that even possible? Sidney grabbed her small overnight bag from the seat, which she had prepared since early that afternoon. She had even stopped at the store not far from town and purchased a lacy black bra with a matching pair of thong underwear for the occasion. Sidney could feel her entire body tremble at the thought of her plot to seduce Jackson. She only hoped she didn't chicken out. She no sooner stepped on the porch when she heard Jackson and Amber in a shouting match, which was nothing new. Before she could even knock, Amber approached the door from the inside, opened it, and glared at Sidney.

"Just in time," Amber announced while moving away from the open doorway.

Sidney reluctantly entered the house and saw Jackson leaning his back against the kitchen counter with a scowl on his face. He met Sidney's gaze and shook his head. Sidney no sooner dropped her overnight bag on the floor when Amber spun to face her, raising her brows commandingly.

"When were you going to tell me?" Amber demanded while folding her arms across her chest.

"Tell you what?" Sidney asked, her heart immediately pounding at the question.

"About the two of you," Amber snapped while pointing at her and her uncle.

"There's nothing to tell," Sidney informed her.

"Nothing to tell?" Amber practically shouted, then pointed at Jackson. "Did you sleep with my uncle?"

"Actually, yes," Sidney replied. "And you tormented me endlessly about it, remember?"

Amber groaned in frustration. "I meant, did you have sex with him?"

"What?" Sidney cried out in surprise. "No, of course not."

Jackson smirked at Amber and threw his hands in the air. "I told you so."

Amber turned her attention back to Sidney. "Greyson saw you and Jackson making out last night in the bed of his truck," she remarked. "And he saw you climbing out of Jackson's truck this morning when he was leaving."

"You mean when he was sneaking out of bed with you?" Jackson launched back.

"Oh, my God," Sidney practically cried out, startling both. "What is it with you two? Is this some sort of competition? The way you two fight is unhealthy."

Amber folded her arms across her chest and stared at Sidney. "Greyson is going to Fort Hood to visit his brother, who is stationed there," she informed her friend, then indicated Jackson. "And ***that one*** tells me I can't go because it's for three nights." She spun to face Jackson. "You can have sleepovers with Sidney, but I can't go with Greyson to visit his brother."

"It's too far, and it's too long," Jackson snarled. "This has nothing to do with Sidney."

"I'm twenty-three years old!" Amber cried out. "I should be allowed to make up my own mind where I go and whom I go with!"

Jackson rolled his eyes and shook his head. "We're not having this conversation, and don't put Sidney in the middle of our ongoing feud."

"I don't need you running my life," Amber shouted at him. "You're not my father!"

"Be grateful I'm not," Jackson shouted back in a rare burst of anger. "Your father was a monster!"

"And you're not?" Amber launched back.

There was a strange, eerie silence between them. Jackson looked like a cobra about to strike, and it actually frightened Amber. Jackson took a quick step toward his niece, which caused her to jump back a step, as he pointed to the stairs.

"Go to your room!"

Amber quickly backed up several steps and shook her head. "No," she replied with a quiver in her voice. "I'm going out." She grabbed her purse and ran from the house, slamming the screen door.

Sidney slowly backed away from Jackson and the enraged look on his face. As Amber's car was heard burning out in the driveway, Jackson turned and threw his fist into the wooden cupboard door. There was a loud bang as the wood cracked and splintered, causing Sidney to jump with surprise.

"Maybe I should go," Sidney announced somewhat timidly.

Jackson stood hunched over the kitchen sink, staring into the drain. "I'm sorry," he whispered. "I didn't mean to frighten you."

"Are you okay?" Sidney asked but refused to get any closer.

He drew a deep breath while straightening, then turned to face her. "No, not really," Jackson replied with a sigh as he clutched his head.

The knuckles on his right hand were scraped and bleeding from punching the cupboard.

"Do you want me to go?" Sidney asked.

Jackson lifted his head and looked at her. "No," he replied. "Having both of you walk out on me is more than I can handle right now."

Sidney gathered her courage and approached Jackson and the sink. She turned on the cold water, then gently took his hand and placed it under the running water.

"We should clean those scrapes and get some ice on your hand," Sidney remarked.

Jackson watched her gently clean his bleeding hand, then glanced at her profile. "I know you think I'm overbearing with Amber," he announced gently. "But there's a lot you don't know. Things I just can't tell you."

Sidney shut off the water and gently dried his hand before meeting his gaze. "Whatever the reason, it's destroying your relationship with her."

Jackson shut his eyes and lowered his head. "Why did I drag you into this?" he whispered, then lifted his head while meeting her gaze. "Amber and I are toxic. We have no business dragging other people into our dysfunctional life."

Sidney held Jackson's hand and gently caressed it with her thumb. "I know you don't want to hear it, but Amber's a grown woman," she informed him. "You can't keep her from dating and eventually moving out."

Jackson groaned, removed his hand from hers, and raked his fingers through his hair. "You don't understand," he muttered.

"You're right, I don't," Sidney replied, making an effort to remain patient and understanding. "Why don't you help me understand?"

"I can't," he replied softly, then finally met her gaze. "She can't go to Texas without me."

"You certainly can't follow her," Sidney insisted.

"I'm pretty sure I can."

"Jackson," she scolded. "She'll never forgive you if you do that."

"She doesn't have to know."

Sidney shook her head, almost defeated. "Whatever your trust issues, it's not normal."

"Nothing about ***this*** is normal," Jackson insisted, then eyed her sternly. "And don't tell her I'm following her either."

Sidney considered his request, and it made her uncomfortable. "Amber is my best friend," she reminded him. "You want me to keep this from her?"

"Yes," Jackson snapped back. "You didn't tell her about us last night in the truck bed, and you don't have to tell her this."

"Fine," Sidney scoffed. "I won't tell her that her clingy uncle is stalking her, but I also don't want any part of it either."

As Sidney headed for the door, Jackson hurried after her.

"Come on, Sidney," he groaned. "Don't go."

She spun to face him. "Do you still intend to follow Amber to Texas?"

"I have to," he insisted.

"No, you don't," she snapped back. "No one is forcing you."

"It's complicated."

"Good night, Jackson."

Sidney left the house, completely forgetting about her bag, and hurried down the porch stairs toward her truck. She heard the screen door open, but she didn't let that deter her.

"Come on, Sidney," Jackson called after her. "Don't leave mad at me."

She paused by her truck and turned to face him on the porch. "The world is full of tough decisions," Sidney remarked. "If you're hell-bent on following Amber to Texas, I think you should be able to give a compelling argument as to why."

Jackson frowned and shoved his hands in his pockets. "I can't do that."

"If you can't confide in me," she announced. "Then I don't know what we're even doing here."

Sidney jumped in her truck, turned around, and drove away. Her mind was reeling at what had just happened. She couldn't believe she had actually considered sleeping with Jackson just half an hour ago. Thankfully, he showed her who he really was before she made that mistake! Still, it made her head and heart hurt.

Chapter 29

The following afternoon, Amber and Greyson flew to Fort Hood, Texas, with their stalker in pursuit. Sidney was disappointed that Jackson felt the need to follow his grown niece like some control freak. It didn't matter. Her relationship with him was too complicated anyway. She was better off alone, as she was meant to be. While having lunch with her G-ma, she was surprised to learn that her grandmother had made plans with a friend to shop and catch a show on an overnight visit to the city. With her grandpa's passing, everyone seemed to change overnight, and she suddenly feared nothing would ever be the same again. Sidney had things to do in the workshop that afternoon, remaining occupied so she didn't have to think about any of it. Grandpa's buyer, Evans, was stopping by that afternoon to pick up several pieces of furniture and have a look at the finished bar.

While waiting for Evans to show up, Sidney heard a car nearby. When she looked outside at her G-ma's house, she was surprised to see a man in his late fifties greeting Helena. He kissed her on the cheek, took her bag, and hurried to the car, opening the passenger side door for her. Sidney stared out the office window with complete astonishment. Her G-ma was going to the city for an overnight with a man? What was happening? Evans's large panel truck pulled up the driveway, alerting Sidney to his arrival. She attempted to calm her rising anxiety. Evans knew her grandpa's work better than anyone, herself excluded. If he realized her grandpa hadn't finished the bar, he might reject it. Finding another buyer for something that big, impressive, and expensive would be difficult.

Sidney crossed the workshop while listening to the backup beep of Evans's panel truck. She opened the electronic bay door and watched the truck back into place. Sidney took several deep breaths while attempting to act and look calm. Relying on payment for the bar could make or break the business. Evans got out of the truck and smiled when he saw her, greeting her with a friendly handshake.

"How are you, Sidney?" Evans asked.

"I'm fine," she replied. "And yourself?"

"It's been difficult since your Grandpa passed," Evans informed her. "All those canceled orders hit me pretty hard, as I'm sure they did you." He clapped his hands together and offered a tiny, tense smile. "If you have that bar for me, it'll be a great burden off my shoulders."

"I have it," Sidney replied and felt her heart flip-flop at the prospect of her little ruse.

"Great," he announced. "Let's have a look at it."

Sidney held her breath while leading him across the workshop to the behemoth bar taking up half of the far workshop bay. Although it appeared massive, it came apart into three sections for moving purposes. Evans whistled when he saw it, then grinned and examined it more closely.

"Looks even better varnished," Evans announced while running his hands along the edges.

When he took his time on the end she had finished, Sidney noticed how closely he inspected every detail of each acorn. She was certain he noticed the slight variation, and panic swept through her. He was going to reject it!

"That's amazing," he remarked, then straightened while staring at the side. "I almost can't tell that it's not Henry's work."

Sidney felt her heart just about stop at his words. Of course, he'd notice! How did she think she'd pull that off? Evans turned toward her and grinned while shaking his head.

"That is truly amazing, Sidney," Evans announced. "Both our asses are saved. Who finished it?"

Sidney finally resumed breathing and forced a tiny smile. "I did," she replied. "You think the client will accept it?"

"Oh, he'll accept it, and he'll never even know the difference," Evans informed her while chuckling.

"What gave me away?" she finally asked. "Was it because my grandpa was left-handed? Did I etch differently because I'm right-handed?"

"Actually, I wouldn't even have noticed if I hadn't been looking for it," Evans admitted. "I was here the day Henry had his heart attack. I knew the last end wasn't finished. When you sent me the pictures, I knew I had to see it for myself." He chuckled warmly. "You did a great job."

Sidney sighed with relief and managed a tiny laugh as well. "I'm so happy to hear," she remarked. "Selling that was the biggest hurdle for the shop."

"You know," Evans announced. "If you can duplicate Henry's work, I may be able to get some of those clients back."

"I can do the artwork," Sidney informed him, then grimaced, "but I'm not a carpenter. I'm not great with all the machinery."

Evans shrugged. "You don't have to be," he replied. "You can hire someone to do the base, copying Henry's style, and then finish the detailed work yourself."

"I can look into hiring someone," she informed him. "But we'd have to take it slowly. I can't be flooded with orders until I know I can fill them."

"Your grandpa started out making rocking chairs," Evans informed her. "Why don't you put together a few rocking chairs? I'll stop by next month and see what you've got. We'll take it from there."

Sidney smiled and nodded. "Okay, I'd like that," she replied and shook his hand.

§

Sidney needed to celebrate her small victory, considering everything that had happened recently. Her family and two best friends were away, and her potential love interest alienated himself from her, choosing to stalk his niece instead. It seemed like a good evening to have a few drinks, take a bubble bath, and have a good cry. She locked up the shop at one o'clock, shortly after Evans loaded up his truck and left. As she headed to her parents' house, she decided she'd order a pizza before the bubble bath and drinking. When she couldn't find her truck keys, she remembered having them in her pants pocket when she got home last night. She headed up to her room and poked around the laundry basket for her keys. They weren't too hard to find. She was about to pick up the phone and place her pizza order when her eyes fell on the picture of her grandmother, grandfather, and mother, taken in front of Norwood Manor.

She removed the picture from her dresser and sat on her bed, studying the photo. Jackson had taken a lot of her focus off her grandpa and what happened with her mother and grandmother. Now, she had time to think about it again. She removed her laptop and looked at the back of the photo, typing the mansion name into a search. Several hits matched her search, and she found the mansion from a picture posted online. Shock and horror immediately swept over her when she read one of the many repeated articles that seemed to pop up on the mansion. "Triple Homicide at Norwood Estate". Sidney read the article four times, attempting to shake the horror she felt. Debra and Ransom Norwood were murdered at their estate during a robbery gone wrong. In an attempt to intervene, their butler, Flynn Murdock, was also killed. Why didn't G-ma tell her that her grandfather was ***murdered***? How could she keep something like that from her?

Sidney realized she could confront her grandmother about the new revelation, but, considering everyone seemed to be lying to her these days, she had a different idea. It didn't take long to find the estate address and locate it on a map. It would be a lengthy car ride to the mansion, but only a short trip by plane. The more she thought about it, the better the idea sounded. Why shouldn't she visit the mansion where her mother grew up? The estate where her mother was raised, and where her grandparents lived happily for many years. They had an entire life there that no one ever talked about. Maybe a visit to Norwood Manor was exactly what she needed. Perhaps someone there remembered her grandparents. Maybe she'd even find another photo of her grandfather, since her grandmother mentioned she had so few. Sidney made her decision. With her credit card and laptop, she booked a flight, a hotel room, and a car for tomorrow morning. She was going to do it!

Chapter 30

After a short plane ride the following morning, Sidney was already in her rental car, driving to the mansion where her mother grew up. Now that she was almost there, she was wondering if she'd made her decision in haste. She was acting out in anger at both Jackson and her grandpa. The end result was driving out to some mansion belonging to people she didn't know, uninvited, yet somehow thinking it was a good idea. Sidney almost changed her mind as she approached the massive, iron gate before the insanely long driveway. Did she think they'd just invite her in?

"Well," Sidney announced aloud to herself. "I'm here now."

As she pulled up to the gate, she felt her heart pounding. She couldn't believe she was doing something so insane. They were never going to let her in. She glanced at the button and the blank television monitor, then took a deep breath before pressing the intercom. A neatly dressed man in a suit immediately appeared on the screen.

"Can I help you?" the man asked.

"Uh, hi," she announced, fumbling over herself. "I'm Sidney Bristol. My grandparents worked for the Norwoods twenty years ago." She could already tell she'd lost the man's interest. "I was wondering if anyone on staff remembers them."

"I don't remember any Bristol's working here," the man gruffly informed her.

"Actually, their names were Helena and Flynn Murdock," Sidney informed the man on the little screen, although she was losing hope of gaining access.

The security guard suddenly sat forward and squinted at her. "You're Flynn Murdock's granddaughter?" he asked, barely finishing the question when the gate began opening. "Keep to the right and pull around back until you reach the garage."

Sidney was stunned to be granted access and quickly threw the car into gear, driving through before they changed their minds. She couldn't get over how long the driveway was and how far she had to drive before the multi-million dollar mansion came into view. The driveway wrapped around a large fountain in front and also branched off to the right. The ten-bedroom, six-bathroom mansion had natural stone siding on all three levels, while white trim gave it a regal appeal. Judging by all the chimneys, there had to be at least four fireplaces. It looked exactly like the picture, but with different landscaping. As Sidney drove along the driveway that branched off to the right, the mansion disappeared from view, and she spotted the eight-car garage up ahead. The garage, with living quarters on the second floor, was made of the same stone and had eight oversized bays with massive electronic doors.

In front of one of the garage bays was an expensive, lovingly cared-for, vintage Rolls-Royce. Sidney pulled up to the garage and parked off to the side, not far from the mansion's kitchen entrance. She barely got out of the car when a tall, clean-shaven, neatly dressed man in his early fifties approached her. The handsome man had neatly trimmed dark hair, peppered with gray, with even more gray in his sideburns. He immediately smiled and extended his hand to her.

"You're Murdock's granddaughter?"

Sidney accepted his hand and felt the firm handshake. "Yes," she replied while adding a polite smile. "You must be Mr. Norwood."

The man suddenly chuckled. "I'm the chauffeur, Lance," he informed her. "Security said you were driving up. I was asked to greet and escort you inside."

The chauffeur then indicated the nearby sidewalk that led to the kitchen entrance. Sidney walked with the well-dressed man toward the side of the mansion. Although her attire was business casual, Sidney felt almost frumpy alongside the well-dressed chauffeur.

"I guess you didn't know my grandfather," Sidney announced. "You seem too young."

"Oh, trust me, I knew your grandfather," Lance announced with a chuckle. "I was twenty years old and had only worked here for a year at the time, but we'd gotten to know each other pretty well in that year. He was one hell of a poker player." The chauffeur maintained his suave and cheerful demeanor. "I'll introduce you to some of the older staff. I'm sure the rumor of your arrival got around before you even parked your car."

As they entered the mansion's kitchen through the side entrance, they immediately headed down a set of stairs into the basement, where the staff quarters were located. Sidney couldn't get over how amazing the place was. As they approached the staff lounge, she was immediately bombarded by two older women in their late fifties to early sixties. Both wore plain black dresses. For a woman her age, Camille had unnaturally dark, thick, and curly hair. She was a robust woman with more than her share of zesty exuberance. Sandra was an attractive, tall, slender woman with shoulder-length platinum-dyed hair. Both women squealed with joy and fussed over Sidney.

"You look just like Casandra," Camille exclaimed. "She was such a beautiful young lady."

"How is that grandmother of yours?" Sandra asked while grinning. "Oh, Helena and I got into so much trouble when we were younger."

Lance laughed at the spectacle. "That's my cue to leave," he announced. "If you need rescuing, I'm star three on the house phone."

As Lance left, Sidney was ushered into the staff lounge. The staff wing living area was extremely cozy, with peach-colored furniture and a mauve-print throw rug over the hardwood floor. The living area had its own fireplace, adding to the warm, cozy atmosphere. Unfortunately, the room had no windows because it was in the basement. While Sidney was bombarded with questions about her grandmother and mother, a tall, slender, proper-looking butler in his late fifties, with a head full of thick gray hair, entered the lounge behind them, smiled, and approached Sidney with his hand extended.

"I'm Jenkins, the butler," he announced. "It's a pleasure to meet you, Miss Murdock."

Sidney shook his hand and returned the smile. "Sidney Bristol," she informed him. "My mother married."

"Yes, of course," the butler replied, then indicated the two women. "The two women smothering you are Camille and Sandra. In case they forgot to introduce themselves."

The women ignored the butler and took Sidney to the sofa, sitting on either side of her. They immediately talked over each other, appearing giddy to meet her.

"So how are Helena and Casandra?" Camille asked, talking over Sandra.

"Well, it would seem my grandmother has a new man friend she neglected to mention," Sidney remarked and added a tiny laugh. "So she's doing well. My mother and father just left for a second honeymoon in Hawaii."

"Oh, I'm so happy your mother met a nice man," Sandra announced. "She was a little reserved and somewhat shy when she lived here."

"Really?" Sidney asked with surprise. "She must have outgrown that."

There was a round of laughter.

"She gets that from Helena," Camille announced, bubbling over. "She was a pistol."

"Still is," Sidney remarked. "I never knew my grandfather, and I guess I was just hoping to connect with people who did know him."

All three were solemn for a moment but retained their smiles. Sidney was sure that comment would get the ball rolling regarding the night he was murdered.

"He was a wonderful man," Sandra informed her. "He started as the assistant chauffeur, then moved up to part-time driver. The Norwoods loved him so much, they brought him into the house as an assistant butler."

"Which is unheard of," Jenkins chimed in. "Chaffed the head butler, since he had to train him in proper etiquette."

"Stop being so dramatic," Sandra scolded, then looked at Sidney and grinned. "He got promoted to head butler over Jenkins. Some sour grapes there."

Jenkins groaned and rolled his eyes.

"We have photos," Camille squealed with delight, swiftly changing the subject. "Would you like to see them?"

"I'd love to."

Camille jumped up from the sofa and hurried for the lounge door. "Make yourself useful, Jenkins," she announced. "Get some tea for our guest."

Jenkins again rolled his eyes and shook his head as Camille left the room.

"You don't need to go to any trouble, Jenkins," Sidney announced while offering a sympathetic smile.

"Apparently, you're not married," Jenkins remarked with a tiny smile. "When your wife says, 'make tea,' you make tea. Excuse me."

Over tea, Sidney spent the next hour looking at old photos and talking with the two maids and the butler about her grandparents. None brought up her grandfather's passing, which kept the mood upbeat.

"So tell us about yourself, dear," Sandra announced with interest. "Are you in college?"

"I was," Sidney replied. "I graduated more than two years ago with an associate's degree in graphic design and architecture."

"So that'd make you twenty-two?" Camille asked, seeming oddly curious about her age.

"Actually, twenty-three," Sidney replied. "I was working with my great-grandfather full-time the last two years until he passed over a week ago. He left the business to me, so I guess I'm going to be a furniture designer now."

"Henry?" Sandra asked with a strange look on her face.

Camille and Jenkins exchanged looks, which Sidney immediately caught.

"Yes, Henry," Sidney replied while eyeing them almost suspiciously. "Helena's father."

All three seemed slightly uncomfortable for a moment, then attempted to cover.

"Why is everyone acting strange?" Sidney asked.

"So Helena moved back home after she left here?" Sandra asked.

"Yes," Sidney replied and studied the strange looks she was receiving. "Why?"

The two women appeared visibly uncomfortable. "No reason," Sandra easily lied.

"I know my grandmother and great-grandfather had a falling out," Sidney informed them. "It's okay. They got past it. She even lived with him for the last twenty-four years."

All three forced smiles and nodded. Camille was quick to hand her the second photo album.

"These pictures were later, after your grandfather passed," Camille informed her. "But there are some lovely ones of your mother and grandmother."

Sidney refrained from opening the album and looked at the two maids and the butler. "I love this stroll down memory lane and seeing photos of my mother and grandmother in their younger days," she announced, then gently cleared her throat. "But I'd like to know more about my grandfather's death."

"Told you so," Jenkins muttered to his wife, then looked at Sidney somewhat sympathetically. "Their son, our boss, doesn't like it when we talk about the murder of his parents, but you have a right to know about the night your grandfather died."

Camille shifted uncomfortably, seeming visibly shaken even after all these years. "Helena and I returned from church bingo that evening close to eleven o'clock--"

Chapter 31

Flashback. Twenty-seven years ago. Two women in their late twenties to early thirties, Camille and Helena, got out of the older car in front of the garage and headed toward the back porch. There was a light on in the kitchen, but the back porch remained dark.

"That's odd," Helena remarked and glanced at her watch. "Why didn't Flynn leave the light on for us? He always leaves the light on."

"He probably forgot," Camille insisted, waving her off. "If he's anything like my husband, he fell asleep in front of the television in the lounge."

"That's not like Flynn," Helena reminded her, then seemed slightly uncomfortable. "He always waits up for me."

"Checking up on you, huh?" Camille teased as they approached the porch.

"No," Helena replied, then fidgeted while attempting to hide her tiny grin. "He likes to give me a 'proper' goodnight."

Camille eyed Helena, who blushed at the admission. "I wish Jenkins gave me a proper goodnight just once," she announced a little louder than necessary.

Both women giggled at the sexual innuendo. Helena paused by the door, then looked back at the garage, appearing curious.

"Huh," Helena remarked and indicated the apartment above the garage. "Lance is still up. I thought he'd be in bed by now. He has an early morning drive."

"He probably passed out and left the light on," Camille scoffed before unlocking the door.

Both women crossed the massive kitchen. Helena set her purse down on the counter and continued toward the main hallway entrance.

"Aren't you going to bed?" Camille called after her.

"In a minute," Helena insisted, then pointed toward the door. "I just want to collect Mr. Norwood's dirty glasses from the study. I'd rather his brandy glass didn't sit all night. Those glasses are so hard to wash once the brandy dries."

"All right," Camille announced and waved. "I'll see you in the morning."

As Helena headed down the hallway toward the dimly lit study, her eyes strayed to what appeared to be blood droplets on the floor. Helena eyed the spots, somewhat puzzled, now slowing her approach. She stepped into the study doorway and immediately froze. Debra and Ransom Norwood were on the floor not far from the desk, blood covering their lifeless bodies. Before she could even scream or react, her eyes strayed a few feet away from them. Flynn was sprawled across the floor with a massive pool of blood surrounding him. Helena screamed and ran for her dead husband, collapsing to the floor and pulling him into her arms. She called out, uncertain anyone would even hear her while crying and clinging to her dead husband, holding his lifeless head to her bosom. Only a few minutes later, twenty-year-old Lance ran into the room and froze at the chilling sight.

Present day. Camille and Sandra were brought back to the current day, appearing solemn and still somewhat traumatized by what had happened that night.

"The killer was never found," Jenkins informed Sidney. "The police are convinced that the missing antique revolver from Mr. Norwood's desk drawer was the same gun the killer used to shoot Flynn."

"Some of the older staff still believe it was an inside job," Sandra informed her.

"Stop that nonsense," Jenkins scolded. "No one in this house disliked Ransom and Debra Norwood, let alone had any reason to kill them."

"But the killer didn't steal anything," Sandra countered, becoming irritated. Apparently, they argued about the killings many times in the past.

"Mr. Norwood's gold watch was missing," Jenkins reminded her, becoming huffy.

Sandra loudly groaned and waved her hand. "He was always misplacing his watch," she scoffed. "Even so, do you really think someone broke into this place to steal a watch? You're really dense, Jenkins."

"Nothing more was stolen because he was caught in the act," Jenkins reminded her. "The moment he fired that gun, Lance was alerted to trouble."

"Lance was passed out drunk," Sandra snapped back. "As he was most nights back then. He told the police he arrived in the study shortly after Helena, but it was more like fifteen minutes later."

"It's true," Camille replied softly with a sigh. "Helena didn't want to correct him in front of the police. He could have lost his job."

"He wouldn't have lost his job for drinking after he was off the clock," Jenkins scoffed.

"If you had seen the way young Mr. Norwood looked at Lance, you'd think differently," Camille insisted, then looked at Sidney. "Their son, Blain Norwood, showed up an hour later just before the medical examiner finished his assessment of the scene. It was awful. Blain seeing his parents like that. I'll never forget that shocked look on his face."

"Security seems pretty tight here," Sidney remarked. "The guard, gate, and cameras."

"Young Mr. Norwood had all of that installed after the murders," Jenkins informed her. "There was an alarm system on the doors and windows, but Mr. Norwood never remembered to set it. Now, this place is locked down like a fort."

"Is this where everyone is hiding?" a man asked from the doorway.

All four were startled by the voice, not expecting someone else in the doorway, and looked at the neatly dressed man. He was a tall, handsome, moderately muscular man in his late twenties. The man had short, dark hair, a clean-shaven face, and carried himself with an air of confidence. Sidney couldn't help but notice the attractive, broad-shouldered man in the expensive suit. That had to be Mr. Norwood, but he didn't look old enough.

"We have company," Camille announced almost arrogantly while cocking her head. "Be polite, Harris."

Harris eyed Sidney with more than a passing interest, even smiling politely. "I don't remember seeing any visitors on today's calendar," he remarked, "but I'll let this one slide just this once."

"Sidney's grandmother worked here over two decades ago," Jenkins informed Harris. "Her grandfather, too."

"Oh?" Harris asked, now interested. "A little before my time, but anyone I might know?"

"Murdock," Jenkins informed him.

"Murdock?" Harris asked with a curious tilt of his head. It was obvious he immediately remembered the name of the murdered butler, but he covered rather quickly. "Did they have the little girl I'd heard Mrs. Norwood adored? I'm pretty sure her name was Murdock."

"Yes, Casandra," Jenkins replied while gently rocking in his chair. "This is Sidney, Casandra's daughter."

Harris's smile increased, and he immediately approached with his hand extended. "Forgive me for being so rude," he announced and shook her hand. "I'm Harris, Mr. Norwood's personal assistant." He then cocked his head, appearing interested. "Forgive me for asking, but how old are you? Casandra Murdock can't be that old."

Sidney smiled and shifted uncomfortably. "Yes, she had me young," she replied. "I was an oopsie."

Harris appeared slightly embarrassed and hid his smile. "I'm sorry," he announced. "I didn't mean to get so personal."

"It's okay," Sidney remarked. "I'm twenty-three."

Harris studied her a moment, his smile never faltering. "Well, don't leave without giving Mr. Norwood a chance to meet you," he announced. "I'm sure he'd love to say hello."

"I'd like that," Sidney replied.

Harris nodded, then looked at Jenkins and raised his brow. "Lunch, Jenkins?"

"Oh, yes," Jenkins announced, then quickly stood before smiling at Sidney. "Don't leave without saying goodbye."

Chapter 32

Within twenty minutes, Harris returned to the staff lounge with news that his boss wanted to meet with Sidney and had asked her to join him for lunch. Although she felt a little awkward about it, since she hadn't even been invited to his mansion, she graciously accepted his invitation. Sidney walked through the mansion with Harris, silently marveling at the old architecture. The place was amazing!

"Are you from around here?" Harris asked, distracting her from the mansion's beauty.

"No, but it was a short flight," she replied. "It would have been a few hours' drive."

"How long are you in town?" he pressed.

Sidney glanced at the handsome man walking alongside her and caught his tiny smile. "Just tonight," she replied. "I leave first thing tomorrow morning."

"So does that mean you're free for dinner tonight?"

When Sidney looked back at Harris, he was grinning at her. She considered the question a moment. Given how Jackson had been behaving, it would be nice to have dinner with a gentleman. Was he actually asking her out? There was one way to find out.

"Yes, I suppose I am."

Harris stepped in front of the door, blocking her path. His smile never faltered. "Great," he announced. "I'll pick you up at six."

Sidney was surprised by his boldness and self-confidence and had to smile. "Sure," she replied. "Why not? But you should know, I didn't pack anything except my laptop. This is as fancy as I get."

"I'll ditch the tie and lose the jacket," he announced cheerfully.

Harris pushed the door open behind him, backed through the doorway, and extended his hand onto the patio. Sidney walked past him and smiled at his charm. There was a small dining section and a comfortable sitting area with white and gray wicker furniture. The back patio was completely covered, with the pool and hot tub only a few steps away, surrounded by professional landscaping. Harris walked a step behind Sidney to the elegant patio table beneath the veranda. A man seated at the table stood and smiled as she approached. Blain was a nice-looking man in his mid-fifties, standing close to six feet tall with a lean build. Although not classically handsome by any standards, he had a certain charm and sophistication. His short, white hair was moderately spikey on top, and he remained clean-shaven. He wore a black suit that was ridiculously expensive and quite possibly hand-tailored. Blain immediately extended his hand, grasping her hand affectionately between his.

"Miss Murdock," Blain announced warmly.

"Bristol," she corrected while returning the smile. "Sidney."

"It's a pleasure to meet you," Blain replied, then gave a quick nod to Harris, sending him on his way.

Blain pulled the nearby chair out for her without taking his eyes off her. Sidney accepted the seat and watched him return to his chair while maintaining his smile. She couldn't deny that his odd way of staring was making her a little uncomfortable.

"I'm sorry for staring," he announced with some embarrassment, as if reading her mind. "You look so much like your mother."

"Everyone's been saying that," Sidney remarked and shook her head. "I don't see it."

"Well, when she was younger," he replied.

"You're younger than what I was expecting," Sidney informed him.

"Helena worked for my parents," he informed her. "My mother adored your mother. I think she would have traded me for her if she'd been given the chance. When my parents passed, I inherited their estate, but I knew your mother and grandmother for years before that."

"I'm glad you agreed to meet with me," Sidney remarked. "I really wasn't expecting it. I'm sure you're very busy--"

"Not too busy to have lunch with a young lady," he replied, then stood and poured two glasses of wine. As he set a glass before her, he grinned almost slyly. "You are legal to drink, right?"

"Yes," Sidney replied with a soft laugh. "I'm twenty-three."

Blain returned to his seat. "Twenty-three," he announced and nodded. "That's about right. Your mother must have had you shortly after they left my employment, then."

Sidney tensed slightly at his odd behavior but managed a smile. "Yes, she did," she replied.

"I'm sorry," he announced and shifted in his chair. "I didn't mean to make you uncomfortable." Blain continued to stare at her, then shook his head. "Did your mother ever mention me to you?"

The question surprised her, and she shook her head. "No," Sidney replied. "She never talked much about her childhood. I didn't even know my grandmother worked in a mansion until my great-grandfather died. That's when I found a picture with my grandparents standing out front of this place."

Blain couldn't take his eyes off her and finally leaned across the table. "Before this becomes too awkward," he announced. "I think there's something you should know."

Sidney stared at him, now curious.

"Your mother and I had a brief romance before she left," Blain informed her.

Sidney stared at the man across from her as the comment registered. Her expression immediately dropped. "Are you suggesting--?"

Blain smiled and nodded. "I know I was your mother's first," he announced somewhat delicately. "When Harris told me Casandra's twenty-three-year-old daughter was here, I immediately knew you were my daughter."

Sidney couldn't take her eyes off Blain, and she wasn't even sure if she blinked the entire time. She didn't know what to say. Did her mother lie to her about her real father? Why not? It seemed as if everything she'd ever been told was a lie.

"My mother told me my real father was dead or in jail," Sidney informed him, barely getting the words out.

"I'm honestly not surprised she'd tell you that," Blain remarked, turning uncomfortable. "And while you're doing the math in your head, she told me she was eighteen. By the time I found out she wasn't, Helena handed in her resignation and took off." He shook his head. "I never got the chance to tell my side of the story, apologize, or even say goodbye."

"You loved my mother?" Sidney asked timidly.

"Oh, very much," Blain replied and sighed. "She was so beautiful. The most beautiful woman I'd ever laid eyes upon." He frowned and fidgeted slightly. "If I had known she was pregnant, I would have done everything in my power to provide for you growing up." He sank back in his chair and drifted into his own world. "I lost my only child many years ago." Blain again met her gaze and offered a warm smile. "I thought I'd never be a father again." He leaned across the table and appeared overjoyed. "This is fate, Sidney."

"I doubt my mother would see it that way," Sidney remarked. "She went to a lot of trouble to keep you a secret from me."

"I'm surprised she didn't give you a hard time when you told her you were coming here," Blain remarked. "She had to know I'd figure it out."

"She doesn't know I'm here," Sidney informed him. "My parents went to Hawaii for two weeks."

"Neither your mother nor grandmother will be happy that you learned the truth," he remarked, then gave it some thought. "Would you be willing to submit to a paternity test to prove I'm your father?"

Sidney didn't see the harm since she hadn't been a minor for years. "I don't see why not," she replied.

Blain turned enthusiastic. "Wonderful," he announced. "Are you in town the entire day?"

"I'm staying at the hotel near the airport," she informed him. "I have an early flight out."

"That works out," Blain remarked. "I can have someone stop by your hotel later this afternoon to administer the DNA test. Then, in a couple of days, I'll let you know the results. Although I'm positive I was the only one your mother had been with, maybe you'll want to hold off telling your mother until the test is back."

"Telling her is a slippery slope," Sidney remarked.

"If you'd feel more comfortable not telling her for a few months, we can get to know each other better first," he announced. "Then you'll see I'm not the monster she'll make me out to be." He smiled cheerfully. "I'll finally have an heir to my estate." Blain indicated the area surrounding him. "This estate has been in my family for many generations. I was worried it would end up in someone else's hands. I need someone to carry on my legacy."

"I'll be honest with you," Sidney announced. "I'm not interested in your money or property. My great-grandfather left me his business and his cabin. I pretty much have everything I want or need."

"Well, that's good, because I don't intend to drop over anytime soon," he remarked with a chuckle. "Maybe you could stay for dinner tonight. We can discuss visitation. I believe I'm supposed to get every other weekend."

Sidney managed a tiny laugh at his joke. "Although it's only a short flight to get here," she informed him, "that's a lot of time spent in airports."

He waved her off. "Forget the airports," Blain announced. "I'll send my private jet to come and get you."

"That's very generous of you," Sidney replied, then shifted uncomfortably. "As for dinner, Harris already asked me out tonight."

Blain raised a brow and eyed her almost suspiciously. "Isn't he the little opportunist?" he muttered, but his smile soon returned. "I understand."

"I only said yes because he seems like a gentleman," Sidney remarked.

"He is," Blain replied. "You're fine."

Despite the awkwardness of their initial meeting, their lunch lasted more than an hour and was quite pleasant. Blain talked candidly about his work, his life, his parents, and the mansion. He was intelligent and incredibly charming. Perhaps it was those traits that fascinated her mother as well. Although it was a pleasant visit, it was a lot for Sidney to take in, and she needed some time alone to process everything. Blain was understanding and promised to give her a guided tour of the estate the next time she visited.

Chapter 33

Despite wanting some time to herself, Sidney's time of reflection in her hotel room was almost immediately interrupted by the woman sent to collect a DNA sample for the paternity test. She shouldn't have been surprised that Blain Norwood was that eager to find out if she was his daughter, but all the fussing was a little overwhelming. She did have time to soak in the tub before her dinner date with Harris, which was somewhat relaxing. Harris picked Sidney up in front of her hotel at precisely six o'clock that evening. When the expensive, red Ferrari pulled up to the hotel curb, Sidney may have stared a little longer than she should have. Harris got out of the driver's seat, hurried around the sports car, and suavely opened the door for her. Despite that he 'dressed down', he still looked classy in his white dress shirt with the sleeves rolled up to his elbows and his black dress pants.

Sidney felt underdressed even in one of her nicer shirts that she'd packed for her return flight home in the morning. She certainly wasn't expecting to go on a date with a man wearing a hand-tailored suit and driving a Ferrari. Sidney attempted to get comfortable in the car that probably cost more than her grandpa's truck and boat combined. She put on a façade of confidence as Harris jumped back into the driver's seat.

"You'll love the restaurant," he insisted. "First class all the way."

"Don't those places usually have dress codes?" she asked, now becoming tense all over again.

He grinned somewhat slyly. "For the average diner, perhaps," Harris announced. "But I have connections in every classy establishment in town."

"Okay," Sidney replied somewhat hesitantly. "I'll trust your judgment."

It was a short drive through town to the restaurant. From what Sidney saw from the outside, it was ***exceptionally*** classy. Harris pulled around back and parked just off the alley. Sidney looked around somewhat hesitantly as he opened the car door for her.

"Should I be worried?" she asked.

"Nah, you're with me," Harris informed her, then held out his arm for her to link onto.

Sidney clutched his arm almost insecurely as he led her to the back kitchen door of the restaurant. Harris promptly knocked on the old door. Within a minute, it opened to reveal a man dressed in a chef's uniform.

"What's the password?" the man dressed in white asked gruffly.

"Let me in, or I'll tell your wife you lost five hundred dollars playing poker last week," Harris scoffed.

The chef grinned, laughed, and stepped out of the doorway. "Table for two, right this way," the man announced and led them across the kitchen.

Sidney looked around the kitchen at the busily working men and women, who took a moment to eye them as well. They immediately approached a door in the back. When the chef opened the door, Sidney entered with Harris. The restaurant's wine room, encased in stone with tall wine racks, had a small round table in the center that comfortably seated four. Above the table was a small chandelier, indicating it was an often-used table, possibly for friends or VIP guests. The setting was very cozy and extremely intimate. Harris pulled out a chair for Sidney as the chef lit the candle in the center of the table, then handed them menus.

"The service in the back is slow, but you can pick your own wine," the chef announced. "On the house."

Once the chef left the room, Harris snorted a laugh and smiled at Sidney. "Pretty lousy restaurant, making us serve ourselves," he announced, then stood and approached the many racks filled with wine. "How about a 1987 Silver Oak Cabernet Sauvignon?" He removed a bottle from the rack and suavely displayed it for her. "He did say anything we wanted 'on the house'. This sells for about eight hundred a bottle."

Harris found a corkscrew and easily opened the bottle, then set it aside to let it breathe. He returned to his seat and opened his menu.

"Do you know what you'd like?" Harris asked while scanning his menu.

"Whatever that is that smells so wonderful," she informed him, then grinned.

"Well, that would be me," he announced, then waved his menu past his face, sending the delightful, musky scent her way. Harris then returned to his menu. "Unfortunately, Blain said he'd castrate me if I made any moves on you, so I'm officially ***off*** the menu."

Sidney laughed while hiding her smile. "You're funny," she remarked.

"So, have you decided from something ***on*** the menu?"

"I think so," Sidney replied.

Harris jumped up from his seat, placed his linen napkin over his arm, whipped a pad and pen from his back pocket, and stood over her.

"What can I get for the lady?" he announced in possibly the worst Italian accent she'd ever heard, but it was enough to make her laugh.

"Are you seriously taking my order?"

"Yes, I will be your waiter this evening," Harris informed her. "The chef wasn't kidding when he said the service back here was lousy." He then eyed her. "Would you like to hear our specials for tonight?"

Sidney stared up at him and laughed. "Uh, sure," she replied.

Harris flipped through his pad and read the specials to her. Sidney couldn't stop laughing at the horrible accent that was supposed to be Italian but sounded more like Pepé Le Pew. An hour and nearly an entire bottle of wine later, Sidney and Harris finished their expensive meal. Sidney had probably learned more about Harris over dinner than she knew about Jackson after years of him living in town. No. She refused to let Jackson ruin her delightful evening with the charming man across from her.

"That was wonderful," Sidney announced.

"You wouldn't be saying that if I had to double as the chef too," he remarked. "Are you sure you don't want any dessert?"

"No, I'm full," she informed him.

"Then I'll get the check, and we'll be on our way," Harris replied before removing the pad from his pocket. He did some quick math, wrote the total, and added a smiling face. He then removed his wallet while eyeing the bill and snorted a laugh. "They recommend a twenty percent tip. There's no way I'm tipping that horrible waiter twenty percent."

Sidney watched him toss two hundred dollars on the table. He then stood, pulled her chair out for her, and offered her his arm.

"Shall we?"

Sidney giggled and linked onto his arm. "Thank you ever so kindly."

§

Once they reached Sidney's hotel, Harris parked his car out front in a no-parking area and opened the door for her. As he walked her to the entrance, she looked back at his car.

"Aren't you worried about getting a ticket?" she asked.

"I'm only parking for five minutes," he remarked, then smiled at her as they entered the hotel lobby. "I'll walk you as far as the elevator. I plan to avoid temptation so I get to keep my favorite man parts." Harris stopped her by the elevator and smiled charmingly. "I had a wonderful time tonight, Sidney. Perhaps, we can do this again when you're back in town."

"Thank you for being such a gentleman," Sidney announced warmly. "I had more fun than I thought I would."

Harris grinned slyly. "You thought I was going to be some stuffed shirt, admit it."

Sidney laughed softly and nodded. "Yeah, kind of."

Harris took her hand and warmly caressed it. He then leaned in and kissed her quickly on the lips, surprising her, and pulled away before she could react.

"Good night, Sidney."

As she waited for the elevator, Sidney watched Harris stroll across the lobby. Her heart immediately sank. Out with a perfectly charming, funny gentleman at a gourmet restaurant, and all she could think about was Jackson. She cursed herself for thinking about him at all. Harris told her half his life story over dinner, and Jackson couldn't even tell her why he was a controlling bastard over his niece. The nerve of him! Following Amber around like some helicopter uncle! How had her wonderful evening circled back around to Jackson? Harris was a great guy. She needed to shake Jackson's memory from her mind and grab onto the good guy before it was too late. Maybe spending time at Blain's mansion was what she needed to sort out the rest of her life.

§

Helena's gentleman friend drove his car up to G-ma's house a little after midnight. The house interior was dark except for a kitchen light Helena had left on for her return from her lengthy overnight trip to the city. As Helena got out of the passenger side of the car, her male companion, Jerry, got out and headed for the trunk. Jerry was a Lebanese man in his late fifties with mostly black hair and, despite his age, only a little gray. Typical for a man of his age, he had his share of wrinkles around his eyes, a slightly receding hairline, and was far from athletic. He removed her overnight bag and some shopping bags, then escorted her to the house. Helena smiled at her friend as she unlocked the kitchen door.

"Did you want to come inside for a while?" Helena asked.

"Tempting," Jerry announced, then smiled warmly. "But what will the neighbors say when they see me slipping out of your house at sunrise?"

"Why didn't the fool stay for breakfast?" Helena teased while grinning.

"That's possible," Jerry remarked, then kissed her warmly on the lips. "I don't want to wear out my welcome, but I'll call you tomorrow."

Jerry set her travel bag and shopping bags just inside the kitchen beyond the open door, then headed back to his car. Before he got into his car, Jerry smiled and waved. Helena entered the house and locked the door behind her. She reached for her bags, hesitated, and then waved them off, leaving them for tomorrow morning. Helena turned out the kitchen light and headed for the stairs, venturing up them without turning on a light. Small nightlights allowed her to see well enough to go up the steps. As she approached her dark bedroom, she heard a faint clunk from Henry's room. Helena hesitated and looked toward her father's dark bedroom. What she heard could have been any one of a thousand sounds. When she didn't hear anything after that, she headed for her bedroom, turned on the light, and partially shut the door behind her. The shower in the bathroom was then heard running.

A few minutes later, Helena's bedroom door slowly opened, and a man dressed in black with a black mask over his face crept across the bedroom with a hunting knife clutched in his gloved hand. He silently approached the partially open bathroom door as the shower ran, covering any sounds of his presence. The intruder paused before the bathroom door and slowly pushed it open a little further. Steam instantly poured out of the bathroom and into the bedroom. The nearly deafening and alarming sound of a revolver cylinder turning echoed loudly through the bedroom. Helena stood behind the man with a .357 Magnum aimed at his head. The intruder froze at the distinctive sound that would send fear through any man. Helena sneered and revealed no fear.

"Went a little heavy on the Old Spice deodorant, didn't we? Smelled you halfway up the steps," Helena scoffed. "My house smells more like green tea and cucumber."

The masked intruder slowly raised his hands in the air, allowing her a view of the hunting knife.

"My father taught me how to use a gun," Helena informed him without emotion. "I know how to shoot, I won't hesitate to pull the trigger, and I won't miss. If you want to live, drop the knife and balls to the floor."

The intruder hesitated and turned his head upon hearing her instructions.

Helena's expression turned to rage, and she shouted, "I said, balls to the floor!"

The man dropped the knife and slowly moved to his knees. A floorboard barely creaked behind Helena, but the sound was deafening to her. Helena's eyes widened in horror as she spun with the gun aimed.

§

Jerry pulled back into the driveway after having circled the block once, apparently changing his mind about the invitation to stay. He got out of the car, hesitating only briefly, and then walked up the porch steps. He paused before the door, adjusted his jacket, and firmly knocked before he had time to change his mind. Jerry fidgeted slightly, then roused his best smile, waiting for Helena to answer the door. When there was no response, he knocked a little louder. The sound of a gunshot echoed from within the house. Jerry's expression immediately dropped as panic set in. He attempted to open the door, but, of course, it was locked.

"Helena!" he cried out while shoving his shoulder against the heavy, handcrafted door. It groaned beneath his weight but refused to budge. "Helena!"

Jerry threw his shoulder forcibly into the door again, splintering the jamb, and the door flew open, striking the opposing wall with a loud crack. He barely had a chance to straighten and recover when a figure dressed in black thundered across the dark kitchen for him. Before he could even let out a startled gasp, the intruder stabbed him with the knife. He clutched his bleeding shoulder and almost instantly dropped to the floor as the intruder bolted from the house.

Chapter 34

Around four o'clock in the morning, Sidney pulled up to her house in her grandpa's truck and parked. Since she hadn't been able to sleep, which was all Jackson's fault, she exchanged her morning flight for a red-eye. Sidney wearily got out of her car while grabbing her overnight bag from the passenger seat. As she shuffled for the house, she glanced across the yard to her grandmother's house. Sidney was a little surprised to see G-ma's gentleman caller's car parked in the driveway. That was interesting, considering how her grandmother had been so discreet regarding her male friend. Sidney again looked across the yard, having to see it to believe it. She hesitated and squinted at the house. The kitchen door appeared to be open. Sidney set her bag on the macadam just before the porch and walked with a quickened pace on the worn path to G-ma's house.

As she got closer, she noticed the door was, in fact, open. She hurried up the porch steps, then slowed her approach when she saw blood on the kitchen floor. Sidney took a step closer to the open door, peered inside, and saw a trail of blood across the tile floor.

"G-ma!" Sidney cried out and bolted across the kitchen.

When she reached the steps, she saw G-ma's motionless gentleman friend partially on the steps, holding a blood-soaked dish towel not far from the bleeding knife wound on his shoulder. His bloodied cell phone was still clutched in his hand. Sidney withheld her frightened scream and approached him, uncertain if he was dead or alive. As she reached down to check for a pulse, his eyes suddenly popped open.

"Helena," he gasped, staring at her. He immediately panicked. "Find Helena."

Sidney removed her cell phone from her pocket with a trembling hand and pressed 911. "It's going to be okay," she insisted. "Try not to move." Sidney placed the dishtowel over his wound and moved his hand on top of it. "Try and keep pressure on it."

"Helena," Jerry again gasped, pleading with her. "Gunshots--"

Sidney felt every nerve in her body suddenly twitch at his words. She darted back into the kitchen, snatched the butcher knife from the knife rack, and hurried back to the stairs, past the barely conscious man.

"911, what's your emergency?" the operator came over the phone, startling her.

Sidney put the cell phone on speaker and cautiously hurried up the steps with the butcher knife clutched in her hand. When she saw the open bedroom doors, she internally panicked. There was no telling if someone was waiting just inside one of the dark rooms.

"I'm at 428 Westmore Road. My grandmother's boyfriend has been stabbed," Sidney gasped while nervously passing each dark room on her way to G-ma's bedroom. "I think my grandmother might be hurt as well. Send help."

Without waiting for a response, Sidney shoved her phone back in her pocket and approached her G-ma's bedroom. She clutched the butcher knife, prepared to strike, as she quietly stepped into the bedroom. To her horror, there was quite a bit of blood on the floor, a spatter on the wall near the door, and droplets leading up to the closed bathroom door. Sidney held her breath and nervously approached the closed door, her knife firmly grasped, preparing herself for what she might find.

"G-ma," Sidney gasped, her voice trembling as she tried the knob, but it was locked. "G-ma, can you hear me?" There was no response, but her grandmother had to be in there. "I'm going to break down the door. If you're in front of it, try to move away."

Sidney took a step back and then rammed her shoulder into the door. The pain was almost enough to paralyze her, yet the door didn't seem to budge. Curse her grandpa and his fine carpentry craftsmanship! She sucked up the pain and struck it three more times before the frame finally splintered and the door opened. Sidney looked across the bathroom and saw her grandmother sitting on the floor between the vanity and the tub. There was blood covering her shirt, and the revolver was still in her hand. As Sidney darted across the bathroom, Helena lifted the gun and weakly opened her eyes. Sidney gasped at the sight of her G-ma aiming the large weapon at her. When she saw Sidney, she groaned and lowered the gun.

"Sidney," she gasped. "Thank God. I can't get up. Help me up."

"An ambulance is on its way," Sidney insisted and just about fell to her knees before her grandmother, dropping the knife to the tile floor with a clatter. She held the hand towel to her grandmother's shoulder and applied pressure to the deep stab wound. "You're going to be okay."

Ambulance sirens could be heard in the near distance. They were only minutes away. Her grandmother just needed to hang on a little longer.

"No," Helena groaned and shook her head. "It's not going to be okay." Her eyes then briefly opened as she met

Sidney's gaze. "No amount of scrubbing is ever going to get that blood out of the tile."

"Sidney!" Greyson was heard shouting from downstairs.

"Greyson?" Sidney gasped, feeling some relief, hearing her friend's voice. "We're up here!"

"I'm coming!"

"No," Sidney called back. "Stay with G-ma's friend! Keep pressure on the wound!"

"Jerry?" Helena suddenly gasped, seeming to come back to life, and frantically struggled to sit up. "Jerry's here? Is he okay?"

"He's conscious," Sidney informed her. "The ambulance is pulling up now. They'll take care of him. You just hold on, okay?"

"I shot him," Helena announced, now turning feeble after her exertion.

"Jerry?"

"No," Helena gasped weakly. "One of the intruders. I shot the bastard, but they got away. Two men."

§

Sidney paced the small and intimate hospital waiting room. There were only twenty padded chairs, most of which were empty, considering the early hour. Greyson sat in one of the chairs, attempting to make a call on his cell phone, but he looked more frustrated than anything.

"I can't get a hold of Amber," Greyson muttered, then looked at Sidney. "I dropped her off right before I passed G-ma's house. She must have turned off her phone when she went to bed."

"Why did you come back early?" Sidney asked, now curious that he had been driving past G-ma's house at four in the morning. "I thought you were going away for three days."

"Her psycho uncle was following us," Greyson huffed and shook his head. "We need to have a talk about your new boyfriend."

"He's not my boyfriend," Sidney scoffed and resumed pacing. "When he even hinted about following the two of you to Texas, I got into an argument with him. A little mystery is romantic, but he takes ***mysterious*** to a whole other level."

Greyson stood and moved closer to Sidney. "I have a really bad feeling," he announced. "I need to check on Amber."

"If you can just wait until G-ma is out of surgery, I'll go with you," Sidney informed him.

"I suppose I really should wait with you," Greyson replied with a soft sigh. "Did you call your parents?"

"No, not yet," Sidney reported. "I don't see a reason to ruin their vacation just yet. If she's okay--"

"She will be," Greyson replied while affectionately placing his hand on her shoulder. "She's a tough broad."

"Considering she shot one of the intruders, I guess she is," Sidney replied. "Tougher than I thought."

"I'm guessing that new boyfriend of hers is a keeper," Greyson remarked. "Despite being stabbed, he just kept asking about her. I'm glad he's in stable condition."

Another twenty minutes passed before a doctor appeared and approached them. Sidney and Greyson eagerly met the doctor halfway.

"Your grandmother is in the recovery room," the doctor informed her, then smiled. "She's going to be okay. That's one tough lady."

"Is she awake?" Sidney asked. "Can I see her?"

"You can, but keep it short," the doctor insisted. "We'll be moving her to the ICU in an hour or so, then you'll be able to visit longer."

"Thank you, doctor."

§

Sidney approached the surgery recovery room and heard her grandmother's voice before she even reached the doorway.

"You don't have to wait on me," Helena announced. "I can take care of myself."

"You just came out of surgery," the nurse informed her. "You're supposed to be resting."

"I'll rest when I'm dead," Helena remarked.

Sidney entered the recovery room and saw her grandmother partially elevated in her bed with a cup of ice chips in front of her. When she saw Sidney, her eyes lit up.

"Sidney," she cried out and motioned her to her bedside. "I'm so glad to see you!"

Sidney approached, holding back tears, and gently hugged her grandmother.

"You need to get me out of here," Helena insisted, then turned confrontational. "I can't be around all these sick people. Tell them I can take care of myself."

"I'm afraid you have to stay," Sidney insisted.

Helena frowned in disapproval. "You're just as bad as those others."

"I can't stay long," Sidney insisted. "The doctor said I can come back after they move you to a room."

"Well, at least he's cute," Helena muttered before her eyes suddenly lit up, meeting Sidney's gaze. "He's single too."

"Please, G-ma, don't start," Sidney groaned, then leaned on the bed railing. "Did they tell you Jerry's recovering nicely?"

"They did," Helena replied. "Think they'd put us in a room together? I don't want to be around strange, sick people."

"You can ask," Sidney informed her, then turned concerned. "Do you remember anything that happened?"

"Every insane moment," Helena remarked dramatically. "I told the sheriff everything when he stopped by before I went into surgery."

"You said there were two intruders," Sidney remarked. "You didn't see who they were, did you?"

"No, they were wearing masks," Helena insisted. "Silly boys. Bringing knives to a gunfight." Her look turned serious. "I shot one of them. He was wearing black, so it was hard to tell where I hit him, but I think I got him in the shoulder."

Sidney was slightly baffled by her G-ma's comment. "Where did you get the gun?" she asked. "I thought you got rid of all Grandpa's guns."

Helena gasped slightly, placing her hand over her mouth like a child caught in a lie. That's when Sidney realized they must have given her grandmother the good painkillers.

"I may have kept one or two," Helena reported, then looked Sidney dead in the eyes and whispered. "You know, ***rapists***." Her eyes widened dramatically, looking stunned. "That .357 slug tore right through him." She shook her head with embarrassment. "I thought hollow-points were supposed to mushroom. Ruined my wall. Did you see the size of that spatter?"

"Actually, I did," Sidney muttered while grimacing.

"There were two men," Helena again reported. "I'm guessing roughly six foot each. Not lean like Greyson or Leon. Broad, like Miller."

"Can you think of anything else that might help?" Sidney asked. "Did they say anything?"

"No," Helena replied and shook her head, then suddenly came back to life. "But the other one, the one that stabbed me, he wore Old Spice deodorant."

"I'm not sure how helpful that is," Sidney remarked.

"How many men wear that particular deodorant?" Helena demanded while glaring at her. "He absolutely reeked of it! Smelled that mother fucker a mile away."

"I somehow doubt that's going to help the sheriff's investigation," Sidney informed her, then eyed the IV drip. "Since when do you curse like a sailor? What drugs are they giving you?"

"Jerry's a bad influence," Helena informed her without missing a beat. "He might look like a Muppet, but he's a stud in bed."

Sidney eyed her G-ma with some surprise, then managed a tiny, awkward smile. "Thanks for sharing that."

Chapter 35

Sidney's pickup truck headed down the long driveway to Amber's farmhouse a little after six o'clock in the morning. As Sidney and Greyson pulled up to the front of the house, they could see both Amber and Jackson's vehicles parked out front.

Sidney shot a quick look at Greyson. "She's still not answering her texts?"

"No," Greyson replied, seeming to feel the same sense of dread. "I get that she may have turned off her cell phone when she went to bed, but if they're home, why isn't anyone answering the house phone?"

Sidney threw the truck into park and just about dived out the driver's side door. Greyson hurried after her, now concerned.

"Whoa, whoa," he announced softly while cutting off her path to the porch. "Maybe we don't bust inside halfcocked here. We don't know what's happened."

"I've got that covered," Sidney announced and pulled one of her grandpa's semiautomatics from the back of her pants.

Greyson eyed the weapon and stepped out of her way. "You're scary, Sidney."

Sidney hurried onto the porch, opened the screen door, and knocked firmly on the exterior door. When there was no response, she tried the doorknob. The house was unlocked.

"Oh, that's not good," Greyson muttered as Sidney opened the door.

They entered the neat and tidy kitchen. Perhaps it was a little too tidy. There was a clean plate with utensils on the table, which suggested someone was about to eat breakfast, but there was nothing on the stove. There was a full pot of coffee within the coffeemaker and a clean mug set just before it. Sidney peered into the sink, then gave a firm nod, directing Greyson's attention to the dirty frying pan that once held eggs and hadn't even been rinsed. Greyson didn't understand and shrugged while shaking his head. Sidney then lifted the lid on the garbage can and peered inside. She immediately frowned. There was a perfectly good omelet in the trash. Greyson strained to look into the garbage can as well. He was now equally alarmed. Sidney nodded to the kitchen door.

"Jackson keeps a baseball bat behind the door in the umbrella holder," Sidney whispered.

Greyson hurried for the door, pushed it shut, and grabbed the baseball bat. He held the bat to his shoulder and gripped the handle while cautiously following Sidney.

"This house is huge," Greyson whispered. "What if they're injured like G-ma? What if they're dying?"

Sidney held her breath a moment, looked at him, and nodded. "Okay."

Greyson approached the stairs, standing to the side, while Sidney peered into the living room.

"Amber!" Greyson called up the stairs. "It's Greyson!"

There was no response. Sidney and Greyson exchanged concerned looks across the kitchen.

"They're not in the living room," Sidney remarked, then nodded to the stairs. "Let's check their rooms."

Greyson's text dinged, startling both of them. He swiftly removed his phone and looked at the screen. His expression turned confused.

"What is it?" Sidney asked.

"It's from Amber," Greyson informed Sidney, then met her gaze. "She said she and Jackson had to leave town for a family emergency."

"Family emergency?" Sidney asked, slightly bewildered, and then squinted. "What family? And both their cars are still here."

Greyson ignored Sidney's questions and immediately texted Amber back. "Are you okay?"

The response immediately came back. "I'm fine."

Sidney fidgeted slightly while releasing a tense breath. "How do we know someone doesn't have her cell phone?" she asked. "Maybe it's not even her."

Greyson glared at Sidney. "Do you have to go there?" he demanded. "You're freaking me out." He shook his head and texted back. "Call me."

Amber immediately texted back. "Can't right now. Will try later."

Greyson groaned and eyed Sidney. "Great," he scoffed. "Now, I'm really freaking out."

"Let's check the garage," Sidney insisted. "Jackson has his collection of muscle cars out there. Maybe they took one of them."

"On a family emergency?"

"Just humor me," Sidney groaned as she grabbed a set of keys from the pegboard near the kitchen door.

§

Sidney unlocked the smaller garage door with the key she took from the kitchen and quietly entered the dark building. She flipped the first switch, lighting only one bay.

Greyson followed her into the garage and looked around at the many vintage muscle cars in varying stages of restoration. None of them were missing.

"That can't be good," Greyson muttered while nervously raking his fingers through his hair. "It looks like they're all here."

Sidney then noticed the large empty spot beyond the door leading into the hangar, and her heart sank.

"What is it?" Greyson asked.

Sidney frowned and shook her head. "There was a small plane back there," she informed him.

Greyson's eyes widened as he stared at her. "They went by plane?"

"It sure looks that way," Sidney muttered, then removed her cell phone. Greyson looked over her shoulder as she sent a text to Jackson that read, "G-ma was attacked and stabbed a few hours ago. Call me. Now!"

Greyson eyed her, then her phone several times. "Did you honestly think that would--?"

Sidney's phone rang, and she answered it immediately. "Jackson," she gasped into the phone. "Are you guys okay?"

"We're fine," Jackson announced over the phone. "We'll be back in a day or two." There was a brief pause. "What happened to your grandmother?"

"Two intruders broke into her house and tried to kill her and her guy friend," Sidney informed him while shifting uncomfortably.

"Is she okay?" Jackson pressed.

"Yes, they're going to be fine," Sidney reported. "She shot one of the men, which is probably the only reason she survived. Both intruders got away, but one of them was definitely injured."

"Are you at the hospital?" Jackson asked.

"No, Greyson and I are at your house," she informed him.

"What are you doing there?" he practically demanded, which instantly irritated her.

"Standing in your garage looking for you and Amber," she huffed in response. "Staring at the spot that was once occupied by a small plane."

"Maybe you should stay with Greyson at his apartment for a few days while your grandmother is recovering," Jackson informed her. "It might be safer there. Amber and I will be back by then."

"I'll do that," Sidney retorted curtly. "In a time of emergency and crisis, he's the only one I can really count on anyway. Sorry to disturb you during your ***family*** emergency."

As Sidney disconnected the call, she saw the stunned look on Greyson's face. "I guess that ends that relationship," he remarked.

"What relationship?" Sidney demanded as her anger continued to spike. "I kissed the guy a few times, that's all. A relationship requires respect, trust, and commitment. He lived here for years, and I still don't know anything about him. Never mentioned any family, but he suddenly has a family emergency after you find out he's stalking the two of you in Texas." Her anger continued to rise. "Emergency, my ass! He's just trying to keep you away from Amber." She shook her head. "He's deranged and maybe even a little dangerous. Meanwhile, my grandmother was almost butchered last night, and he pawns off my safety onto you." Sidney was now fuming. "Where's my goddamned white knight? I'm so close to losing it, and I have no one to talk me off the ledge."

"Well, you technically have me," Greyson reminded her, then offered a tiny smile and pulled her into his arms.

Sidney resisted his hold, but he refused to release her. She held back her sobs and finally clung to her friend.

"You're too good for him, Sidney," Greyson gently announced while comforting her. "He doesn't deserve you."

She finally pulled away and wiped a stray tear from her cheek. "Can I stay with you tonight?" Sidney asked. "I don't want to be alone."

"Of course you can stay with me," Greyson replied warmly. "You're welcome to stay anytime."

"Thanks," Sidney whispered, then sniffed and looked around. "Let's get the hell out of here."

Greyson reclaimed his baseball bat and placed it against his shoulder. "FYI," he announced. "I'm keeping this. I'll protect you."

"You don't need that," Sidney muttered, not wanting any reminders of Jackson. "I have about fifty handguns and rifles in my grandpa's cabinet in the workshop office."

"Then let's go arm ourselves to the teeth," Greyson teased while grinning.

Sidney finally managed a smile and a tiny laugh. "Maybe we should just stay at my house," she remarked. "We won't have to lug the guns to your apartment."

"Even better," Greyson remarked. "Your dad has all the good television channels."

Chapter 36

After visiting her grandmother in the ICU later that morning and discovering she could share a room with her gentleman friend, Sidney felt better. Helena was in fine spirits, especially since she had Jerry recovering by her side. Both were still hooked up to IVs and monitors, but emotionally, they were feeling good. Companionship and the good drugs. They'd probably both be in the hospital for a couple of days, recovering from their ordeal, which would keep them safe. Helena was happy to see Greyson and was pleased that he was staying with Sidney so she wouldn't be alone. After visiting hours ended around eight o'clock that evening, Sidney and Greyson returned to Sidney's house and locked themselves in for the night. They did a sweep of the house, making sure doors and windows were locked, and that there were no monsters under the beds or in the closets. They were about to enjoy their pizza and a movie when Sidney's cell phone rang. She saw the unfamiliar number and answered it.

"Hello?"

"Sidney, it's Harris," came the somewhat familiar male voice.

"Oh, Harris," Sidney announced, noticing the look Greyson gave her. "What a pleasant surprise."

"I just wanted to make sure you got home okay," Harris informed her. "Once you start taking the private plane, I can escort you home properly."

"Wow," Sidney remarked, then eyed Greyson. "That's possibly the nicest thing I've heard in a while. How gentlemanly of you."

"Well, I wouldn't go that far," Harris replied from the other end. "I just really enjoyed spending time with you last night, and I look forward to spending more time with you in the future."

"You don't know how much I needed to hear that," Sidney announced while choking back her urge to cry. "That's sweet of you."

"Sidney, is everything okay?" Harris asked somewhat firmly. "You don't sound right."

"I'm sorry," she announced while holding back her tears. "Someone tried to kill my grandmother last night, and she's lucky to be alive." She wiped her tears and sniffed. "I'm just so upset right now."

"Sidney, I'm so sorry for what you've been through," Harris announced in a gentle, comforting tone. "Is there anyone with you?"

"My friend is here with me," she remarked and glanced at Greyson alongside her as he handed her a tissue.

Greyson mouthed the word, "Harris?"

"I can have the private jet prepped in less than an hour," Harris insisted. "An hour flight. I can be there in about three hours."

"You'd actually drop everything and fly out here for me?" Sidney asked with some surprise.

"I want to be there for you, Sidney," Harris replied warmly. "And I'm sure Blain would be happy that I'm looking after you."

"That is so sweet," Sidney announced, feeling countless emotions at the offer. "As much as I appreciate the offer, though, it's not necessary. Greyson is staying with me tonight, and I'm probably going to be spending a lot of time at the hospital tomorrow. I don't want you going to all that trouble--"

"It's no trouble, Sidney," Harris insisted.

"The offer is enough," she replied. "I appreciate it."

After a few warm sentiments, Sidney said goodnight and disconnected the call. Greyson continued staring at her with his mouth hanging open.

"Who the hell is Harris?" he practically demanded. "And did he just offer to come stay with you?"

"He's just some guy I met yesterday," Sidney informed her friend and couldn't help feeling herself blush.

"A guy you just met yesterday wants to run out here and look after you?" Greyson remarked and shook his head. "He wants to get in your pants."

"Greyson," she scolded. "It's not like that."

"Oh, sure it isn't," he muttered. "Complete strangers always rush to the aid of an emotional woman for selfless reasons." He clucked his tongue, disgraced. "With how naive and innocent you are, how are you still a virgin?"

"You know, there are nice guys out there, Greyson."

"Yeah, right," he scoffed. "Name one."

"You."

Greyson sneered and shook his head. "You really don't play fair."

§

It was just before midnight when Greyson and Sidney decided to head to bed. Greyson would stay in the spare bedroom, which was right next door to Sidney's room. As they were about to head up the stairs, Greyson's cell phone rang. He removed it from his pocket and saw

Amber's name on the caller ID. He groaned with relief and pressed the green button.

"Amber," he announced into the phone, catching Sidney's attention. "Where are you? Are you okay?" There was a pause as she responded. "I'm so relieved. I'm glad you called. I was so worried."

Greyson entered the kitchen and paced while talking on his cell phone. Sidney frowned and leaned against the staircase railing. Now, she needed to know what Amber had to say. While she waited for her friend, her cell phone rang as well. She recognized the number as Harris's. She answered the phone and smiled, despite the fact that he couldn't see it.

"Harris," she announced. "Hey. I didn't think you'd be up this late."

"Sorry to call you so late."

"It's okay," she replied. "I wasn't in bed yet."

"I told Blain what happened with your grandmother," Harris informed her. "Long story short. We just landed at the airport, half an hour from your town."

"You did?" she asked, surprised, as her eyes welled with tears again. "I can't believe the two of you did that for me. That's so sweet of you."

"Well, good intentions only go so far," Harris informed her. "The car rental counter is closed for the night. Option number one. We could take a taxi to your house, but we probably wouldn't get there until almost one in the morning. Option number two would be to get a room here at the airport and rent a car in the morning."

"Option two would be easiest," Sidney informed him. "Don't go out of your way anymore tonight. I was going to bed anyway. Greyson's here. He's got my back."

"As long as you're certain," Harris replied.

"Yes, and thank you very much, Harris," she announced. "Goodnight."

"Goodnight, Sidney."

Sidney disconnected the call and could hear Greyson still talking on the phone with Amber. She couldn't believe how much two men she barely knew cared about her. She wasn't even sure what she saw in Jackson to begin with. While waiting for Greyson to finish his call, her phone dinged with a new text message. She checked the message. To her surprise, it was from Jackson.

It simply read, "Are you still up?"

Sidney considered ignoring it. She didn't need to get into another 'debate' with Jackson, especially when all he did was deflect her questions and concerns. She finally gave in and responded.

"Still up; still mad."

Jackson texted back, "Can we talk?"

She groaned in frustration, then replied, "Not by text. Call me."

He immediately responded. "Would prefer face-to-face."

Sidney typed back, "There's an app for that, too."

Jackson responded, "I'm at the kitchen door."

She reacted to the text, looking at the kitchen door, and saw a faint outline of someone outside. Sidney cocked her head, hesitated, and approached the kitchen door, catching Greyson's attention. Sidney pulled back the small curtain and saw Jackson standing on the porch staring back at her. Sidney drew a sharp breath as her heart skipped a beat, then unlocked and opened the door.

"You came back," she remarked, somewhat surprised to see him.

"You were pretty mad," Jackson reminded her. "I needed to fix things with you or live with that regret, and I'm already overloaded with regret."

Sidney stepped away from the door, allowing Jackson to enter. Her eyes followed him as her heart pounded in response. She couldn't believe how much she missed him and regretted her harsh words with him, whether she was right or not. What had gotten into her? It then dawned on her as she took in a sweeping eyeful of Jackson. She loved him. Greyson eyed Jackson, now standing in the kitchen, then returned to his phone conversation with Amber.

"Why does your uncle get to be here and not you?" Greyson asked in a stern tone. When he heard the response, his expression suddenly changed. "I'll be right there." Greyson disconnected his call and pointed to Jackson. "The two of you need to work this out. I'm going to Amber's house."

Both watched Greyson slip out the kitchen door, then returned their attention to each other. Once the initial rush of lust and desire wore off, she remembered why she was mad in the first place.

"You just don't get it, Jackson," Sidney informed him. "I shouldn't have to guilt you into coming here."

"You didn't," he insisted, then fidgeted while raking his fingers through his hair. "I know I seem unstable at times, emotionally repressed, whatever. Pick one." He groaned and leaned against the counter. "***I*** was the family emergency." Jackson stared at her a moment while she waited for him to finish his thought. "After Greyson dropped off Amber around four in the morning, I was driving out to see you, hoping to smooth over the mess I had made, when I came across an abandoned car on the back road. When I saw someone slouched in the passenger seat, I stopped." Jackson held his breath a moment. "The driver was dead. He'd been shot in the chest."

Sidney's expression immediately dropped as she swiftly put it together. "The man who attacked my grandmother?" she gasped.

"Possibly," Jackson replied, then shifted. "It would seem he bled out."

"But what about the second man?"

"He probably took off," Jackson informed her.

"But you didn't even know what had happened to my grandmother when you found him," Sidney then remarked. "Why wouldn't you simply call the sheriff?"

"Because I recognized the dead man, Sidney," Jackson informed her, appearing tense. "I'm certain he was looking for me."

"Looking for you?" Sidney just about gasped, attempting to understand. "Why would he be looking for you?"

"Because there are people who want to kill me," he informed her with a low groan. "And they'll kill anyone that gets in their way."

"But why do these people want to kill you?" Sidney asked.

She wondered if he was making the entire thing up to gain her sympathy. He wouldn't do that. Would he? And what did any of that have to do with the guy attacking her grandmother?

"Let's just say I rubbed some pretty nasty people the wrong way," Jackson remarked. "Amber and I have been hiding from them for a long time. I thought we were safe here, but I'm still afraid to let her out of my sight. I don't know what they'll do to her to get to me." He groaned softly and shook his head. "I didn't know what happened to your grandmother when Amber and I took off, I swear, but I don't see how it could be related to us. She's too far removed from Amber and me."

Sidney considered everything he'd told her, and her concern was growing. "You shouldn't have come back," she insisted, then groaned. "You could have just explained this to me over the phone." She shook her head, now feeling foolish. "I got mad because I thought you were just trying to keep Amber away from Greyson. I didn't think it was an actual life or death situation."

"Greyson humping my niece is the least of my worries right now," he insisted. "We need to hide out for a while and monitor the situation from a safe distance. If no one else comes looking for me, then maybe that man being here was just a really bizarre coincidence, but Amber and I have to leave first thing tomorrow morning." He stared into her eyes for a long moment. "I don't want to leave you, Sidney, but I can't stay either. I could be putting you in danger just by being here."

"What if I'm already in danger? Maybe I should go with you," Sidney announced, then immediately backpedaled on the comment. "I mean, Amber's my best friend. I should be with her."

"What about your grandmother?" Jackson reminded her. "With your parents away for two weeks, you can't just leave her alone."

Sidney fidgeted while staring into Jackson's eyes. "I'm afraid if you leave, I'll never see you again."

When Jackson pulled her into his arms and held her tightly against him, Sidney clung to him, burying her head into his chest. She couldn't believe how strong her feelings were for him. All those wasted years, and now she felt as if she was losing him forever. It just didn't seem fair.

"I already made a mess of my life as well as Amber's," he whispered into the top of her head. "I couldn't live with myself if I ruined your life as well." Jackson hesitated a moment. "Honestly, it'd be better for you if I didn't come back."

Sidney abruptly pulled away and eyed him. "Just because something is less complicated, that doesn't automatically make it better," she informed him.

"Being hunted and killed isn't a minor complication," Jackson reminded her. He groaned and ran his fingers through his hair and seemed to consider his options. "Greyson is already heading back to my place. I don't want you staying here alone. You should stay with us tonight. Greyson can bring you home tomorrow morning."

Sidney smiled gently and nodded. "That's a reasonable compromise; for now."

Chapter 37

It was a little past midnight when Jackson's truck pulled up to his farmhouse. The porch light and the kitchen light were on, brightening the area in front of the house. Sidney got out of the passenger side and approached the house with Jackson. He unlocked the door, opened it, and allowed her to enter first. As she stepped into the kitchen, Greyson appeared in the archway with a shotgun aimed at her. Sidney cried out with surprise. Greyson breathed a sigh of relief when he saw it was just Sidney and Jackson.

"Jesus," Sidney gasped, startled by the sight of her friend with the shotgun.

"Sorry," Greyson announced. "Just being cautious."

Amber appeared from behind Greyson and sighed with relief when she saw Sidney. She hurried to her friend and hugged her. When Jackson saw Amber wearing Greyson's shirt that barely covered her buttocks, he frowned his disapproval but didn't comment. Amber pulled back and appeared sympathetic.

"Is G-ma okay?" Amber asked.

"She's recovering," Sidney remarked. "She's tougher than she looks."

"No kidding," Amber muttered, then briefly eyed her uncle. "Did he tell you why we left?"

Sidney nodded. "A little light on the details, but he explained the situation."

"Amber wasn't heavy with details either," Greyson remarked.

"It's better that way," Jackson insisted somewhat dryly as he locked and bolted the door. "The less you know, the better off you'll be." He then turned and looked at Amber. "Five A.M. wake-up call."

"That's in less than five hours," Amber cried out. "I'll be exhausted."

"Fine," Jackson announced. "Six o'clock."

Amber groaned and turned back to the stairs. Greyson managed a tiny smile and backed away from Jackson.

"Look at the time," Greyson announced. "It's late. I should be getting to sleep. You know, in the guest bedroom."

"Yeah, whatever," Jackson scoffed.

Greyson turned and hurried up the kitchen stairs.

Jackson fidgeted slightly as he glanced at Sidney. "You, uh, can make yourself comfortable in the guest bedroom," he announced. "If you'd like."

Sidney knew he didn't actually want her sleeping in the guest bedroom, but she had to give him credit for his politeness.

"I thought you brought me here so I'd be safe," Sidney remarked while raising a skeptical brow. "I'd be safer in your room, wouldn't I?"

He hid his tiny smile and continued with the charade. "It'd be safer, yes," Jackson replied. "I just wasn't sure if you'd already had enough of me for one day. Or maybe a lifetime."

"No, not yet," she remarked.

Jackson chuckled softly and extended his hand to her. Sidney placed her hand in his and allowed him to escort her to the kitchen stairs.

§

Upon entering his bedroom, Jackson shut the door and began his usual nightly ritual, almost forgetting Sidney was there. He removed his shirt, then hesitated and looked back at her, and gently cleared his throat.

"You left your overnight bag here the other day," Jackson informed her, then nodded to the bag that now occupied the chair in his room, not far from his bed.

Sidney found it interesting that he had placed her overnight bag in his room rather than the guest room.

"Did you need something to sleep in?" Jackson asked as he tossed his button shirt onto the wooden chest at the foot of the bed.

Sidney hesitated, distracted by his broad, bare chest with just the right amount of chest hair. She didn't want to stare, but she hadn't actually ***seen*** him bare-chested before. The night she was drunk, they were both under the covers, and at the campsite, they were in the sleeping bag in the bed of his truck. Sidney avoided looking at him and then snatched his discarded shirt.

"This will do," she replied, then indicated the bedroom door. "I'll, uh, just change in the bathroom."

When Sidney returned to Jackson's bedroom only moments later, Jackson was sitting on the bed in a pair of old, frumpy shorts. She understood that they didn't need things to be any more awkward than they already were, and she had to give him credit for remaining polite. Sidney wasn't sure why she was feeling so insecure at that moment. Perhaps it was being in his room with him after everything that had happened. Or it might have been because she was wearing his shirt as a nightshirt. Jackson's shirt reached partway down her thighs, and she had to roll the sleeves up to her elbows, since they would have been very long on her. She pushed her anxiety aside and shut the door behind her, then hesitated.

"Do you lock the door?"

He smiled and chuckled. "If I did, you never would have crawled into my bed last week."

Sidney smiled, somewhat embarrassed by the truthfulness of his statement, and subconsciously folded her arms across her chest, rubbing them slightly. Jackson noticed and pulled the covers back for her.

"Is it chilly tonight?" he asked. "I hadn't noticed."

Sidney climbed into bed alongside him and pulled the covers over her legs for added warmth. "No, it's just a little ***awkward***," she timidly replied. "It seems as if so much has changed in the last week." She sighed softly and drifted into her own thoughts. "Actually, everything has changed. I feel like a stranger in my own life."

Sidney finally looked at him, where he sat above the covers. Her eyes instantly fell upon the tattoo on his right upper arm. The six- to eight-inch tattoo was a Colt .45 semiautomatic pistol fitted with a silencer, featuring a skull and angel wings.

"You have a tattoo?" she asked before being able to stop her mouth.

All those years, and she never knew that. She actually thought Amber was kidding when she commented on his tattoos. Jackson subconsciously placed his hand over the tattoo and fidgeted slightly.

"Oh, yeah," he replied and managed a tiny smile. "I've had that one for years." Jackson then gently cleared his throat. "Among others." He tensed slightly while studying her. "Does it bother you?"

"No," Sidney replied, then offered a tiny, insecure smile. "It's just, well, I've never actually ***seen*** you without your shirt on before."

"Back at you," Jackson announced, then grinned somewhat slyly.

Sidney felt her cheeks flush, and she hid her smile. "You're bad," she informed him.

"Well, you're not wrong," he replied with a defeated sigh. "Part of the reason why I'm on a hit list." He then turned off his bedside light.

As he slid under the covers, Sidney did the same and immediately nestled against him. Jackson placed his arm around her and held her against his chest as she clung to him almost insecurely. He nuzzled her hair with his cheek, kissed the top of her head, and then groaned softly.

"I love you, Sidney," he whispered.

Sidney stiffened when she heard his words, then gently caressed his chest. "I love you too," she whispered back. She hesitated only a moment, then kissed his chest near where her head rested. "Will you make love to me?"

It was Jackson's turn to tense. His arms instinctively tightened around her, and he might have stopped breathing for a moment. He finally groaned softly.

"I can't," he just about whimpered into her hair, causing her heart to sink. "I can't take your virginity and then leave in the morning. It wouldn't be right."

"But what if something happens to you?" she asked. "I don't want that regret."

"You'll meet someone else," Jackson gently insisted while clinging to her. "You deserve someone better anyway."

"I don't want anyone else," she replied firmly with conviction.

"When I can promise you a future," he announced, "that's when I'll make love to you."

Sidney was disappointed and a little frustrated. It was the first time she'd ever wanted a man, and somehow, he was able to turn her down. He was right, though. When he left in the morning, it would tear her apart. If she gave herself to him, his leaving would hurt even more. She sank into her own thoughts for a moment and lightly strummed her fingers on his chest.

"I had a thought," she then remarked.

"No," Jackson replied almost firmly.

"Hear me out," she insisted.

"Sidney, no."

"As long as I keep my underwear on--"

Jackson's hand covered hers, and he gently caressed her lower arm. "Okay, I'm listening," he responded.

"Everything else comes off, and we can work around that," she remarked.

Jackson suddenly groaned and just about tackled her to the bed. She let out a tiny, startled scream, then giggled softly.

Chapter 38

Jackson held Sidney in his arms as the rising sun poked through the part in his bedroom curtains. He sighed contentedly and kissed the top of her head.

"Did you get any sleep?" Jackson asked while grinning.

"No, but I don't mind," she replied while caressing his side.

He groaned softly with embarrassment. "I can't imagine what you must think of me," Jackson remarked. "I acted like a horny teenager that had never seen a pair of breasts before."

Sidney giggled at the comment, knowing it was sort of true. "I kind of liked that," she announced.

"You just kept winding me up," he informed her.

"I couldn't help it," Sidney announced, then lifted her head and met his gaze while grinning. "Who would've thought a man's manly parts would be so much fun to play with?"

"Every man ever born," Jackson remarked, then chuckled warmly. "Of course, it's always better when you can share your toys." He kissed her warmly, then looked at the bedside clock and groaned. "I have just enough time to grab a quick shower and then prep the plane."

As Jackson sat up in bed, Sidney clutched the sheets to her naked upper body and smiled somewhat deviously.

"Would you like some company in the shower?" she practically cooed.

Jackson looked at her and groaned, a pleased smile on his face. "I'd love to say 'yes,' but then that quick shower turns into a marathon shower," he informed her. "And if you're completely naked, the temptation would be way too high."

Sidney groaned and collapsed onto the bed in an unintended sexy pose. "If that's how you feel--"

Jackson just about pounced on top of her, pinning her to the bed, and stared into her eyes.

"It's not how I feel," he informed her while smiling almost sadly. "It's just the way things need to be right now." He kissed her quickly but passionately before once again meeting her gaze. "You get a little sleep. I'll wake you before we leave."

Sidney reluctantly nodded. He kissed her again and sprang from the bed. She nuzzled the pillow and, surprisingly, fell asleep almost instantly. She woke what seemed like only minutes later to the bedroom door opening loudly. Sidney just about flew up in bed with a gasp as Jackson stormed into the room, enraged.

"She's gone," he huffed and quickly changed out of the old clothes he'd worn to the bathroom and into clean ones.

"What?" Sidney asked with surprise and some confusion while holding the sheet to her partially naked body. "Amber? How?"

Jackson handed her the note, then finished dressing. Sidney read the note Amber had left for her uncle. Amber and Greyson apparently took off in the middle of the night. His niece didn't want to go into hiding without Greyson, and he refused to leave her. Amber ended the note by wishing her uncle happiness. If he didn't have to look out for her safety, he could hide out on the farm and not have to leave. In a week or two, when it was safe, she'd return home. Jackson tossed Sidney her cell phone.

"Call those dimwitted friends of yours," he huffed. "Maybe they'll actually pick up if they see your name. I'm going to check Greyson's apartment first. I'm sure he'd want to pack some things and grab some cash. Maybe I can catch them there."

"I don't have my car," she reminded him.

"I'm sure they took Greyson's truck," he informed her. "You can take Amber's car back to your place. Let me know if you hear from them." Jackson then hesitated and approached her on the bed. "I'm sorry, I'm running out like this. I didn't want this to happen, Sidney. That damned girl will be the death of me." He kissed Sidney quickly on the lips and met her gaze. "I promise I won't leave without stopping at your place first."

"I need to go to the hospital and visit G-ma," Sidney reminded him, "but I don't have to stay long. Let me know what you want me to do."

"I'll meet you at your house at noon," Jackson replied. "If neither of us has found her, we'll need to work on a contingency plan."

Sidney nodded.

§

Sidney still hadn't heard from Jackson, Amber, or Greyson by the time she'd changed and showered at her own house. She didn't know what her friends were thinking, taking off like that on their own. She doubted they had any sort of plan. Where did they honestly think they were going to go where no one would find them? Sidney suddenly stopped.

"No," she remarked, then considered her thought only a moment longer. "Those sons-of-bitches." Sidney swiftly removed her cell phone and pressed Jackson's number.

Jackson immediately answered his phone. "Sidney," he announced. "Did you hear from them?"

"No," Sidney replied while grabbing her truck keys, "but I think I know where they went." She heard someone knocking on her front door. "There's someone at the door. I'll meet you at your place in ten minutes."

Sidney disconnected the phone before Jackson could respond, then hurried to the front door and unlocked it. When she opened the door, she was moderately surprised to see Blain and Harris on the porch. Blain held a bouquet of expensive flowers.

"Hey, Sidney," Blain announced while smiling. "I left a couple of messages this morning and got worried when you didn't call back." He extended the flowers to her. "These are for your grandmother. You can tell her they're from you."

Sidney stared at Blain and Harris for a long moment as her mind reeled. She'd completely forgotten about them. She put on her best smile and accepted the flowers.

"That's very sweet of you," Sidney announced, then stepped onto the porch with them. "I was just on my way to the hospital. I, uh, overslept and was running late. I didn't even check my messages since last night." She locked and shut the door behind her.

"Understandable," Blain replied while maintaining his smile. "Harris and I are here for you."

Harris smiled warmly, then moved in and gave her a warm kiss on the cheek. As he pulled back, she returned the smile and stared at the handsome man. They had an amazing date, and he was undoubtedly a wonderful man, but all she could think about was Jackson. There was no doubt that Jackson was the only man for her.

"Is there anything we can do to help?" Harris asked. "Anything at all."

"Not that I can think of," Sidney replied, since all she could think about was finding Amber and Greyson before they did anything stupid. She glanced at both men. "Maybe we could meet up later for lunch or something."

"That would be terrific," Blain replied, then hesitated. "I know you're in a hurry, but I wanted to talk to you for just a moment."

"Okay," Sidney replied and indicated the porch furniture.

When Blain took a seat on the porch swing, Sidney joined him, giving him her full attention despite feeling rushed. Blain removed a folded piece of paper from his pocket and handed it to her.

"I had them put a rush on it," he informed her as his smile brightened. "They faxed it to the hotel last night."

Sidney accepted the paper. Before she could even look at it, Blain continued.

"The paternity test came back a positive match," he informed her cheerfully. "You're my daughter."

Although she was slightly shocked by the news, she somehow knew it would be the case. Sidney glanced at the paper, then looked back at Blain and smiled.

"I kind of suspected I was," Sidney replied somewhat timidly. "I hope you understand that I'm going to need some time before I talk to my mother about, you know, this."

"Absolutely," Blain replied cheerfully. "Take all the time you need." He placed his hand on hers in an insecure way. "Just as long as we can spend some time together in the meantime. You know, get to know each other."

Sidney nodded as her mind raced. "Yes, I'd like that," she replied. "After my grandmother gets out of the hospital and can look after herself, I'll gladly visit for a weekend."

"I'm looking forward to that," Blain replied.

Although Blain appeared pleased, Harris was overly enthusiastic. Sidney immediately saw her next conflict. It was only one date and one little, one-sided kiss. He'd understand, wouldn't he? She'd think about that later.

Sidney returned the paper to Blain and stood. Blain stood as well.

"I should get to the hospital," Sidney announced. "There's a restaurant in town. We could meet there at noon for lunch."

"We'll be there," Blain replied, then hesitated and opened his arms to her.

Sidney was a little apprehensive, but she moved in and hugged him. As she walked past Blain, Harris offered his hand to her.

"I'll walk you to your car," Harris announced.

Sidney felt her heart pounding with the awkwardness of what she was feeling, but she accepted his hand and let him escort her down the porch steps and to her truck. He was so polite and suave, but she couldn't get her mind off Jackson. Anything she thought she'd felt for Harris seemed to vanish the moment she saw Jackson on her back porch last night. Getting into her truck, Sidney was relieved to get away from her house. Blain and Harris would be a complicated issue for another day. Right now, she needed to meet up with Jackson and find her friends. Although she headed in the direction of town and the hospital, Sidney eventually turned around and headed on a back road that would take her to Jackson's farmhouse.

Chapter 39

Sidney sat in the front passenger seat of Jackson's truck and talked with her grandmother on her cell phone while Jackson drove along the back road.

"Are you sure you're okay?" Sidney asked. "You're okay with me stopping by later this afternoon." There was a pause. "I'm glad you're feeling better. I'll talk to you later. Bye."

Sidney disconnected her phone and glanced at Jackson, who cast looks at her from behind the wheel, silently questioning her grandmother's condition.

"She said the food sucks, but she's enjoying Jerry's company," Sidney informed him, then smirked. "I guess he's a keeper."

"Why do you suppose she kept her budding romance a secret?" Jackson asked.

"She probably didn't want anyone butting into her relationship," Sidney replied. "You know, the way she gets involved in everyone else's."

Jackson snickered softly, only a moment before his expression suddenly turned serious. "Do you think you'll tell anyone about us?" he asked.

"I'll make you a deal," Sidney announced. "You come back from this in one piece, and I'll tell everyone about us."

He offered a tiny, pleased smile. "Deal."

Both looked out the windshield, returning their attention to where they were going as they drove down the long, grown-over roadway. When Henry's cabin in the woods came into view, both could see the front bumper of Greyson's truck.

Jackson shook his head. "You missed your calling as a detective," he informed Sidney.

"For Greyson, this is the perfect hiding place," Sidney informed him. "He enjoys roughing it, and the property is secluded."

"Not exactly roughing it," Jackson insisted.

As Jackson's truck pulled up alongside Greyson's, Sidney stared out the windshield with a somewhat startled look on her face. The entire exterior of the cabin had been renovated, including refinishing the log walls, new plank flooring on the entire porch, new railings, new steps, and replacement storm windows. What stuck out most was the addition to the second floor, expanding the single bedroom into two. Sidney got out of the truck and continued to stare at what used to be a rundown little cabin. Both eyed the large red bow on the front door as they walked onto the porch.

"What in the world--?" Sidney gasped.

The door was suddenly thrown open to reveal Greyson holding Jackson's shotgun. He saw them and groaned while lowering the weapon.

"How did you find us?" Greyson demanded as Amber peered over his shoulder.

"I just put myself in your shoes, so it wasn't that difficult," Sidney informed him.

"You two," Jackson snarled while pointing an angry finger at them. "Deep shit."

"Didn't you get my note?" Amber announced, as if that would make everything better.

"Yes, very helpful," Jackson scoffed.

"I thought it was," Amber insisted. "You stay at the farmhouse, and I stay here with Greyson. If neither of us goes to town for a few weeks, no one will ever find us. It's a win-win."

"I can see how that seems like a good idea," Jackson remarked, "but it's reckless and dangerous."

"It ***is*** a good idea," Amber protested.

Jackson forced Amber inside the cabin so they could speak, or quite possibly have another shouting match. Sidney pointed to the bow on the front door.

"What's with the bow?" she asked.

"I don't know," Greyson replied, then invited her inside her own cabin. "It was there when we arrived."

Sidney followed her friend inside and immediately stopped to look around. The entire kitchen had been gutted and was replaced with all-new custom cabinets, granite countertops, a double sink, and new appliances. There was even a dishwasher. The original flooring had been sanded and refinished, keeping the vintage cabin feel, while the old, rickety steps to the second floor were replaced with a new staircase. The old wood-burning stove was cleaned up, but it now sat on a fieldstone pad, and the wall behind it was constructed of light stone rather than old red brick. To complete the cabin, the living room had all-new furniture, including one of Henry's custom rocking chairs, a coffee table, and end tables.

"There's a card on the table," Greyson informed her, then indicated the table. "It has your name on it."

Sidney approached the kitchen table and picked up the card. She opened the sealed envelope and read the birthday card. It read, "Happy Birthday, Sidney. I know this is six months early, but I couldn't wait until your birthday. The cabin, lake, and all the acreage now belong to you. Love always, Grandpa." Sidney stared at the card, then looked around the cabin while Jackson and Amber lightly argued within the kitchen portion.

"That's why he was bringing me up to the cabin for the weekend," Sidney gasped and felt tears welling in her eyes. "He was going to surprise me."

"Some surprise," Greyson announced while nodding his approval. "When my grandfather says he has a surprise for me, it's usually followed by 'pull my finger'."

"He did all of this for me," Sidney remarked and continued to look around. "He may have had his faults, but he was trying to make up for them." She finally glanced at Greyson. "He loved me."

"Was there ever any doubt?" Greyson asked while raising an arrogant brow.

Sidney smiled warmly. "No, I suppose not."

Once they were finished arguing, Jackson approached Sidney and pulled her aside. "She's being annoyingly insistent," he remarked. "How would you feel about Amber and Greyson staying here for a couple of weeks? I can bring them weekly groceries early in the morning."

"You're actually okay leaving the two of them here without your supervision?" Sidney asked with some surprise.

"She's in more danger by running off than staying put," he replied. "Of course, I may want to borrow your boat and anchor it in the middle of the lake the first few nights to keep an eye on her."

"If I say yes," Sidney announced and smiled slyly. "Does that mean you're not leaving?"

He managed a tiny chuckle. "No, I wouldn't be leaving," Jackson replied. "But I also won't leave my farm either. Just for grocery runs."

"But I can stay with you?" she asked.

Jackson considered the question and noted her devious smile. He groaned softly and hid his smile. "Yes, you can stay with me," he replied, then turned stern. "But you can't tell anyone there's anything between us for at least two weeks."

Sidney turned giddy. "I can agree to that," she replied. "I'll just tell everyone I'm going away with my friends for a couple of weeks. Miller and Leon will think I went with Amber and Greyson."

"What about your grandmother?" Jackson then asked, turning concerned.

"I'll send her and Jerry away for some recovery time until my parents get back," she informed him. "A nice, relaxing retreat."

"Are you sure?"

"Yes," Sidney replied happily. "I'm sure."

While Jackson went to share the information with Amber, Sidney was reminded of Blain and her promise to him. As far as Blain needed to know, she could just tell him she was going away with her grandmother for her recovery and that she would visit him in two weeks, when everything had blown over. The plan seemed almost too perfect.

Chapter 40

While on her way to visit G-ma in the hospital that morning, Sidney was concerned with how she'd broach the subject of her grandmother taking a relaxing vacation. The woman could be incredibly stubborn at times. When Sidney entered the hospital room, Jerry was sitting on Helena's bed with her while they did a crossword puzzle together. Both were wearing pajamas and had his-and-hers IV bags and poles on their respective sides of the bed. They were just a little too cute, in Sidney's opinion. And possibly a little too happy for two people who were nearly killed just the other night. They didn't even notice her until she cleared her throat, catching both their attention. Jerry appeared slightly flustered.

"This isn't how it looks," Jerry insisted.

Sidney managed a tiny laugh and shook her head. "It looks like you're doing a crossword puzzle together," she remarked.

"Oh," Jerry replied, then offered a tiny grin. "Then I suppose it is what it looks like." He then shifted looks from Helena to Sidney. "Would the two of you like some privacy?

If so, I could go back to my side of the room and pull the curtain."

"No, that's not necessary," Sidney replied while maintaining her smile. "The nurse at the nurse's station said the two of you are being released tomorrow. In light of what happened, I think it's best if the two of you take a little relaxing getaway while the sheriff conducts his investigation."

"Go where?" Helena asked, lightly cocking her head. "You'd be going too, wouldn't you? We can't leave you at home alone."

"No, it would be better if I stayed at Amber's house," Sidney informed her.

"I can stay at Jerry's house," Helena insisted.

"I'd rather you were a little further removed from all of this," Sidney remarked.

"All of what?" Helena asked. "They found the intruder I'd shot, dead in his car alongside the road. It's only a matter of time before the sheriff connects the dots and figures out who his partner was."

"I agree," Sidney replied. "But until he connects those dots, the second man, the man who actually stabbed both of you, is still at large. I'll even pay for your little two-week relax-cation. Anywhere you want to go."

Helena frowned, then looked at Jerry. "What do you think?"

Jerry grasped her hand, kissed it, and smiled. "I'll go anywhere, as long as I'm with you," he insisted. "Did that sound corny? I think that sounded corny."

Helena smiled and gently patted his face. "You're sweet," she replied, then looked at Sidney. "Okay, we'll take a little trip and spend some time away while we recover. It might be fun."

§

After visiting for an hour with her G-ma in the hospital, Sidney met Blain and Harris for lunch at the only restaurant in town. Despite that Sidney was right on time, Blain and Harris were already seated in the diner. Both men politely stood as she approached and joined them. Harris was quick to pull out her chair for her while maintaining his schoolboy grin. Sidney could feel several prying eyes upon her and her meeting with the two strangers.

"How is your grandmother?" Blain asked with genuine concern.

"She's being released tomorrow morning," Sidney replied, then cast a quick look at Harris and the way he smiled at her. She was already uncomfortable around the handsome man and had to keep reminding herself that it was only one date. She didn't owe him anything. It wasn't as if she were breaking off an engagement. "Considering everything that's happened and the second intruder still on the loose, I'm taking my grandmother away to recover for a couple of weeks."

"I'm sure she appreciates that," Blain announced, not seeming the least bit worried about the interruption in their bonding time. "Maybe you could come up for a weekend once you're back in town."

Sidney immediately smiled and nodded, thankful he seemed to understand. "Yes, I'd like that," she replied. "And I appreciate your understanding."

Blain chuckled and waved her off. "Having lunch with you today is enough to make me happy," he replied. "We have plenty of time to get to know each other."

Naomi approached their table to take their order and, despite how poorly their overnight camping trip had ended, she smiled politely. Maybe a little too politely.

"Hey, Sidney," Naomi announced, then glanced at the two men, immediately taking an interest in Harris. "Who are your friends?"

Sidney knew Naomi was the gossip queen in town. More than hearing it, she loved spreading it. But by the way she was checking out Harris, Naomi seemed less interested in gossip and more interested in the handsome man. Sidney managed a smile as she indicated the two men.

"This is Blain, and that's Harris," Sidney informed her. "Friends from out of town."

Naomi introduced herself, flirted lightly with Harris, and then took their drink order before resuming her work.

"People in this town are so polite," Blain remarked cheerfully.

Sidney snorted a laugh. "And everything you say and do can and will be used against you," she remarked. "Naomi's the town gossip. Be careful what you say within earshot of her."

Blain and Harris chuckled at the comment.

"Small towns," Harris announced and cast a glance around the restaurant to see who was watching. "Gotta love them."

"I got you a little something," Blain informed Sidney and removed a slim velvet box from his pocket. "It seemed a bit premature before the test results came back, but I knew the test would be conclusive."

Blain placed the box on the table in front of her. Sidney stared at the jewelry case for a moment with surprise, then picked it up apprehensively. She opened the box and saw the exquisite, possibly vintage diamond-and-opal tennis bracelet set in white gold. Sidney stared at the expensive bracelet for a moment, then looked back at Blain.

"This is too much," she insisted and shook her head. "I can't accept this."

"Of course you can accept it," Blain informed her. "It's a family heirloom. The family jewelry has been sitting in the safe, collecting dust, for too many years. I'm just glad that I finally have someone to pass it on to."

Sidney studied the hopeful smile on Blain's face and knew she couldn't disappoint him. She couldn't fault him for being wealthy, and it was only natural for him to want to share his wealth and family heirlooms with her, his only living child.

"It's beautiful, Blain," she replied and nodded. "I appreciate it very much, but I want you to know I'm not interested in your money."

"That's very refreshing," Blain replied, then removed the bracelet from the box and indicated for her to hold out her wrist. He attached the bracelet to her wrist and admired it a moment. "I'll try not to spoil you too much, but I must warn you, it's in my nature."

Sidney caught a glimpse of Naomi eyeing their table. By the look on her face, she'd seen the generous gift Sidney received. That would spread around town like wildfire. It was good that she was getting her grandmother out of town for a while. She didn't want anyone finding out that Blain was her father until she had a chance to discuss it with her family first. Especially her mother, who went out of her way to tell her that her birth father was in prison. During lunch, Blain did most of the talking, telling exciting and engaging stories. He was an interesting man who led an exciting life full of travel, and Sidney was looking forward to getting to know him better. Of course, that wouldn't change how she felt about her father. Her father, Kingston. No matter what, Kingston would always be her father.

Harris was mostly quiet during lunch, but he kept a watchful eye on Sidney, smiling the entire time. She was glad she had two weeks before she'd see him again. A lot could change in two weeks, and telling Harris about Jackson would be easier later. When Naomi returned with the check, she thanked them and placed the check in front of Harris. Her smile was a bit too seductive, and she looked at him with what could only be described as 'bedroom eyes'. Harris accepted the check and offered an obligatory smile. If he knew she was flirting, he certainly didn't seem to care. Sidney couldn't deny that Harris was very much a gentleman, refusing even to acknowledge an attractive woman while taking an interest in another. Still, Sidney's heart and mind remained filled with Jackson, and she couldn't wait until she saw him again. When Harris looked at the check, he snorted a tiny laugh, catching Blain's attention.

"Something unusual on the bill?" Blain asked, glancing at the check as well.

"You could say that," Harris remarked, allowing his boss to see the check.

When Sidney saw Naomi's name and number on the check, she shouldn't have been surprised, but she was. It was a little bold of her to assume Harris hadn't been the one to give her the bracelet. Maybe she assumed he did, and that prompted her reaction. When Naomi thought Jackson had been flirting with Sidney, she suddenly wanted to slip into his sleeping bag. Thinking Sidney was interested in Harris may have been reason enough for her to give him her number. Although Harris was tall, dark, handsome, and gave off a wealthy vibe. She easily dismissed Naomi's flirting with Harris. Whatever her reason, Sidney simply didn't care.

"Awfully bold of her," Harris remarked, then glanced at Sidney, possibly attempting to gauge her reaction. "Can I assume she's not a friend of yours?"

"She's used up most of her friends," Sidney replied, possibly a bit too honestly. "She specializes in stealing other women's boyfriends."

"In that case," Blain announced, extending his hand to Harris.

Harris grinned and handed Blain the check. Blain appeared a little too humored.

"I'll be right behind you two," Blain informed them while grinning slyly. "I have a waitress to flirt with and thank for giving me her number."

Sidney was barely able to hide her humor at Blain's boyish glee. He had a slightly devious mind. Now, at least she knew where she got that from.

Chapter 41

After lunch, Blain insisted that Sidney show him her grandfather's workshop. He rode with Sidney in her truck while Harris followed them in their rental car. It gave Blain and Sidney a few minutes alone to talk, although there really wasn't a lot to say that hadn't already been said. As Sidney pulled up to the workshop and garage, she saw Jackson's truck parked in front. Her heart pounded with surprise. What was Jackson doing here? The last thing she needed was Jackson seeing Blain and asking questions she didn't want to answer just yet. She'd have to tell Jackson; there was no way around it, but she didn't want to do it here and now. She parked the truck, then turned to Blain in the passenger seat.

"I need to have a quick conversation with my visitor," she announced. "Why don't you and Harris wait in the office, and I'll get rid of him?"

"Sure," Blain replied cheerfully, not even concerned that she was attempting to hide him from everyone she knew. Even he had agreed that might be for the best for the foreseeable future.

Sidney hurried for the open bay door while Blain and Harris headed for the office door. Sidney entered the workshop and saw Jackson rooting through some tools in one of the toolboxes.

"I wasn't expecting to find you here," Sidney remarked, trying to hide her surprise as she approached him.

"I just needed a few tools," Jackson informed her. "I had a little trouble with your boat."

"There are some guys with me wanting to check out my grandpa's furniture, and I don't want them asking all sorts of questions about you," Sidney informed him, which was actually the truth.

"Yeah, and I'm sure I don't want to be answering any either," Jackson replied before finding the tools he needed, then glanced at her and smiled almost slyly. "See you back at my place?"

"Yes, I'll see you in about an hour," she replied while fidgeting. "I have a lot to tell you."

"Yeah, me too," Jackson announced and drew a deep breath. "I'll bring the Crown Royal. It's going to be a long night."

Sidney offered a tiny, seductive smile. "Was there any doubt about that?" she asked.

Jackson smiled, then chuckled. "I love how your mind works," he announced, then kissed her quickly before heading out the bay door.

Sidney hit the garage door button, electronically closing the door behind him, then hurried back to the office. She found Blain and Harris checking out the photos mounted on the wall. Blain indicated the picture of her and her grandfather standing on the deck of his boat at the lake with the cabin in the background.

"That's a fine ship," he announced cheerfully, then pointed to Henry. "Is that your great-grandfather?"

"Yes," Sidney replied and approached. "That was taken last year at his cabin on the lake."

"You know," Blain announced. "I've always wanted to try sailing and never got around to it. I should really look into that. Maybe you could help me skipper a yacht."

"I know the basics," she remarked, then laughed. "But not these fancy ships out there today."

Harris stood by the office door as Jackson's truck was heard leaving. He then looked back at Sidney and indicated the door.

"Who was that guy?" Harris asked, almost sounding jealous. "Does he work for you?"

"No," Sidney replied while attempting to act casual. "He was just stopping by to borrow some tools."

Harris nodded and again looked out the door window before shaking his head while returning his attention to Sidney.

"Maybe I'm just less trusting," Harris remarked. "I was never very good at sharing my things."

Sidney met Harris's gaze and saw the strange look on his face. Was he actually jealous of some guy he didn't even know? They'd only been out on ***one*** date! Did he think she suddenly belonged to him? If Harris had a problem with Jackson stopping by her shop, what would he think of her best friend being a man? Greyson, Miller, and Leon were three of her four closest friends. The way he was fishing for information wasn't sitting right with her, and it made him less attractive and almost unappealing. That might explain why he seemed so outwardly charming yet somehow remained single.

"As long as friends and neighbors return what they borrow, I've never had a problem with it," Sidney informed him somewhat sternly.

Harris straightened as his entire demeanor seemed to change before glancing at his boss. "I'll wait for you in the car," he announced, then left the shop.

Sidney was surprised at how easily she bruised Harris's ego, but it made her job of telling him they wouldn't be going on a second date that much easier.

Blain watched his man leave, almost as baffled as Sidney, before eyeing her. "What's gotten into him?" he asked almost suspiciously.

"A little insecurity, perhaps," Sidney remarked, then shook her head.

Blain stared at her a moment longer then cocked his head. "It's none of my business," he announced, then pointed at the door, "but did something happen on your date with Harris that I should know about? If he did something in appropriate--"

"No," Sidney insisted, then managed a tiny smile. "Nothing happened, and certainly nothing to warrant any fits of jealousy."

He stared at her a moment as if putting the pieces of what she said together. Blain then groaned, smiled, and nodded.

"I see," Blain announced, then snorted a laugh. "Your tool borrowing visitor was handsome and age-appropriate." He waved off the conversation. "You can do better than Harris. I know what he makes. I can find you dozens of terrific men from good families."

"Thanks, Blain," she replied, offering a tiny, amused smile. "But I'll manage."

Blain's cell phone rang, interrupting them. He removed the phone from his pocket, looked at the caller ID, and groaned.

"This will just take a second," Blain announced, then took a step away from her while answering his phone. "Yeah, what's up?" There was a moment's pause, and Blain suddenly appeared interested in the call. "Oh, that is rather urgent. I'll call you back in a few minutes." He disconnected the call and turned back to face Sidney. "I'm terribly sorry I have to cut this short. An urgent matter just came up, and I need to deal with it right away."

"I understand," Sidney replied, and was actually kind of relieved since she had important things to do herself.

Blain took a swift step toward her, giving her a quick hug and a kiss. "You have a wonderful trip with your grandmother, and I'll call you in a couple of days."

"Sounds good," Sidney announced, then watched Blain leave.

Sidney decided she'd give Blain and Harris a few minutes' head start before packing a few things for her extended stay with Jackson after her grandmother was safely on her way.

§

Sidney's truck pulled up to the farmhouse later that afternoon, around three o'clock, and parked alongside Jackson's truck. She grabbed her overnight bag but left her larger suitcase in the back for now, since it could wait. Sidney couldn't stop thinking about spending two weeks alone with Jackson at his farmhouse. Mostly, she was thinking about jumping on him. As she approached the house, lost in her lustful thoughts, she saw Jackson leaning against the doorframe, his hands in his pockets and an oddly twisted smile on his face. Sidney caught his look, her heart pounding with anticipation, and smiled.

"What's that smile about?" she asked as she walked up the porch steps.

Jackson stepped onto the porch, allowing the screen door to fall back into place, and approached her. "I know we need to sit down and have a lengthy conversation first, but I have this strange urge to pick you up and carry you over the threshold."

"I can't decide if that was romantic or presumptuous," Sidney remarked.

"Let's go with romantic," Jackson announced, somewhat humored. "In the spirit it was intended."

Jackson took her overnight bag and slung it over his shoulder, then gathered her in his arms, kissing her passionately while lifting her off her feet. Sidney placed her arms around his neck, clinging to him, not even minding that her feet were off the ground. He broke off the kiss while setting her back down, then met her gaze and grinned.

"Yep," he announced. "It's a carry her over the threshold moment."

Jackson swept her off her feet as she let out a surprised scream before giggling. He then carried her to the entrance, easily opening the screen door, and took her inside. Once inside, he kicked the main door shut with his foot. He kissed her quickly but warmly, then set her down just inside the kitchen.

"I'd better behave," he insisted, then indicated her overnight bag. "Is this everything?"

"No, my suitcase is in the bed of the truck," she informed him.

"I'll get that," he announced, then nodded across the kitchen. "I have dinner warming in the oven and a bottle of champagne chilling in the fridge."

"Hmm," she cooed. "Someone's planning a romantic evening."

"You'd better believe I'm taking advantage of this situation," he remarked while grinning. "Two weeks of playing house with you could be a lot of fun, but we do have to talk first."

Jackson again kissed her quickly, then headed outside. While Jackson retrieved her bag, Sidney removed the covered roasting pan from the oven. She stood there only a moment before grabbing her overnight bag from alongside the door. Only a moment later, Jackson returned to the house with Sidney's suitcase, locking and bolting the door behind him. When he looked around the kitchen, Sidney was gone.

"Sidney?" he asked and headed for the bathroom, but the door was open. He turned back around. "Sidney?"

Sidney appeared in the archway to the living room dressed seductively in a black bustier, black lacy panties, and black stockings with a matching garter belt. She held the bottle of champagne and two glasses while smiling playfully.

"I thought maybe we'd skip dinner for now and get right to dessert," Sidney announced.

Jackson groaned, unable to hide his grin. "I would love nothing more," he informed her while taking a couple of steps toward her. "But we should talk."

"All I could think about all afternoon was you grabbing me, taking me to your bed, and having your way with me," Sidney informed him. "The last thing I want is any kind of serious conversation killing that fantasy."

Jackson again groaned, pulled her into his arms, and kissed her passionately. "Yes, ma'am," he announced, then immediately swept her off her feet.

Sidney cried out playfully at the sudden movement, trying to cling to him without dropping the glasses or the bottle. She met his gaze with her own seductive one.

"And if it helps, I watched a few training films," Sidney informed him.

Jackson groaned at her words, then kissed her somewhat aggressively before carrying her up the back stairs.

Chapter 42

Jackson rolled off Sidney while panting heavily, then immediately gathered her in his arms, holding her against him. Sidney gently caressed his chest, feeling his heart pounding.

"Are you okay?" Jackson whispered, then kissed her forehead. "Was I too rough?"

"I feel a little lightheaded, but not in a bad way," she informed him and added a tiny giggle. "I have to say that was even better than I'd imagined."

Jackson chuckled softly and caressed her hand on his chest, gently brushing his thumb over the bracelet she wore. "I'm glad you weren't disappointed," he remarked. "I was a little rusty." He then groaned softly. "I'm pretty sure my soul left my body once."

"Do guys your age have heart attacks?" she asked.

Jackson tilted his head and met her gaze with a somewhat stern look. "Again, only eight years older than you," he remarked, then laughed.

"Well, you did do most of the work," she reminded him.

Jackson again chuckled, then groaned. "You're something else," he announced while cuddling her in his arms. "Maybe you should climb on top next time. Do some of the work and spare me that heart attack."

"I may need to watch another training video," she informed him.

Jackson had to laugh and kissed her again. "Not a problem," he replied. "I'm sure there's ***one*** around here somewhere." He then cringed. "Don't judge me too harshly. Remember. Celibate for over two years. Can't expect a man to give up all his vices."

Sidney giggled at his comment. "I borrowed the ones I watched from my mom's 'private' nightstand drawer," she informed him. "I'm not judging anyone."

Jackson chuckled as his thumb again flicked past the bracelet. He finally lifted her hand, appearing interested.

"What's this?"

"You like that?" she asked. "I thought it looked nice with the stockings."

Jackson looked more closely at the bracelet in the dim lighting. He hesitated, then sat up and turned on the light, startling her. Sidney sat up as well and clutched the sheet to her naked body.

"Is something wrong?" she asked.

Jackson captured her hand and looked at the bracelet again. His expression immediately dropped, and he met her gaze, practically startling her with the way he stared. She was almost concerned by the look on his face.

"Where did you get this?" he just about demanded, frightening her.

"It was a gift," she insisted, but was hesitant to tell him from whom.

Jackson stared at the bracelet a moment longer, then met her gaze again. "Who gave this to you?" he insisted.

Sidney didn't quite know how to tell him it was a gift from her biological father, but she didn't want to keep things from him either. Still, the way he was acting frightened her, and she was unsure how to respond.

"What's wrong?" Sidney asked while nervously pulling her hand from his. "You're scaring me."

"That's my mother's bracelet," Jackson announced without taking his eyes off her. "She gave it to my sister. My sister was wearing it when we buried her."

How? How could she be wearing Jackson's dead sister's bracelet?

"Sidney," Jackson just about gasped while moving closer to her. "***Who*** gave you that bracelet?"

Sidney was now trembling and unable to think straight. "My, uh, my biological father," she finally blurted out the words. Horror suddenly crossed her face as she stared at Jackson. "He told me it was a family heirloom."

Sidney and Jackson stared at each other for what felt like an eternity. The first thing that ran through Sidney's mind was absolutely gut-wrenching. Jackson and Blain were related! Which might also mean--

"Your biological father?" Jackson gasped, unable to take his eyes off her. "Sidney, who's your ***biological*** father?"

Sidney's heart was pounding so hard, she almost couldn't hear him speaking. "Blain Norwood," she whispered, then waited for Jackson to tell her what she feared hearing most.

Jackson was unable to move a moment while staring at her, and Sidney could almost hear his heart pounding in time with hers.

"Your father is Blain Norwood?" he gasped.

"Yes," she whispered, then trembled at what she had to ask. "Is he your father, too?"

Jackson was nearly stunned by her question. "What?" he gasped, startling her with the abruptness of his response. "No! Oh, my God, no!" He ran trembling fingers through his hair and shook his head. "No, but he was married to my sister."

It seemed like a lifetime for Sidney to grasp what he was saying. "Blain was married to your sister?" she gasped. Her eyes then widened. "Amber's mother?"

"This is bad," Jackson remarked, then jumped from the bed and hastily dressed while trembling. "This is so bad."

"Amber and I are half-sisters?" Sidney asked, now unable to think straight.

Jackson fumbled with his shirt while attempting to collect his thoughts, then shot a look at her. "Was he here?" he asked, then practically leapt across the bed to her, staring at her in horror. "Was he the one who was at the workshop today?"

"Yes," Sidney replied somewhat timidly.

"Did he see me?" Jackson asked, further alarmed.

"No," she replied, then hesitated. "But his associate saw you."

"Who's his associate?"

"Harris."

Jackson shut his eyes for a moment, then groaned. He suddenly came back to life, jumped from the bed, and started tossing her clothes at her.

"Get dressed," Jackson cried out. "We need to go. Now!"

Sidney grabbed her clothes, jumped from the bed, and quickly dressed. "I don't--"

"Blain is the one who wants me dead," Jackson launched while removing a semiautomatic from his nightstand drawer. "He killed my sister, but I couldn't prove it. After her funeral, someone tried to kill me, so Amber and I faked our deaths and took off."

"You're saying Blain Norwood is a bad man?"

"Yes," Jackson groaned loudly while frantically raking his fingers through his hair. "He's a mob boss, Sidney. He's a ***very*** bad man."

"Are you sure?" she gasped.

Jackson straightened and glared at her. "Yes, Sidney, I'm sure," he announced firmly. "Eight years ago, ***I*** was Harris."

"What?"

"I was Blain's general," he informed her.

"Blain is a mob boss, and you were his second in command?" she just about gasped.

"And now he knows I'm alive," Jackson informed her. "Which means he suspects Amber is alive, too. He wants her back and me dead." After placing the gun holster down the back of his pants, he removed a shoulder holster containing another weapon and slipped into that as well. He suddenly hesitated and looked at Sidney. "When did you find out Blain was your father?"

She looked at him as she finished dressing. "The day after you flew to Texas," she replied.

"***When*** on that day?" he just about demanded.

"That afternoon," she replied, not sure what he was getting at.

Jackson stared at her a moment, then cocked his head. "How did he meet your mother?"

Sidney tensed then released her breath. "My mother grew up in Norwood Manor," she replied. "My grandmother worked for his family."

Jackson's expression was even more shocked, if that were possible. "Did your grandmother know Blain was your father?" he asked.

Sidney uncertainly shook her head. "I don't know," she replied. "Why?"

Jackson groaned, then cursed softly under his breath and again met her gaze. "The man who attacked your grandmother, the one I recognized. He worked for Blain," he informed her. "And now it finally makes sense. Blain sent those men to kill your grandmother."

"What?" she gasped in horror. "Why?"

"Because he didn't want her telling you the horrible truth about him," Jackson informed her. "Did he want you to keep it a secret from your family?"

Sidney considered the question, then nodded. "Yes, but even if he had killed G-ma, my mother would eventually tell me about him."

"Not if your parents had an accident on their way home," Jackson remarked and shook his head. "Trust me, Sidney. Blain specializes in accidents."

Horror swept over her as her mind reeled with the new information. It all suddenly made sense. Blain had a private jet, which would have given his men plenty of time to reach her grandmother that evening after he found out she was his daughter. He had all her contact information and knew where to find Helena. She willingly gave it to him, and he used it to put a hit on her grandmother!

"What are we going to do?" Sidney asked.

"Your grandmother is still in the hospital," Jackson reminded her. "As long as she's there, she should be safe. We need to get to Amber at the cabin." He eyed her. "He doesn't know Amber's your friend, right?"

"No, she never came up."

"Think hard," Jackson announced. "Did he see any pictures of her?"

Sidney shook her head. "No, he never made it inside my house," she informed him.

"What about in the workshop office?" he asked. "Do you have any photos of Amber there?"

"No," Sidney replied, somewhat relieved that she didn't.

"When he saw me earlier, did Harris ask you anything about me?" Jackson pressed.

"Yes," she replied, frowning, but then grew hopeful. "But I didn't tell him who you were or my relationship to you. Honestly, I thought he was jealous, so I thought it best not to say anything."

"Jealous?" Jackson asked, surprised, and seemed to hesitate. "What makes you think he would be jealous--?" He eyed her and raised an arrogant brow. "Did that fucker make a pass at you?"

Sidney now tensed, recognizing the hostility in Jackson's eyes. "Well, no," she replied. "But we sort of went on a date."

He stared at her with a strange look of surprise. "How long was I gone?" Jackson demanded. "When did you have time to go on a date with Harris?"

"He asked to take me out to dinner that evening," Sidney remarked, then turned angry. "You ran off to Texas, and I was pissed at you, so I said yes."

"Of course," Jackson scoffed. "He's very charming. Most psychopaths are."

"He's a psychopath?"

"I'll let Amber tell you all about him," Jackson muttered. "Okay, Harris saw me, which means he probably got my license plate number. He's already had a few hours to work with that information, so we definitely need to move before he finds us here."

Jackson removed a snub-nosed revolver from his dresser drawer and handed it to Sidney, then rushed her from his bedroom.

Chapter 43

Sidney and Jackson hurried down the stairs but cautiously entered the dimly lit kitchen, leaving the lights off. Although Sidney was almost positive Jackson was being a bit overly cautious, his paranoia was making her extremely anxious. If he was right, it meant she practically gift-wrapped and handed him to Blain on a silver platter. Jackson moved alongside the kitchen door and peered out the window, mostly obstructed by the curtain. He hesitated a moment, then looked back at Sidney.

"Harris would know your truck," Jackson informed her. "If he's out there, he won't risk you getting caught in the crossfire."

"What do we do?" Sidney asked, rubbing her shoulders nervously. "Maybe he's not even out there."

"We have to assume he is," he replied. "We can't lead him to Amber. They might be watching the trucks, but they won't be watching the garage. We need to get to one of the cars in the garage. I can drive it through the path in the woods with the headlights off. That'll take us out to the back road without them seeing us."

"How do we get to the garage without being seen?" Sidney asked.

"His private jet isn't that big," Jackson informed her. "So we can assume he only brought four men, not including himself and Harris. That means there would be at most four guys casing the place. Two guys watching the back door, and two watching the front." He looked back at Sidney. "He won't have enough coverage to watch the entire house. We can slip out the side window, head into the woods, and sneak into the garage from the back."

Sidney eyed him somewhat suspiciously. "You're surprisingly good at this."

"I faked my own death by running my car over a cliff," Jackson informed her. "I've had quite a bit of practice at disappearing."

§

The mostly dark outside world surrounding the farm was eerily quiet except for the deafening sound of crickets. Just because they didn't hear anything, that didn't mean Blain's men weren't out there. Jackson slipped out of the dining room window first, visually scanned the area, and then helped Sidney. They took another moment to glance over the area. When they didn't hear or see anything, Jackson indicated the woods. It was possible that Blain's men weren't even there, and they were doing all of this for nothing. In a life-or-death situation, it was better to be safe than sorry. Jackson nodded, and they both kept low while hurrying for the nearby woods. They stopped behind a larger tree and scanned the area again. Still, nothing moved. Sidney followed Jackson through the woods in the direction of his garage.

The outside light illuminated the area, allowing them to see almost everything around the garage. They approached the old barn from the rear and entered through a smaller back door. The outside vapor light provided enough light inside for them to move around objects without bumping into anything. Jackson grabbed a set of keys and hurried her to the car closest to the rear bay door, which was the black Chevrolet Chevelle. He reached inside the car through the open window and fiddled with the dome light, manually switching it off, then quietly opened the door for Sidney. She climbed into the driver's seat and inserted the key in the ignition. Jackson shut the door as quietly as possible, although doors on older cars all had that distinctive, metal-scraping-metal sound. He leaned in through the open window and commanded her full attention.

"I'm going to open that bay door," he informed her. "Once I have it open, you need to start the car and pull up to the opening for me. The car isn't loud. Just don't rev it. Anyone down by the house probably won't even hear it. It's an old car, so the headlights don't come on automatically." He raised his brows. "Do you think you can maneuver in the woods in the dark?"

Sidney nodded despite every nerve in her body screaming she couldn't. Jackson kissed her quickly, then hurried for the bay door. He flipped a switch and manually opened it with a rope pulley, making as little noise as possible. Once the door was open far enough, Sidney pinched her eyes shut, held her breath, and turned the key in the ignition. It was louder than she thought it would be, but she resisted panicking and stepping on the gas as she shifted into drive. If she burned out, they would definitely hear that. She let the car roll for the opening, then coasted to a stop near Jackson and the door. She feared putting her foot on the brake, not wanting anyone to see the glow of the red brake lights. Jackson quietly climbed inside and gently shut the door. Sidney barely tapped the gas and let the car roll out the back door.

It was tough seeing the path in the woods without any headlights, and it was much narrower than she thought it would be. When they reached a safe distance, Sidney stopped the car, and they switched seats. As she was rounding the car, both looked back at the garage in the distance. Sidney felt panic sweep over her when she saw the garage light come on.

"Get in," Jackson announced and pushed her around the car. "Someone just opened the garage door. The lights in front come on automatically."

Sidney jumped into the passenger seat while Jackson got in the driver's side and quietly closed their doors. Jackson shifted the car into gear, kept the lights off, and drove along the path a little faster than Sidney had. He had been right, Blain's men were watching the house. When they were far enough away and close to the back road, Jackson turned on the headlights. Sidney felt relieved for the first time and finally glanced at him.

"So," she announced while eyeing his profile. "What is your real name?"

Jackson managed a tiny, tense smile and snorted a laugh. "Max," he replied. "Max Archer."

Sidney stared at him a moment, then smiled. "Max," she announced. "I like that."

"See if you can get a hold of Greyson," Jackson remarked. "Tell them I've been made, and they need to stay put until we can get to them."

Sidney tried Greyson's cell phone. When he didn't answer, she tried Amber's. She frowned and disconnected the call.

"Neither is answering, but there's virtually no cell phone service in that area," she remarked. "There's a landline, but I don't know the number." Sidney then sank into thought before looking at Jackson. "There's no possible way Blain could find them at the cabin, right? I mean, even if he knew about the cabin, there'd be no reason he'd suspect you or Amber would be there. And even if he did, he wouldn't know where to find it."

"Does he know about the cabin?"

"Well, I suppose I mentioned that my great-grandfather left me the cabin in his will," Sidney informed him.

"If he saw your truck at my house, he may very well assume you're friends with Amber, assuming he suspects she's alive, and your truck at my house also means you know me pretty well," Jackson remarked. "If he wanted to find that cabin, all he'd have to do is ask around. I'm sure someone in town would give him that information. All he has to do is flash my picture at the diner. I'm sure Naomi or Randall would happily give me up."

Sidney now stared at Jackson's profile, feeling concerned all over again. "What if someone does tell him where to find the cabin?" she asked while fidgeting.

"Just as a precaution, we're going to drive into the woods where we set up tents the other day," Jackson informed her. "We'll leave the car there and take the boat across the lake to the cabin. No one will see or hear us approaching if we cut the engine and coast to the dock."

Chapter 44

Henry's boat coasted silently across the lake the moment the cabin came into view. It would take some time to reach the dock without the engine, but they didn't want to risk being seen or heard if someone was hiding out in the woods. Sidney leaned on the partition separating the helm from the small set of steps leading down below and stared at Jackson, who sat behind the wheel, keeping the rudder steady so they would drift toward the dock. She studied his profile for a long moment in silence. Jackson didn't even have to look at her in the dim moonlight to know she was staring at him.

"I know you want to ask," Jackson remarked almost timidly, unable to look at her. "You have every right to know about my past."

"When you say you were Blain's general," Sidney announced, now visibly uncomfortable. "What sort of ***things*** did you do for him?"

"Bad things," Jackson replied softly. "I was a bad person who did bad things to other bad people."

"What about innocent people?"

"No," Jackson replied. "It never went that far. Blain's operation wasn't on a broad scale. He wasn't as well-established as city crime bosses. My main job was beating up other guys like me."

"Just beat them up?"

"Yeah, mostly," he replied. "I won't go into any details. Gives you plausible deniability."

"Mostly," she muttered without taking her eyes off him.

"That part of the conversation is closed for discussion," Jackson informed her.

"Did you ever hurt any women?"

"Not physically and definitely not sexually," Jackson replied, then frowned. "Although I could have been a little more tactful with the women I picked up in bars when I was younger. I was notorious for the wham, bam, thank you, ma'am. That'll even piss off women only looking for a hook-up." He glanced at Sidney, then had to look away, somewhat ashamed. "I was a real dick from sixteen until around twenty-two, the year before my sister died. Honestly, I treated Amanda and Amber pretty shitty during that time as well."

"What happened?" Sidney asked, delicately, fearing to press him for answers. "What made you that way? What eventually turned you around?"

"Amanda was ten years older than me," Jackson replied. "I was only six years old when our parents died, and we were placed with our crazy grandmother. The following year, Amber met Blain." Jackson frowned and shook his head. "She was seventeen, he was thirty-two." He snorted a slightly disgusted laugh. "He ***always*** liked them young." They were married the following year, and Amanda begged him to take me in. I was mostly raised by my sister and Blain's servants, which I guess went all right, in the beginning. Before Blain's seedier associates influenced me. By the time my sister was nineteen, she was pregnant with Amber, well, Alexa."

Sidney cocked her head while eyeing him somewhat suspiciously. "Is my math not adding up?"

"No, your math is just fine," Jackson replied, then managed a tiny smile. "Amber is only twenty-one. We adjusted her age up two years, in case Blain was watching schools for a fifteen-year-old."

"Wait," she announced. "So when I took her out for her twenty-first birthday--"

"Yeah, she was nineteen," Jackson admitted. "That's why I was a little pissed."

"If she's twenty-one, and I'm twenty-three," Sidney remarked. "And Blain met her mother two or three years before Amber was born--"

"Yes, he met my sister around the same time he impregnated your mother," Jackson replied.

Sidney made a face but remained silent, allowing Jackson to finish his story.

"I was already a bit of a nuisance by the time I was fifteen," Jackson informed her. "By the time I was sixteen, Blain's enforcers decided to put my aggressive behavior to good use. I was already driving the Rolls at sixteen. By the time I was eighteen, I was working alongside his enforcers. They were a wonderful influence. Drinking, philandering, and a lot of fighting. I guess I showed a lot of promise. By the time I was twenty, I was Blain's right-hand man. Passing Harris for the position. That's where things really took a turn for the worse."

"But you said you turned things around when you were twenty-two," Sidney reminded him. "What happened just two years later?"

Jackson was visibly uncomfortable. "When I was around eighteen, Amanda started complaining about the way Blain treated her," he remarked. "For years, I ignored all her concerns, including the cheating, because he showered her with gifts, and she was living a lifestyle she never would have had otherwise. We both were. I suppose I assumed that should have been enough to make her happy. I never heard the verbal abuse." He held his breath a moment. "When I was twenty-one, my niece practically attacked me, crying about the way her father treated her mother. I made Amanda show me the bruises. That's when I started working on their exit plan. I shifted her money and my money into untraceable accounts, selling off her jewelry for her, and quietly seeking a divorce attorney on her behalf. Figuring out how to keep Amber away from Blain was the real challenge. We needed proof of abuse. That was the tough one. It was around that time that Blain took an interest in a young woman. She was possibly only seventeen. I didn't ask. I'd heard rumors that he wanted to move the new girl into the house, which actually pleased me because I thought he'd divorce my sister. Problem solved."

Sidney watched Jackson as he suddenly shifted uncomfortably.

"Divorce meant giving up some of his wealth. Divorce meant losing control over his daughter," Jackson informed her. "Even though he kept me out of his plans, it didn't take long for me to figure out he didn't intend to divorce Amanda. He planned on becoming a widower. I redirected my efforts and focused on alternate identities for Amanda and Amber." Jackson sank into a darker world. "Unfortunately, Blain put his plan into effect before I could implement mine. Two days after Amanda died in her ***car accident***, Amber and I similarly faked our own deaths, except I pulled it off a hell of a lot better than Blain had. I used the money I'd originally put aside for their exit to buy the farm, make repairs, and afford a decent living for both of us. My side hustle with car restoration jobs kept us quite comfortable on top of what was left in the untraceable account."

"Sounds like you really stepped up to the plate," Sidney remarked.

"Yeah, except Amber was miserable being stuck in the middle of nowhere with just her 'man whore' former enforcer uncle," Jackson informed her. "Until the day she met a seventeen-year-old girl fishing in the stream near the farm. I tried to keep the two of you apart, but that didn't work out at all."

"You always said I was the bad influence on her," Sidney remarked, then raised her brow. "You realize it was the other way around, right?"

"Yeah, I kind of suspected," Jackson muttered. "She's too much like me." He stared at her for a long moment, looking broken and insecure. "You had every right to know about my past before things went too far." Jackson raked his fingers through his hair. "And I really wanted to tell you, but I let my dick overrule my head. I feel like I betrayed your trust for my own selfish desires." He was silent for a moment, then glanced at her with a defeated look. "On a scale from one to ten, how mad are you at me? Is there any way you and I can recover from this now that you know about my past?"

"Everyone kept this massive secret about my real father from me," Sidney reminded him. "If I had all the facts about Blain Norwood from just one of you, we wouldn't even be in this mess, because I never would have flown out to that mansion. I'm the one who brought him here, and I'm the one who jeopardized the lives of the people I love most."

"Maybe, but you didn't know," Jackson insisted. "You're exonerated from any wrongdoing." He then hesitated. "And I'm going to do everything I can to stop him from hurting anyone else." He stared at her as if his entire world had crashed down around him. "I'm so sorry for all the pain I've caused and for hurting you, Sidney. I never should have put my filthy man-whoring hands on you, and I can't apologize enough for that."

Sidney studied him a moment in silence. "The only thing you need to apologize for is stalking Amber when she flew to Texas," she informed him somewhat sternly. "If you'd kept your ass at home, I never would have visited Norwood

Manor because we would have spent three days in bed together instead."

Jackson stared at her a moment, puzzled. "Wait, what?" he asked.

"I hadn't brought my overnight bag to hang out with Amber all weekend," Sidney informed him. "I intended to stay with you."

His mind seemed to reel with the information she'd provided. "I told you about my tainted past, how all of this is my fault, and how guilty I feel about taking your virginity, and you're upset about Texas?"

"That's because I don't care about your past," Sidney insisted. "And as far as you taking my virginity, I gave that to you--quite happily. I don't regret that at all."

Jackson leapt up from the helm and pulled her into his arms, holding her against him in a tight embrace. "If I get out of this with my testicles intact, I'll do everything in my power to make up for ruining your first time."

Sidney pulled back just far enough to meet his gaze and smiled warmly. "You didn't ruin my first time," she insisted. "I thought it was amazing."

"I gave you two minutes of post-sex cuddling before zipping up," he reminded her. "I've been having horrible flashes of 'barroom hook-ups past' since we boarded the boat. That was definitely not how I envisioned the evening going."

"Well, you were more concerned about us being killed at the time," Sidney reminded him. "I'm willing to give you a hall pass on that one."

Jackson hesitated a moment, then gently brushed the hair from her face. "I want you to know, Sidney," he announced almost timidly. "You're the first woman I've ever made love to and the first woman I ever loved. You weren't just some conquest or a meaningless fling."

Sidney stared at him, somewhat surprised by his admission. "What about--?"

"Naomi was just a ***month-long*** hook-up under false pretenses of a relationship," Jackson informed her. "There was never anything emotional from either of us. I certainly didn't love her, and I'm pretty sure she didn't even like me. She just liked the whole 'bad boy' image."

Sidney realized that Naomi's behavior at the campsite was starting to make sense. Naomi had witnessed Jackson's blow-out in the bar the night he came to Sidney's rescue, and it reinvigorated her desire to have him. When she saw the tender moment Sidney and Jackson shared on the dock, it made Naomi want him even more.

"When the 'bad boy' didn't play her games in the bar, she lost interest," Jackson informed her.

"So you purposely took a beating," Sidney remarked.

Jackson managed a tiny smile and nodded. "I wasn't going back to beating up people on someone else's orders," he replied. "And the last thing I needed was people in town gossiping about my fighting skills. I didn't need any more attention placed on myself either."

Sidney clung to Jackson, nuzzled her head against his chest, and sighed softly. "When this is all over," she announced. "You can make it up to me."

"Anything," he replied while brushing his cheek against the top of her head. "I'll do anything to keep you."

"I want to spend a weekend in bed with you," she announced without hesitation. "Romantic to raunchy and everything in between."

Jackson's arms tightened around her, and he groaned lowly into her hair. "Talk like that could get you a two-minute ride on the Jackson Express."

Sidney laughed and pulled away just far enough to meet his gaze. "Two minutes?" she asked. "What can you really do in two minutes?"

"You don't want to know," Jackson insisted while hiding his smirk. "And you're certainly not ready for that."

Sidney eyed the distance to the dock, then looked back at Jackson and seemed to consider it. “We’ve got at least six minutes until we reach the dock,” she informed him, then raised a cocky brow.

Chapter 45

As the boat approached the dock, Jackson was already springing into action. He dropped his heavy duffel bag on the deck near the gangway and darted for the bow line. Sidney grabbed the duffel bag, groaning softly at the weight, and got into position to disembark on his command. Once they reached the dock, Jackson jumped from the deck and tied the bow and stern lines. As soon as the boat was tied, Sidney handed him the duffel bag, and he helped her onto the dock. Jackson opened the bag and removed two rifles and a shotgun, handing Sidney the shotgun. He slung one rifle over his shoulder, the duffel bag over his other shoulder, and carried the second rifle. They hurried along the dock as quietly as possible while scanning the surrounding area. The woods were dark, and it would be nearly impossible to tell if someone was lurking behind any of the many trees. They continued toward the cabin and hurried onto the deck to the back door.

Sidney fiddled with her keys and unlocked the door as quickly as possible. Once the door was open, she slipped inside the dark cabin with Jackson only a step behind her, shutting and locking the door. They silently crossed the living room and nearly reached the kitchen when they heard the sound of a shotgun being pumped. Both froze as the lights came on. Greyson once again stared down the barrel of the shotgun at them. He groaned when he realized it was Sidney and Jackson and lowered his weapon.

"You've got to stop sneaking up on me like that," Greyson scoffed.

Amber poked her head around the corner, then groaned as well. "What are you two doing here?" she demanded. "I thought you were playing 'house' together at the farm."

"We were," Jackson remarked. "Until our hideout was compromised."

"What?" Amber gasped, then nervously rubbed her hands along her arms. "How?"

"Remember when Sidney discovered Kingston wasn't her biological father?" Jackson asked.

"Yeah," Amber replied, now somewhat confused. "What does that have to do with--?"

"Blain Norwood is her biological father," Jackson announced.

Amber's expression suddenly dropped to something resembling shock. She then looked at Sidney as reality hit her.

"You're my half-sister?" Amber gasped.

"Apparently so," Sidney reported.

Amber squealed with delight and hugged Sidney. "Oh, my God," she gasped excitedly. "We're sisters!"

"Hold off the celebration," Jackson remarked with less enthusiasm. "Turns out Blain was visiting Sidney this afternoon, and I was spotted at her workshop."

Horror immediately swept over Amber. "He's here?" she gasped.

"We're pretty sure his men were at the farm tonight," Jackson informed his niece. "Someone was lurking around.

If the two of you would answer your phones now and again, we wouldn't have needed to sneak up on you."

"Our phones never rang," Amber scoffed, clearly irritated with her uncle.

"Spotty cell service," Sidney reminded Jackson.

"Do they know about this place?" Greyson asked with concern.

"We're not sure," Sidney replied. "We'll need to keep quiet and wait it out until morning."

Greyson seemed slightly uncomfortable while glancing at Sidney and Jackson. "So, uh, stupid question," he announced and focused his attention on Sidney. "Is Jackson your uncle as well?"

All three grimaced and groaned at the question.

"Gross, Greyson," Sidney scoffed.

"My mother was Jackson's sister," Amber reminded him. "Sidney and Jackson aren't blood related."

"That's good to know," Greyson replied, appearing relieved. "I mean, if he were Sidney's uncle as well, I'd probably want to throw up."

"You and me both," Sidney muttered.

Jackson and Amber brought Greyson up to speed on the situation with Blain and his men, and the very real possibility that Blain ordered the hit on Sidney's grandmother.

"I don't understand. Why would Sidney's biological father want to kill G-ma?" Greyson finally asked. "Sidney is a grown woman. If she wants to have a relationship with him--"

"That's just it," Jackson informed him. "Helena and Casandra would tell Sidney why they didn't want her to know her real father. Once she found out the sort of man he was, she'd turn her back on him. He didn't want her to find out."

"But I would eventually find out," Sidney announced to Jackson. "It's not as if he could keep that information from me forever. Killing off my grandmother and mother wouldn't change that."

"And why are the two of you still on the run from him?" Greyson asked the logical follow-up question. "Amber is twenty-three years old. I understand why you had to avoid him when she was just a kid, but he has no authority over her now."

"Actually," Amber announced and smiled timidly. "I'm only twenty-one."

"How can you be twenty-one?" Greyson asked, his brows knitting. "We went to school together."

"The first few years we lived in town, I homeschooled her to advance her learning," Jackson remarked. "Blain would be searching for a younger girl. If I aged her, he might overlook older kids. Altering her appearance was necessary."

"I'm not really a redhead either," Amber admitted. "I'm blonde. And being two years older had its advantages." A sly grin crossed her face. "I got to drink when I turned nineteen."

Jackson's eyes narrowed as he sneered at Amber. "That still chaffs my ass," he muttered. "You knew you were only nineteen. You should have known better."

"My driver's license said I was the legal drinking age," Amber reminded him then rolled her eyes. "As if you weren't drinking when you were nineteen--" She then mumbled, "More like fifteen."

"Yeah, and look how I turned out," Jackson scoffed.

"Back to my original question," Greyson remarked. "Why are you still hiding from Amber's father? He has no control over her. She's an adult now."

"Yeah, try telling him that," Jackson muttered.

"If he finds us, he'll kill Jackson, then drag me back to his mansion," Amber informed him. "My mother was practically a prisoner in that house. She wanted to leave him, but he kept tabs on everything she did. He was never going to let her leave him."

Amber stared down at the floor while rubbing her chilled arms. Greyson placed his arms around her and held her, comforting her.

"I knew Blain would always be suspicious of our accidental deaths," Jackson informed them. "That's why we changed our names and stayed hidden for so long."

"He's never going to leave us alone," Amber whispered. "Once he realizes I'm alive, he'll keep hunting for me until he finds me." She then glanced at her uncle. "And he'll put Jackson in the ground."

"After he gets a little payback," Jackson remarked. "I'd be lucky if he ordered his men to kill me on sight."

Amber stared at her uncle for a long moment. "I'm tired of running," she informed him. "You need to fake your own death again, Uncle Jackson. I can stand up to him now, but he won't stop hunting you until you're dead."

"I'm not leaving you, Amber," Jackson insisted. "We're in this together."

"I'm a grown woman now," Amber reminded him. "He's not going to hurt me. With law enforcement's help, I can get a restraining order against him. You're the only one in any real danger. You need to look after yourself. If I stop running, he won't be as eager to get his hands on you."

"If I do that, I lose both of you," Jackson insisted, then looked at Sidney. "I can't do that."

"What if Blain went down for his crimes?" Sidney asked. "If he went to jail, you'd both be free, right?"

"He'd still have power and money," Jackson informed her. "His men will continue to hunt me down."

"Then we need to take away his money and power," Sidney announced.

"How do you intend to do that?" Jackson asked.

There was a moment of silence.

Amber suddenly came back to life. “I’m still his heir,” she announced. “If he goes to jail, I’d control his assets. He loses his money and his power.”

“He probably has an accountant for that,” Jackson informed her. “You’ve been AWOL for years.”

“I can get that reversed,” Amber insisted.

“Yeah, by going back with him,” Jackson scoffed, then shook his head. “No, you’re not going back there.”

“It would only be for a few months,” Amber remarked. “Then we can find a way to put him in jail.”

“No,” Jackson repeated firmly. “You’re not doing that. Not even for a day. First thing in the morning, we’ll take the boat to my car and get as far from here as possible. When we’re someplace safe, I’ll work on a long-term plan.”`

“Running was a good idea when I was little,” Amber informed him. “I don’t want to run anymore. I want to stay here with Greyson and Sidney, but you need to go. If he catches you, he’ll kill you.”

“Then we stay and fight,” Jackson announced boldly. “I’m willing to give up my home, but I won’t give up my family. I’m staying here with you and Sidney.”

“That’s suicide,” Amber cried out.

“I’ll go with you,” Sidney informed Jackson, surprising everyone.

Jackson stared at her for a moment, stunned. “You’d be willing to leave your home and family for me?” he asked.

“If it keeps you alive,” she informed him.

“What about your mother and grandmother?” Jackson asked. “What if Blain goes after them again?”

“He won’t,” Sidney insisted. “His only reason for going after them was to keep me from learning the truth, but I know the truth now.”

“That’s no guarantee,” Jackson reminded her.

“Yes, I know, but I like the odds.”

Jackson pulled Sidney into his arms and kissed her quickly but warmly. “We’ll see that it’s not forever,” he informed her. "We'll continue with our original plan of leaving for two weeks. That should give me enough time to come up with something to get us out of this and maybe get Blain out of our lives forever."

Chapter 46

Just before sunrise the following morning, Sidney, Jackson, Amber, and Greyson sat at the kitchen table within the cabin and discussed their plan over coffee and tea. Despite all their plotting, they still weren't sure whether or not Blain had found the cabin. They were treating the situation as if their location had been compromised, but they also had a contingency plan in case the cabin was safe.

"Okay," Jackson announced with a weary sigh, having gotten very little sleep last night. "Is everyone up to speed on the plan?"

"I'm the scout," Greyson replied. "Blain's never seen me. I take my truck, go to Sidney's house, raid her cash drawer, clean out all the cash from the workshop, and then go to the diner for breakfast. When I'm sure no one is following me, I drive out to the old motel on the interstate where Amber and Sidney are waiting for me to rent a room under my name and credit card."

"Jackson, Sidney, and I head for the boat at the dock," Amber remarked. "We get Jackson's hidden sports car on the other side of the lake and drop him off at Greyson's parents' house."

"Where I'll borrow Greyson's sports car that he keeps at their house," Jackson announced.

"Greyson and I leave Sidney and her money in the hotel room, and then we take the long, roundabout way to the rendezvous," Amber reported.

"When I'm sure I'm not being followed," Jackson announced. "I meet up with Sidney at the motel, and we check out via the key drop box. We then take a two-day drive and meet you two at the rendezvous."

"I'll call Miller and Leon later this morning from the motel parking lot and ask them to pick up G-ma and Jerry at the hospital," Sidney remarked. "And they drop them off at a secured location for the next two weeks."

"If Blain's men are outside when we're ready to leave," Jackson announced, "all four of us make a run for the boat and take off in my car on the other side of the lake."

"Sounds like a solid plan," Greyson remarked, then eyed the others. "It's starting to get light. We should observe the woods on all sides for a little while."

After about an hour, when nothing moved outside, Greyson boldly left the cabin for his pickup truck. He carried some fishing gear and his and Amber's overnight bags. He loaded up the truck under the watchful eyes of his friends waiting in the cabin. Greyson attempted to remain casual and not look around too much, in case another interested party was watching him. He finally got in his truck and drove down the long, private lane. Fifteen minutes after Greyson left, the cabin phone rang. Amber immediately answered it.

"Yeah?"

"I don't think I'm being followed," Greyson reported over the phone. "I didn't see any hidden vehicles near the driveway either."

"Thanks, Greyson," Amber replied with some relief. "See you soon."

Once Amber disconnected her call, the three continued their watch over the cabin. If Blain's men really weren't out there, it was a pity they had to leave the safe house. Unfortunately, it was just a matter of time before Blain stumbled upon the remote cabin. He'd ask the right person and learn its location.

Jackson moved away from his position alongside the window and eyed both women. "It's our turn," he informed them.

"I should go first," Sidney insisted. "If he's out there and sees me, it won't look suspicious. I'll untie the boat and start her. That'll be your cue to haul ass."

"As much as I hate the idea of you going first," Jackson remarked, "that is the best plan. I'll bring up the rear, in case anyone attempts to stop either of you." He hesitated a moment, then released the breath he'd been holding. "If you hear gunshots and I'm still in the cabin, just make it to the boat and leave without me."

That was the part of the plan Sidney really hated, and she wasn't sure if she'd actually stick to it, if it came down to it. Even though Blain and his men wouldn't have any reason to harm her, Sidney was still nervous for her friends. She grabbed her overnight bag, as well as a fishing pole, and left, making a straight shot for the boat dock. She shot looks out of the corner of her eyes, attempting to watch the woods even though Amber and Jackson were doing that for her. She placed her things on the boat, then swiftly untied it from the dock. As she made her way to the helm, she took a little more time scanning the woods. Nothing moved, but she didn't want to put down her guard just yet. Once she started the boat, Amber headed out next with Jackson lagging behind. Jackson and Amber both wore oversized fishing hats and carried fishing poles as well.

Amber carried Jackson's overnight bag while her uncle carried the weapons duffel bag. Sidney held her breath and watched the woods as both casually walked along the dock for the untied boat. Once they were onboard, Sidney swiftly and skillfully backed the boat away from the dock and deeper into the lake before turning it and speeding to the other side.

§

Despite running into no issues, Sidney and Amber remained in constant contact with Jackson and Greyson via their cell phones. Sidney breathed more easily once Jackson successfully secured Greyson's sports car from his parents' house. Amber and Sidney pulled into the motel parking lot a little after ten o'clock that morning, as planned. The no-frills motel was two stories of bland cream-colored siding, with small, boxy motel rooms. The parking lot had seen better days. There were many cracks in the macadam, and the white parking space lines were barely visible. At least the place wasn't falling apart, but it certainly wasn't anything to write home about. They purposely picked that particular out-of-the-way motel since they knew Blain was staying at the hotel near the airport.

Sidney called Miller and Leon from the parking lot and asked them for the favor regarding her grandmother. Thankfully, both men happily agreed to make the trip. Now, they needed to wait for Greyson, who wouldn't be along for another hour. Within the hour, Sidney's cell phone rang, revealing Leon on the caller ID. She answered the phone with some concern. The hospital was supposed to be releasing her grandmother, so there shouldn't have been any complications just yet.

"Yeah, Leon," Sidney announced into the phone. "Do you have my grandmother?"

"Oh, yeah," Leon replied from the other end. "We have her and her partner in crime. There is one little snag, though."

"Snag?" Sidney just about gasped. "What snag?"

"She's fussing over everything you packed for her trip," Leon reported.

"I am not *fussing*!" Helena was heard from the other end.

"Okay," Leon scoffed, sounding irritated. "Then you were bitching!"

Amber glanced at Sidney in the driver's seat on her cell phone. Apparently, she heard Leon's colorful language directed at Sidney's grandmother.

"Really, Sidney," Helena cried out so she'd hear her through the phone. "You're letting these boys drive us nearly two hours one way? Does this car even have a muffler?"

"Sidney," Miller was heard in the background. "This deal is about to be off. She can insult me all she wants, but she's not allowed to insult my car!"

"I'm surrounded by children," Sidney muttered.

"Sidney said to stop acting like a child," Leon announced, presumably to G-ma.

"She said that?" Helena cried out.

"Jesus," Sidney scoffed into the phone. "If I have to come over there, there'll be hell to pay!"

Everyone within Miller's car seemed to quiet down, having heard Sidney's outburst. Sidney groaned with frustration.

"This is serious, Leon," Sidney informed him. "You need to take them to their destination sooner rather than later. I can't stress the importance of it enough."

"Does this have to do with the men who attacked them?" Leon suddenly asked.

"What?" Helena was heard screeching. "Is that what this is about?"

"Leon, you tell her whatever it takes to get you on the road fastest, you understand?" Sidney announced.

"Yeah, I hear you," Leon replied through the phone. "We'll stop by her place, throw a few of the things she wants into her bag, and get out of Dodge."

"Thank you," Sidney moaned and disconnected the call. She allowed her head to fall back against the headrest. "I should have just done it myself."

"It's going to be fine, Sidney," Amber insisted. "Leon and Miller may be a lot of things, but in this sort of situation, they'll rise to the occasion."

"I hope you're right."

§

Half an hour later, Miller and Leon darted across Helena's bedroom while she chased after them with her fuzzy pink slipper.

"Sorry, sorry!" both guys yelled while attempting to dodge the 'slipper of fury'.

"Never, never touch a lady's unmentionables drawer," Helena shouted as she chased them.

Jerry sat comfortably on the chest at the foot end of the bed and watched the spectacle with little reaction and no comment.

"Come on, G-ma," Miller protested while avoiding the slipper as he turned to face her before her open bedroom door. "Sidney said we had to leave right away."

"This is important," Leon added while holding his arm defensively in front of his face, just in case he got walloped again by Helena's slipper. "We don't have time for this nonsense."

Jerry placed his hand over his eyes, lowered his head, and groaned at the comment.

"Nonsense?" Helena cried out. "My unmentionables are nonsense?"

"Jerry," Miller pleaded. "Help us out here."

"Never argue with a platinum blonde brandishing a fuzzy slipper," Jerry informed him.

Chapter 47

Jackson approached motel room number four just before noon with his overnight bag over his shoulder and the weapon's duffel bag in his hand. He lightly rapped his knuckles on the door.

"Hey, it's me," he announced softly through the door and awaited a response.

He tensed when no one responded. Jackson was about to knock again when the door unlocked and opened, revealing Amber. Jackson stared at his niece, surprised.

"I thought you and Greyson would be long gone by now," he remarked.

"Slight problem," Amber muttered and walked away from the door, allowing her uncle to enter.

Jackson stepped into the small motel room, shutting the door behind him. The motel room was actually nicer than the exterior suggested. The carpeting, although dated, was a dark peach color, and the two double beds had handmade quilts. Sidney stood near the bathroom door with her arms folded insecurely across her chest while Greyson appeared to be calming her.

"What's going on?" Jackson asked. "What's the problem?"

Sidney frowned and met Jackson's gaze. "My parents are on their way home," she informed him.

"What?" he asked, then cocked his head. "Why?"

"Apparently, someone from town called my mother in Hawaii and asked her how G-ma was doing after her attack," Sidney informed him. "I missed several calls from my parents while we were at the cabin without cell service. Naturally, when G-ma didn't answer her cell phone, they called the sheriff, and he told them everything."

"Great," Jackson muttered with a low groan as he collapsed onto the nearby bed. He then met Sidney's gaze. "You need to call them right away and convince them to leave with your grandmother."

"Yeah, about that," Sidney scoffed. "Since they'll be on their way home from the city airport later this evening, G-ma doesn't want to leave either. She feels ***safer*** staying at home with them."

"And maybe she will be," Jackson remarked, "but I'm not willing to gamble with their lives like that."

"I need to tell them about Blain," Sidney informed him.

"That's a bad idea," Greyson insisted. "If you go home, you risk him or his men following you."

"He's right," Jackson announced. "If you want to tell them about Blain, you need to do it by phone."

"I can't have that conversation with them over the phone," Sidney protested. "It's going to be difficult enough telling them what I did."

"Oh, by all means," Greyson announced sarcastically while indicating Jackson. "Tell Uncle Jackson your theory."

Jackson kept his gaze fixed on Sidney. "What theory?"

Sidney drew a deep breath, then sighed. "If I talk to my mom and grandmother about Blain, he won't have any reason to hurt them. It'll already be too late. I confess to Blain that they know, and they told me everything about him."

"Maybe," Jackson remarked, then shook his head, "but that's just a theory, Sidney. That doesn't make it gospel. His big plan for you could be to kill off your family just so you'll move in with him and be the daughter he lost."

"That's ridiculous," Sidney scoffed. "This is my home. Even without my parents and grandmother, it's still my home. There's nothing that would make me move in with him, especially with what I now know."

"It may sound ridiculous," Jackson insisted, "but that doesn't mean it's not a possibility. You don't know Blain. You don't know what I went through to rescue Amber from that place."

"It's true, Sidney," Amber remarked while frowning. "He's all about control and power, even over me. Just because I'm a grown woman now, that doesn't mean he won't resort to kidnapping me just to get me back into that house and under his thumb. Don't put it past him to do the same to you."

"If he actually did hire thugs to kill my G-ma and her boyfriend, I'm guessing he's capable of just about anything," Sidney remarked, then groaned while flinging her hands down to her sides. "I need to go home and sort this out with my parents. I can leave you and Amber out of it, but I need to tell them what I've done."

"It's a mistake," Jackson remarked while standing. "But if you insist on going, you're not going alone."

Sidney snorted a laugh, smirked, and shook her head. "You're certainly not going back with me."

"I'll ride in the trunk, and you can pull into your parents' garage," Jackson insisted, then shrugged. "Blain will never know I was there."

"Unless he comes looking for me and accidentally sees you," Sidney remarked.

"Maybe we should all stick together," Amber suggested, then looked at her uncle for approval.

"No," Jackson huffed while glaring at her. "You and Greyson continue with the original plan. We'll catch up with you in a few days. If we don't show up, you don't come back looking for us."

"Seriously?" Amber shot back while folding her arms across her chest. "You've looked after me since I was thirteen. I'm not going to abandon you when things get dark."

"And I'm not abandoning Sidney either," Greyson insisted. "I'd die for her."

"Then it's settled," Sidney announced boldly. "We'll plan on leaving here so we reach my house around nightfall. My parents will be home by then, and that'll give added protection against prying eyes."

Jackson shook his head. "This is not how I imagined today going."

"I wonder who called your parents about your grandmother," Greyson remarked. "I mean, everyone knew they went to Hawaii and wouldn't be back for two weeks. Most people would refrain from saying anything so they ***wouldn't*** worry unnecessarily, cut their vacation short, and return home."

§

Casandra slept peacefully to the soft sounds of classical music playing from the car radio. When the music was turned off, the silence woke her. She looked around the dimly lit interior of the car, then eyed Kingston behind the wheel.

"Are we almost at the rest stop?" Casandra asked, somewhat disoriented.

"Actually, we're about twenty minutes from home," Kingston informed her while offering a slightly sympathetic smile. "I didn't have the heart to wake you. You'd been awake almost twenty hours."

Casandra straightened in the passenger seat, pushing against the seatbelt, and attempted to get comfortable. "It was a long flight," she remarked, then shook her head with something resembling disgust. "I can't believe neither of them called to let us know what happened. I hate that we had to find out from one of her book club friends that Mom was in the hospital."

"They probably didn't want us worrying and catching the next flight out from Hawaii," Kingston informed her. "I'm sure Helena is fine." He suddenly eyed his rearview mirror, immediately distracted by what he saw. "That guy behind us is coming up awfully fast." Kingston placed both hands firmly on the wheel while shifting looks into the mirror.

Casandra looked into the side mirror. "I don't see--"

The car jolted with a loud bang, startling both. Casandra grabbed the door and the dashboard, while Kingston clung to the wheel, trying to keep the car on the road. The car behind them swerved into the passing lane, sped up alongside them, and rammed them in the back driver's side door. Kingston shouted a profanity while Casandra screamed. The car swerved off the road, narrowly missing a tree, and flew across the gravel. Kingston fought to keep the car from wrecking while braking heavily. The car sped past them and continued down the road. Kingston stared after the speeding car, stunned. Once his rational thinking returned, he unbuckled his seatbelt and leaned across the console to Casandra, who was rigid in her seat, eyes wide with panic.

"Are you okay?" Kingston asked, visually inspecting her for any injuries.

"I, uh, think so," she just about gasped, then looked at him. "What the hell just happened?"

"That fucker ran me off the road," Kingston announced, becoming angry now that the shock wore off.

Casandra stared out the windshield, eyes wide, and gave a tense nod. "Kingston," she announced. "He's coming back."

Kingston looked out the windshield and saw the same car, heavily damaged on the front fender, driving back down the road.

"At least he had enough sense to come back," Kingston scoffed and reached for the door lever. "I can't imagine what excuse he has for running us off the road."

Before Kingston could open the door, Casandra grabbed his arm as horror crossed her face.

"He's picking up speed," she gasped.

Both saw the car careening toward them and froze in fear. Just then, blue and red flashing lights brightened the darkening road as a police car pulled up behind them. The damaged car swerved back into its own lane and sped away. The deputy got out of his car, paused to watch it take off, then grabbed his hand radio from his belt and reported the license plate.

Chapter 48

After sending Miller and Leon home, Sidney and Greyson joined Casandra, Kingston, and Helena in G-ma's living room for evening tea. Before her parents could retell the tale of their near-death experience on the road, they heard someone in the kitchen. Sidney's parents and grandmother were a bit surprised when Jackson and Amber entered the house through the garage entrance and joined them. Before anyone could even question their evening visitors, Sidney spoke. Jackson and Amber offered nothing while Sidney told all three what she'd done, and that she brought Blain to their little town. Sidney's father seemed mildly uncomfortable, but her mother and grandmother were stunned into silence. Once Sidney finished recapping everything that had happened since her parents left for Hawaii, there was an unusual silence. After a long period of quietness, Sidney fidgeted. It was as if she reached into their chests and ripped their hearts out.

"I wish one of you would say something," Sidney remarked timidly.

"Well," Casandra began, then shifted uncomfortably. "I had honestly hoped I'd never see the guy again, and he's certainly not welcome in my house."

"My house, either," Helena scoffed, seeming less uncomfortable and more enraged. "Do you know what kind of monster that man is?"

Sidney gently cleared her throat and nervously ran her fingers through her hair. "I do now," she replied while sheepishly glancing at Jackson. "Jackson, uh, used to work for him before he came here with Amber."

Helena shot Jackson a look and immediately cocked her head. "So that's it, is it?" she just about demanded. "You didn't move here. You were ***hiding*** here. Hiding from your former boss."

Jackson frowned and nodded. "Let's just say that I didn't leave on good terms with him," he remarked. "If he finds me, he'll kill me."

"Yes," Helena hissed. "That's what monsters do." She then studied Jackson, who sat hunched in the chair, his hands clasped between his knees. "What sort of work did you do for Blain?"

"The dirty work," Jackson replied honestly while meeting her gaze. "And I know what you're probably thinking. I know. I'm not much better than he is."

"Actually, I'm thinking you got suckered into Blain's fast and exciting lifestyle," Helena remarked. "Well, you're lucky you got out when you did. Eventually, he'd want you to do something so heinous that you'd refuse, and then he'd have one of his ***other*** goons get rid of you."

Jackson shifted uncomfortably, knowing she was correct with her assessment. "That's kind of why I had to get out," he informed her, then appeared curious. "You seem awfully knowledgeable about his practices. I mean, most of the house staff never saw that side of him. They had no idea what was going on inside that house."

"Which is why I had to get out, too. I couldn't exactly prove it," Helena remarked, "but I'm confident he was responsible for the deaths of his parents and my husband." She lightly tapped her fingernails on the arm of the handcrafted rocking chair and eyed those within the room. "I'm going to tell every one of you something I've never told anyone in my life. Something I've carried with me for twenty-seven years."

Flashback. Norwood Manor. Helena headed down the hallway toward the dimly lit study. Her eyes strayed to what appeared to be blood droplets on the floor. She eyed the spots, somewhat puzzled, now slowing her approach. She stepped into the study doorway and immediately froze. Debra and Ransom Norwood were on the floor not far from the desk, blood covering their lifeless bodies. Ransom's pearl-handled, antique Wild Bill Hickok .38 revolver, which he'd kept in his desk, was in his outstretched hand. Before Helena could even scream or react, her eyes strayed a few feet away from them. Flynn was sprawled, face down on the floor with a massive pool of blood surrounding him and a bloodied hunting knife clutched in his hand. Helena screamed and ran for her dead husband, collapsing to the floor and pulling him into her arms.

Helena yelled out, uncertain anyone would even hear her while crying and clinging to her dead husband, holding his head to her bosom. She again looked at the bloodied knife in her husband's hand, the bullet wound to his chest, and the antique revolver in Ransom's hand. Horror immediately swept over her at what she was seeing. The scene overwhelmingly suggested that Flynn murdered Debra and Ransom Norwood, but not before Ransom shot and killed the murderous butler. No! Helena refused to believe what she was seeing. Flynn was not a murderer, and he didn't kill Debra and Ransom Norwood.

Helena leapt from her dead husband's side, grabbed the handkerchief from Ransom's pocket, and wiped Flynn's fingerprints from the knife. She tossed the knife between her employers' bodies, then grabbed the gun, wiped it clean of prints, and looked around. She could hear Lance calling from within the kitchen. Helena hurriedly wrapped the revolver in the handkerchief and stuffed it down her cleavage as far as

she could manage without hurting herself. She returned to Flynn's fallen side, pulled him back to her bosom, and cried out loudly, allowing her tears to once again consume her. Lance ran into the room and stopped in the doorway, horrified at what he saw.

Present day. When Helena had finished telling her story, everyone was transported back to the here and now. Jackson shifted uncomfortably and met Helena's gaze.

"My sister, Amber's mother, was married to him," Jackson informed her. "I suspect he was responsible for the accident that killed her as well."

Helena, Casandra, and Kingston looked at Jackson with surprise, then at Amber, as if putting it together.

"Oh, I see," Helena remarked and nodded. "He killed your sister, and you took off with his daughter. It's no wonder he wants you dead." There was a moment of silence. Horror suddenly crossed her face. "Those men that came after Jerry and me--?"

"They were Blain's men," Jackson delicately informed her. "I recognized the one they found dead in the car alongside the road."

Helena's mouth hung open at the revelation. "He wanted me out of the picture before Sidney told me she'd met him," she gasped.

"More than likely," Jackson replied.

Helena drew a deep, shaken breath. "And that's why family should never keep secrets," she remarked. "If we'd told Sidney about her real father, if we'd told her ***everything,*** she never would have gone to see him."

"Now that we know everything, he has no reason to come after you and Mom," Sidney insisted.

"No," Helena remarked with a defeated sigh. "You don't know everything."

"He more than likely killed my grandfather, and he tried to bump you off," Sidney cried out. "Possibly had Mom and

Dad run off the road, too. How much more could there be? How much worse can it get?"

"Oh, it gets much worse," Helena replied with a sigh. "And it's not pleasant."

Everyone sat in total silence, waiting for Helena to tell her story.

"After the death of my husband, Blain started with the sexual advances," Helena informed them. "Naturally, I resisted at first, but I started feeling pressure, as if my job depended upon it. I eventually gave in." She frowned while sinking into a darker world. "It became almost part of my job. Just one more thing to do. Keeping him happy lasted about three years, but then the unthinkable happened." Helena appeared visibly uncomfortable as her eyes flicked up, settling upon Casandra. "Blain always liked them young--"

Jackson immediately shifted, knowing where the story was going.

"His attention shifted to Casandra," Helena reported everyone's worst fears. "She was just sixteen." She shuddered and insecurely rubbed her chilled shoulders. "She was young and naive. He convinced her that she needed to fulfill his desires or we'd be kicked out, so she did as he demanded." Helena drifted off into another world but swiftly returned with a vengeance as her voice turned angry. "When I found out he'd manipulated my daughter into sleeping with him, I tried to take Casandra and leave, but he threatened me. I pulled his father's revolver on him. I wanted to kill him. Everything in me told me to pull the trigger, but I couldn't do it." She hesitated only a moment. "Instead, I took my daughter and fled the mansion with little more than the clothes on our backs. We had little choice but to return to my family home. At least I knew Casandra would be safe there."

Jackson, Amber, Sidney, Greyson, and even Kingston stared at Helena after she told her story.

"So his motive for wanting you dead goes way beyond telling Sidney what kind of monster he is," Jackson remarked while shaking his head. "He has a personal axe to grind with you as well."

"Yeah, pretty much," Helena replied. "I mean, I wasn't worried he'd come after me, but now that he knows Casandra had his child, and I took her away from him, that would certainly press a few buttons."

"The weapon used to kill your husband that you removed from the crime scene," Jackson remarked to Helena. "Was that the same gun you pulled on him before you left?"

"Well, yes," Helena replied. "It was the only weapon I had at my disposal. I'd kept it hidden in my room all those years."

"If he killed Debra and Ransom Norwood and staged it to look as if your husband was the killer," Jackson began, "when he saw that you had the revolver he'd planted on the butler, he probably realized you'd tampered with ***his*** staged crime scene. That gun could clear or convict him. It's possible his men were looking for that gun when they attacked you."

Helena stared at Jackson a moment while considering his words, concern growing in her eyes. "I never thought about that."

Sidney groaned and rubbed her eyes. "I can't believe this is all my fault," she gasped, then looked at her family and friends. "I'm the reason he's here. I'm the reason everyone is fearing for their lives."

"That's not true, Sidney," Jackson remarked somewhat sympathetically. "I earned my death sentence years ago. ***I'm*** the reason he wants me dead."

"And I'm the reason he wants me dead," Helena insisted.

"Yes, but ***I'm*** still the reason he's here," Sidney informed them. "I'm the one who contacted him."

"But you didn't know," her mother insisted. "That's just as much our fault. If you had known, you would have made different choices."

"I have a lot of years of pent-up anger and hostility for that man," Helena informed them while holding her head up proudly. "If I had pulled that trigger twenty-four years ago, none of us would be where we are today."

"It's just as much my fault," Jackson informed her. "If I had gotten my sister out of there sooner--"

Helena sighed and pulled herself from the rocking chair with some discomfort after her surgery. "Well, I for one am done letting that man ruin my life," she announced. "Let him come and get me." Helena removed the pearl-handled, antique revolver that had been safely tucked away down her ample cleavage. "There's a bullet in this gun with his name on it, and it's twenty-four years overdue."

Jackson suddenly grinned and chuckled while removing his semiautomatic from his hidden shoulder holster. "I've got your back, G-ma."

Kingston groaned and shook his head. "Now, let's not all go off half-cocked," he announced, then removed a shotgun that had been carefully hidden alongside his chair by the fireplace. "I prefer fully cocked. And two barrels are better than one."

Greyson sighed and opened the duffel bag on the floor. "This is one fucked up family," he announced, then removed his own shotgun. "Let's go high noon on his ass."

Sidney smiled and removed her semiautomatic from her pants as well. "Giddy-up."

Amber rolled her eyes, then groaned and removed the small semiautomatic hidden within her boot. "Yeah, yeah, yee-haw," she muttered, lacking enthusiasm. "You're all nuts. I hope one of you mentally disturbed nutcases has a really good plan."

"I have a plan," Jackson replied.

"Someone other than Uncle Jackson," Amber announced. "Preferably one that doesn't end with a shootout at the O.K. Corral."

Chapter 49

The following afternoon, Blain and Harris walked up the steps to Sidney's house while talking quietly between themselves. Harris knocked on the door, and both men were now silently waiting for someone to answer. When Sidney opened the front door, Harris and Blain smiled upon seeing her.

"Thanks for inviting us over for lunch," Blain announced cheerfully.

Sidney smiled and stood aside, allowing both men to enter her house. "Well, I thought we needed some time to clear the air a little," she insisted, then shut the door behind them.

They followed her into the kitchen, where Helena and Casandra stood by the kitchen counter. Blain and Harris stopped partway into the kitchen and stared at the two women. Blain's expression immediately dropped. Casandra was visibly uncomfortable while Helena smiled like a serial killer.

"Hello, Blain," Helena hissed.

Blain attempted to hide his surprise and managed a smile. "Hello, Helena," he announced, attempting to sound polite.

"Sidney's grandmother?" Harris asked his boss, somewhat stunned.

"And that's Casandra," Blain informed his man. "Sidney's mother." He then looked back at Sidney. "I thought you didn't want to tell them just yet. Kind of caught me off guard here."

"After what I'd learned," Sidney remarked. "I felt I had to tell them, and I'm glad I did. Seems there's a lot more to the story than what you told me."

Blain glanced from Sidney to Helena and Casandra. "What's she talking about?" he asked almost politely. "Trying to turn my daughter against me?"

Helena was about to erupt, but somehow held it together. "You coerced Casandra into having sex with you," she snarled in anger, although her strange smile remained. "You knew she was only sixteen and you still went after her."

"I didn't know she was only sixteen," Blain shot back. "She said she was eighteen."

"Liar!" Helena cried out, now looking more like a cobra ready to strike. "You pursued my sixteen-year-old daughter and told her you'd fire me and toss us both out of the house if she didn't do what you wanted."

"If she told you that, she lied," Blain launched back then sneered at Casandra. "I never threatened her. ***She*** came on to me!"

"Bullshit!" Casandra finally cried out.

"Spin it anyway you want," Helena snarled in response. "Sidney knows the truth!"

Blain sneered at Helena, then turned to face Sidney while perfecting his innocent look. "You can't possibly believe any of that is true," he remarked to Sidney, attempting to play on her sympathies. "Your mother and grandmother have been lying to you since the day you were born."

Sidney raised a condescending brow while folding her arms across her chest. "You pressured my grandmother into having sex with you for three years," she announced. "And when you grew bored with her, you went after her sixteen-year-old daughter. When my grandmother found out, she tried to take her daughter and leave, but you threatened her."

"All lies," Blain insisted while adding a tiny, tense laugh.

"I don't know," Amber remarked while walking into the kitchen from the garage. "I remember you threatening my mother in a similar situation."

Blain stared at Amber with shock as his mouth fell open. "Alexa," he gasped softly, then smiled, overwhelmed. "You're alive."

He made a motion to approach her when Jackson suddenly stepped in front of her with his weapon aimed, pointed at Blain's face.

"That's close enough," Jackson snarled, a cold and menacing look on his face.

Harris immediately went for his gun within his hidden shoulder holster when the barrel of a shotgun poked him in the back between his shoulder blades.

"Take your fingers off that weapon very slowly," Kingston snarled from behind him while holding the shotgun.

Harris delicately removed his hand from beneath his jacket and held his hands up in front of him. As Blain stared at Jackson standing between him and his long-lost daughter, Jackson couldn't hide his emotions and the anger he felt for his former employee and brother-in-law. Sidney wasn't sure who was more intimidating at that moment. She wanted to say it was Jackson, but G-ma didn't even blink while looking mentally unhinged.

"I should have known you weren't dead," Blain scoffed at Jackson, turning emotional while still somehow playing the victim. "You son-of-a-bitch! You abducted my daughter!"

"I didn't abduct her," Jackson snarled. "I took her away to protect her from you."

"She wasn't yours to take," Blain cried out.

"Alexa was my niece," Jackson growled. "My sister's daughter. You remember my sister, don't you?"

"Is that what this is about?" Blain demanded. "You're still blaming me for what happened to Amanda?"

"Yes, actually, I am," Jackson shot back. "I don't know exactly what happened to her, but I have a pretty good idea."

"So you're accusing me of killing my wife?" Blain snapped back and indicated Amber. "Is that what you've been telling my daughter? Poisoning her with your lies. Trying to convince her I'm some sort of monster? Maybe you should tell her what sort of monster you are."

"Maybe you should tell her," Jackson remarked, then cocked his head. "Tell her the sorts of things you wanted me to do. Tell Alexa and Sidney all about your work and my job."

Blain sneered at Jackson.

"That's right," Jackson announced. "They know everything, and you're afraid if you implicate me, you'll also be implicating yourself."

"Right now," Blain remarked. "You're the one holding me at gunpoint. I believe that's called kidnapping. Something you know a lot about."

"Actually," Kingston announced from behind Harris. "You're trespassing in my house."

"I was invited," Blain scoffed in response.

"So you claim," Sidney remarked without flinching. "Everyone here knows ***who*** and ***what*** you are. I suggest you leave and ***never*** come back. You aren't wanted here. Not by me and certainly not by Alexa. Stay out of our lives."

"And if anything happens to any of them," Kingston announced. "You'll be the ones having an unfortunate accident."

"You heard the man," Helena scoffed and nodded. "Get the hell out of my daughter's house."

Watching the two men leave had to be one of the tensest moments of Sidney's life. Despite having all the guns aimed at them, it felt as if the entire situation would erupt into one big shootout, destroying everyone she loved in an instant. Once Blain and Harris left and the door locked behind them, Jackson returned his gun to his shoulder holster, then eyed them.

"You know it's far from over, right?" Jackson remarked to the others.

"One step closer," Helena announced.

"Yeah, but closer to what?" Amber muttered, rubbing her chilled arms.

§

Harris and Blain entered the diner later that afternoon during the slow hours between lunch and dinner. Naomi saw them enter and just about did a double-take, immediately checking out Harris. As they claimed a quiet booth near the back, Naomi quickly pounced on them, offering her most pleasant smile.

"Back again, huh?" Naomi announced and handed them menus. "Just two this afternoon."

"Sadly, our lunch plans fell through," Blain informed her, then minded his menu.

Harris seemed to pay more attention to Naomi than to his menu and offered her his most charming smile. "Turns out Sidney had plans with some other guy," he remarked. "Tall, dark-haired fella."

Naomi groaned and rolled her eyes. "Jackson," she scoffed. "I don't know what's up with those two. I didn't even think they socialized outside of him being Amber's uncle, but when I saw them sleeping in the bed of his truck during our overnight camping trip, I'll admit, I was a little surprised. Jackson and I used to date, you know."

Harris maintained his charming smile while cocking his head. "You dated that guy?" he asked, then shook his head. "You seem a little too classy for a guy like that."

Naomi practically blushed, turning all gushy on him. "Well, it was years ago," she informed him. "I outgrew him."

"Are there a lot of places to camp around here?" Blain asked, interrupting their conversation.

"I suppose so," Naomi informed him. "We went to this lake last week. I thought Sidney's great-grandfather had a cabin there, but I didn't see one."

"My associate and I are into real estate," Harris informed Naomi. "We'd heard about some cabin properties in the area. Sidney was going to show us her grandpa's cabin. She said it was on a lake." He then frowned. "Unfortunately, she had other plans tonight and couldn't show us around."

"We thought we'd check it out on our own," Blain insisted. "But her directions weren't the greatest. Got lost for an hour instead."

"Do you know where her great-grandfather's cabin is?" Harris asked.

"No," Naomi replied, appearing sympathetic. "I saw the lake, but I didn't see any cabin."

Harris suavely leaned back in the booth seat and maintained his charming smile. "I wouldn't mind seeing the lake," he announced. "Maybe you could show me where it is."

Naomi studied him a moment, her smile never faltering. "That might be fun," she replied, then glanced briefly at Blain.

Harris immediately waved off his boss. “Blain has a ton of phone calls to make this evening,” he assured her. “It’d just be the two of us.”

Naomi seemed pleased to hear and struck a sexy pose. “I get off of work at five o’clock,” she informed him. “That should be plenty of time to take a little walk around the lake. Let you have a good look around. Maybe we’ll even find the cabin.”

“That sounds fantastic,” Harris announced, oozing with charm. “I’ll pick you up here at five.”

As Naomi left their table, she passed Jerry, who stood at the counter picking up his to-go order. Jerry eyed Naomi and then the back booth.

Chapter 50

Greyson and Amber showed Helena, Casandra, and Kingston around the recently remodeled cabin. The three were pleasantly surprised, if not a little stunned, at the renovations Henry had made before his death.

"Henry must have spent months updating this place," Kingston remarked while looking around the living area.

"According to the card he'd left for Sidney," Amber remarked, "it was an early birthday present for her."

"Yes, the two of them did share a strange love for this place," Helena remarked as she lovingly caressed the countertop. "We had that sort of relationship when I was a little girl. That changed when I fell in love with Flynn."

Casandra looked around and shuddered slightly, despite the fact that there was no chill. "Are you sure we're safe here?" she asked.

"***Safer***," Greyson replied. "We have a duffel bag filled with weapons and ammo, in the event that we're not. If you're concerned, Leon and Miller can always take the three of you to someplace further away."

"I'd feel better if Sidney were staying with us," Kingston insisted. "I don't know why she wanted to remain with

Jackson. He even admitted Blain wants him dead more than the rest of us. Why would she want to go with him?"

"Sometimes, it's what we need to do," Amber informed him while clinging to Greyson's arm. "He can protect her, and she can watch his back. That's why Greyson and I are staying here with the three of you."

"You told Jackson you were going to Greyson's apartment," Kingston reminded her, now confused.

"It's easier to tell Jackson things he wants to hear," Amber assured him. "You guys are safer while I'm with you. My father won't risk turning me into collateral damage in his quest to get even with any of you. I'm your ace in the hole."

"I'd better call Jerry," Helena announced, seeming almost defeated. "I want to check on him. He was pretty upset about being excluded from our little intervention earlier this afternoon. Probably drowning his sorrows in a hot fudge sundae." Helena looked at her cell phone, then held it up in a few different places before groaning. "Huh? Guess Grandpa still didn't get any kind of internet up here, though."

While Helena stepped into the kitchen to make her phone call on the landline phone, the others made themselves comfortable in the living room. Helena's conversation with Jerry was brief and didn't seem to cheer her up at all. If anything, she seemed more depressed after hanging up.

"I'm going upstairs to take a nap," Helena informed them, "since I probably won't be getting much sleep tonight."

"I hate that she blames herself for all of this," Casandra reported somewhat insecurely while watching her mother disappear up the stairs. "In many ways, this mess is my fault too."

"You were just a teenager," Kingston reminded her. "Blain took advantage of you."

"He didn't take advantage of her," Amber insisted while sneering. "He manipulated and threatened her into complying. The same way he brought my mother into his life, and it would have ended with the same violence that took her out."

§

Helena dangled from the first floor porch roof while attempting to place her foot on the porch railing. She grimaced, then groaned at the effort it took.

"This was easier when I was fifteen," Helena muttered.

She finally caught the railing with her foot and managed to grab onto the support beam with one hand. When Helena attempted to lower herself on the railing, she lost her balance and fell onto the ground, landing on her buttocks. She groaned lowly, then slowly picked herself up.

"That's going to leave a mark," Helena muttered before hurrying down the driveway.

Halfway down the driveway, she saw Jerry's car approaching. When he stopped, she rounded the car and jumped inside. Jerry looked at her dirt-covered pants, shoes, and elbows.

"Are you sure this is a good idea?" Jerry asked.

"No," Helena replied while belting herself in. "But I caused this mess over two decades ago. I'm damned well going to clean it up. I need to protect my family. Is Naomi still at the diner?"

"She said she was working until five," Jerry informed her.

Helena glanced at her watch, then eyed Jerry. "Well, don't sit there and dawdle," she announced, motioning them onward. "Beat feet. Let's go."

Jerry put the car into reverse and attempted to hide his smile. "If I wasn't terrified for our lives," he announced. "I'd be a little turned on right about now."

Helena eyed Jerry, then grinned. "I knew you were a keeper from the moment I met you."

Jerry turned the car around on the dirt driveway, threw it into drive, and looked at Helena while grinning. "Tighten your bra straps," he announced, then appeared focused while looking out the windshield as he gripped the steering wheel. "I'm about to go forty in a thirty-five zone."

As he stepped on the gas, Helena cried out excitedly. "Whoo-hoo!"

Two minutes later.

Helena glared at Jerry behind the wheel while he frowned and handed the deputy his driver's license and registration.

"You could have outrun him," Helena scoffed.

"He knows who I am, Helena," Jerry insisted while waving his hands around. "He would have found me. Forty in a thirty-five zone. What was I thinking?"

§

Jerry entered the diner a little after four o'clock and casually looked around. He didn't seem to notice Blain sitting in the corner booth, talking on his cell phone, but he did notice Naomi was conspicuously missing. Jerry approached Randall at the counter.

"Twice in one day," Randall announced, somewhat humored. "What's the occasion?"

"No occasion," Jerry replied, despite seeming down. "Where's Naomi? I thought she was working until at least five."

"She had a date," Randall informed him. "Nice, well-dressed man. He showed up early, so I told her to go."

"That's unfortunate," Jerry remarked, then gently cleared his throat and managed a smile. "She's a good listener when it comes to, you know, troubles with relationships."

"You?" Randall asked, then hesitated and nodded. "Oh, that's right. Your little side romance with Helena that you've been trying to keep hush-hush."

"Yeah, well," Jerry remarked in a dreary tone. "Those things don't stay hush-hush too long when you're taken by ambulance to the ER."

"No, I suppose not," Randall replied while managing a smile. "Helena giving you trouble since you've been out? Women will do that, you know."

"Yeah," Jerry groaned softly. "She's not speaking to me. Again. I got a speeding ticket, and she was giving me grief about it."

"Everyone speeds from time to time," Randall insisted. "She needs to cut you some slack."

"No, she wanted me to lead the deputy in some high-speed chase," Jerry informed him, surprising the diner owner. "Helena was hell-bent on getting home. I don't know why. It's not as if there's anyone there. Then, she told me she wanted me to leave. Practically threw me out." He shook his head. "I swear, I don't know what women want. Just told me to leave her the hell alone." Jerry sighed and shook his head. "I guess I'll take a turkey sandwich to go and hang out at my place all alone."

"Sorry your evening plans were scrapped," Randall replied, then smiled. "I'll get you that sandwich and even throw in dessert for free."

Blain walked past Jerry, who didn't even seem to notice him, and left the diner.

Chapter 51

Sidney entered Jackson's farmhouse only a step behind him. After he shut and bolted the door, he turned toward her with a hard-to-read expression on his face. She nervously rubbed her chilled arms while looking around.

"Are you sure this is a good idea?" she asked.

"No, and I specifically remember telling you to go with your parents and grandmother," he remarked somewhat sternly.

She glared at him, not humored. "There are three people Blain wants," Sidney informed him. "You, me, and Amber. If I'd gone with them, he'd send his men after us. My family is safer without me."

"And you're safer without me," he reminded her. "I'm the one Blain wants dead. He wants you and Amber alive."

"Which is why I don't understand why you'd make it easier for him to kill you," she scoffed, then indicated the remote farmhouse. "There's no one around. We're in the middle of nowhere. His men can easily come after you without any witnesses."

"Which is exactly why I want ***them*** out here," he informed her.

Sidney stared at him a moment before reality hit her. "You want them to come after you," she just about gasped. "Custard's last stand."

"If I want to defeat Blain, I have to play by his rules," Jackson informed her. "The police can't stop him, because he has to break the law before they can go after him."

"I understand your logic," she reported. "But what makes you think they'll come after you first and not go after Amber and Greyson?"

"Because they're at Greyson's apartment in town," Jackson informed her. "Under the watchful eyes of dozens of busybodies. Small towns aren't like the city. He can wait her out." Jackson shook his head. "No, I'm the bigger threat. If he gets me out of the way, he has an easier path to Amber. I'm the direct threat."

"At least tell me you have some sort of plan," Sidney remarked. "Something other than sitting on the porch with a shotgun, waiting for him."

Jackson gave her a curious look. "You have something against that plan?"

Sidney's eyes widened in horror. "That's your plan?" she practically gasped.

Jackson chuckled and placed his arms around her, pulling her against him. "No," he announced while grinning, then quickly kissed the top of her head before releasing her. "Bugging out was always my first choice, which is why I got the plane and my pilot's license. But running isn't always an option, so you need a backup plan."

"So what's your backup plan?" she asked, now concerned.

§

Harris's rental car pulled into the deserted campsite and parked not far from the bonfire pit. When Harris got out of the car, Naomi sprang from the passenger seat and joined him. She couldn't take her eyes off the handsome man, while he seemed more interested in the docked boat, recognizing it from the photo in the workshop office.

"Gorgeous spot, isn't it?" Naomi asked while perfecting her seductive body language, attempting to get the brawny man's attention.

Harris removed his cell phone, then looked at her and offered a charming but seemingly distracted smile. "Yes, this area seems perfect," he announced while taking a picture of the boat on the lake.

Naomi giggled when he attempted to send a text. "There's no cell service out here," she informed him while taking a few steps closer. "It's ***very*** secluded."

When Harris realized she was right about the cell phone service, he hid his irritation and again smiled, replacing his phone in his pocket.

"Some might say that makes the spot more ideal," Harris informed her.

"Complete seclusion," Naomi remarked as she paused before him, giving her best come-hither smile. "Two people could do just about anything out here without being interrupted."

Harris grinned at the comment before swiftly pulling her into his arms with enough vigor that it seemed to steal her breath away. She immediately ran her hands along his broad, muscular chest and pressed her body against his.

"I know I could think of a few things this place would be good for," Harris replied.

"A little skinny dipping, perhaps," Naomi suggested.

"I was thinking more like a little boat ride on the lake," Harris remarked. "We could weigh anchor in the middle and make use of that little sun deck on the stern."

Naomi's smile faded, and she pouted. "I don't think Sidney would appreciate us taking her grandpa's boat out without permission. I'm not exactly her favorite person."

"If we get caught, you can tell her it was all me," Harris replied with a tiny shrug. "She seems to like me. I think she'd go easy on me."

"I doubt she left the keys onboard," Naomi informed him as her hands affectionately caressed his massive chest and broad, muscular shoulders. "You're really turning down skinny dipping?"

Harris maintained his grin while placing his hand on her neck. "I didn't say that," he insisted, then brushed his lips past hers. "People always leave a spare set of keys on boats. I'll make you a deal. If we don't find the keys, we'll go skinny dipping."

He suddenly kissed her with aggression, taking control and instantly thrilling her. Naomi returned the kiss, enjoying the way he dominated her. When Harris broke off the kiss and offered a sly yet seductive smile, Naomi blushed and nodded. Harris took her hand, led her to the boat at the dock, and helped her onboard, flexing his muscles, which turned her on even more. He eyed the steps to the galley and nodded.

"Why don't you see if there's any alcohol in the galley, and I'll look for a spare set of keys."

Naomi did as he suggested without even questioning him. The moment she disappeared down the stairs, Harris leapt into the control seat and pulled some wires. It took him under a minute to hot-wire the boat. Naomi returned to the deck, having heard the motor start, as Harris cast off the bow and stern lines.

"You found the spare keys?" Naomi asked, somewhat surprised.

Harris grinned and returned to the helm. "People are predictable," he informed her, then indicated the comfortable seating. "Better sit down. I'm going to give her a lot of ***thrust***."

Naomi giggled and moved to the padded seats just before Harris launched the boat forward. The boat sped along the lake, headed toward the small island, and then turned to round it. He slowed the boat when he saw the renovated cabin and a parked car in the distance, then cut the engine.

"This is a perfect spot," Harris informed her.

Naomi looked around, not even noticing the cabin nestled just inside the woods' edge. "Very romantic," she replied, then indicated the sun decks on the bow and stern. "Bow or stern?"

"Stern," he replied while grinning slyly as he snatched a nearby blanket. "It's closer to the water. Was there any alcohol in the galley?"

"I never made it to the fridge," Naomi replied, then offered a lustful smile. "I'll be right back."

As Naomi disappeared into the bottom of the boat, Harris's eyes narrowed while studying the cabin in the near distance.

"Take your time." Harris then muttered, "We're not going anywhere."

Chapter 52

Harris rolled off Naomi with a pleased groan after their aggressive sexual encounter. Naomi immediately moved against him, clinging to him while he panted, attempting to catch his breath.

"That was incredible," Naomi cooed while affectionately caressing his chest. "I could easily get spoiled."

Harris chuckled softly as he caressed her body in response. "Stick around a little while longer," he announced. "I'll do things to you you'd never imagine in your wildest dreams." He kissed her quickly on the lips, then sat up. "I'm going to see if there's another beer in the fridge." Harris smiled slyly while taking in a sweeping glance of her naked body. "Why don't you do a little nude sunbathing until I get back?"

Naomi giggled at the comment, then watched him slip into his pants and shirt, although it seemed unnecessary for him to dress, considering there was no one around to see them. As he walked across the deck toward the galley stairs, he flicked his used condom into the lake. Naomi pondered it a moment longer, then sat up and slipped into her clothes. She headed across the boat, about to follow him into the galley below, when her eyes fell upon the steering wheel. Naomi hesitated and took a step closer, seeing several wires hanging below the panel. She was momentarily puzzled, attempting to figure out what she was seeing. When she heard him on the steps returning from the galley, Naomi didn't even have time to turn. He placed his muscular arm around her neck and shoulder and his other arm around her waist, holding her in a somewhat warm but constricting embrace from behind. Naomi gasped with surprise, then managed a tiny laugh at her own reaction.

"You scared me," she gasped while smiling, although she was now uneasy.

"It's the little thrills that make it that much more exciting," Harris informed her while gently caressing her body with both hands as he pressed against her.

Naomi relaxed as he kissed her neck from behind, enjoying the sensation.

"You know what I mean," he insisted between kisses. "Like the thrill you get from having sex with another woman's man."

Naomi tensed slightly at his words. "What do you mean?" she asked, somewhat surprised and possibly guilt-ridden. "You never said you were dating Sidney."

"You assumed I was," Harris informed her in the same seductive tone while continuing to kiss her neck. "Admit it, you like how it feels."

"Sidney is with Jackson," Naomi informed him as her body tensed despite his affectionate kisses.

"Not anymore," Harris replied warmly right before his arm tightened around her neck, placing her in a firm chokehold.

Naomi gasped and fought the muscular arm around her neck despite knowing there was no way to loosen his grip. Without thinking, she rammed her heel onto his bare foot, smashing his toe. Despite his height and strength over her, the surprise was enough to loosen his grip. Naomi rammed her elbow into his ribs, giving her enough room to maneuver away from him. She looked around only a second, knowing there was nowhere to go, and she'd only succeeded in pissing him off. When he lunged for her, Naomi jumped overboard, splashing into the water. Harris looked over the railing and cursed while striking his palm against the wood. Naomi had already surfaced and swam for the small island. Harris re-engaged the wires, starting the boat, and weighed anchor. He turned the boat and drove it toward the swiftly swimming woman. Naomi reached the shallow area before the island, preventing Harris from following any closer with the boat. When she darted into the small section of trees, Harris cursed and rounded the small island, looking for a place to drop anchor while watching her.

"Hey!" a faint, male voice called out.

Harris suddenly became alert and looked back at the campsite dock. A man, whom he could barely make out, stood on the dock and waved to him.

"Jackson, over here!" Miller called to him.

Harris sneered and glanced back at the island. Naomi was within the trees somewhere. If he went after her and she screamed, the man on the dock would hear her. Harris cursed and turned the boat for the dock, needing to get rid of that man. He would come back for Naomi later. When he looked back at the island again, he saw Naomi disappear on the other side. To his surprise and horror, she was swimming for the cabin dock on the other side of the lake. If he went after her, he'd risk being seen by someone within the cabin. As the boat approached the dock where Miller waited for him, Harris stuffed the wires back under the console and slipped into his shoes. Miller was already grabbing the bowline and working to secure the boat. Harris removed his switchblade knife from his pants and hid it in his hand as he approached the stern. He tossed the rope to

Miller to tie it off as well. Miller eyed Harris for a moment, confused.

"Are you a friend of Sidney's?" Miller asked.

Harris offered his most charming smile and nodded. "Yes," he replied. "She said I could take the boat out and have a look around the lake."

"I guess she found the spare keys," Miller remarked, then tied off the stern.

Harris jumped onto the dock while flicking his switchblade open and took two steps toward Miller's back as he bent over, tying off the line.

"Miller," Leon was heard calling.

Harris retracted the blade with a seamless motion and looked back to dry land. Leon approached the dock and eyed Harris almost suspiciously.

"Hey," Leon announced, giving him a quick once-over. "Are you a friend of Sidney's?"

"Yes," Harris replied, oozing charm as he approached with his hand extended while keeping the switchblade close to his leg in his left hand.

Two men in close proximity. Take down one before the other even notices, then swoop in and get the second.

"Leon," Carrie called out from near the newly placed logs in the fire pit. "Did you remember the wine coolers? I only see beer."

"Found them," Emily called to her from the open passenger side door of Miller's truck.

"Never mind," Carrie announced to Leon, then eyed Harris and smiled. "Are you a friend of Sidney's?"

Harris's once confident smile was now little more than a tense smirk. "You know," he remarked, fidgeting slightly. "I should probably go. This looks like a couple's afternoon, and I don't want to intrude. I'll return Sidney's boat keys when I see her."

Before Miller or Leon could respond or possibly ask for the boat keys that he didn't have, Harris headed for his rental car. Miller and Leon watched the man jump into his car, back up, and then drive down the overgrown lane.

§

Harris's rental car raced along the back, country road around the lake. The driver had one hand on the wheel and his cell phone in the other, finally getting a signal.

"I found the cabin," Harris announced over his cell phone. "The waitress got away, and she's heading there now. If I hurry, I can beat her there. I'll need a couple of the guys to help get rid of her and any extra baggage while I retrieve the girls."

"No," Blain announced firmly from the other end. "You need to abort your mission. Sidney and Amber can wait for another day. If they're all there together, it'll get too complicated."

"But the waitress got away," Harris insisted. "She knows what I intended to do to her."

"In this hick town?" Blain remarked. "I think you're safe from her accusation. There's no proof, is there?"

"No," Harris replied. "It's her word against mine. Are you sure you want me to abort?"

"Yes," Blain insisted from the other end. "Right now, I just want to tie up a couple of loose ends. The girls can wait until they lower their defenses in a few months. I need you to take care of Jackson. We need him out of the picture now."

"Where should I look for him?"

"When the guys checked out his farm, they found a personal plane in a hangar by the barn," Blain reported. "Take some of the guys and look for him there. I have my own loose end to tie up."

"What if Amber is with him?"

"She won't be," Blain informed him. "He thinks she's safe with her friends. He's secure, thinking he's protecting her by leaving."

"Okay, I'll check out the farm with a few of the men," Harris replied, then eyed the nearly hidden dirt driveway to the cabin. He frowned while disconnecting his call, then continued past the driveway.

§

Naomi reached the ladder to the dock, pulling herself from the lake in near exhaustion from her lengthy swim, and just about collapsed. Just because Harris didn't follow her across the lake didn't mean she was safe. Naomi only took a moment to catch her breath, then heaved herself to her feet and attempted to run for the cabin in the near distance. Despite her attempt, her waterlogged body only moved so fast, especially in her bare feet. She finally reached the cabin door and promptly pounded on it. When the door opened, she was greeted by the barrel of Greyson's shotgun. Naomi cried out and jumped back a step before realizing it was Greyson holding the weapon.

"You have to help me," Naomi cried out, barely even able to speak after her traumatic swim.

Greyson lowered the shotgun and immediately looked around outside behind her before meeting her gaze. "Come inside," he announced, stepping away from the door.

Naomi entered the cabin and just about collapsed, then saw Kingston also aiming a shotgun at her. She was momentarily alarmed before looking back at Greyson.

"A man Sidney introduced me to the other day just tried to kill me on the lake," Naomi informed them.

Kingston lowered his shotgun while staring at her with horror in his eyes. "Out here?" he asked.

Naomi nodded. "He and his business partner were supposedly buying this cabin from Sidney," she informed them. "I offered to show him the lake, and that's when he attacked me."

"Did he see the cabin?" Amber asked as she appeared from the back, where she'd been hiding.

"We were just alongside that little island in the middle of the lake," Naomi informed her, then nodded. "I think he saw the cabin." She shook her head, practically in tears. "Why did he want to kill me? I thought he was Sidney's friend. She was having lunch with him the other day. He even gave her jewelry."

"Those two men lied and manipulated Sidney," Amber informed Naomi. "The older man is my father, and he wants to take me back home. He doesn't care who he has to hurt to achieve that goal."

"He wanted to kill me to keep anyone from knowing he'd found you?" Naomi gasped, horrified.

Casandra now entered the room and approached Naomi while cocking her head. "You willingly went to a secluded location with a man you didn't even know?" she demanded. "Why would you gamble with your safety like that?"

"Not the time," Kingston muttered softly to his wife.

Naomi stared at Casandra, looking her in the eyes, as she attempted to find a response to the question. She then frowned and shook her head.

"I thought he was Sidney's friend," Naomi replied timidly. "He seemed ***nice***."

"You mean, you thought he was handsome and wanted to lure him away from Sidney," Amber remarked almost callously.

Naomi frowned and nodded. "I may have acted in haste," she replied.

"We need to get out of here," Greyson informed them. "The cabin has been compromised. There's no telling when Blain or Harris might show up, and with additional backup."

"I'll get G-ma," Casandra announced and hurried up the stairs.

Amber returned with a towel and handed it to Naomi, who accepted it with a shaking hand. She attempted to dry off while trembling.

"We should call the police," Naomi insisted.

"You're more than welcome to," Amber informed her. "But I guarantee my father already has a contingency plan in place for that. You've put yourself on the same hit list as everyone else in my life."

Naomi stared at Amber with fear in her eyes. "Do you think he'll come after me again?"

"It's possible," Amber replied with a dreary sigh. "You're a loose end. Welcome to my world."

Naomi now looked as if her entire world had shattered. "Is that why Jackson never wanted to share anything personal about himself?"

"When you're hiding from hitmen, you don't exactly tell people your life story," Amber replied.

Naomi slowly shook her head, unable to take her eyes off Amber. "I'm so sorry, Amber," she whispered. "I didn't know I led Harris right to you."

"You were played like everyone else," Amber reminded her.

"I suppose I was," Naomi replied softly. "I actually thought he liked me."

"You should be thankful you're alive," Amber informed her. "Harris is a monster with a million-dollar smile. My mother was terrified of him."

Casandra thundered down the stairs and swung the banister at the bottom. "G-ma is gone!"

"Gone?" Kingston cried out. "You mean, she was abducted?"

"No," Casandra scoffed. "The crazy woman escaped out the bedroom window!"

"Why?" Greyson asked, dumbfounded.

"With the way her mind works, there's no telling what she's up to," Casandra replied.

Chapter 53

Helena sat on the living room sofa while daintily sipping her tea from a china teacup. She had just finished her tea when the grandfather clock chimed midnight. The witching hour. She set the teacup and saucer on the coffee table and consulted her watch. As if on command, a text message came through on her phone. She removed her phone from her pocket and opened the message from Jerry.

It simply read, “Sorry about earlier. Really want to apologize in person. Can I come over?”

She responded to his text with, “No, but you can call me in twenty minutes before I go to bed.”

Helena then stood and headed up the stairs to get ready for bed. By twelve-thirty, the lights were already out in her bedroom, and she was nestled under the thick comforter. A cool breeze blew in through the open bedroom window, but with the comforter on, Helena didn’t seem to stir. The partially open bedroom door creaked softly as it opened a little wider. Blain, dressed entirely in black, entered the bedroom with a Bowie knife clutched in his gloved hand as he silently crept closer to the bed. He paused before the bed and, without hesitating, plunged the knife into the mass through the comforter. He immediately pulled the blade out, appearing dumbfounded at the squishiness of the kill. The bedroom light suddenly popped on, surprising the man. He spun away from the bunched-up comforter, scanning the room, and saw Helena, dressed in a pair of white satin pajamas, standing in the bathroom doorway with the pearl-handled, Wild Bill Hickok revolver in her hand, aimed at him.

"Is this what you came for?" Helena casually asked, indicating the gun. "Tying up some loose ends from twenty-seven years ago."

Blain stared at the weapon aimed at him before meeting Helena's gaze. A somewhat charming smile then crossed his face.

"Why would you think that?" Blain asked.

"I saw the way you stared at the gun this afternoon," Helena informed him without showing any emotion. "It was you. You killed your parents and tried to frame my husband."

Blain stared at her a moment longer in silence as his smile faded and his brows rose. "The police never suspected Flynn in my parents' murder," he reminded her.

"Yes, I know," Helena replied. "The crime scene wasn't the way you had left it, and that made you very nervous, especially since the gun was missing." She cast her eyes upon the gun in her hand. "This gun. Your father's gun from the desk drawer."

Flashback. Debra stumbled a few steps, attempting to reach the open study door while the intruder followed casually, unhurried. When she was nearly there, he snatched away her hope as he grabbed her from behind and slit her throat. Debra staggered a step or two, clutching her throat as the blood gushed from the gaping wound. She fell beside her husband. Ransom forced his eyes open in time to witness his wife collapsing near him. The last thing he heard was thundering footfalls in the grand hallway. Help was on the way, but it would be too late. Ransom managed to look

away from his now dead wife and saw Blain standing over her with the bloodied knife in his hand and a vacant expression on his face, showing no remorse. The footfalls from the hallway grew louder. Flynn entered the study, pausing a moment in the doorway, and saw Debra and Ransom bleeding out on the floor.

Ransom twitched and attempted to gasp a warning to his faithful butler. Flynn took several quick steps closer to Ransom, then looked up when he saw movement in the dark corner near the desk. Blain cocked his head as if to say, 'Oh, well,' and then raised the antique gun. Before Flynn could even react, Blain pulled the trigger. Flynn didn't even have time to clutch the fatal chest shot before dropping to the floor. Blain leapt into action, while carefully stepping around the rapidly spreading blood, placing the bloodied knife in Flynn's hand and the revolver in his father's hand. When the stage was set, Blain darted out the exterior study door, removed a snub-nosed revolver from his pocket, and fired it into the air, effectively waking the young chauffeur, who was undoubtedly sleeping off a bender in his apartment above the garage. Blain had plenty of time to slip through the woods to his car that was parked far enough away from the mansion.

Present day. Blain stared at Helena from across the bedroom and shook his head.

"It was all planned so perfectly," Blain remarked, the tiny smirk never leaving his face. "I guess I didn't count on you restaging my staged crime scene."

"I knew Flynn wouldn't kill the Norwoods," Helena announced, showing no emotion. "I was positive someone framed him, and I wasn't going to allow that. I didn't know it was you, but I had my suspicions."

"Bullshit," Blain scoffed and even chuckled, mocking the woman with the gun aimed at him. "If you thought I'd killed Flynn, you never would have carried on an affair with me for three years."

"What's that old saying?" Helena remarked while cocking her head. "Something about keeping your enemies close."

"Go ahead, Helena," Blain announced bluntly. "Call the police. Tell them you suspect I killed my parents and your husband twenty-seven years ago. I have an alibi for that entire evening. The most you'll do is inconvenience me." His eyes then turned dark and cold. "On the other hand, I'll make sure you lose everything and everyone you ever loved."

Helena smiled sweetly while tilting her head. "Oh, Blain," she announced in a warm and sincere tone. "You won't do anything of the kind, ***dear***." She maintained her smile. "I don't want you arrested for murdering my husband." Her smile twisted into something wicked, yet somehow remained almost sweet. "I want to put you in the ground."

§

Kingston's car pulled into Helena's driveway, where a police car with its flashing lights was already parked. The car didn't even fully stop before Casandra jumped out of the passenger side and ran up to the house.

"Mom," she cried out and nearly blew past the police officer standing just outside the door.

The deputy stopped her, holding her back. "I'm sorry, Casandra," he announced. "This is an official crime scene."

"Mom!" Casandra screamed from the patio through the open kitchen door.

Helena appeared in the doorway holding a bloodied rag to her forearm while Jerry held her close to his side, guiding the severely disheveled, distraught woman from the house. Her satin pajamas were spattered with blood, and she looked as if she were in shock.

Casandra ran to her mother and looked her over as an ambulance siren wailed in the near distance, approaching fast.

"What happened?" Casandra cried out.

"It was that awful man," Helena announced while gesturing and trembling like a frightened old woman. "My former employer, who'd been stalking Sidney." She shook her head, possibly in shock. "I was talking to Jerry on the phone while in bed, watching some television, when I thought I heard someone in the house. Naturally, I thought it was you or Sidney. When I called out, Blain Norwood burst into my room with a knife, demanding to know where Sidney was." Helena placed her hand on her chest and shook her head, perfecting her feeble old woman routine. "It all happened so fast. I tried to jump out of bed, and he slashed me with his knife. The whole time, he just kept shouting, 'Where's Sidney?' I screamed that I didn't know while running to the bathroom." Her trembling hand dramatically moved to her forehead. "That's when he pulled a gun on me." Her eyes widened. "It was the same gun that disappeared from Ransom Norwood's desk all those years ago. The one used to kill your father. I recognized it. I screamed, 'It was you! You killed your parents and my husband!" She shuddered and clung to Jerry for support. "He admitted he did it. He admitted that he killed his parents and your father, and that he was going to use the same gun to kill me!"

Casandra stared at her mother with horror in her eyes. "What happened, Mom?"

"It all happened so fast," Helena again insisted in an award-winning performance. "I tried to stop him from shooting me. The gun flew across the floor, and I just ***lunged*** after it. I barely remember the gun being in my hand. He was practically on top of me, clutching the knife. I don't even remember pulling the trigger." Her eyes remained wide as she shook her head. "I can't believe I actually shot him. Two intruders in less than a week." She then looked at Jerry, her eyes wide in horror. "Does that make me a serial killer?"

"It was self-defense," Jerry reminded her, firmly rubbing her shoulder as he held her, then looked at Casandra. "I was on the phone with her the entire time, racing here in my car. I wanted to call the police, but I was afraid to hang up. I heard everything. His confession, his murderous threats, and the final gunshot that stopped him from killing your mother."

Kingston waved the paramedics to the patio. "Of course it was self-defense," he remarked to Helena while gently touching her shoulder. "You must have been frightened out of your mind. I just wish you had reconsidered and stayed with us at the cabin instead."

Helena smiled sweetly at Kingston and affectionately patted his face. "You're a wonderful son-in-law, Kingston," she informed him.

As the paramedics guided Helena, with Jerry by her side, to their ambulance to check her injury, Kingston pulled Casandra into his arms. He held her as both grimaced, pretending to believe the story Helena told.

"Your mother is one scary woman," Kingston muttered to his wife.

Casandra clung to Kingston. "Be thankful she's on our side."

Kingston then released her and indicated Helena by the ambulance. "Stay with your mother," he announced. "I'm going to call Greyson and Amber. Tell them what's happening over here. They should remain at that hotel until we're sure it's safe."

Chapter 54

Harris, along with two men dressed entirely in black, paused alongside Jackson's garage, putting them within view of the old farmhouse from the rear. There appeared to be one or two lights on within the house despite it being after midnight. Harris studied the house while placing his hand radio close to his mouth and speaking into it without raising his voice.

"Team two," Harris announced into the radio. "Are you in position?"

"About twenty yards from the front porch," a man from team two replied.

"Make your way to the front," Harris informed him. "We bust down the doors in two minutes. Remain invisible. We don't want him alerted to our presence." There was a pause. "Proceed now."

Harris and his team of two men darted from behind the barn for the back of the house. Harris stumbled on something, noticing too late that it was a trip wire. There was a split second of uncertainty about what would follow. Still, none were prepared for Richard Wagner's "Ride of the

Valkyries" blaring over hidden loudspeakers, echoing loudly across the quiet farm. Flood lights then popped on from nearly every corner, both front and back, giving the men no cover.

"Converge!" Harris yelled into his radio, pressing the men to continue with the plan.

Harris and his two men reached the back patio and immediately attempted to bust down the door. With maximum effort and some intense pain, the door didn't even budge. Harris motioned for the man behind him to pick the lock.

§

Three men, also dressed entirely in black, reached the front porch and effortlessly busted the door down. It seemed almost too easy. The first man entered with his automatic rifle aimed and ready to fire. There was no one within the dimly lit kitchen. He cautiously crossed the kitchen but still saw no one. The second man entered behind him and scanned the area as well. The third man was about to cross the threshold when a trap door opened and swallowed him. He let out a startled gasp as the door closed swiftly behind him. The first and second man looked back, curious about what had happened. Both were surprised when they didn't see their teammate. It was almost as if he'd vanished. Despite losing their man, they continued cautiously through the kitchen.

The second man headed for the kitchen stairs while the first man approached the living room. A hidden door opened up behind the second man directly before the stairs. Jackson, also dressed in black, grabbed the man from behind, placing him in a chokehold with a cloth over his nose and mouth. The man briefly struggled while being pulled into the hidden compartment and lost consciousness just inside the opening from the chloroform. The hidden door closed a second before the first man turned in the living room archway, looking back for his man, but he was already gone. The first man looked around, now moderately spooked, possibly wondering how two men could vanish so silently and without a trace. The hand radio on his belt softly crackled.

"Team two," Harris announced, keeping his voice down. "Are you inside?"

The last man standing slowly backed across the kitchen toward the entrance, not responding to his radio. He then turned and bolted out the kitchen door. The same trap door sprang, swallowing him whole, dropping him into some dark oubliette. His startled scream was cut short as the door fell back into place.

§

Harris's man picked the back lock, immediately stood, and kicked the door open. Both men entered ahead of Harris with their automatic weapons aimed as they fanned out across the living room. Harris stood in the doorway holding his hand radio, still attempting to contact team two. When they didn't respond, he cursed and followed his men inside. Harris motioned for the first man to take the kitchen and the second man to take the living room stairs to the second floor. The first man entered the kitchen with his weapon leading the way, but he didn't see anything. He paused at the bottom of the back stairs and aimed his weapon up them, unaware of the hidden door right alongside him. He cautiously headed up the stairs, attempting to remain as quiet as possible.

Within the hidden compartment, Jackson jumped over the unconscious, zip-tied man, grabbed onto a metal vertical ladder, and swiftly climbed it to the second floor. Jackson pushed open the hidden door within the second floor hallway just far enough to poke the barrel of his semiautomatic through. He could hear the man rumbling up the kitchen stairs, and a distant, creaking floorboard told him another man was at the top of the living room stairs. Jackson fired his weapon at the man already in the hallway and quickly shut the hidden doorway. The man from the front stairs took cover and aimed his weapon, firing the moment he saw the man at the end of the hallway by the kitchen stairs.

"I got him, Harris," the man announced through his hidden ear transmitter as he ran along the hallway toward the fallen man. He aimed his weapon at the lifeless man and stared at his own comrade. "Son-of-a-bitch!"

"Can you confirm the kill?" Harris announced into his ear transmitter.

The man lowered his weapon while turning, about to respond to Harris, when he saw Jackson standing directly in front of him. He didn't even have time to gasp. Jackson struck him on the head with the butt of his rifle, dropping the man to the floor with a loud thud. Without a second to spare, Jackson grabbed the unconscious man and dragged him into the guest bedroom. Sidney shut the door behind him and his unconscious prisoner.

"Tie him up," Jackson announced.

Sidney immediately crouched alongside the man and zip-tied his hands behind his back.

"How many are left?" she asked, her body trembling with fear.

"Just Harris," Jackson replied as she straightened. "He won't go down as easily. Blain put years' worth of training into me before I was even eighteen. Harris is a highly skilled fighter and killer."

Sidney stared into his eyes through the dim lighting, feeling her heart aching for his safety. "Be careful," she whispered.

Jackson smiled and gently touched her face. "I'm coming back for you, Sidney," he insisted. "You're my unfinished business." He kissed her quickly but passionately before turning to the door.

Chapter 55

Harris stood rigid in the dimly lit living room with his radio in his hand, waiting for a response from his men, but the look on his face conveyed he knew there wouldn't be any.

"All right, Jackson," Harris called out while casting his hand radio across the floor with a loud clatter. "Let's see how tough you are in a face-to-face, one-on-one fight!"

"Awfully bold of you," Sidney announced from the darkness. "Assuming it was Jackson who eradicated your men."

Harris looked across the living room to the kitchen archway and saw Sidney appear with a semiautomatic in her hand, aimed at him. Harris released his automatic rifle, letting it dangle from his shoulder, and held his hands up only as high as his chest.

"This isn't your fight, Sidney," Harris informed her.

"Oh, it's my fight," Sidney replied. "It's been my fight since the day I was conceived. Your boss manipulated and exploited both my grandmother and my mother. Now, he wants to manipulate and exploit me."

"Your hatred for your father is between you and him," Harris informed her. "Go take it up with Blain. I'm here for Jackson."

"Blain Norwood is ***not*** my father," Sidney hissed while sneering.

"I'm not discussing your daddy issues with you," Harris replied, then turned almost sympathetic. "And I'm not here to hurt you. I'd never hurt you."

"Of course you wouldn't," Sidney replied while snorting a laugh. "That would ruin everyone's plans, wouldn't it? I mean, Blain's second in command marries his daughter. I live under daddy's thumb while you keep the little wife in line."

"You think I was playing you?" Harris just about demanded. "Where would you come up with something like that?"

"Straight out of Blain's playbook," Sidney informed him. "That's what he did to Amber's mother. Once Amber was born, Amanda could never leave him. Well, until he decided he wanted to trade her in for a younger model. Then, she'd outlived her usefulness, so he arranged for her little ***accident***."

"I suppose Jackson told you that," Harris remarked. "Jackson is a conman and a killer. Everything about the man is a lie. Even his name. He's using you the same way he used Alexa and Amanda. He siphoned money off his sister for nearly a year before her mysterious car accident, then he manipulated his thirteen-year-old niece and stole her away from her father."

"Max," Sidney remarked.

"What?" Harris asked, bewildered.

"Max Archer," she replied. "That's Jackson's real name, and I've known him my entire adult life. I have every reason to trust him but zero reason to trust you. If you're the good guy in all of this, prove it. Prove you're the good guy and leave us alone."

"If that's what it'll take for you to trust me," Harris announced, then nodded. "I'll do as you ask."

Sidney kept the gun trained on him as he backed away from her, his hands still where she could see them, and maneuvered closer to the door. Harris suddenly darted up the stairs. Although Sidney should have been expecting it, she was still caught off guard. She also didn't have any shot from her position in the kitchen archway. Sidney cursed and ran into the living room, slowing near the stairs. There was a loud clunk followed by Harris tumbling down the steps. Sidney jumped back with surprise. Harris was on his feet and lunged for her and the gun before she could even aim the weapon. He snatched the gun from her while simultaneously shoving her backward. As Sidney fell to the floor, landing on her backside, Harris aimed the gun at the stairs and waited, panting heavily from whatever had happened to him prior to falling down the steps.

A panel opened from beneath the staircase, only a step or two behind Harris. He saw something from the corner of his eye and spun, but Jackson was already mid-kick, striking him in the chest and sending him flying across the living room. The gun flew from his hand and slid under the sofa as he crashed into the staircase banister.

Jackson glared at Sidney while cocking his head. "Did you actually chloroform me?" he demanded.

"I was afraid you might do something stupid," Sidney replied.

"You do plenty of stupid stuff, and I've never once chloroformed you," Jackson huffed in response.

When Harris straightened, prepared to lunge for Jackson, who was preoccupied, Sidney indicated the situation to him.

"Less talk," she remarked.

Harris threw his fist at Jackson's face, which he easily blocked, then backhanded him with a slap that was heard halfway across the farm. Harris stumbled a step or two from the surprisingly hard slap, then immediately straightened, sneering at Jackson.

"I'm going to kill you," Harris snarled.

"Who's stopping you?" Jackson demanded while holding his arms out to his side, almost taunting him into his circle.

Harris swung with his right fist, which Jackson immediately blocked, but then punched him across the face with his left. Jackson deflected the next blow but couldn't avoid the kick to his chest that sent him backward into the stairs. Harris seized the opportunity and practically jumped on Jackson, clutching his shirt and punching him several times in the face. Having seen Harris dominate Jackson, Sidney frantically searched for her discarded gun. She didn't give a shit about it being a fair fight. She wasn't going to let Harris kill Jackson. The gun was under the sofa. She could just about see it, but couldn't reach it. Sidney lunged for the fireplace and grabbed the fire poker as a means to retrieve the gun.

"You couldn't hack working for Blain because you're weak," Harris shouted, almost mocking Jackson's inability to defend himself. "You can't even defend yourself. How did you think you'd ever save your sister?"

Harris clutched Jackson's throat and attempted to squeeze the life out of him while Jackson gasped, struggling to free himself. When Sidney saw what was happening on the staircase, she shifted direction from the gun to using the fire poker as a weapon.

Harris leaned closer to Jackson's ear and whispered, "Your sister fucked me so I wouldn't tell Blain that you betrayed him," he snarled, then grinned and chuckled. "In fact, this is exactly what she saw right before I snapped her neck."

Jackson suddenly sneered and punched Harris in the throat, knocking the wind out of him. Sidney gasped and took a step back with the fire poker still gripped in both hands. She wasn't sure if she should interfere. Jackson just about flew up into a sitting position on the stairs. He thrust his booted foot into Harris's abdomen, launching him across the living room and against the sofa. It loudly screeched several inches across the hardwood floor. Jackson sprang to his feet, gasping only briefly, and took two steps toward Harris, who moved to his hands and knees while looking somewhat stunned and still attempting to catch his breath.

"Yeah, I suspected it was you," Jackson snarled. "But I wanted to hear you say it. What will be the last thing ***you*** see before I snap ***your*** neck?"

Harris straightened on his knees with Sidney's discarded semiautomatic in his hand, aimed at Jackson only a few feet from him. Sidney was horrified when she saw Harris holding her gun aimed point-blank at Jackson's chest. When the gun fired, Sidney gasped, feeling as if she'd taken the bullet herself. Jackson took the shot to his chest and stumbled back a step, striking the banister and doubling over. Harris managed a low chuckle while pulling himself to his feet. He aimed the gun at Jackson, where he remained hunched over, still unwilling to go down.

"I guess you'll never know," Harris replied, answering Jackson's question.

Sidney cried out in anger while swinging the fire poker, striking the gun in Harris's hand, forcing him to drop it to the floor. Harris clutched his hand in surprise and shifted his attention to Sidney. The look of raw rage on her face was almost frightening as she swung the hooked end of the poker with surprising force directly into Harris's crotch. He immediately cried out with a mix of horror and pain, clutching himself as she pulled the poker free, ripping his pants and taking some flesh with it. Harris clutched himself as blood seeped between his fingers from whatever damage she had obviously done to his nether regions. Harris gasped several times, attempting to endure the pain and compose himself before dealing with his boss's daughter. Despite the pain, he met her gaze and sneered at her.

"Fuck Blain," Harris snarled, the pain evident in his tone. "You're dead, bitch."

As Harris attempted to grab Sidney with his bloodied right hand, it was deflected. Harris turned his head, startled, and saw Jackson standing directly before him, his face filled with rage and hatred.

"***I'm*** the last thing you see--"

Before Harris could even comprehend how the man he'd shot was still alive and standing before him, Jackson grabbed his head with both hands and swiftly snapped his neck. Sidney cried out and jumped back, stunned by the horrendous sound and what she had just witnessed as Harris dropped to the floor. Jackson released two deep breaths, then groaned loudly before gingerly rubbing his chest.

"I probably should have warned you to look away," Jackson remarked with some sympathy.

Sidney was finally able to look away from the dead man on the floor, his head turned in an unnatural position, and met Jackson's gaze.

"How are you still alive?" she gasped.

Jackson lifted his shirt, revealing his bulletproof vest. "You don't take on the mob without body armor," he informed her, then reached down his pants and removed a support cup. "One of these is also rather useful." He tossed the support cup over his shoulder, then shook his head while eyeing Harris's bloodied crotch and cringed. "Guess someone should have told Harris that."

Sidney eyed the blood and flesh still dangling on the hook of the fire poker, immediately made a face, and tossed the poker aside.

"I think I'm going to be sick," she muttered.

Jackson pulled her into his arms and held her as if his life depended upon it, or maybe he just needed a little extra support from feeling as if he took a sledgehammer to his chest. "I promise I will ***never*** piss you off," he informed her.

"Back at you," she whispered while clinging to him.

Chapter 56

One week later. Jackson left the farmhouse carrying a large box out to his awaiting pickup truck while Greyson followed him carrying another box. The truck's bed was already partially loaded with boxes and various personal items. Sidney and Amber followed the guys from the house, talking and giggling about something. After their boxes were loaded, Jackson shut the tailgate and then turned to the young women.

"Are you sure you'll be okay out here by yourself?" Jackson asked Amber.

Amber chuckled and shook her head. "Well, I won't exactly be by myself," she informed him.

Greyson hid his smile and refused to look at Jackson, who glared at him through narrowed eyes.

"Oh, come on," Amber scoffed at her uncle. "You're moving into Sidney's cabin with her, but you have a problem with Greyson staying with me?"

"That's different," Jackson remarked.

Sidney and Amber folded their arms across their chests while casting stern looks at Jackson.

"Oh, how so?" Sidney demanded.

Jackson noticed the looks he was receiving and hesitated slightly. "Because we're older," he replied with some cockiness.

"Oh, so now you're dropping my age back to twenty-one, huh?" Amber remarked. "How convenient for you."

Jackson groaned and avoided looking at both women. "Just--" he began, then hesitated. "Just stay out of my garage. I'll still be working on restoring cars during the week."

"I'll be lucky if he's really actually gone," Amber muttered to Sidney.

"He'll also be helping me out part-time at my grandpa's workshop, making furniture," Sidney reminded her friend. "He'll be gone more than you think."

As an older pickup truck drove down the driveway toward the farm, everyone looked up.

"Mailman," Amber announced, indicating the truck belonging to their local mail carrier, then glanced at her uncle. "What did you order now?"

"A few car parts," Jackson informed her. "Huh? They came fast."

When the truck stopped, the older mailman got out but didn't have any packages, only a large envelope.

"I have a certified letter for Amber," the mailman announced while approaching them.

Amber was slightly surprised. "A certified letter? For me?" she asked, then eagerly signed his electronic pad. "That's interesting."

The mailman handed her the letter, then returned to his truck. Jackson approached and looked at the envelope she held. It was from a lawyer's office.

"What's that?" Jackson demanded.

Amber stared at the address on the front and appeared surprised. "It's addressed to Alexa Norwood, care of Amber Ford," she remarked, then eyed her uncle. "Should I be concerned?"

"No, but you might want to prepare yourself," Jackson remarked. "Blain knew you were alive for an entire afternoon. Plenty of time to do something weird and creepy."

"You're weird and creepy," Amber muttered, then drew a deep breath and opened the envelope. She removed the single sheet of paper from the lawyer's office and read it. Amber then gasped and looked at her uncle. "It's from my father's estate." Her eyes again fell upon the paper. "It says my sister and I are the beneficiaries of his estate." Amber cast a quick look at Sidney, who was equally surprised. She then looked back at the paper. "Apparently, he revised his will after he found out Sidney was his daughter." Her eyes scanned the letter. "One of the estate employees informed my father's lawyers that I was alive and gave my information to them."

"It's all yours," Sidney remarked and waved her off. "I don't want any part of Blain's estate."

"Does that include the old Rolls-Royce?" Jackson asked, now looking over her shoulder at the paper.

"I assume so," Amber replied, then glanced back at her uncle while making a face. "Why? Do you want the Rolls?"

"Hell, yeah!"

Amber looked at Sidney and cocked her head. "Come on, Sidney," she announced. "For everything he'd put our families and us through, you owe it to them to split the estate with Uncle Jackson and me. You can give your share to your mother and grandmother for their sacrifices, pain, and suffering."

Sidney considered the comment, then nodded. "Okay, for my mother and grandmother," she replied, then gave a quick nod to Jackson. "And give Jackson the Rolls."

"We can give a percentage to the staff as well," Amber remarked. "Some of them helped raise me."

"I'd met some of them," Sidney replied, then nodded. "I think that's a good idea."

"We should all drive up there for the weekend," Jackson informed them. "I'll bet he still has some of Amanda's things in storage."

Amber glanced at her uncle as her expression dropped. "Do you think he still has her old photos?"

"Probably," Jackson replied.

"We should go," Amber announced with conviction. "All of us."

Sidney hesitated, then looked from Amber to Jackson. "I think my mother and grandmother should come along," she announced. "Reunite with some of the old staff and replace those bad memories with some good ones."

"So let's go," Jackson announced, then indicated his pickup truck. "I'll park the truck in the garage, and we can leave on the next flight out."

"Are we actually doing this?" Greyson asked with some surprise.

"Yes, I think we are," Amber replied, then smiled. "I left a lot of my childhood behind when Jackson and I took off. I think it's about time I got it back."

Other books by Holly Copella!
Reviews left on Amazon are appreciated!

"The Battle for Andrea Maria"

A cruise ship attack turns six survivors into overnight celebrities after they take credit for the heroic act of a stowaway who died saving them.

The cruise is just what Jess needed--a bit of harmless fun far from her daily grind. But what begins as a relaxing vacation turns into a desperate fight for her life when terrorists take over the ship and start piling up bodies. Teaming up with a mysterious stowaway, Jess attempts to send out a distress call but knows they cannot wait for help to come. If she or the few remaining passengers have any hope for survival, Jess must act now. The papers dub it "The Battle for *Andrea Maria*," but to Jess it is the moment she fought side-by-side with her enigmatic Romeo, saving the ship--and losing him. She thinks the story ends there, but really, the nightmare is just beginning...

"Insanely Deadly"

When the dead return to life, it's up to an admiral's daughter and a mildly insane, former war hero to save their small town.

Jetta Cross, a Navy Admiral's daughter, is tasked with keeping her father's comrade, a former war hero turned town crazy, grounded in the real world. Capt. John Hunter is still fighting the war in his head, where imaginary dead people are part of his world. When a viral outbreak brings about a zombie uprising, Hunter is left to his own devices. He must resume his role as a one-man commando unit in order to destroy the ravenous undead. With Hunter still fighting his own inner demons as well as the undead, the townspeople fear their zombie neighbors may not be the only threat. Stranded at the island's luxurious resort with a handful of workers, Jetta is forced to live up to her father's reputation and take charge of the deteriorating situation at the hotel. She must wage her own war against the infected before the government declares her hometown a total loss.

"Deadly Institution"

A town recluse suspected of killing his wife teams up with a young woman in order to stop a killer.

After being accused of murdering his wife, Konrad Churchill turns his back on the town that once adored him. Ten years later, he still holds his grudge and the title of the most feared man in town. With the reopening of the burned mental institution, where his wife had died, former employees are now murdered one by one, throwing suspicion back on Churchill. A young local reporter, Jacey, is forced to reveal her long-time friendship with the infamous recluse in order to clear his name not only in the recent murders but to exonerate him in the death of his wife as well. Will Jacey's relationship with Churchill invite the killer closer to her? Or is the killer already in her life?

"Death Displacement"

A grief-stricken man travels back in time to seek revenge on the woman who murdered his girlfriend, but inadvertently falls in love with her.

Kane is about to marry the woman he loves. His life is perfect. A few weeks before the wedding, a vindictive woman from his girlfriend's past mysteriously arrives and kills her. He learns of a traumatic accident that happened five years earlier, which triggers Riley's hatred for his girlfriend. Distraught over his girlfriend's death, Kane uses an antique time machine to travel into the past in order to find and destroy the woman responsible. When he runs into Riley's younger self, he realizes she's not the monster she later becomes, and he can't bring himself to destroy her. With a little help from his oddball friend from the past, they formulate a plan to prevent the accident that sends Riley down her destructive path. Kane's plan backfires when he falls for the younger Riley. His new tortured existence is further complicated when future Riley, his girlfriend's killer, shows up with her own devious agenda that doesn't include him. Will he be able to stop the time ripple, which ultimately ends with his girlfriend's death? Or will future Riley take him out of the timeline forever--

"Dead Village"

After strange happenings isolate a small resort town from the rest of the world, nearly one hundred residents seek refuge at the closed hotel. Only eight survive the night. And that's just the beginning...

One day after the entire population of Fox Ridge Village disappears, a car wreck forces several unsuspecting crash victims to seek help at the closed summer hotel. Within the hotel, they discover the grisly aftermath of a brutal slaughter. Crash victims Vander and Devon, a reluctant clairvoyant, team up to solve the riddle of the "haunted hotel" and the mass hysteria plaguing the remaining survivors. By the time they discover the hotel's secret, they're already drawn into the hysteria. As the body count continues to climb, it's a race to isolate the source and bring everyone back to reality before they kill one another. Will Devon be able to communicate with the traumatized spirits before their fate becomes her own?

"Town Darling"

After surviving a brutal attack that claims the lives of those she loves, a young woman seeks revenge on a corrupt town.

Going back home is never easy, but for Casey, it means returning to her corrupt hometown, where she barely survived a brutal attack. Accompanied by two family friends, she seeks justice for the night that destroyed her life. Her physical scars are nothing compared to her emotional ones, forcing the local sheriff to believe that the town darling is back for revenge. As the conspiracy for her revenge appears to be leading up to the coveted town fair, the sheriff is determined to stop her from fulfilling her vengeful scheme...but guilt over his role on that fateful night continues to haunt him. Will his desperate need for Casey's forgiveness be his undoing? Or will Casey's desire for revenge destroy them both?

"Basement Dwellers"

A viral outbreak at a hospital leaves a mortician, sheriff, and coroner fighting for their lives against a horde of undead and the CDC.

After a massive car wreck leaves several survivors in critical condition at the local hospital, a surgeon uses experimental drugs on his critical patients and accidentally causes a zombie outbreak. When local mortician, Lexx, receives an infected corpse as her client, she becomes stranded in the hospital basement during CDC quarantine along with the local sheriff and the coroner. The infamous surgeon struggles to find a cure for his infectious blunder by using the other survivors as test subjects. Meanwhile, Lexx and the sheriff attempt to locate his missing sister, who's stranded somewhere in the battle zone that once was the emergency room. It's a race against time and the ravenous undead. Can they survive the undead before the CDC sanitizes the hospital of all infection?

"Misfits, Inc."

A seemingly ordinary young woman meets four misfits who claim she has given them supernatural powers.

While on a business trip to a remote island paradise, a bored secretary, Hailey, has her world turned upside down when her path collides with a psychic freak, Skyler. He attempts to convince her that they had met in his dreams, and she had chosen him as one of her four mystic warriors. After Skyler foresees a woman's death, they discover an unidentified creature has killed one of the guests. They are joined by a lounge pianist and a rich playboy, who also claim they had met her in their dreams. If Skyler's prophecies are genuine, the evil entity controlling the ravenous creatures needs to destroy Hailey to ensure its survival. Reluctantly accepting her fate, Hailey has to locate the last and most powerful of her chosen warriors, The Guardian. Their fate is in doubt when The Guardian turns out to be a self-absorbed, former cat burglar with a bad attitude. Can Hailey turn her company of misfits into an elite team of mystic warriors? Or will The Guardian's secret agenda destroy them all?

"Deadly Institution 2"

When blackmail turns into murder, a young woman finds herself caught in the killer's crosshairs.

The small town of Stony Ridge is no stranger to scandal and persecution of the innocent. When a brutal killing shakes the town's prestigious country club, Jacey McMurray seeks help from a self-proclaimed vigilante, Konrad Churchill. As her professional and personal worlds collide, Jacey fears the stress of the country club killings have finally taken their toll on Churchill. Can a stressed-out vigilante stop the killer before he strikes again?

"Witness Protection"
Also available in audiobook!

After witnessing an execution, a resourceful young woman attempts to disappear while being pursued by a hitman and a handsome federal agent.

A helicopter pilot, Jackie Remus, reluctantly agrees to go on a date with one of her clients, but her date is unexpectedly cut short when she witnesses a man being murdered. After narrowly escaping with her life, she is placed into protective custody. When the safe house is breached, Jackie makes a daring escape from both the hired killers and the handsome FBI agent, who wants to return her to protective custody. With a little help from her sly and crafty friend, Monroe, Jackie is convinced she can disappear until the trial. While on her journey to meet with her friend, she solicits help from a few shady but lovable characters along the way. Although she manages to stay one step ahead of the hired killers, the federal agent remains in hot pursuit. Will Jackie reach Monroe before she's captured by the FBI and returned to protective custody? Or will the hired killers silence her first?

"Unconditional"

A young woman puts her life on hold to care for an unstable, highly skilled combat soldier, who believes someone is trying to kill him.

A botched military coup leaves a team of elite fighters injured, with one clinging to life in a coma. When Harlan wakes from his coma, he's left with no memory of his past life. His commander's daughter, Indy, takes it upon herself to care for the fallen war hero. She's challenged with more than just his physical care as she combats with not only his memory loss but also his newly found desire for her. His infatuation with her becomes the least of her worries when he sinks back into his role of a combat soldier. Believing his life is in danger, his fighting skills emerge, transforming him into an unpredictable and dangerous man. Will his memory return to him before Indy is forced to commit him? Or will he finally find his nemesis, "the coyote", and possibly claim the life of an innocent person?

"The Pen Pal"

In order to save her friend, she must enter the mind of a serial killer.

When her best friend is abducted, no one believes Jolynn saw it in a psychic vision. With nowhere to turn, Jolynn reluctantly joins Agent Harris Slade and his team on their hunt for a sadistic serial killer known only as "The Pen Pal". Finally confronted with the killer, Jolynn realizes she must enter the mind of the psychopath in order to stop the brutal killings. But when her vision reveals a particularly disturbing death, can Jolynn sacrifice her lover for her friend?

"Witness Protection 2"
The Return of Whiskey Tango Foxtrot

Believing she holds the clue to millions in missing laundered money, a young woman is placed into the protective care of a former Navy SEAL team.

Feeling sorry for her recently separated co-worker, Leeann invites Wiley to join her and her friends on their night out. Little does she know that finding her co-worker murdered is just the beginning of her nightmare. Leeann unknowingly holds the key to fifty million dollars in potentially laundered mob money. With hired killers pursuing her, the FBI places her into a different kind of protective custody. Former Navy SEAL team Whiskey Tango Foxtrot reunites to keep Leeann alive at their secret hideaway. What should be an easy assignment takes an unscheduled turn when secrets, lies, and betrayal threaten to derail their mission. Is the team prepared for a war on their own doorstep? Will Leeann's misguided trust endanger the lives of those sent to protect her?

"Witness Protection 3"
Alpha Mike Foxtrot

A helicopter pilot risks her life to help a team of retired Navy SEALs rescue two girls from a killer.

When former Navy SEAL team Whiskey Tango Foxtrot asks for a simple favor, Jackie reluctantly offers her air-taxi services. What could go wrong? What begins as a search and rescue for two girls turns into a fight for survival against a heavily armed drug cartel. Wanted by the law with the cartel in hot pursuit and their home base breached, the team is forced to call in a favor from a questionable ally. Unfortunately, their new safe house isn't what it seems. Without knowing who the real enemy is, can Jackie and the team save their young witnesses from the hands of a killer?

"Already Dead"
Supernatural Collection

From the already dead to the undead. Three supernatural tales of "things that go bump in the night".

"Bloodletting" - A vampire-themed resort allows guests to *participate* in their Bloodletting Ritual to celebrate the island's legendary vampires.

"Reaper of Souls" - A young woman must outwit an evil sorcerer in order to save her brother or become one of his minions forever.

"Already Dead" - When Flight 220 crashes, ten passengers make it to an isolated island, but only one man lives to tell the lie.

"Witness Protection 4"
O-Dark-Hundred

A simple assignment turns deadly when a retired Navy SEAL team uncovers a plot to kill a notorious mob boss.

When Whiskey Tango Foxtrot embarks on a simple stalking case, they're not prepared for a trip to a private island paradise owned by an infamous mobster. With one of their own suffering from traumatic head injuries, the team is left scrambling to decide what is real or imagined. The situation escalates even further when they uncover an assassination plot where everyone is a suspect. Now targets themselves, can the team survive their trip to paradise?

"Witness Protection 5"
Outside the Wire

After suffering several casualties on their last assignment, a retired Navy SEAL team discovers their misery is just beginning.

When Whiskey Tango Foxtrot returns home after suffering a devastating loss, they're hit with even more bad news regarding the rest of their team. Their grief is cut short when they discover their names are all on the same hit list. Hunted by relentless assassins, the scattered team must decide whether to remain safely hidden or find the man who put the price on their heads. Against the wishes of her teammates, Jackie strikes out on her own in order to save a friend who wants her dead. In a kill-or-be-killed situation, will Jackie's emotions finally betray her?

"The Murder of Emily Fisher"

After finding their favorite teacher murdered, the lives of two teenage girls are forever changed.

Everyone loved Emily Fisher. While walking home one afternoon, two teenage girls, Sidney and Trisha, stumble upon a gruesome murder scene. The brutal murder of Emily Fisher, a young, attractive schoolteacher, shocks the small town of Marilina. After graduation, Sidney moves far away from the memories of the small town, while Trisha retreats deeper into denial. Eight years after the murder, Sidney receives a desperate call from her childhood friend, forcing her to return home. Trisha believes Emily's killer was falsely accused, and she manages to turn the entire town against her while attempting to prove it. When Trisha receives a death threat, Sidney realizes there may be some credibility to her friend's wild accusations. Is Trisha's mental breakdown a result of childhood trauma? Or is the real killer actually attempting to silence her? In order to save her friend, Sidney must answer the eight-year-old question. Who murdered Emily Fisher?

"Once Upon a Disaster"

A young homicide detective finds herself at the mercy of a hitman in the aftermath of an earthquake.

While investigating the murder of a hitman, Detective Jade Wesson pursues a lead connecting the dead man to a break-in at a computer programming company. She's drawn into the world of a nightclub owner and front man for the mob, Cody Riley. Her investigation continues to point to Cody's right-hand man and possible hitman, Vahn Lott. Despite her efforts to keep her investigation on track, Vahn has plans of his own for the attractive detective. When an unprecedented earthquake rocks their east coast town, Jade must put her life in Vahn's hands if she wants to survive. Can she trust a man who might be the killer she's hunting?

"Awaken the Dead"

A grieving innkeeper struggles to keep her haunted hotel out of foreclosure.

After losing her parents in a suspicious boating accident, Harley Brandon is determined to keep the family hotel out of foreclosure. Unfortunately, the hotel ghosts have other plans. Built with tainted money, the century-old Horizon Hotel thrives on a tradition of murder, scandal, and suicide. As the paranormal activity increases to alarming levels, Harley discovers the truth about the hotel and its residents. Can Harley save her friends from the hotel's frightening hidden secrets?

"Castle Bloodshed"
Murder Collection

From a deadly island paradise to haunted castles. Three novella-length tales of murder, mystery, and malicious intent.

"Castle Bloodshed" – A tour of Wesley Castle turns into a fight for survival as six stranded tourists discover the haunting secrets within the castle walls. A mystery writer teams up with an uptight butler in order to stop a killer who may already be dead. Novella-length paranormal murder mystery.

"Fleshies" – Is Uncle Rutger crazy? Five years ago, four business partners died within their newly purchased, fixer-upper castle. Their bodies were never found. The surviving partner, Rutger, claims a demon keeps him as its slave. Rutger's nephew schemes to save his uncle by sacrificing the lives of a group of stranded motorists and a high-profile novelist. Novella-length supernatural murder mystery.

"Demon Island" – A group of strangers are invited to a remote island for the reading of a will. The guests soon discover they were brought to the island to be executed one by one. It's up to a private detective and a tenacious young woman to solve the murders and find a way to escape paradise. Novella-length murder mystery.

"Brighton Island"

When a psychic visits a haunted island mansion, he inadvertently awakens the ghosts' tortured souls.

Something's not right with Simon. When Jacklyn brings her eccentric friend to her uncle's island mansion, she doesn't expect him to slip into psychic overload. As Simon attempts to solve a decade-old double homicide, Jacklyn is confronted with the possibility that she could be next to join the mansion ghosts. When they find themselves stranded on the secluded island, her Uncle Hyland wages his own war to save them from a flesh-and-blood killer. Will her uncle's "shock and awe" military tactics save them or get them killed? Can Simon bring peace to the tortured souls or unexpectedly join them?

"A.L.F. Resort"

A fantasy vacation turns into a nightmare when the resort's artificial life forms are compromised.

Welcome to A.L.F. Resort, where you can live out your fantasies with safe, state-of-the-art artificial life form robots! When a young journalist and a photographer are sent to A.L.F. Resort to do a story for their magazine, Shay and Becka believe they've hit the jackpot of all work-cations. The engineers pull out all the stops to make their fantasies a memorable experience. Unfortunately, the newly designed A.L.F., the Gen X, is smarter than his programming and creates havoc within Shay's fantasy. A computer malfunction removes their safety inhibitors, and the A.L.F.s play out their own hostile fantasies. Zombies, bikers, and mobsters run amok, turning fantasies into nightmares. Shay gets more of a story than she anticipates, but will she survive long enough to write it?

"Jungle Princess"

While stranded on a prison island, a young woman discovers a creature of "unknown" origin.

After their cruise ship sinks, Alex and two of her shipmates are stranded on a deserted, tropical island. Unfortunately, the castaways soon realize they're not alone. They discover an abandoned prison with over two dozen inmates living on the island's south side. While avoiding the prison on the far side of the island, Alex discovers a strange but loveable creature of unknown origin. When one of her fellow castaways is in trouble, Alex reluctantly seeks help from the prisoners. After the brutal murder of several inmates, their questions surrounding the abandoned prison are about to be answered. What really killed over one hundred prisoners? And is it still out there?

"Murder in Wax"

A series of brutal murders plagues a quiet farming community when beautiful women audition for the same acting job.

While all the young women in town are fighting over a once-in-a-lifetime acting opportunity, Devon Vincent is excited about her new job at the local wax museum. Although supportive of her friend's acting aspirations, Devon has a hard time understanding the rivalry among the women in town. When the aspiring actresses are brutally murdered one by one, Devon fears her friend may be the next victim. Devon finds herself in the middle of a murderous revenge plot that leads back to the wax museum's doorstep and possibly implicates her boss as the killer. Will Devon's newly found feelings for her boss bring a killer closer to her? Or is the killer already in her circle?

"Witness Protection 6"
Alpha Dogs

An easy rescue turns into a wild ride for retired Navy SEAL team Whiskey Tango Foxtrot when everyone wants to kill their client.

It was a simple task. Rescue a young woman from her mob boss father-in-law. Little did Jackie and company realize that rescuing the young woman was the easy part. Keeping her alive would be a massive undertaking, especially when everyone wants a piece of the mafia heiress. The team fights for survival against their toughest adversaries yet. How many innocent people must die in order to save one woman? Can the team survive the ultimate battle between mercenaries and assassins?

"Midnight Requisition"

A series of brutal murders leaves a traumatized young woman on a hunt to find a killer.

When they were just babies, Scorpio and her twin brother, Kane, tragically lost their parents under mysterious circumstances. Refusing to accept his father was dead, Kane set off on a mission to find a man he'd never met. A home invasion gone wrong leaves Scorpio grieving the loss of those she loves. Out of the tragedy of her loss, two fallen heroes are thrust upon her. Scorpio soon realizes someone wants her dead, and the killer may already be in her circle. As her entire life unravels in a web of betrayal and lies, can Scorpio trust her new, slightly questionable friends?

"Until Death"

Liars, cheaters, blackmail, and murder. It would be a wedding no one would forget.

Despite knowing he's making the biggest mistake of his life, Raina Steele reluctantly attends her father's third wedding. What should have been a boring reception turns into a web of lies, betrayal, and murder. With no one above suspicion, Raina must put aside her feud with the arrogant yet insanely handsome butler in order to catch the killer before he finds his next victim. With a murderer waiting to strike and lives hanging in the balance, the real question remains...the bride is wearing white? Seriously?

"Tainted"

What happens at the Dark Forest Hotel, stays at the Dark Forest Hotel...for all eternity.

What secrets surround Dark Forest Hotel? After her parents die under mysterious circumstances, sixteen-year-old Jeri escapes foster care and seeks refuge at a "closed for the season" hotel. Over the next six years, Jeri graduates from teenage runaway to the hotel's assistant general manager. When she learns a convention is secretly held every year in her absence, she demands answers from her boss, friends, and co-workers. After getting conflicting stories, Jeri sets out to discover the truth. She's suddenly thrown into a horrifying new world where vampires and vicious creatures are craving her virgin blood. After six years of being lied to, is there anyone she can trust?

"Witness Protection 7"
Bravo Foxtrot

An Army deserter on the run brings mayhem to a retired Navy SEAL team when his teenage daughter is caught in a mercenary's cross-hairs.

A weekend of fun turns into a race for survival as Monique and Colleen's surrogate big brother, Bogart, rescues the girls from mercenaries hunting Colleen's Army deserter father. With the girls safely stashed at their Colorado hideaway, trouble brews when the team discovers Colleen's father was framed by his former commander over a stolen, high-tech weapon. In order to clear Colleen's father and bring him home, the team must fight one of their toughest adversaries yet...a high-ranking military officer with countless mercenaries and the U.S. military behind him.

"Midnight Requisition 2" Amateur Night

A brother and sister duo team up to catch a potential kidnapper.

After finally reuniting with her not-so-dead brother, Scorpio and her friends are taunted into helping him with his new case. A wealthy cattle rancher believes someone wants to abduct his daughter, but the team suspects her ex-boyfriend is pulling off an elaborate scheme to win her back. What appears to be a slice of paradise in the Colorado Mountains turns out to be a venomous snake pit filled with lies, lust, betrayal, and murder. Surviving the depraved family becomes the least of the team's worries when a botched kidnapping turns into murder.

"Cemetery Stalkers" Horror Collection

Four tales of horror from flesh-eating alien monsters to blood-sucking vampires.

"Night Creatures" – When a rescue party becomes stranded on an abandoned cruise ship, they discover the terrifying secret unleashed from the cargo hold. What starts out as a rescue mission rapidly deteriorates into survival as a frightening creature with a taste for human flesh hunts the small group. Novella-length horror book.

"Ravenous" – After escaping a carjacking in the back woods, a young woman seeks refuge in a mysterious mansion with a terrifying secret. Despite promises of a ride to town in the morning, she's convinced she's being held prisoner by a cult leader. Short paranormal story.

"The Feast" – Five years ago, a killer went on a murderous rampage at the church picnic. Despite eyewitness accounts of a non-human killer, the local law refused to believe the town's citizens. When a group of teenagers stumble upon the contained remains of the killer, they unwittingly set him free to continue his terror upon the small town. Novella-length paranormal book.

"Cemetery Stalkers" – When 'The Reaper' stalks a cemetery, death follows. Following a series of bizarre incidents within the cemetery, a young woman fears for the safety of her friend, who lives in the middle of spook central. Short horror story.

"Jumpers"

When a cruise ship is exposed to a deadly virus, the fate of the world rests in the hands of a lounge dancer and a conman.

An infectious outbreak threatens the passengers and crew of the "Queen Anita" and the entire world if the virus escapes back into civilization. Lounge dancer, Maxine, must find a way to prevent the destruction of the world, but in order to do that, she needs to trust a conman with unique insight into the virus.

"Witness Protection 8"
Midnight Requisition

A brother and sister duo find themselves on an explosive collision course with a team of retired Navy SEALs.

Obsessed with the belief that his father is still alive, Kane Wayland embarks on a foolhardy mission to confront the elusive former Navy SEAL, Zack Kinsley. Despite heavy protests, Kane's sister, Scorpio, joins him on his quest. The disastrous "reunion" comes with a steep price that none are prepared to pay. With the haunting reality of the botched mission, Midnight Requisition, still looming over each of them, can the two teams pull together in time to prevent another tragedy?

"Midnight Requisition 3"
Circular Run

A brother and sister reopen a hotel with a tainted history, only to discover its past refuses to stay dead and buried.

Scorpio and Kane Wayland finally realize their dream of reopening their grandfather's old, cliffside hotel in Maine. With the hotel's checkered past behind it, the relaunch is a dream come true. Unfortunately, history has a tendency to repeat itself. When guests mysteriously vanish, the hotel's somewhat seedy clientele are all now suspects. In order to save their hotel, Scorpio and Kane must stop a killer. When your guests are mercenaries, bounty hunters, and mobsters, who can you trust?

"Raven Force"

An innkeeper becomes involved in a game of espionage after picking up a mysterious hitchhiker.

After surviving a nightmare of a date, Maxine Croft didn't think her evening could get any worse...until she nearly hits a stranger on a dark back road. This unprecedented meeting would turn Max's world upside down as she's thrust into a world of murder, corruption, and deception within her own backyard. As she gets in deeper with an elite, special task force, Max inadvertently puts her sisters' lives in danger. Will Max and her sisters become just more "collateral damage" to facilitate the team's mission?

"Midnight Requisition 4"
Charlie Foxtrot

A mob convention at a remote cliffside hotel has murderous consequences.

Hotel owner, Scorpio Wayland, reluctantly books a "mob" convention at her quiet, cliffside resort. What could go wrong? When former mob boss Salvatore Romano invites friends for a "family" reunion, disaster swiftly follows.

"Witness Protection 9"

S.N.A.F.U.

A notorious mob boss turns to a retired Navy SEAL team to keep his son alive.

They were made an offer they couldn't refuse. When his son is accused of murdering known mobsters throughout Colorado, Giovanni turns to the retired Navy SEAL team of Whiskey Tango Foxtrot to keep his boy alive and prevent a war between the "families". With the mobster's son in the crosshairs of every hitman and bounty hunter on the West Coast, Jackie and the boys need to find Marco and go completely off-grid. But is the team risking their lives to protect a serial killer?

"Witness Protection 10"

Bravo Zulu

It's all hands on deck when the mob declares war on the team and those they love.

Whiskey Tango Foxtrot reunites with Midnight Requisition when war is declared by a notorious mobster and his army of highly trained soldiers. After several deadly attacks shake both teams, their skills, loyalties, and limitations are tested in an explosive and bloody rampage that will scar and change their lives forever.

"Pretty Little Dead Things"

Romance, scandal, and an unsolved murder. Welcome to snob central!

After a disastrous evening at the exclusive country club gala, Marley Temple doesn't think her life can get any worse. When someone close to her is murdered, Marley is left devastated. Although everyone else seems to move on after the unsolved homicide, Marley can't let it go. She's suddenly thrust into the inner circle of a wealthy playwright recluse, whose stage actress wife was brutally butchered just two years earlier. Although Marley fears falling for the infamous Devlin Ryker, forming a strange alliance with him brings her closer to solving the perplexing murder. But as she gets closer to learning the truth, the killer gets closer to her. Will Marley discover the killer's identity before she becomes his next victim?

"Dead Again"

After barely surviving a murderous attack, a young woman believes a cold-hearted cattle rancher holds clues to that night.

After the murder of her mother in an attack that nearly claimed her life as well, Sage Remington believes moving to the country with her sister will heal her emotional scars. Sage's near-death experience leaves her with memory loss surrounding that fateful night. A bizarre encounter with an infamous cattle rancher, Jackson Morgan, brings back fragments of Sage's lost memory. If she wants to piece together what happened to her mother, Sage needs to get closer to Jackson, who somehow holds the clues. Unfortunately, discovering Jackson's secrets opens the door to a whole other world where nothing is what it seems.

"Dead Woods"

Two magazine reporters get more of a story than they want while investigating strange happenings in a cursed forest.

While interviewing a small-town hero, two adventure-seeking magazine reporters, Kara and Lenox, hike into the infamous Dead Woods in search of a story. Their simple outing takes a chilling turn, and they soon find themselves involved in the town's haunted history filled with curses, witch burnings, and zombified minions. Narrowly escaping with her life, Kara runs into local legend Daemon Archer, a distant relative of a man accused of witchcraft and burned in Town Square in the 1800s. In order to survive a panic-stricken village prophesizing 'evil will take a mate', Kara has to trust the town's most feared citizen.

"Cinderella of Yardley Manor"

Never believing in love at first sight, a young woman finally thinks she's met the man of her dreams, only to discover he's the wrong man.

After graduating college, Ramsey O'Connell reluctantly agrees to travel with her uncle on his business trip to England. However, when she discovers her uncle's true intention--to fix her up with his wealthy colleague, William Yardley —she has some reservations. Falling in love was the last thing she expected, but falling in love with an emotionally unavailable man turns her fairytale into a nightmare.

"Protect and Serve"

Celebrating her birthday with friends on a luxury cruise ship, a young heiress is looking for a little romance on the high seas. Instead, she's confronted by kidnappers and assassins.

Kasey's birthday celebration cruise was supposed to be ten days of sun, sea, and fun with her friends. That is, until her uncle insists she take her bodyguard along. Although her bodyguard, Hunter, is undeniably handsome, he's a little rough around the edges. When her uncle's enemies exact their revenge on Kasey, the cruise turns into a nightmare. If they want to survive, they have to trust Hunter. But sometimes, the enemy is not who you think.

"Crime Scene"

The cast of a popular television crime show finds themselves stranded in a small town after a real-life murder mystery intrudes on their world of make-believe.

After weeks of filming on location, the cast of a highly acclaimed crime show becomes stranded when their luxury bus breaks down in the middle of nowhere. An inconvenient overnight in a small town turns into the beginning of a murder investigation with the cast of "Crime Scene" high on the suspect list. To save the cast's reputation, the show's writer assists the handsome but guarded sheriff and his K-9 deputy in the murder investigation. As alibis unravel, lies pile up, and the suspect list grows, can they catch the killer before he strikes again?

"Midnight Requisition 5"
Sierra Hotel

A Christmas wedding, mistletoe, and murder.

Only a few days before Christmas, a very pregnant Scorpio and her friends are planning Mac and Maverick's wedding. Little did they know that Santa would be delivering a few early presents. What was supposed to be a merry Christmas turns into an epic whodunit when a helicopter crashes on the hotel grounds, leaving eight stranded passengers and a dead man. Their once silent night is filled with accusations, alibis, and mayhem. With the assistance of former Special Agent Holden Falcone, can they solve the murders before the next body drops?

"The Rancher's Daughter"

When her town, ranch, and life are threatened, a young woman teams up with the enemy's top enforcer to reclaim what is hers.

Skyler Winchester's small hometown has become more corrupt in the five years since her parents' car accident. Little by little, wealthy business tycoon Marcus has been buying buildings, property, and people. As one of the largest ranch owners and the object of Marcus's lust, Sky has always been immune to the corruption and dirty dealings, but her friends aren't so lucky. After forming an unholy alliance with one of Marcus's top enforcers, it appears that Sky's immunity has been revoked. When her life is threatened, will the man she trusts most be the one sent to eliminate her?

"Beyond the Fence Line"

In the dust of a modern cattle ranch, a girl with wrangler dreams and her childhood protector build a bond that falters under unvoiced desires.

On a sprawling modern cattle ranch, two kids bound by loss forge an unbreakable bond. After losing his mother when he was only ten years old, Brandt wants nothing to do with the fatherless five-year-old ragamuffin, Mazie, whose mother runs the ranch house. But as years of dust and dreams shape them, he becomes her protector, and she his constant shadow, chasing her goal to wrangle cattle alongside him. Their friendship is unshakable until one reckless night sparks a truth Brandt has always known: he loves her. Mazie can't see past their childhood bond, and the rift tears them apart. Several years later, with the ranch as the only home they've known, they must confront their past, their pain, and the love that's waited years to claim its truth. A story of resilience, loyalty, and a romance forged in the grit of the open range, spanning years of heartache and hope.

"Nature of the Beast"

She claimed her father's cursed mansion...where the ghosts within the walls have long been waiting for her.

When Brandy Holloway inherits a sprawling country mansion from the father she never knew, she expects secrets, not literal skeletons in the closets. The gothic estate has all the comforts of the "Psycho" house and all the charm of "The Addams Family" home. The young maid swears it's haunted, and the handsome, mysterious butler hides secrets of his own. After Brandy invites her friends for a weekend escape, the fun turns deadly when, one by one, they vanish into the house's endless depths. Trapped in a ghostly home that hungers for souls, Brandy must team up with her eccentric butler to uncover the mansion's bloodstained secrets before she becomes its prisoner...forever.

"Past Lies"

Some inheritances are handed down in love. Some are guarded in silence. Some are protected at any cost.

When Sidney Bristol inherits her great-grandfather's lake house and workshop, she also inherits a single photograph that stirs questions about her family's past long held in silence. Her grandmother's careful reserve. Her mother's childhood never fully shared. Then there's Jackson Ford. The reclusive man her best friend, Amber, calls "uncle", the one who has always watched from the shadows, who has kept Amber close, who seems to carry more than he will ever say. Sidney has known him for years. Enough to fear him, enough to trust him, enough to wonder why her heart races every time he looks her way. But the deeper she looks into the past her family and friends have kept hidden, the more she realizes some things were never meant to be uncovered. Some family stories end with love. Some end with a locked door...and someone waiting on the other side.

"Hell's Paradise"

A tropical paradise where the most dangerous thing is the company.

When a luxury yacht wrecks on a beautiful but deadly tropical island, what begins as inconvenience for the wealthy and privileged quickly spirals into violence, betrayal, and depravity. As the masks slip, heiress Harley McBride learns the jungle isn't the greatest threat; the people she's trapped with are. Harley's only protection is her devoted butler and Damon, the silent but lethal bodyguard she once feared and despised. But the more the group unravels, the more she realizes the man she was warned to avoid might be the only one worth trusting. On an island where civilization dies fast and primal instincts take over, desire might be the most lethal force of all. Harley must decide how far she'll go to survive...and whether falling for the dangerous man beside her is the biggest risk of all.

ABOUT THE AUTHOR

Holly Copella has been writing since the age of twelve when her frustration at a book's poor plot drove her to author her own story. Over the last decade, she's written a number of screenplays, some of which she's now adapting into novels. Her fascination with zombies and other darker material lends an edge to her writing, which tends to lean toward horror. As a fan of Agatha Christie, she appreciates the craft of a good plot and the importance of creating significant characters.

Hailing from Pennsylvania, Copella lives in the Endless Mountains on a farm with her new horse, Maverick, and other animals. In addition to writing and reading fiction, she enjoys riding horses and traveling to Las Vegas.